IDENTITY CRISIS

BOOK ONE OF THE ARBITER TRILOGY

CLAYTON PULSIPHER

Book Cover by MiblArt
Illustrations by Taylor Pulsipher
1st Edition 2023

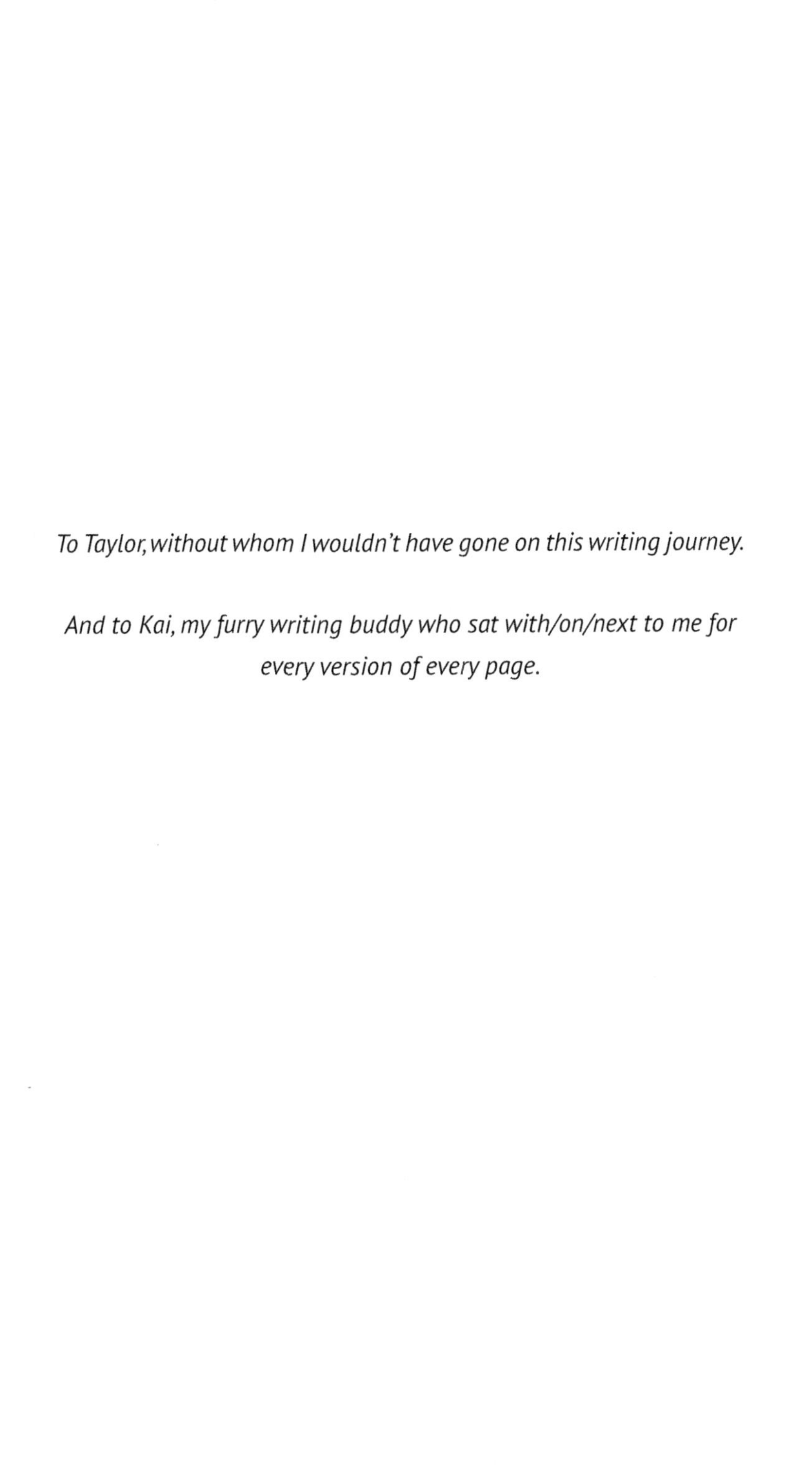

To Taylor, without whom I wouldn't have gone on this writing journey.

And to Kai, my furry writing buddy who sat with/on/next to me for every version of every page.

CONTENTS

PROLOGUE

"Do you believe in fate, Torin?" Elama gazed through *Pioneer's* front window, basking in the planetary elegance that was Rixxon Prime, and tested the appearance modifier on her wrist.

Bit by bit, her body stretched up and tinted emerald green.

"I believe in *you*, commander." Torin, her second, mirrored her actions, similarly transforming his physical form. "If you say it is fate, I cannot help but agree."

A smile stretched across Elama's newly elongated face. "I will never understand why some do not—"

"Commander!" Torin's long, hooked toenails clacked on *Pioneer's* steel flooring as he strode forward. "Is that... a Guild vessel?"

In the distance, a small, black spacecraft—one proudly displaying the insignia of the Prospectors' Guild—descended toward the planet's eastern hemisphere.

"Well," said Elama, "if we had any doubts before, it's become clear: now is the time."

Torin nodded, eyes fixed forward. "How is the boy doing?"

"He's no longer a boy," Elama replied with a chuckle, "and in fact quite large in stature by human standards." She lowered to a seat, stumbling as she grew accustomed to her altered form's extra leg joints. "I thought all was lost when war came to the jungle all those years ago, but he and his brother have overcome much and blossomed into quite the pair."

"It is astounding how easily the Rixxonians accepted him. Your decision to place him here was wise."

"Though they are primitive, the Rixxonians are a mindful, sensible people. Their belief system centers around the importance of personal strength and fortitude, and they embrace the fact that there is much to this universe they do not know. The people are thus driven by a constant, open-minded thirst for knowledge as they strive to better themselves in both body and mind. In their own words, the deities they worship are merely avenues of gratitude for the indescribable."

"Sounds like an ideal society."

"As are many at this stage of development. Things only get more complicated."

They shared a soundless moment admiring the two-toned world. Encased in perpetual night, the eastern mountains shimmered a dim gray *just* visible on the void's black canvas; brightened by constant sun, the western jungle's unending green leapt from the dark backdrop; and twinkling between them, a snaking blue river divided the globe in two.

"It is a beautiful planet," Elama said, rising to her feet and joining Torin at the front window.

"I am unsure any like it exists."

She pressed a hand on the glass. "I do not understand the meaning of these events—and I cannot even attempt to predict what will come of them."

She nodded to herself.

"But perhaps we will finally learn how humans came to be here, some two and a half million light years away from Earth."

ACT I

The Mysterious Visitors

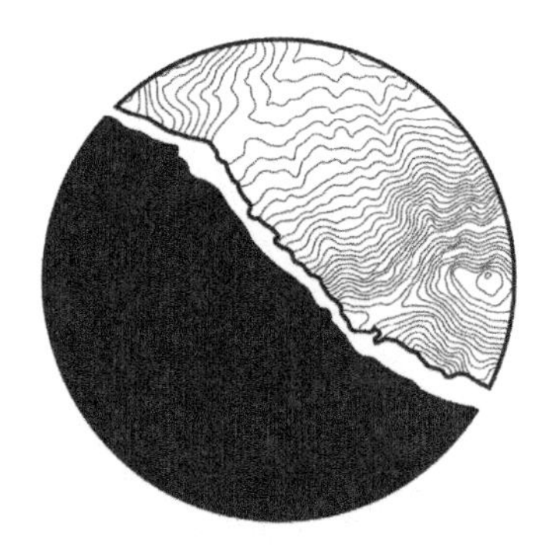

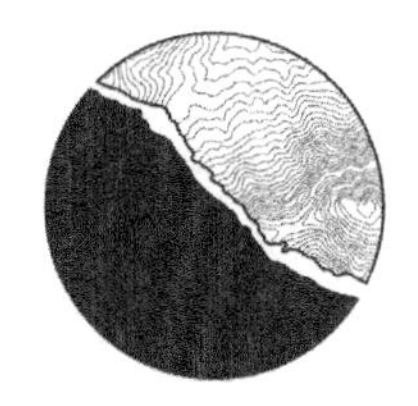

Chapter 1

It'd been just over 135 hours since the last eclipse, the Rixxonian jungle's only relief from the scorching sun. That meant they had about five hours to finish the hunt and head home.

Good thing Jag didn't miss. All he needed to do was find his prey.

Crossbow in hand, he lowered to a crouch and crept through the undergrowth. The cerulean sky peeked through the perpetual green a short way off—a break in the all-consuming thicket. Jag pressed toward it. And with each step, the ever-present, all-too-familiar rays penetrated the brush about him, baking into his skin and bringing a soft warmth to his face.

Jag found solace in hunting. Making himself scarce, becoming one with his surroundings—it comforted him. He had one goal, and one consequence for failure: no fresh meat for him and Sixxis. This fed his instinct, clearing out everything but his will to survive—which was usually *great* for days like today when he was having trouble shutting his mind off. Not even hunting was helping today, though. He couldn't shake his thoughts.

It all seemed so... *loud*.

The brush thinned as Jag made his way to the cliff's edge. There, he pressed his back against a tree.

This was probably his favorite spot in the jungle, the one place close to home offering an unobstructed view of the Rixxonian expanse. The imposing canopy blanketed the rolling hills before him. Green faded to blue as forest met sky, everywhere save a distant, pointed peak that rose above it all.

Were he closer to the mountains, Jag might've been scared; after all, it *was* the mountain dwellers who invaded his village and scattered his people all those eclipses ago. But he was safe here. He could admire the peak for what it was: a glimpse of a world beyond his own.

Like him, it was unique, unlike anything around it.

Jag had always known he was different from the other Rixxonians. It ate at him sometimes—on days like today. His mind would spin on wondering where he came from, why he was so... *peculiar*. But he always felt ashamed for feeling out of place. Sure, some of the village kids poked fun at his non-green skin and smaller body when he was younger—especially when they grew up so much faster than him—but the jungle folk were otherwise kind and accepting.

Not that it mattered anymore. It was just him and Sixxis these days.

Jag drew a deep, cleansing breath and ran his fingers through the grass.

Ages ago, he used to ask his father why no one seemed to care that he was different.

"Through the winds of change, we stand tall as trees," his father would say, reciting the tribe motto. And when Jag would push back on how terrible a response that was, he'd add, "A tree has no feud with its neighbor, so long as that neighbor means it no harm."

Father's interpretation of the words never did it for Jag. It was Adira who taught him their *true* power.

Skies, Jag hadn't even seen Adira in probably fifty eclipses—the chief, either. Hopefully they were okay.

"Through the winds of change..." he muttered to himself.

Leaves rustled across the way, snapping him to the present as a big, white bird blasted onto the blue backdrop. Its flapping wings echoed through the ravine as Jag dropped to a knee, followed its flight—and *SHOOP!*

"Nice shot!" Sixxis hollered as the bird's momentum carried it into the trees.

Jag popped up and turned to find the athletic, emerald-green frame of his brother strolling toward him. "Hope you're hungry!"

"You know me." Sixxis' stomach gurgled—on cue. "I'm always hungry!" He held up his forearm.

Even though Jag had finished growing and filling out, Sixxis was still more capable than him in every physical arena. He'd developed into the ideal Rixxonian: a whole head taller than Jag, lean, and agile.

"This session really dragged on." Jag bumped Sixxis' forearm with his own. "I wasn't sure we'd find anything."

Sixxis tossed his shoulder-length, flaming-orange hair to the side. "Lucky for you that birdie was so big," he said, pumping his fiery brows and flashing that signature grin. "Would've been a real shame if you missed."

Jag narrowed his eyes and tilted his mouth. "And it'll be a real shame if *you* can't find where it landed."

"Challenge accepted!" Sixxis trotted ahead. Bending at each of his three leg joints—one at the ankle, one at the knee, and one in between—he launched upward and cleared the first two levels of the tree with ease. Landing softly on a thick branch, he craned his neck to look up.

Jag and Sixxis had been together since the beginning, or at least as far back as Jag could remember. They were the same in many ways, in many others they were complete opposites—but they'd always been inseparable. Good thing, too! Sixxis was so reckless, he would've gotten himself killed ages ago if Jag wasn't around. But he made up for it in a lot of other ways.

"Aha!" With some effortless hops and skips, Sixxis ascended the tree, grabbed the bird, and slid down a nearby vine. Padding into the dirt in front of Jag, he tossed a thumb over his shoulder and winked. "No problem!"

Jag rolled his eyes and shoved his brother's head.

"Hey now!" said Sixxis, jumping forward and smoothing out his hair, running his hands across the thin braids that started above his ears and met in the middle of his head.

"Who are you trying to impress?" Jag asked, one eyebrow raised.

"You never know who we'll run into!"

His eyes then drifted past Sixxis—and he gasped. "Adira!?"

The name made Sixxis whip around so fast he almost fell over.

And Jag couldn't help but laugh. "Come on," he said, bumping past and starting for home. "We should have plenty of time before dark."

"Oof." Sixxis unclipped the rope from his belt, lashed it around the bird's legs, and tossed the carcass over his shoulder. "That wasn't very nice."

"Says the guy who says *I* take things too seriously."

The brothers' banter continued as they snaked through the enormous tree trunks, pushing branches and brambles from their path and weaving down the familiar trail home. It was especially hot in the jungle—especially quiet, too. Despite Sixxis' levity, the loudness of Jag's intrusive thoughts invaded that quiet, quickening his heartbeat and tightening his chest.

Something felt off—he couldn't shake it.

"Six," he said as they approached the big stone wall propping up their lonely lean-to, "do you—"

"Shh!" Sixxis stopped dead in his tracks. "Do you hear that?" He dropped the bird and sprang onto a high branch.

Nothing. Jag didn't hear anything. "What are—"

A voice grunted from inside their home.

"Skies!" Jag slotted back and glanced up at Sixxis. "Grab me!" He shot himself up, kicking off the tree trunk and catching his brother's hand.

Growing up in the dense jungle had given Jag plenty of practice, so he was no slouch when it came to climbing. Still, he was no match for the other jungle folk. His shorter, bulkier frame gave him less reach, and he didn't have the long, spindly fingers and toes that helped the others keep their grip and balance.

Stabilizing on the thick bough, he crawled forward.

Did someone actually find their home? Jag and Sixxis had done such a good job camouflaging it that no mountain patrol had ever bothered them. Adira and the chief even had a hard time figuring out where they were hiding.

A man in black pulled the bracken cover aside and stepped into the open. He walked forward a few paces, looking down at something in his hand—as *another* man in black emerged behind him. But the black wasn't what caught Jag's eye.

These men—they weren't green!

"Who are these guys?" Sixxis asked. "And what are"—his face exploded open as a beam of sunlight glinted off something on the second man's belt. "Is that my machete!?"

Jag grabbed his brother and almost got pulled out of the tree. "We don't know what they're about, Six!" he whispered. "We can't just run at them."

Typical Sixxis—never thinking before he did anything.

"But—"

"Just take a beat," Jag said.

Jag may have had disadvantages to the Rixxonians, but his eyesight was far superior. He was also hyper aware of all the ways he could die at any given moment. This was a product of the loudness, but not a bad trait for someone growing up in a dangerous jungle. Add in his hunting skills, and he was great at breaking down a situation.

"Can you tell what they're saying?" he asked.

Sixxis shook his head. "Sounds like some other language."

Another language...

All his life, Jag had never seen *anyone* else who looked so different from the other Rixxonians. They were green, he wasn't. They bled purple, him red. But now these men... one yellow, the other pale like the clouds in the sky.

Eyes glued on the object in his hand, the yellow man grabbed the pale man's arm and pointed into the distance. They nodded to each other, then started up a hill.

And for the first time all day, every thought left Jag.

"We have to follow them."

It was slow going for Jag and Sixxis. To avoid being seen as they trailed the men, they stayed high in the trees—a task that proved more difficult for Jag. But the men luckily stopped now and then to check the handheld object. These moments helped the brothers stay close.

The jungle grew denser as they traveled, mimicking the compounding collection of thoughts that enveloped Jag's mind. Who were these men? Where had they come from? Were they a link to Jag's past—to the truth?

He couldn't turn it off. Question after question poured in, and no answers came out.

Then came the memories. Jag found himself transported back to a time when he was taller than Sixxis—when their parents were still alive.

Their parents...

There was obviously something they'd never told him. What if—

"Jag." Sixxis elbowed his ribs, breaking his unrelenting stream of consciousness. "Look." He nodded forward.

The forest thinned out ahead of them, revealing four wooden platforms connected by a series of ladders, circling and ascending a mighty tree. Atop each sat a bungalow that fully encased the tree's trunk. Beyond the first group of familiar huts, Jag counted four more.

"The Forbidden Village..." he mumbled.

There was no mistaking it. Even though Jag hadn't seen the village since the flight, its imagery was imprinted on his mind. He and Sixxis lived here ages ago—back when it wasn't forbidden. It'd been lost to the depths of the jungle since.

Yet somehow these men had led them straight to it.

"What could this mean?" Jag said.

"Not sure." Sixxis hopped forward a bough. "But let's go check out our old place!" He skipped across a series of branches.

"Six—wait!" A wave of discomfort washed over Jag, stretching up from his toes and through his constricting chest. He dropped to a seat and leaned against the tree trunk.

Everything changed that night.

The mountain dwellers were on them before anyone could react. Those who survived the initial attack fled into the dark jungle, running for their lives from an enemy they could barely see. Then mother and father organized the last defense, a diversion so anyone left could escape.

That was the last time Jag saw them. And now he was back, approaching this world forgotten by his day-to-day life.

Curiosity and excitement, fear and dread—it all hit him at once.

"It'll be dark soon," said Sixxis, pointing up at the sky's somber, navy coloring. "We'd better get out of the trees."

Practicality. Yes—that's what Jag needed.

He grasped at the branch and ran his fingers across the bark, noting every groove in its ribbed texture as he surveyed the village structures. "Our old hut should be on the third level of..." He pointed. "That tree!"

Sixxis grinned. "You're not that much older than me, you know."

"Right," Jag said with a nod. "Sorry."

"*Relax*, brother."

Relax—easier said than done.

A chilling breeze blew past as Jag glanced up at the sky. Taking in the almost full eclipse, he whispered, "Through the winds of change..."

"What?"

"Nothing." Jag drew in a deep, regulating breath. "I'm fine." He dropped to a lower branch. And after plotting his way across a slew of sturdier limbs, he skipped forward, bit by bit until he reached the nearest high platform.

Making it look effortless, Sixxis followed and joined him. "Should be easier now," he said, tiptoeing toward a plank bridge.

"Careful," Jag said. "If I remember right, these bridges can be—"

CREAK!

"Go!" Jag tucked into a quiet run behind Sixxis as they bolted across the bridge, took a hard left, crossed another bridge, and ducked into a bungalow—*their* bungalow.

Or what was left of it. Beds were broken, chairs overturned—the place had been picked clean.

Sixxis shrugged. "Guess the village wasn't so forbidden after all."

Stepping inside the open doorway, Jag turned and gazed out at the platform—the precise spot where he had one final conversation with his parents.

"Six, do you—"

His eyes darted to his brother, widening at a sudden realization: someone was coming.

"Hide!" Jag jumped aside and pressed against the wall. Clutching at his chest, he did everything he could to control his breathing—but to no avail. He was starting to lose it.

Years away, he'd finally come back—and for what? Who were these men? Were they dangerous?

Sixxis ducked under a nearby windowsill. "Focus," he whispered. "What do you see? What do you hear?"

A light knocking signaled the men's arrival to the platform, rattling Jag's attention free from worry. All that remained was the situation. Catching Sixxis' eye, he flashed five fingers: Five sets of footsteps; two people on opposite bridges, one coming up the ladder.

Jag and Sixxis weren't exactly in the best position, cornered in their old bungalow with no exits but the open doorway and two windows. But that was beyond the point now.

Reaching behind his back, Jag drew two arrows and held one in each hand—as the yellow man came to the window and peered inside. Scaled face, beak mouth—Jag had never seen anything like it! But before he could get a better look, the pale man appeared in the doorway, a menacing expression coating his rounded features.

Just then, a high-pitched call broke the silence. "Eyoooo!"

Both men whirled about and took a few steps forward—as an arrow flew through the darkness and pierced the pale man's arm.

"Agh!" he called out, gripping at the arrow as he teetered off the platform and plummeted to the ground.

Another man—this one tall and red with a long, swishing tail—drew a small device and pointed it into the jungle. A terrifying noise erupted through the trees as flashes of light flew from its barrel.

Seemingly scolding his companion, the yellow man shouted and stormed toward him.

"Six!" Jag hollered through the chaos. "Now!" He dashed through the doorway, lowered his shoulder, and rammed into the yellow man. At the same time, Sixxis grabbed the top of the windowsill, swung forward, and plunged his feet into the red man's back.

Both spilled over the lip of the platform.

Arrows still in hand, Jag brought himself upright and faced down the remaining two. Clad in that same black armor, they looked almost identical to the yellow man.

One of them drew his device and pointed it at Jag. His beak mouth clicked as he said something unrecognizable—then another arrow flew through the black and flung the device from his hand.

Yelling into the night, the second man unloaded his weapon on their unseen attacker.

Jag seized his opening and jumped on the offensive. He threw a punch at the unarmed man's face, then spun around him and drove the arrow into his back—but it shattered on impact with the armor.

The man grunted as he whirled around and swung at Jag's stomach—but Jag was ready. He hopped back to avoid the blow, then clasped his hands above his head and brought them crashing down onto the man's head. And as his opponent toppled forward, Jag threw a shoulder into his body to pick him up and force him over the edge.

"Ready to join your friends?" said Sixxis, gripping the last man's leg. And with spin, he heaved him off the platform, into the darkness.

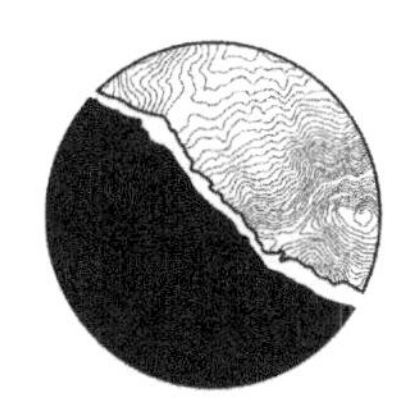

Chapter 2

Answers—here one second, gone the next.

Jag leaned out over the platform's edge. The short night shrouded the forest floor in darkness, the jungle quiet consuming the moment's intensity.

"See anything?" Sixxis asked beside him.

"No."

But Jag didn't need to see. Nothing could've survived that fall—right?

He leaned out further. "We should—"

"Hey!"

Sixxis popped upright. "I'd recognize that voice anywhere!"

"Since the mystery's been solved," Adira's words murmured through the gloom, "will one of you come give me a hand?"

"You go ahead," said Sixxis, patting Jag on the back as he turned for their bungalow. "I need to look around some more."

Add that to the day's list of strange things. Sixxis *never* missed a chance to help when someone needed it, no less Adira.

"Hello?" she called out. "Are you—"

"Coming!" Jag tucked into a jog, creaking his quickened steps onto a plank bridge, rounding right, and creaking onto another. And as the bridge rocked and swayed with his rapid motions, the image phased into his reality.

Beams were scattered about, charred marks littered the tree—the man's weapon had all but destroyed the hut.

"Under here!"

Adira's tight, orange top bun gleamed beneath the rubble as Jag rushed to her side. "Are you—"

"Yeah, I'm fine," she said, gripping round a beam with her long fingers. "It's just my leg." She tried to push up with her body. "It's stuck."

Jag dropped to a crouch and threw his hands under. "One... two... three!" They lifted the splintered wood enough so she could wriggle free.

"Thanks!" Adira brushed off her Therulin tribal tunic, flicking dust and dirt from its white and purple threads, then hopped to her fallen longbow. "I don't know what I would've done if I lost this." She slung it over her shoulder.

"I'm just glad you're okay," Jag said.

"Me, too." Standing tall, finally looking at him, she offered a smile. "It's good to see you."

That was an understatement for Jag—*he* was thrilled!

Other than Sixxis, Adira was the only real friend Jag had ever made. They just had so much in common. She too struggled with loud thoughts, and she too had responsibility piled on her when she was young. Suddenly, everything they'd known the first stretch of their lives was erased, scattered into the night by invaders. Adira tended to her injured father, Jag kept close watch of his reckless brother—all while avoiding the mountain dwellers' patrols. And so passed some 250 eclipses.

Then things slowed down. The patrols lessened, even stopped. And one day, Jag and Sixxis just stumbled upon her and the chief—a glorious reunion not unlike this one.

"Thanks for the help," Jag said, returning the smile.

"Where's Sixxis?"

Jag shrugged. "Said he needed to look around some more."

"Always on the move, that one," she said, rolling her eyes in a way she only reserved for Sixxis.

"How'd you find us?"

"I was coming to talk to you, then I saw those men at your lean-to—so I tailed them. And it's a good thing I did!" She shook her head. "I didn't need a close look to know they were bad news."

"Why—because they looked different!?"

"What?" Adira scowled. "Where is *this* coming from?"

"Sorry," Jag said, hanging his head. "It's been a weird day, and—"

"You thought those two would be your connection to something about yourself."

Blinking, darting his eyes about—focusing on anything *but* her—Jag muttered, "...ye ah."

"Don't snap at me." Adira whirled around and took a few powerful strides away. "If I wasn't here, they wouldn't have connected you to anything but the dirt."

She was right. Jag wanted to believe he had a handle on the situation, but he didn't.

With slow, somber steps, he came to her side. "Did you ever think we'd be back here?"

Adira nodded. "Not this soon, though. I don't think I'm ready."

"Ready for what?"

"Father is dead," she said, squeezing her eyes shut. "He became the soil with the last eclipse."

"I... I'm sorry."

"It's all right. He'd been ill a long time—almost fifty eclipses."

Skies. That explained why Jag hadn't seen her in so long.

When they reconnected, Adira and the chief said they were searching for their scattered people, and that a return to the village was forbidden until they had more numbers; fear of the mountain dwellers' return was too great. And so the jungle folk stayed together but separate, gathering periodically for communal hunts. Then the hunts stopped without explanation.

Adira lifted her head, casting her gaze into the shadowy woodland. "Do you remember that day?"

Remember? Of course Jag remembered.

"I don't think I'll ever forget."

"Father always blamed himself, you know." She plucked at her bowstring. "He said it was his fault the village wasn't prepared."

"We were as prepared as we could've been."

That much Jag knew. The tribe just didn't stand a chance against the Rinx tribe's metal weaponry.

"I still see them," he said, staring forward.

Adira tilted her head to face him.

"When it's dark—especially now that we're here—I can see them running off while I—"

"There was nothing you could've done," she said, placing a gentle hand on his shoulder. "We were so young."

"I barely even got to say goodbye."

"Goodbyes are overrated."

Maybe she was right. Jag's goodbyes to his parents left him with nothing but questions.

"Jag," mother said, kneeling in front of him, "you have grand purpose ahead of you. You *must* survive this night." And as she walked away to say goodbye to Sixxis, all father did was recite the tribal words. Next thing Jag knew, Sixxis was pulling him away.

Grand purpose... now and again, mother's words came back to Jag. He found himself questioning if there truly *was* more. And now, being back in the village, having seen not one but *five* men who were clearly *not* from the jungle...

"Through the winds of change..."

"We stand tall as trees," Adira finished with a smile. "Glad to know the words are still alive in you."

They were more than alive in him—they carried him forward in life. And it was all thanks to Adira.

"Trees can't predict the winds and the rains," she told him one day long ago. "They don't know what's coming or what might affront their existence on a given day. But no matter what comes—no matter how strong it is—they stand tall."

This explanation brought out the words' power. And so anytime things were *loud*, when it seemed like Jag couldn't do anything to escape his thoughts, insecurities, or fears, he used this simple phrase to remind himself that there was always more to the situation—that at almost every moment, there were things at work beyond his control.

"I bet it's been loud for you since losing the chief," he said.

Adira nodded.

This was the foundation of their relationship, this almost daily experience they shared—when inner body revolted from all sense of logical thought. Sometimes it was helpful to focus on what they knew to break out of it: sights, sounds, smells, things they could touch. Other times, all that helped was to step back and acknowledge that they knew nothing—to surrender control by admitting they had no control.

And sometimes nothing worked.

"Jag?"

His eyes creaked open, bringing him back to the present. "Sorry, I—"

"It's okay. This isn't easy for me, either."

Jag half-smiled, then turned toward the ladder. "We should make sure those guys aren't going to come after us."

Sixxis stopped in the doorway and took a long, sweeping look at the remains of their old home.

For a while now, he'd had this crazy idea: Find the village and bring Jag to it. He'd ventured out several times searching and failed—but now they were here! Things were going *exactly* according to plan.

Okay, maybe not exactly. Those goons—wherever they came from—they weren't part of the plan. Neither was Adira, but Sixxis wasn't complaining about that.

Grinning to himself, he re-entered the bungalow.

How long had it been since he saw her? Somehow nothing had changed; his heart started doing flips the moment he heard her voice. It would've been *great* to go out and talk to her—but he had something to do first. More accurately, he had something to find.

Sixxis had already rifled around a bit, but obviously the men had interrupted him. Now with Adira distracting Jag, he could rifle in peace.

Jag had always been hard on himself; took things too seriously, too. He'd get stuck in these slumps, lost in his head, never bringing Sixxis along. But that was okay; Sixxis knew what was happening. And despite it all, Jag had spent their entire lives taking care of him. Sixxis had been waiting for the right moment to return the favor—and that moment had finally come! Now was *his* chance to take care of *Jag.*

He'd find the answers his brother craved.

His eyes panned left to right, passing from a pile of debris, across the central tree—to a small, overturned cabinet by one of the broken cots.

"There you are!" Sixxis bounded across the room and lifted the cabinet upright. Dropping to a knee, he yanked open its lone drawer—and his shoulders sank.

Empty.

He shoved his hand in and rooted around—still nothing—then flopped backward.

This whole time, his mind had been locked on a particular item from their past: their mother's journal. It *had* to be here. He'd seen her put it in this drawer loads of times, and there was way too much going on that day. She couldn't have done anything with it, right?

"Where *are* you?" With a huge sigh, he lifted his head and knocked it into the floor.

RATTLE.

His eyes popped open, and he knocked the floor again.

RATTLE—inside the cabinet!

Sixxis rolled onto his knees and shuffled over. He went for a more artful approach this time, drawing his fingers along the drawer's inside edges.

"Aha!"

Slipping a fingernail into a crack on its side, he lifted the bottom wood and revealed a hidden compartment. Nestled inside was his mother's journal.

Yes!

He pulled the small, leather-bound book into his hand, then crossed to the center tree and leaned against it. There, he opened to the first page:

> *I discovered today that I am with child. Despite the uncertainty of these times, Wazzaru and I could not be happier to—*

Boring! This was obviously about Sixxis. He flipped forward several pages.

> *Jag is taking to our home nicely. He is a curious little thing, always—*

Nope; too far. He turned back, this time skimming as he flicked the pages—until his jaw dropped.

> *Wazzaru took me there today, to the place where he found him. It's odd, a sort of metal orb. We told the chief about it, and a party is being sent to excavate what they can from the wreckage.*
>
> *It's strange. I felt a severe sense of cold from the orb, yet I feel nothing but warmth from the child who has come to be my son.*

Whoa—this was *huge!*

Beaming ear to ear, Sixxis pocketed the journal, fully intent on sharing it with his brother when they were in a safe place. He shoved off the tree and started for the door—then something glistened in the corner of his eye.

"Ooh!" With a hop in his step, he moved over to a pile of wrecked furniture and started digging, tossing things over his shoulder left and right. Then his smile stretched even wider.

Arrows. Five of them. And they were made of the most lustrous, silvery metal he'd ever seen—just like his machete.

"I'll take those, thanks!" He'd give the arrows to Jag now and save the journal for when they got home. "Hey Jag!" Skipping past the door, he vaulted through the open window. "Where'd you get off to?"

"Down here!" echoed his brother's voice from below.

"Be right there!" Sixxis jogged toward the edge, then crouched and grabbed the platform to drop himself to the next, then the next—*THUMP!*

Down on the ground, Adira jumped. She turned and threw a glare his way.

Sixxis gave his fiery brows two quick pumps, then sprang into a backflip off the final platform. And after landing gracefully on the soft soil, he sauntered her way. "Oh—hey, Adira. Sorry, I didn't see you there!"

Skies, she was incredible. Sixxis' feelings for her had only grown since the flight. He spent so many days wondering if she was okay, hoping he'd see her again. And every time he *did* see her, his feelings hit him that much harder.

"Where have *you* been?" she asked, rolling her eyes.

Heh—always resisting his charm. But Sixxis didn't buy it.

"I wanted to spend a little more time at home," he replied with a shrug.

Adira lifted a single eyebrow. "This is hardly the—"

"Why so tense?" Sixxis moseyed over and started reaching an arm around her shoulder. "It's a lovely night, and—"

Adira ducked his arm and sent him stumbling. "Sorry—didn't see you there."

An enormous grin stretched across his face. He'd missed their banter.

This was *exactly* why Sixxis had been into her for years. She didn't take anything from anyone! She was beautiful and strong—inside and out—the fiercest, most tenacious woman he'd ever met.

Then again, he hadn't met many women.

The truth was that Adira reminded him a lot of his mother—what he remembered about her at least. Mara was an unyielding warrior, which is why she stayed behind to lead the final defense as they fled.

But still, that wasn't what Sixxis *really* saw in Adira.

Warriors weren't hard to come by among the Rixxonians. It *was* hard to find true leaders, people who not only cared enough to make a difference in the lives of others, but consistently acted on it—people like Adira and the chief, like Jag.

"Thanks for helping us out up there." Sixxis shifted his weight and leaned in toward her. "Especially with how dark it's gotten, it's amazing you were able to nail that guy right in the arm!"

"Well"—the corner of her mouth twitched—"someone has to keep an eye on you two, and I know you don't have anyone else."

A smile radiated from Sixxis' face. "Can't say I'm complaining."

"What are those?" she asked, pointing at the arrows in his hands.

"Oh, these? I found them in our old place!" He gave one a twirl. "Pretty, aren't they?"

"They're beautiful."

"*You're* beautif—"

"Hey you two." Ahead, somewhat obscured in the twilight, Jag knelt on the ground beside two bodies. "Come check this out."

Adira's emerald cheeks flushed orange like her bun. Shaking her head out, she turned and trotted toward Jag.

Sixxis stretched his long, lean frame as high as it would go, then brought his hands behind his head. He traipsed forward with a swagger, arrows still firmly in one hand.

"Here you go," said Jag, pulling the machete from the yellow man's belt.

Oops! In all the excitement, Sixxis had almost forgotten about the stolen machete. Not great, considering it was a gift from father.

"Look here, too." Jag pointed at a small, quiver-like object attached to the man's calf. "Arrows, and it looks like they're made of the same metal."

The silver sparkled in Adira's eye. "Sixxis, aren't those—"

"Yeah!" Sixxis tossed his arrows on the ground beside Jag. "I found these up in the bungalow just now. Do you think this is why they're here? Are they looking for this metal? And how did they find it so easily? It's hard enough to—"

"Will you *please* slow down?" said Adira, rubbing at her temples.

Jag lifted a small object from the man's belt. "Maybe this? I did notice them looking—"

A bright light exploded from the object, illuminating their faces on the dim avenue.

"...what in the world?" Jag said.

"What else do these guys have?" Sixxis pulled the sheath from the yellow man's body, wrapped it around his waist, and stowed his machete. As he then scanned the man further—probably because of what he read in the journal—two small metallic spheres caught his eye. "Ooh!" He grabbed one.

"No pulse," said Adira, kneeling between the bodies with two fingers on each neck. "Both dead."

"Nothing could've survived that fall," Jag added.

Sixxis stopped listening, fully distracted by the curious orb. He ran his fingers along the shallow grooves in its cold body—until he found a button that he didn't hesitate to press.

BEEP!

"Waaah!" he screamed, throwing his hands in the air and letting it fall to the ground.

"What was that?" Jag said. "I've never heard anything like—"

BEEP BEEP!

"I don't like this thing *one bit!*" Sixxis reared his leg back and gave the orb a powerful kick—searing pain into his exposed toes. "Yeow!"

BEEP BEEP BEEP!

A deafening explosion broke the still of the jungle. Flames erupted from the tiny sphere, brightening the area in a blaze and sending the three Rixxonians diving for their lives. But Sixxis' kick had luckily sent the object both away from them and into the village's only clearing. Before long, all that was left to show for it were a few smoldering branches.

Flat on his stomach, hands over the back of his neck, Sixxis peeked over his shoulder. "That was close."

"*Too* close!" Adira yelled, storming toward him and yanking him off the ground. "What were you *thinking*? You could've killed us!"

Uh oh—now he'd done it.

"I'm sorry! I didn't mean—"

"Of *course* you didn't mean to! But that doesn't make it okay!"

"Guys," Jag muttered, looking into the distance.

"I just—I don't know. I got a little carried away."

"A *little!?*"

"Guys," Jag said, this time a bit louder.

"But we're okay! Doesn't that count for—"

Jag grabbed their arms and spun them to face the forest edge. "We're not alone."

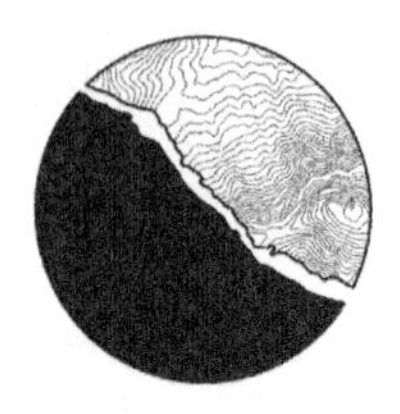

Chapter 3

Jag didn't even consider giving Sixxis grief about this one; Adira seemed to be handling that just fine. Besides, he'd learned not to get too bothered by his brother's carelessness. It was just part of who he was.

But this was not good.

A creature had emerged from the brush, creeping through the settling dust that shimmered in the waning eclipse's faint light. Low to the ground, it ambled about on all fours. A horn jutted out from the thick skin of its gray snout, less terrifying than the broad spikes shooting from its sides.

Jag had met this creature once before—the night of the flight. He didn't need to see its teeth to know they were sharp.

As he motioned for the crossbow on his back, two more fiends crawled out from the thicket. So he instead grabbed the others and pulled them behind a nearby hut, off the main road.

"Zerns," he whispered, leaning out to keep an eye on the beasts.

"Zerns?" Sixxis repeated.

"Don't you remember? The Rinx mounts? They were here—you know—the last time *we* were."

The lead zern stuck its snout into the air. Finished exploring the charred ground, its companions crept toward the black cauldrons lining the avenue, all but completing Jag's mental flashback.

There was a time when the flames in these cauldrons illuminated the night. Every eclipse, villagers snaked between them and danced about—even on *that* night, that fated final night when everything changed.

They'd never been lit since.

"He's right," said Adira, leaning out over Jag. "Those gray hides have clearly never seen the sun." She whirled back to cover and shook her head. "I don't understand, though. According to the Treaty of the Rixxon Tribes, they aren't allowed out of the mountains. The—"

"Treaty?" Jag repeated, spinning back to face her. "What treaty?"

"Father brokered peace with the mountain chief before he fell ill. Evidently, the—"

"I don't think these zerns have read the treaty," said Sixxis, reaching for his machete.

"We're bound by that same treaty!" Adira whispered with more intensity. "If we harm them, it's an act of war!"

"Well—isn't *that* convenient?" Sixxis folded his arms. "The one time we run into these beasties, and—"

"We can't," she said. "It took father years to reach the agreement. If—"

SNARL!

Startled, Jag leaned out to get a look. All three zerns weaved between the cauldrons, making their way toward the companions' hushed voices.

"I *really* don't think these things care about all that," Sixxis reiterated.

Jag sighed. "Adira's right. We don't know why they're here, but we can't hurt them."

"*Fine*." Sixxis sheathed his machete.

"There are only two things this could mean," Adira added, flopping against the hut, "and neither are good."

Jag kept his eyes locked on the beasts.

"In one scenario," she continued, "these creatures have merely escaped. That feels unlikely, but if it's true, there are probably more."

"And the other?"

"The Rinx have once again declared war on the jungle, and it's just a matter of time before they're here."

"But why would they do that!?" Jag whipped back, heart racing. "We've been scattered for years!"

Adira shook her head. "It doesn't make sense to me either."

It was too much to be coincidence. On the same day Jag couldn't shake his edge, non-Rixxonians appeared in the jungle and led them to the Forbidden Village, a place long since abandoned—a place none of them had even *seen* since fleeing all those years ago. Now there were beasts from the mountains in that same village, just like the night they left.

No, there was something at work here—something big.

"There's got to be more to it," said Jag, shaking his head. "What if those guys are to blame?"

"It's definitely possible," Adira replied. "But seeing as they're dead..."

"Well, I don't know about you two," said Sixxis, "but I'd rather not become something's snack and join them." He clapped his brother on the shoulder. "What's the plan?"

Jag stood tall. "We make a break for it."

"We can't run into the jungle," said Adira. "The zerns are too fast; they'll overtake us."

"We're not going back. We're going to the Great River—and we're going to cross it."

"*Cross it?*" Sixxis spewed—too loudly. He ducked into a crouch. "Why?"

"I can't help but think this is all connected," Jag said. "And even if it's not, we need to get to the mountains to figure out what's going on."

"He's right," agreed Adira. "We have no choice."

Sixxis looked at Jag, then Adira, then back at Jag. He shrugged. "You know I'm with you."

"We don't know what we'll find over there," Jag continued. "We should grab everything we can just in case."

Sixxis offered his forearm. "Right behind you."

With a nod, Jag bumped arms with his brother, ducked low, and dashed into the open. Kneeling beside the bodies, he removed the quiver from the yellow man's calf and slung it over his head. His eyes then lingered on the second metal sphere. He didn't want to think he'd need it, but the day had already not gone as planned—so he grabbed it.

Slinking past, Sixxis scooped the arrows off the ground, then came up behind Jag and loaded them into the quiver.

"Guys," said Adira, still behind the hut. "Our friends are gone."

Jag popped upright.

Why would they leave? They had to have—

Sixxis tapped his shoulder, then pointed at a zern creeping out from the brush—right by them. Jag's eyes then darted about the village, and sure enough, he found the other two.

They were surrounded.

"Well," said Sixxis, standing back to back with his brother, "so much for that."

Skies! What was Jag thinking? He'd run into the open—dead center of the avenue, totally exposed. Now the zerns circled them, growling and gurgling at their soon-to-be prey. What did he expect?

At least there was some light now.

The avenue ran straight ahead between the two lines of cauldrons. At its end, the great Ancestor Tree stood resolute, looming over the gloomy village whose inhabitants had abandoned it. If Jag remembered correctly, the avenue stretched east to west, meaning the river was a straight shot from their position.

PAT... PAT... PAT... The beasts continued their slow crawl around the brothers.

"Adira." Jag shifted his gaze toward her. "Do they know you're there?"

She shook her head.

Good—one more convenient thing.

Jag had confidence in his straight-line speed; he could outrun the zerns, at least until he ducked back under the brush. Sixxis and Adira weren't quite as fast on the ground, but they could use the trees in ways Jag couldn't.

"We'll need to split up," he said, "but we won't get anywhere without a distraction."

Adira drifted to the ground and picked up a rock.

"The river is due east," he continued, nodding down the avenue. "I'll run down the road and try to draw them. You two scatter and hit the trees. Redirect and make for river when you can."

Sixxis bonked Jag's head with his own. "What happened to not outrunning them?"

"I should be fine with nothing blocking my path."

"I don't like that word '*should.*'"

Neither did Jag, but that was beyond the point. Run or get eaten—there wasn't much choice.

Still hidden, Adira pointed north and mouthed the word, "Bridge."

Jag nodded. "Once you clear the jungle border, head north. We'll meet up and find a crossing point."

"Got it," said Sixxis, digging his toes into the dirt.

"One..."

Jag bent at the knees.

"Two..."

Rock in hand, Adira slotted back.

"Three!"

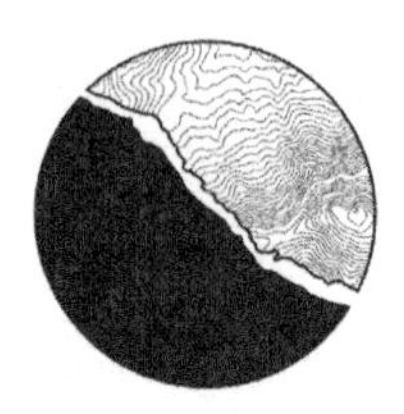

Chapter 4

Jag exploded through the zern pack as Adira's rock banged between two trees. Tearing down the dirt-laden avenue at full speed, he kept his focus forward and pumped his arms with every step—as *THUMP THUMP THUMP,* his hunter's drubbing feet made it clear how close he was to death.

The sun peeked its way out high overhead, revealing just how far he had to go before he could rest. But at least he had a marker to run for. Towering over the main village square, the mighty Ancestor Tree was impossible to miss; it dwarfed everything around it, carrying the souls of those who'd passed into the skies above—or at least that's what everyone had always said. It was different for Jag, though. The Tree offered a sort of otherworldly comfort, maybe because it was different from all the others in the jungle, maybe because no one understood it.

It would've been great to see it again—not running for his life.

After a full-minute dead sprint, Jag came within a reasonable distance of the Tree. If it was still standing, the chief's villa blocked his way east on the other side. He'd have to go around.

Jag drifted to the left side of the avenue. It would've been too hard to redirect sharply and maintain his pace, so he aimed to hit the square at a diagonal. And if he angled it right, he'd just brush past the southern tip of the villa.

Pumping out three quick breaths to count down, Jag planted his foot and shot into an altered course.

Success! He cleared the edge of the villa, keeping his distance from the trailing beast. Good thing, too—because it huffed and snarled behind him, not losing a single step.

Redirecting east, Jag burst under protection of the brush. *Finally*, he could start looking for a spot to catch his breath. And when he found one, he ducked down and pressed his body against a large trunk.

Betrayed by its low sightline, the zern lost track of him and continued past—but not for long. It slowed to a stop and sniffed the air.

Jag couldn't keep running forever; that much was obvious. And what would happen when he got to the Great River? As far as he knew, it'd been forever since any jungle dweller made the crossing. How could he be sure it'd be simple? It's not like anything else had been that day.

He couldn't risk it. He needed to lose his zern.

Short of breath, Jag searched for his solution. It was tough to see much of anything, so he floated upright—ever so slowly so as to not reveal himself—and poked his head into the open. Still nothing; all he found was unending green, the same unending green in every other part of the jungle.

Skies!

The zern scoured the ground a ways ahead, seeking its prey. The brush seemed to taper just beyond it—maybe a pit, or a ravine? If Jag could just trap the zern, maybe—

SNAP! He leaned too hard on a fallen twig, catching the beast's ear. It took no time to relocate and charge at him.

Out of options, those skin-tearing teeth screaming toward him, Jag came up with a crazy idea. He shot out three quick breaths and launched himself forward—right at the zern. Closing the gap quickly, he feigned preparation to jump.

The zern responded by leaping toward him—exactly as he hoped it would.

Jag dove and slid feet first under the beast, then popped up on and continued his sprint toward what he *hoped* to be some sort of dropoff.

The zern screeched to a halt, rustling the surrounding undergrowth as it turned and renewed its pursuit.

Jag confirmed his suspicion as he drew closer: there *was* a dropoff, a small pit just deep enough to trap the beast. He pounded to a stop, threw his gear aside, and turned to face his hunter.

Baring its teeth, showing its fatal intentions, it surged from the ground.

Jag threw himself down and slammed his back into the dirt. He guided the beast's jump with his hands and feet, sending it over the edge with nothing more than a few scratches on his arms. And then for the first time in what felt like hours, he laid back and caught his breath.

The zern snarled up at him.

"You stay down there, okay?" he said, rolling onto his stomach and pushing himself up. The pit was fairly wide, so he'd need to navigate around it—but that wouldn't be hard now that something wasn't trying to eat him. Hoisting his crossbow over his shoulder, he fixed up the rest of his equipment and set out at a trot.

Before long, he broke the eastern barrier of the jungle.

It was astounding, the impossibly straight treeline bordering the clearing, running north and south along the river's edge. But more confounding for Jag was the open space before him. Save a few scattered on the river's other side, there wasn't a single tree beyond the jungle border. And so the unending green was consumed by brilliant blue, the jagged gray peaks poking up into it.

Jag's pace lagged, lost in a wonder that both trapped his mind and spurred it forward with a sort of inward purpose. On another occasion, he would've lingered to marvel at the beauty.

Not now, though—he was still in danger.

He stopped to survey the steep hill before him. North of his position were two wooden poles, seemingly posts of a plank bridge—just what he needed!

Finally feeling somewhat safe, Jag jogged up toward the posts. As he crested the ridge, a collection of red-stained buildings on the other side filled his view; maybe they'd be nice places to lay low and lose the zerns.

A wave of relief, one that'd been missing from the previous parts of the day's adventure, washed over him as he continued his jaunt up the hill—only to discover his true obstacle.

The bridge had been cut.

Things were no longer going as planned.

Thanks to Sixxis' carelessness, their stint in the Forbidden Village was short-lived. He could've killed them all—as Adira didn't hesitate to remind him—and now that task had been left to the zerns. One was hot on his tail. Another was behind Adira as far as he knew, but he hadn't seen her in a bit.

"Stupid," he said to himself, running the wrong direction as the zern nipped at his heels. "Let's see how well you climb!" He picked up his pace for a few steps, found his footing, and leapt upward, landing flawlessly on a high branch.

Easy!

But the beast surged up the trunk, latched on with its impressive claws, and started to climb.

So much for that.

"...right—bad idea!" Guessing which direction was east, Sixxis took off and bounded through the branches, as the zern released from the tree and continued its pursuit on the ground.

Talk about persistence! How could something so vicious ever be trained as a mount? There's no way *anyone* could've ridden that sucker—not in a million eclipses!

Sixxis couldn't lead it to the rendezvous point; that wouldn't go well. He needed a new plan. So turning north—he was pretty sure—he continued skipping across limbs, running parallel to the Great River. Then some rustling drew his attention left.

He grinned. "Adira! Over here!"

"Not a good time!" Also dashing through the trees, she gave an exhausted nod to the ground—to the other zern racing in step with her. "You're going the wrong way!"

"No I'm not—trust me." He veered in her direction. "And follow me!"

In turn, she angled toward him until they were running side by side. Her zern, on the other hand, didn't change direction so gracefully; it collided with Sixxis'.

Finally—a chance to take a break! They both slowed to a stop.

"If we lead them to the river," Sixxis let out between breaths, "we're not really escaping. Plus we're putting Jag in danger." He blew out a load of air. "We have to lose 'em."

"I *did* think of that," said Adira, doubled over, "but I hadn't quite figured out what to do about it."

Sixxis popped tall and propped a hand on his hip. "Then it's a good thing you ran into—"

"Can you stop trying to impress me and just get on with it?"

Sixxis scratched at his head, offering a weary yet warm smile. "Now that we're leading them away from the river, we should rise in the trees until we're out of sight. They'll assume we're still moving and keep chasing, allowing us to"—he walked two fingers across his forearm, then nodded east—"get away."

"That could work!"

Below, the dazed and hungry zerns shook themselves out and put their paws on the tree's trunk.

"We should get going," said Adira. "These things can climb pretty well!"

"Yeah," Sixxis replied with a nervous laugh, "I learned that the hard way." He waved his arms and gave an exaggerated bow. "After you, m'lady."

"You're impossible," she groaned.

The two took off through the trees, only this time, each leap brought them to a higher bough. Steadily, they rose through the understory and into the canopy, and it didn't take long to get out of sight. Sixxis soon slowed to a stop; Adira did the same a few branches ahead.

"Bye bye!" Grin plastered to his face, Sixxis twinkled his fingers at the ground as their predators zoomed past.

"Yes! It worked!"

Sixxis lifted a playful eyebrow."Do I detect a tone of surprise?"

"Maybe a little," Adira replied through a slight smile. "And you really *should* stop trying so hard to impress me."

"But is it working?"

Her smile widened. "Maybe a little."

Jag scanned the towering treeline, and the lush meadow that stretched all the way to the massive drop-off at his feet. The rope-and-plank bridge hung loose across the gap, swaying and rattling into the rocky face. No sounds or even signs of movement came from the buildings above. And the Great River raged on far below, slapping the cliffside.

Things were *not* looking good.

There wasn't much of a way forward with the bridge gone. Falling from such a height would surely kill them, and if it didn't, there was a good chance the powerful current would—but none of that would matter if Sixxis and Adira were *already* dead. It'd been a while since Jag stopped running, and still no sign of them.

Day had finally arrived, but it wasn't the same day he knew from the jungle. It was dimmer, quieter, almost like he stood in the shade despite the cloudless sky. Jag couldn't decide if it was calming or creepy—but again, that didn't matter.

"Come on, Six..." he muttered. "Where are you?"

Just then, they exploded from the trees south of him—looking tired but otherwise fine!

"Sixxis, Adira—up here!"

"Jag!" Sixxis shouted, wiping sweat from his forehead. He charged uphill.

Jag charged back and grabbed him by the shoulders. "I'm glad you're okay!"

"Likewise, brother," Sixxis replied, touching their foreheads together. "So what do we do now?" They broke apart. "Can we cross?"

"Not here," Jag said, pointing at the lifeless bridge across the chasm.

"*That's* inconvenient."

Adira jogged to the edge. "Our friends?"

Jag's mouth wrinkled. "Probably."

"At least we're clear of the beasties!" added the ever-positive Sixxis. "We led ours very much in the wrong way."

"I trapped mine in a pit," Jag said. "It's not permanent, but it'll give us time to figure out what's next."

Sixxis leaned out over the precipice. "You know, it's not that far. I bet I could clear it in one jump!"

"*You*, maybe,“ Adira retorted. "Not us."

Leave it to Sixxis to confidently present a wholly unhelpful plan. Then again, Jag didn't doubt him; he probably *could* have cleared the gap. That wouldn't have been much help to Jag or Adira, though.

Then Jag's eyes fell on his brother's rope. "That's it!"

"Umm, what's it?" Sixxis lifted an eyebrow. "Care to bring us along?"

"Toss me your rope," Jag said, dropping his crossbow and drawing one of the arrows from the village. He tied it tight to the rope, took aim, and fired.

The special metal almost glowed as it whizzed across the gorge. And it didn't just pierce the building on the other side—it flew straight through the wall!

Sixxis grabbed the other end of the rope and took off down the hill. "I think I see where you're going with this!" He leapt up a tree on the line, pulled the rope taut, and lashed it to the trunk, then plucked at it and signaled back with a big thumbs up.

"You first," Jag said to Adira.

"Got it!" She jumped up and gripped the line with both hands, then brought her legs over top and crawled across. And when she hit the grass and turned back—her face exploded open. "They're back!"

Jag whipped southward as the two zerns launched up the hill at him. "*Skies*!" He grabbed the rope and climbed across, then dropped to the ground and turned to find Sixxis still in the tree. "What are you doing!?"

"I'm not leaving this behind!" In rapid, subsequent motions, Sixxis drew his machete, cut the rope, and catapulted himself from the tree, hitting the grass mid-stride and breaking into a sprint. The sudden movement seemed to catch the zerns by surprise, but they redirected toward him in no time.

Adira rushed to the cliffside. "What is he *doing*?" She turned to Jag. "Is he crazy?"

Skies.

Jag grabbed the rope and started coiling as fast as he could. "I think you know the answer to that question!"

Sixxis didn't slow his gait. He raced uphill, looping the rope around his waist and tying it tight. And with the zerns chomping at his feet, he ran right to the end of the line and launched into the air.

Time stopped as Sixxis hurtled across the gap. Frozen in place, Adira looked on in horror.

"Adira!" Jag snapped, cutting the silent tension as he hustled toward the building's open entryway. "Help me weigh it down!" He wrapped the rope around his arm and planted his feet.

Adira rushed over, grabbed his other arm, and held fast to the doorframe. They braced themselves.

Sixxis *just* made it across. He planted his left foot and tipped backward into the gorge—lurching them forward—but their combined strength proved enough.

They caught him!

Stunned, Jag and Adira just stared.

"Uhh..." Mouth agape, body at an angle, Sixxis balanced with his toes hooking the cliff. "...could you pull me up?"

"Right," Jag said, shaking his head out. "One, two, three!" They heaved, yanking Sixxis forward and flattening him onto his stomach.

"Are you kidding me?" Sixxis lifted his head up and looked at the others. "There's no way that worked." He rolled onto his back, whipping his flaming hair about as he roared out in laughter. "Seriously—tell me there's no way that worked!"

Adira stomped over and smacked him. "You idiot! I can't *believe* you!"

"You're lucky I know you as well as I do"—Jag flashed a haggard grin—"and that Adira was here. I don't think I could've caught you on my own."

"You're right!" With his signature grin stretched across his entire face—vertically *and* horizontally—Sixxis jolted upright. "I *am* lucky to have you two."

"Flattery won't get you out of this!" Adira shouted with a scowl. She marched off. "How could you be so reckless!?"

Sixxis scratched at his head. "Oops."

With the heat of the moment—or rather, string of moments—passed, the day's drama flooded Jag's mind. "She's right, Six." He approached his brother and helped him up. "That was too close."

"It worked out okay, though."

Jag shook his head. "You've *got* to stop using that as justification. It's not always going to work out."

Sixxis had trouble taking things seriously his whole life. It rarely put him in any *real* danger, though, probably because he always had Jag behind him.

"I don't know how to explain it," Sixxis said. "I just... had a feeling, you know? We don't know what we'll find up there, but I think this rope is going to come in handy—probably the same reason you grabbed that fireball."

Jag's head tilted. "Fireball?"

"You know—the little explodey thing? I saw you grab it off the yellow guy's belt." He shrugged. "After what happened earlier, I could argue that was a major risk."

Sixxis had a point. Jag didn't have time to think it through all the way, but he had that same thought back in the village. For whatever reason, he felt this "fireball" might be necessary on the road ahead.

"Well, it's a good thing I'm the one carrying it." He gave his brother a shove. "It'll be a while before I let you play with explosives again!"

Sixxis erupted into another bout of laughter. "Yeah," he said, wiping tears from his eyes, "probably best to not let me touch it." His grin returned. "I have to admit, though—I loved it!"

Jag rolled his eyes and joined in on the laughter.

Then Adira's voice trembled from beyond the building, "Boys... you're going to want to see this."

Jag caught Sixxis' eye, then trotted toward her. She stood a ways ahead as they rounded the building, just past where its walls ended. And when she didn't say anything further or even turn, they picked up speed.

"What's going on?" Jag asked, keeping his eyes on her as they came to her side. "What'd you find?"

Adira still didn't speak. She just nodded up the hill.

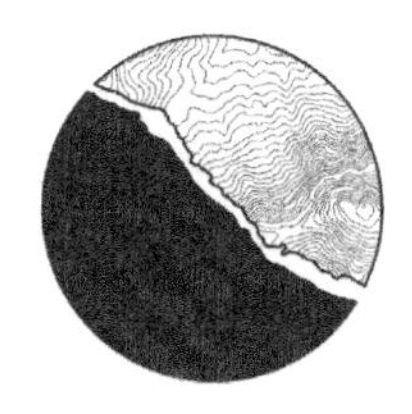

Chapter 5

It was horrifying.

What must have once been little more than a farm—a pleasant place at the foot of the planet's peaks where mountain folk tended to their fields—was now a battered wasteland riddled with death.

Beyond the first collection of red-stained buildings, the terrain expanded into a sea of quiet barns and meadows. Short fences partitioned off a series of pastures, leading up the slope and into the mountains. And all over, coagulated streaks of crimson and lilac connected the mangled corpses of paled Rixxonians, zerns, and livestock.

A cool breeze swept through the area, filling Jag's nose with the unmistakable smell of blood. "What..." He trailed off, unable to finish his sentence.

Even Sixxis—one who never failed to bring levity to a situation—didn't have much to say. He walked forward and dropped to a knee beside the purple-stained remains of a leather-clad Rixxonian. There, he finished Jag's question: "What happened here?"

Adira knelt beside him and ran a finger along marks on the body's leg. "Teeth... The zerns must have had their way with these people."

The gruesome scene stretched through the pastures, past the faded grass line, and up into the mountain pass. A lump rose in Jag's throat as he considered the way forward through the carnage.

"You must've been dead a while, huh?" Sixxis asked his fallen kin.

Adira pressed a hand into the man's neck. "Still warm."

"Then why's he so pale?"

"Remember what I said about the zerns? The same is true of the mountain folk; their skin has paled from lack of sunlight."

"That's something I'll never forget," said Jag, finally summoning the strength to speak. "On the night of the attack, their pale green bodies all but lit up in the darkness." He squeezed his eyes shut as his heart began to race.

Life had been difficult since the flight. The jungle was dangerous, but nothing *ever* compared to this massacre—not even close.

"Until now, that was the most terrified I'd ever been."

Adria floated upright. "All the more reason not to linger."

"You're right; we should keep moving." Jag took the lead. He tried to focus on each solemn step as he came to the building's other side, breathing through his mouth to avoid the overwhelming stench.

"Could this have been those guys?" Sixxis asked.

"I'm not sure," Jag led them into a narrow alleyway. "After what their weapon did to that hut back in the village, I think we'd know if they did this."

"Makes sense."

"I wouldn't be so quick to make a prediction," Adira cautioned. "Indirect means of sabotage can be more effective."

Jag stepped out of the alley and onto a dirt pathway. It led uphill past three fenced-in meadows, each filled with the scattered carcasses of white, woolen field beasts. But it was a straight shot into the pass.

The way into the mountains was clear.

Jag took in a deep breath, then let it out. "There's only one way to know for sure."

Jag gripped the stone platform and hoisted himself up. Before him, a battered, rocky road led between two soaring cliffs.

It'd been a difficult, surreal journey since the farm. As the three companions ascended the slope, the terrain shifted from luscious green to jagged gray. The rocks lining their path scaled with its steepness; before long, they were using both hands and feet to keep balance as they traversed the talus field. And adding to the eerie setting, the slow brightening of the day never came to fruition. As they moved further east, away from the fixed location of the Rixxonian sun, it only grew darker.

None of them had spoken since departing the scene below.

The quiet allowed Jag's mind its first bit of space since they encountered the men. There was no doubt: Each and every event from the day was connected. If he could just keep moving, he might find answers—what caused all this death, the origins of the mysterious men, maybe even his own past.

And if he stopped moving—well—he'd probably go crazy.

Sixxis hopped up onto the platform, then turned to help Adira. "Would you look at that view?" he said as she stabilized on the plateau. "You can see the entire jungle!"

Jag didn't turn. The only view that mattered to him led forward.

Adira brushed dirt off her legs as she came to Jag's side. "Father always told me of the 'Old Road' leading from the mountain pass into the Rinx settlement." She took a few steps forward, kicking at the rocks with her elongated toes. "This must be it."

With a nod, Jag set off into the canyon with purpose.

While the way forward snaked, turning every which way as it progressed deeper into the mountains, the height of the massive cliffs on either side never diminished. Every rock-rattling step echoed, bouncing wall to wall as it rose up and dissipated into the perpetual dusk. The trek was otherwise silent, save elegant, far-off birdsong that twittered down from the canyon's rim.

A constant, gentle wind blew past their bodies. Jag pressed on, grateful for his boots in the stone-laden gorge.

It was unsettling here. Various creatures inhabited every corner of the jungle, and even the smallest movement rustled some portion of the dense foliage. Pair that with the ever-present rushing of small streams, and the region never afforded this sort of quiet.

Jag could almost *hear* his thoughts.

For a time, these thoughts dwelt on the day, trying to make sense of everything. And they kept drawing Jag back to that final conversation with his mother—to his "grand purpose." He still had no idea what any of it meant, but with this wild string of events, there was a feeling he couldn't shake—that it was all part of something greater.

Was there such a thing as destiny? Was Jag born here different from everyone else for a reason?

Was all this death somehow *his* fault?

Heart pounding, Jag lifted his head and felt the cool breeze on his skin. Concentrating on the crisp mountain air, he felt an odd sense of familiarity—but that was impossible. He'd never been out from under the canopy.

"We stand tall as trees," he whispered, shuffling to a stop as the walls expanded outward.

Adira stepped in beside him. "This must be it."

Before them lay a tremendous valley, still and quiet beneath the endless night sky. Stone platforms peppered the space, connected by a series of bridges. On each platform stood hosts of wooden-bodied, metal-framed buildings.

"Something's not right," Jag said. "Where is everyone?"

From the massive, rectangular structure in the distance, through the deserted stone streets, and across the simple rope bridge at the base of the their slope, there wasn't a single trace of movement. But there *was* another dead body—propped against the first bridgepost.

"There!" Jag pointed.

Sixxis bounded ahead and knelt by the woman, pressing two fingers into her neck. He turned and shook his head.

A distant, foreboding thunder grumbled through the mountains, unsettling Jag and calling his attention to the sky. Eyes locked on the growing cloud cover, he fell in behind Adira as they wandered down from the plateau.

"More zerns?" she wondered aloud.

"These don't look like teeth marks to me," Sixxis replied.

"Civil war?"

Jag stepped onto the bridge, still keyed in on the sky's increasing black. "We'll only know if we keep moving." He led the way across the wavering catwalk, onto the first terrace of the lonesome stone village. After passing a series of structures—which remained intact despite the inhabitants having either died or abandoned them—they held fast to another worn-down bridge. And on the other side, they entered an open-air market.

Jag stopped at a faint rattling sound. "Did you hear that?"

"Don't move!" shouted a deep voice, jolting the companions' attention.

"Who's there?" Jag called out.

"Drop your weapons," directed the same voice—as one by one, mountain dwellers appeared atop the surrounding buildings, arrows fixed on the travelers.

Skies!

"We mean no harm!" Jag said, lowering his crossbow. "We just want to know what's going on!"

"We were hoping *you* could shed moonlight on that," declared a smoother, warmer voice, as a stunning woman emerged into the marketplace. Wrapped in heavy armor, her pale-green body clinked as she strode forward and stopped before them. Her helmet's impressive plumage gave her a full head's height over Sixxis.

"Jungle folk," she said, sweeping her eyes across them, "your presence here is unusual." She focused on Jag. "And *you*... you are unusual regardless of where you are."

"I've known Jag since we were infants," said Sixxis, leaping between them. "He's just as much Rixxonian as you and I!"

The woman squinted. "And yet he is not the first strange being I have seen this day."

"The black-armored men?" Jag pushed Sixxis aside and stepped forward. "We followed them through the jungle. They're—"

"My name is Adira," she interrupted, standing tall, "daughter of the late Salaf Therulin and chieftain of the Rixxonian jungle. I—"

A bloodcurdling roar broke the still of the night, trembling the earth.

Evident fear washed over the woman. "We must go—now!" She whipped around and twirled an arm through the air. On her command, the soldiers hopped from their perches and closed in on the jungle folk, taking their weapons and binding their hands.

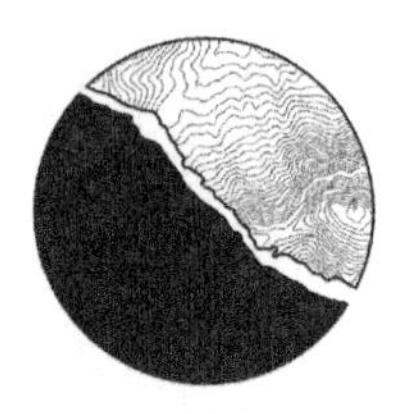

Chapter 6

Captured, strung to his companions by a line of rope, Jag stumbled through the village streets. Sound had once again abandoned the valley; all was silent save the thumping of their retreat.

"What *was* that?" Sixxis whispered behind him.

Nothing good—*that* was for sure.

"And did Adira say she's chief now?" he continued. "When did that happen?"

"She told me back in the village," Jag said. "The—"

"Hush!" commanded the imposing woman. "I will not have you be the reason I lose my soldiers!" She charged ahead, bursting onto the largest stone platform. And after a double take at its center, she signaled them toward a prominent villa tucked against the opposite mountain.

A cool, damp wind swept across Jag's body as they hustled across, flapping the muted tapestries that hung loose on either side of the open doorway.

He was a long way from home.

"Inside—hurry!" She led them through three rooms that hooked around the villa's center. And when they came to an open den full of plush seating and banquet tables, she approached the rear paneling and knocked once, then twice.

What in the skies was going on? Was all this necessary? And where were they going?

Jag might've been more patient had he not almost died so many times that day. Now he was a prisoner—which was just ridiculous! He hadn't done anything wrong. If anything, they were here to help!

A loud bang reverberated behind the wall as it lurched to life. Its two sides opened outward to reveal a cramped, rocky passageway lit by rows of mounted torches.

The woman stepped inside. "This—"

A horrible noise boomed in from outside—another roar, this one chilling Jag to the bone.

"Quickly!" She tore forward, leading the group through a snaking series of tunnels—as *BANG!* The wall closed behind them. Before long, the cavern widened into a dank chamber lined with bunk beds.

Scattered about, a host of mountain dwellers talked amongst themselves.

Before Jag could finish counting, a strikingly beautiful, pale-green woman trapped his gaze at the room's center. A collection of small braids wrapped about the sides of her head, all converging and joining a large central braid that fell past her shoulders with the rest of her pale-orange hair. Despite her simple attire, her energy and presence made it clear she was someone important—maybe the tribe's chieftain.

The armored woman shuffled ahead to speak with her.

Impatience continued to brew within Jag, slowly pooling to the top of his body. And the two women just continued their conversation, glancing over their shoulders and acting like their visitors were some great threat.

He'd had enough!

"We saw the men you fear"—Jag surged forward—"and we killed them! We've since been chased by *your* creatures—creatures not allowed in the jungle by the treaty *you* signed—and walked through a valley of death to come to you!" A soldier grabbed his arm and tried to pull him back, but he yanked himself free.

"We're not a threat!"

The chief stepped out and nodded; following her orders, the soldiers loosened the travelers' restraints.

"Thank you," Jag said, rushing forward, rubbing at the rope burns on his wrist. "Please—we just want to know what's going on."

"Very well," she replied with a kind expression. "I suppose we cannot deny you an explanation."

The other woman drew a massive greatsword from behind her back, thrust its tip into the ground, and placed her hands on its hilt, eyeing the visitors with clear intentions.

The chief chuckled. "I must apologize for the rough reception," she said, gesturing to the woman. "Jade is both my guard captain and my lifemate. She merely aims to protect me."

"Talk about a power couple," Sixxis whispered.

"I am Kithara, Chieftain of the Rinx Tribe. I can only imagine how difficult your journey has been."

Adira stepped forward and offered a bow. "Thank you for speaking with us, your eminence. I—"

"Please," Kithara said, waving a hand in front of her. "No need for such formalities. Call me Kithara."

"Thank you, Kithara." Adira smiled, but just for a moment. "I am Adira, daughter of the late Salaf Therulin. This here is Jag and Sixxis."

"So Therulin has passed." Kithara's eyes fell to the ground. "Time has taken much from us of late."

"We followed five mysterious men to our old village," Adira continued. "There, we were ambushed by a group of feral zerns and forced to flee for fear of endangering the treaty. We then crossed the Great River just west of a farm."

Kithara's ears perked up. "Tell me," she said, looking to Jag, "is the valley of death you spoke of?"

Jag nodded.

"So the carnage has spread beyond the mountains..." Kithara hung her head for a silent moment. "Your actions were honorable indeed," she said, lifting her gaze and offering a smile. "You would be worthy of official commendation were circumstances different; however, I fear now is neither the time nor the place."

"Chief," said Jag, "we've—"

"Please—Kithara will do. I have only been chief a short while."

Jag nodded. "We've encountered nothing but death since crossing the river, even your own people lifeless in the streets of your village." He paused, looking to Sixxis for confidence. "What exactly is happening here?"

Kithara's expression sank.

"Look around you," she sighed, opening her arms to indicate the huddled masses. "This is all that remains of our people—or rather, this is all we *know* of what remains. Our scouts continue to bring more back to us."

"This..." Adira rotated her head round the cavern. "This is all that's left?"

Kithara nodded. "As you may know, mining is our way of life. We excavate the caverns in search of precious metals and minerals and use them to build our civilization." Her gaze drifted past the travelers. She stepped through them to follow it.

"It seems we have angered the mountains. No longer do we question what lies deep beneath the earth."

She paused.

"Three days ago, our clearing specialists triggered an explosion to open a new area in the central mine not far from here. This action is commonplace. All the usual precautions were taken."

Slowly, she turned toward them.

"Not long after, miners began disappearing. I sent Jade to investigate." Her gaze floated across Jag, Sixxis, and Adira, resting on each as they passed. "It was then... that I *heard* it."

"Heard what?" Sixxis asked.

"A *terrible* roar."

"The same one we heard in the village just now?" Jag said.

She nodded.

"What is it?"

"Perhaps Jade can take it from here." Kithara turned to the captain. "My love, please describe what happened when you looked into the disappearances."

"Certainly, my chief." Clapping a fist to her chest, Jade bowed her head in compliance. "I set out with eight guardsmen, five of whom you met moments ago. We discovered a trail of blood as we neared the mine. And when we followed it to the plateau, we witnessed something dragging one of our people into the shaft."

"Something?" Jag repeated.

Jade nodded. "From a distance, it looked no different from our zern mounts, so I let out a holler. It dropped the man, reared back on its hind legs, and charged us full speed. We stepped back and prepared to receive it, but every bounding step it took revealed how wrong I was: it was far larger than any zern."

Jag struggled to imagine a more terrifying creature than the vicious beasts from the village. "How did you get away?"

"It came straight for me," Jade replied, meeting his gaze. "My first officer shoved me out of the way and sacrificed himself—setting the rest of us into a wild rage. But it was no use; nothing we did pierced its hide. Six of us escaped to warn—"

"And we rushed to gather the villagers in this sanctuary built by my grandfather." Kithara placed a warm, comforting hand on her lifemate's shoulder. "Jade and her guard saved our race."

"Not all of them," Jade said, releasing her weapon, clanking it onto the stone ground as she dropped to a knee. "The beast had yet to leave the plateau before we goaded it." She hung her head. "It followed us—we *brought* it here. And it feasted on our people. Worst of all, my chief..."

Kithara removed the captain's mighty helmet, revealing a close haircut with intricate symbols shaved into it. "It's all right, my love." She cradled Jade's head against her hip. "You did everything you could."

"I wasn't strong enough."

"Nobody is as strong as you."

Adira knelt and drew her eyes level with Jade's. "I know your feeling." She looked up to Kithara. "And yours. I watched my own father fall to an untimely death, and I too was thrust into a position I was not at all ready"—she shot upward—"I apologize. I only mean to—"

"It's all right," laughed Kithara. "Whatever the circumstances, the two great tribes have been brought together again."

This was all good and fine, but Jag still had questions.

"Kithara, this beast—what is it exactly?"

"We fear it is an ancient ancestor of the zern that until recently found its home deep in the under caverns. It looks much like the creatures we have come to domesticate, train, even love—but it is many times larger." She shook her head. "A beast of legend... we call it the Thakk."

With that, Jag realized the full weight of the situation. It didn't take a wild imagination to know what would happen if the monster was left to run freely.

Grand purpose...

He turned to Jade. "You said I wasn't the first strange being you've seen today."

She nodded. "I saw two men in the distance as we fled the beast. I would not have noticed were it not for their bright yellow coloring."

"Sounds like our friends," said Sixxis, cocking a foot back and folding his arms. "Guess we were right after all."

Despite confirming their suspicions, Jag's unease only grew. "Do you think they released the beast?"

"It's possible," Kithara mused, "but to be honest, the Thakk has only been a part of our worries. Once it ravaged the town, our citizens were scattered and forced away from the village. Driven wild, our zerns then turned on us, almost as if the monster had some sort of ancestral control over them."

Jag darted a glance to each of his companions. "So the beast drove them feral?"

"I saw it," said Jade, drifting to her feet. "Once the creature roared, something shifted behind the eyes of our mounts. They were dangerous in an instant; it didn't take them long to develop a taste for our flesh."

"Well, there are three in the jungle now—but the bridge is out." Sixxis shrugged. "That should keep any more from crossing."

Kithara sighed. "That is the first relieving thing I've heard in some time. Perhaps it will keep tragedy from escaping the region."

Escaping the region? That wasn't much of a relief. This Thakk was a threat to all life on the planet.

For the third time that day, mother's words rang in Jag's mind.

He bent at the waist. "Might we have a moment?"

"Certainly," replied Kithara, bowing in turn.

The companions retreated back a few steps and tightened into a circle. "You know what we have to do, right?" Jag said.

"Isn't it obvious? We've got to take that thing down!" Sixxis gave his brother a shove. "You know I'm with you."

Jag could always count on Sixxis.

"Me, too," said Adira. "I can't stand by—not while I know I can help. Besides, if we don't do anything, it's just a matter of time before this monster finds its way to the jungle, and our weapons aren't nearly as strong as the ones made here. Things will only get worse."

They were a long way from the jungle. And just as it had been all day, the next step was clear—but that didn't make it any less terrifying.

Jag turned and approached the powerful women. "Kithara, captain—we request a guide to the mining plateau."

"I cannot allow you to do that," Kithara replied, shaking her head. "This is our battle."

"With all due respect"—Sixxis stepped up beside Jag—"this is our battle, too."

Adira fell in on Jag's other side. "Though it originated here, this conflict will carry itself beyond the mountains before long."

"It's our duty to all life on this planet," Jag finished with a nod.

Kithara let out a heavy sigh. "Very well. But I will not force anyone to—"

"I will guide you," said Jade, rising to her feet. "And I will fight by your side."

"Are you sure, my love?"

"These travelers speak of duty. Despite being far from home, they do not shy from this task I've already failed to complete. My honor would be lost if I did not assist."

"If you are sure"—Kithara gripped her lifemate at both shoulders and pressed their foreheads together—"I will not stop you." She turned to her visitors. "Jade will see that you are properly outfitted before you depart."

"Thank you," Jag said with a bow.

"I will return, my lady." Jade placed a gentle kiss on Kithara's cheek, then hoisted the sword onto her shoulder. "This way." She started for the entrance. At the snap of her fingers, the soldiers scurried to return the confiscated weapons to their owners.

Sixxis fell in behind Jag, whispering, "She's quite the woman, isn't—"

Thump! Adira gave him a swift kick.

Jade escorted them to an adjacent chamber with weapons, armor, and ammunition strewn about, all lumped into disorganized piles. "This is our makeshift armory," she said. "Take whatever you please."

Jag dropped his crossbow and surveyed the messy room. Unsure what he'd need, he pulled arrows from a nearby barrel and filled his quiver before rummaging around.

"Jag—check this out." Sixxis tossed him a small barrel.

Oil. Not bad, Six. If this thing really was used to the deep darkness, it might not like firelight.

"Good thinking!" Jag said. "Grab one more."

Adira combed through a small pile, then equipped two ankle scabbards and sheathed a small dagger in each.

"Six." Jag gestured to a machete the same size as his brother's.

"Ooh!" Sixxis' grin stretched wide as he grabbed it by the handle, drew his own weapon, and twirled both about. "Not a perfect balance, but it'll do."

Hah—showoff.

"Ready?" Jag said, heaving his crossbow over his shoulder.

Jade's head tilted. "Do you not want thicker armor?"

"Nah." Sixxis squatted low and hopped. "We're more nimble this way." He moved to the room's center and thrust his fist forward. "Shall we?"

"For the jungle," declared Adira, similarly outstretching her arm.

"For the mountains." Jade added her fist.

Jag stepped forward and joined in. "For all of Rixxon."

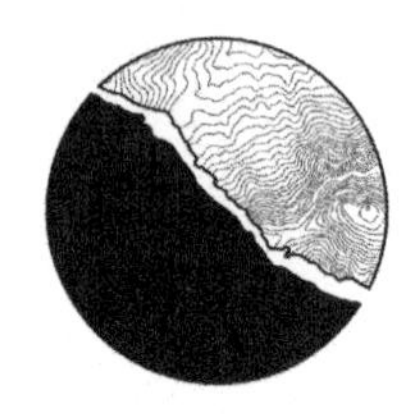

Chapter 7

Gone were Jag's hesitation and fear. All that remained was the memory of his mother's words.

With Sixxis and Adira in tow, he followed Jade through the deserted village. They came to the final bridge before long, its lifeless planks glowing in the faint moonlight.

Thunder rumbled through the shifting clouds, reverberating off the distant peaks. Jag's grand purpose rumbled with it as they crossed and stepped onto an incline flanked by soaring stone walls.

"Here we are," Jade said as they came to the top. "The mining plateau."

It was almost perfectly square in shape. Steep cliffs surrounded their position, reaching into the foreboding sky. And opposite them, a colossal doorway loomed over the flat face.

"We'll want to steer clear of those," Jag said, pointing to the sheer drop-off on both sides. "That'd be a nasty fall."

"What is that?" Adira gestured to the platform's center, where a collection of words and symbols carved a marvelous and symmetrical work of art into the stone floor.

"The engravings designate the importance of this place," Jade explained. "The center message is our tribe motto: 'Strength and wealth from deep within.'"

Adira smiled. "A beautiful senti—"

SCRAPE!

Three of them jumped back, dropping below the lip of the incline. Sixxis stayed still, prone, peering across the plateau.

Jag crept forward to join him, as the Thakk dragged a corpse from its lair.

Just as Jade had described, it looked like a big zern. But it had jagged scales in place of the smaller species' side spikes, and sharp spines jutted from its backbone.

Stopping atop the engravings, it began to feast.

Jade furrowed her brow beside Jag. "It appears *this* will be our arena."

The pitter patter of rain added to the monster's quiet crunches; more thunder rolled through the swelling storm.

"The moon's position was perfect for this assault," she continued, looking to the sky. "Now I fear we are at a disadvantage."

"Not if we're clever." Jag rolled down the hill and offered his barrel to Adira. He pointed at a high ledge to the right of the opening. "Can you light up the ground?"

"Good thinking," she replied with a nod.

"Six, did you get that other barrel?"

Sixxis rolled the barrel down the slope without looking.

"I'll support from the other side," Jag continued. "My shots will be slower, so you'll probably draw its attention first." He shuffled up and put a hand on Sixxis' shoulder. "We'll need you to distract it. Try not to step on any fire."

"No problem." He still hadn't taken his eyes off the Thakk.

"This beast is very smart," Jade warned. "It won't be long before it sees what we're doing." She nodded at Jag and Adira. "I will defend your positions."

"Thanks." Jag stepped out, hugging the left wall with Sixxis close behind. He placed his barrel on the ground halfway to the drop-off, then popped its lid and loaded a wooden arrow into his crossbow.

Adira followed the wall in the other direction, leaving Jade at the opening. In deft silence, she ascended the rock face and settled into position atop the high cliff.

Sixxis crouched. "Ready brother?" he said, drawing and applying oil to each machete

The rain surged, pelting Jag's face, cooling the warmth exuding from the moment's heat as he closed his eyes. "We stand tall as trees," he whispered.

It was time.

After a single, deep breath, Jag opened his eyes, nodded—and lit his barrel ablaze. Adira did the same across the way.

With a flaming machete in each hand, Sixxis let out a war cry. He charged the monster, leaping into the air as he drew closer, *just* avoiding the protruding spines as he thumped onto its back.

The Thakk responded with a howl of its own, one that shook the arena.

"Six!" Jag launched a blazing arrow. "Are you crazy?"

"Meant to go over—whoa!"

The Thakk thrashed about, bucking Sixxis to the ground. He landed on his feet, then crouched and waited as the monster's tail came sweeping toward him. Surging into a backflip, he hacked as he rotated over.

CLANG CLANG! Sparks flew. He may as well have been cutting rock.

The Thakk's roar trembled the earth.

"Don't bother with the tail!" Sixxis yelled. "Too strong!" He hit the ground and took off running—and the Thakk gave chase.

Using the flaming machetes to guide his aim, Jag launched a special arrow at the beast. But even the precious metal, the arrow that flew cleanly through the barn wall—the presumed reason those men were here in the first place—wasn't strong enough to pierce its hide.

High on the cliff, Adira lit arrow after arrow, showering the plateau with light. Before long, the boundaries of the battleground were in view.

Sixxis kept running, his distraction proving perfect until a flash of lightning ignited the scene. Though brief, its intensity provoked another terrible cry from the monster.

Then one of Adira's shots rebounded off its leg. Abandoning its pursuit of Sixxis, it took a beat to locate the high flame and bounded off.

"Adira!" Sixxis sprinted after the beast.

Skies!

Thinking fast, Jag lit an arrow and heaved his barrel at the charging Thakk. As it then ricocheted between two spines, he pumped out three quick breaths and let a fiery arrow fly, inflaming the beast's oil-coated backside.

"Yes!" he celebrated—too soon. If anything, the fire only made the Thakk pick up its pace. Now bounding faster than ever, it continued on, back ablaze.

Jade erupted from her position. Clasping her enormous greatsword with both hands, she whirled it above her head and sliced at the behemoth's front leg.

The beast's outcry boomed through the mountains as it stumbled forward and crashed into the cliff.

Adira was quick to action: before the Thakk hit the wall, she leapt from the cliff and landed gracefully on the ground, tossing her head toward the captain. "Nice one, Jade!"

But this revealed her position—and the Thakk pounced, throwing her onto her back.

Rolling side to side, Adira managed to avoid two vicious bites, and when the third came, she wedged her longbow in the beast's mouth.

The Thakk reared its head back. Stretching its neck toward the sky, it snapped the bow in two and brought another attack down on the defenseless Rixxonian.

She threw her arms in front of her face—then *THUD!* The enormous creature lurched aside. Rounding the battlefield, Sixxis had accelerated to full speed, lowered his shoulder, and rammed it as hard as he could.

Its meal interrupted, the Thakk turned its fury on the disoriented Sixxis.

"Back, you devil!" yelled Jade, stepping between them. She lifted her greatsword over her head—one hand on the hilt, the other on the blade—as the Thakk lunged. And with a wide stance, she caught its mouth and held it in place.

Even in the heat of the moment, Jag's jaw dropped. Kithara wasn't kidding when she said nobody was as strong as Jade. How could anybody hold such a monster like that?

Sixxis' head wobbled side to side beneath the struggle.

"Six, get out of there!" Jag said.

"...what?"

"Go!" Jade shouted, startling him enough to send him scurrying. Once he was clear, she screamed into the night and rotated the blade, slicing her hand and drawing blood from the beast.

With crimson dripping from its maw, the Thakk cried out and brushed Jade aside with its tail. Fully depleted, the Rinx captain had no chance of avoiding the attack: it launched her toward the drop off, and the beast launched toward her.

Another push would've meant Jade's death; Jag needed to do something. And so standing in the direction of the charge, he took careful aim with one of the metal arrows, held his breath—and let it fly.

The arrow squished into the monster's left eye, bringing it to a screeching halt.

Ever so slowly, rain pummeling and splashing into its enormous body, the Thakk turned to face Jag—and to his absolute horror, elevated itself onto its hind legs, reached backward, and ripped a spine from its back.

Nothing stood between Jag and the beast that now approached him on two legs wielding its own spine as a weapon. It let out the most terrifying of sounds as it reared its arm back and brought a strike down.

Move or die! Jag dropped his weapon and dove to the side.

Missing only slightly, the Thakk once again hoisted its blade and swung at him—but missed. The momentum sent it stumbling.

Its one-eyes vision was betraying it—that was good at least. They had no hope of defeating the demonic creature, though. They needed a new strategy.

Jag didn't wait for the Thakk to regain its balance before putting distance between them. Heart racing, he rushed toward the center of the plateau and turned to take in his surroundings, hoping *desperately* that a plan would present itself. Forward and to the left, Sixxis helped a beleaguered Adira to her feet. Forward and to the right, Jade lay stunned from the beast's tailsweep.

The Thakk renewed its pursuit, the hammering of its steps matching the cadence of Jag's pounding heartbeat. It heaved its weapon above its head.

CRASH! The smooth terrain exploded into rocky pieces as Jag rolled from harm.

He couldn't keep this up. He was thoroughly exhausted, and it seemed like the beast hadn't tired one bit. They were running out of time.

The sound of rocks smashing into the ground drew Jag's attention to the archway, where the force of the monster's blow had caused portions of the mine's entrance to collapse.

Skies! It was crazy—and it probably wouldn't work—but it was their only option.

"Six!" Jag yelled through the storm, pointing to the crumbling arch. "We have to get it into the—"

"Jag, watch out!"

CLANG!

Jag couldn't believe his eyes. Straddling his grounded body was Jade, holding her weapon once again above her head. She'd clashed swords with the Thakk, catching its strike and absorbing the blow.

She'd saved his life.

Without a word, Jag leapt to his feet and started for the doorway. And as suspected, his eye-gouging arrow marked him as the monster's prime target: it swept its other hand at Jade and knocked her aside before taking the bait and following him toward the mine.

Jag burst through the archway, unsure what to do next. Turning, he came face to face with the menacing beast, his arrow sticking from its eye socket.

Behind the Thakk's nightmarish frame, Sixxis finished helping Adira, then caught Jade's attention and signaled forward with his head. Jade responded with a nod, and the two warriors converged on the monster with a resounding yell.

Jade shrieked out as she heaved her blade overhead and thrust it into the beast's calf. And as she drew it from the wound, another deafening roar filled the mountains, shaking the earth.

Finally provoked away from its pursuit of Jag, the brute rotated to face her.

"I do not fear you!" she wailed, setting her feet to prepare for the onslaught.

The Thakk swung its blade at her; she parried. Lashing out in horrifying rage, it struck once more—but again, she deflected it.

Blinded by its ire, the Thakk failed to notice Sixxis climbing its spines.

"Six!" Jag yelled. "The rope! Swing the rope around its neck!"

"You got it!" Perched atop the highest remaining spine, Sixxis unclipped the rope from his belt and slung it around the monster's throat—then plunged a flaming machete into the hole left by the spine-turned-sword. As the Thakk then lurched upright in the doorway, he hopped to the ground. "Here!" He shoved the rope into Jag's hand and took off running.

Jag wrapped the two rope ends around his forearms. "Bring it down!" he yelled, heaving with everything he had to pull the staggered monster into the cavern. "Bring it down!"

As the Thakk teetered backward, Adira drew her daggers and picked up speed. She dropped down and slid under its erect and imbalanced body—slicing at the insides of its legs as she passed—then bounced from the ground, rebounded off the wall, and exited back through the doorway.

Jag kept pulling.

Retreating back a ways, Sixxis and Jade dropped their weapons to put in one final, coordinated assault: Side by side, they sprinted at the beast. And side by side, they jumped high on its body and gave it a strong kick to the chest.

"Brother!" Sixxis called out as the beast tumbled toward Jag and slammed onto its back.

With no time to lose, Jag took the fireball in hand and surged into a sprint. "Heads up!" He clicked the button and hurled it toward his brother.

BEEP!

"Shit!" Sixxis turned and ran in line with the flying fireball.

BEEP BEEP!

In one motion, he jumped, caught it, turned midair, and lobbed it toward the top of the stone gateway.

BEEP BEEP BEEP! The explosion rattled the mountain. Sixxis, Adira, and Jade turned tail and ran as the arch started to cave in.

Jag veered side to side, dodging the rock that rained down around him. Barely clearing the threshold before the bulk of the gate collapsed, he joined his companions in flight. And after a series of resounding crashes, bangs, and thuds, it was finally over.

Countless tons of rubble now lay between the Thakk and the free world.

Jag dropped to the ground with the others, laying in silence for a time. He was unbearably hot despite the endless night; steam radiated from his body. Thankfully, the ice cold rain cooled him down.

"Well," he said between wheezes, "that was something."

"Are you kidding me?" Sixxis rocketed to his feet. "That was incredible! And Jade—YOU'RE incredible!"

"Strength and wealth from deep within..." Jade had come to a knee, her sword on the ground before her. "You all... you helped complete my mission. You saved my people, and you saved me in the process." She bowed her head. "I fear I will never repay this debt."

Jag stood and approached her. "You don't need to repay us," he said, offering his hand with a smile.

Jade returned the smile. "Shall we tell everyone the good news?"

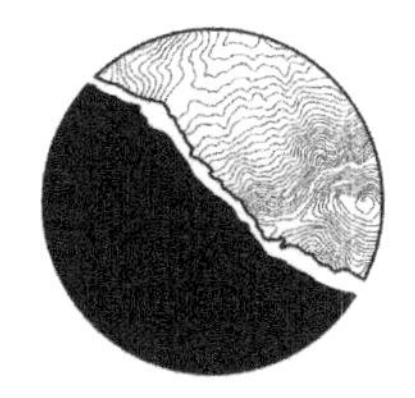

Chapter 8

Jag rolled over to face the wall by his sanctuary bunk. With the caverns vacated, the crisp, cool air enveloped his body, as the scurrying sounds of mountain folk murmured down from the villa.

It'd been about five hours since their triumphant return. Joyful celebration erupted throughout the sanctuary the moment they announced their victory—but it wasn't long before reality set in: the people of the mountains were still scattered, just like those in the jungle.

That's when the panic started. But it too was momentary.

With both Jade and Adira by her side, Kithara radiated a quiet, stately confidence as she calmed the troubled crowd. The celebration was put on hold, and all were sent out in search of their loved ones. Those who'd been lucky enough to keep their families together were tasked with assessing damage to the village and making preparations for a grand ceremony.

Jag elected to not join his companions at the front of the group. Yes, he'd been a major player in the Thakk's defeat. But when the dust settled, he felt more out of place than ever.

He should've been happier, but his mind hadn't stopped bouncing back and forth, racing between his thoughts as it tried to make sense of the day. Time and time again, he lingered on the fact that the mysterious men—the most likely causes of all this pain and suffering—were dead. And their secrets, their unknown motives were gone with them, as was anything they could've revealed about Jag's past.

He let out a heavy-hearted sigh; it evaporated into the sanctuary's silence.

With the mountain dwellers repairing their broken lives, the jungle folk were the only ones given opportunity to rest after the chaos. Sixxis was the only one who'd slept, though.

Jag couldn't help but laugh at his brother. Throughout Kithara's entire speech, he was almost drooling as the three women promised to lead the people through the tragedy. Now he was sleeping soundly, letting out the occasional snore from the bunk above.

Jag hadn't been so fortunate. He had yet to fall asleep, at least for any meaningful amount of time; there was just too much on his mind. And it'd been hours since he'd seen Adira. She was clearly awake and about, probably doing what she could to aid in the recovery.

"Sorry, Adira," Sixxis mumbled in his sleep, "I didn't mean... to..." A drawn out snore swallowed his apology.

Giving up on sleep, Jag decided he'd be better served moving around. He swung his legs to the ground and sat up. "Wish I could drop everything and relax like you, Six," he said through the upper bunk, knowing full well he wouldn't wake his brother.

A light click-clack echoed in from the stone corridor—probably Adira. Jag pressed to his feet, tiptoed over, and peeked his head through the entryway.

"Ah, here you are," said a Rinx woman with the shortest hair he'd ever seen. She continued toward him, past the crackling torches lining the walls. "I've been looking for you, Jag."

"Did Kithara send you?"

"No," she replied with a smile. "I come of my own accord. I was wondering if I might speak with you."

Jag hadn't been around the mountain dwellers long, but none he'd seen dressed this way. A pristine white layer of cloth stretched from her neck to her ankles, staying tight to her skin all the way down—so it looked, at least. She wore a looser, more traditional Rixxonian tunic over top of it. The tunic's coloring didn't match any tribe Jag knew of.

Had he not seen so many strange things that day, he might've thought twice about her. But recent events had left him tired and unguarded.

"Sure," he said.

The woman glanced up the tunnel, then ushered him into the sanctuary. "I must congratulate you on your victory over the Thakk. The battle must have been horrific!"

"We did what needed to be done for our people."

"That you did," she said with a smile. "In any case, allow me to get on with my purpose." She approached a bed opposite the room from Sixxis and gestured for Jag to sit. "Please."

"I think I've spent enough time in bed for now. What is it you'd like to talk about?"

"Through the winds of change, we stand tall as trees—is that right?"

Jag nodded. "Our tribe motto."

"Wise words indeed. I ask that you keep them top of mind as we speak."

Jag folded his arms and leaned back against the bunk.

"I—or rather *we*—have been watching you for quite some time."

"You've been..." His head tipped to the side. "...watching me?"

The woman's eyebrows lifted. "I..." She stood up straight and rubbed her hands together. "Years ago, we thought it odd you were so out of place—so different from those around you. And so we watched you. It didn't take long to discover your seemingly limitless potential, something this latest development in your life's story only confirms. You've far exceeded our expectations—and your timing could not be more opportune."

"I'm sorry," Jag said, expression unchanged. "I appreciate your kind words and all, but who exactly *are* you? And what do you mean you've been watching me? I've never seen you before."

She let out a chuckle. "We are exceptional at remaining unseen."

"Why are you here?" Jag asked, narrowing his eyes.

"Surely you must have sensed it by now."

"Sensed what?"

"Jag." Their eyes locked. "You are not of this world. I come to you now, asking you to fulfill your destiny among the stars." She stretched out her arm and pressed two fingers into her wrist.

Impossibly, a small image of the night sky appeared, floating above her hand.

"Many worlds find themselves in peril," she said. "*You* can save them, just as you saved this one."

"I..."

Jag's momentary resistance faded; he couldn't deny the events of the day. The only logical explanation behind the men was that they came from elsewhere. Their physical appearances, odd clothing, strange devices—it's why he'd been so interested in them.

But this didn't make any sense. How was it that this Rixxonian spoke of such things? And how did she shrink the stars and bring them into the cavern?

"Who are you?" Jag asked.

"My name is Elama Singh." She tipped forward into a diplomatic bow. "I am the outreach coordinator for my race."

"But you don't look any different from the other mountain dwellers."

"It is a simple modification," she said, presenting her other arm and nodding to a metal band wrapped around her wrist. "This device allows me to adjust my appearance and project as a being with whom you are more comfortable speaking. To you, this technology is unfathomable; to my people, it is rather uncomplicated."

"How do I know you're telling the truth?"

Closing her hand, Elama took away the stars and clicked something on her wristband. Bit by bit, a vibrant yellow washed over her pale-green body; she shrunk in stature; and scales poked out from her skin.

Jag's jaw dropped.

"You've seen this being today, haven't you?" clicked her beaked mouth. "This is the form of a Lommorian from the planet Lommoria."

"Whoa—watch out!" Sixxis sprang from his bunk and broke into a sprint toward them.

"It's okay, Six!" said Jag, rushing toward him "She's... well—"

"She's Rixxonian now?" Sixxis pushed past. "What just happened? Who are you?" He grinned. "And how'd you do that?"

"I am Elama Singh," she said with a bow.

"She's here to, uhh"—Jag scratched at his arm—"ask me something."

Elama fiddled further with her wrist.

"I'm confused," Sixxis said, scrunching his face together. "Wait—what just happened?"

Jag had noticed it, too. Moments ago, the villa's faint sounds trickled in through the tunnels. Now that noise had disappeared. Previously, the mountain gorge was the most complete quiet he'd ever experienced.

This was something else.

"I've created an audio-visual barrier." Elama continued tapping on her wrist. "Think of it as a large bubble. Passersby will be unable to see or hear anything we do."

"Well." Sixxis folded his arms. "That's something."

"But why?" Jag wondered aloud.

"What I'm about to share with you is extremely confidential." Seemingly finished with what she was doing, Elama brought her eyes to meet Jag's. "This merely prevents anyone from interfering. In fact"—her eyes darted to Sixxis—"I would ask your brother to step away were I under the impression you wouldn't tell him everything." She let out another chuckle.

"How do you know so much about me?"

"As mentioned, I've been watching you for some time. I know your bond with your brother is strong." She smiled. "I wouldn't ask you to keep anything from him. If you are to assist my people, I must have your full trust and cooperation."

"Who exactly *are* your people?"

"We call ourselves *Arbiters.* We travel the cosmos doing what we can to maintain peace in the galaxy. With no governing body to claim, we operate in secrecy and do most of our work via indirect means. When direct mediation is required, we work through contracts with mercenaries and diplomats. Our appearance modification technology allows us to come and go from these interactions while preserving our anonymity."

Jag's brow lifted as his eyes drifted past her.

Unhelpful explanation. What did it even mean?

"Say you go through what you have to say, and I refuse." His eyes snapped back to Elama. "Will we ever see you again?"

"To your knowledge, no."

"Why all the secrecy?" asked Sixxis.

"The unfortunate truth is that too many actions are guided by politics. Since we claim no governing body, we do not take sides in any matter. Rather, we act when a problem merits a solution that will benefit all. And this brings me to my purpose today." She double-tapped her arm below the shoulder.

And the stone ground swept from beneath their feet.

Startled, the unsuspecting Rixxonians stumbled before taking in the scene that now encased their reality: gone were the beds, the torches, and the cavern.

Somehow, they stood in the black void of space.

"As with my appearance modification," Elama continued, "this is a simple projection. We are still on your home planet."

"Amazing..." Sixxis craned his neck, basking in the wonder of the black. "Truly amazing."

"As I mentioned, Jag, you are far from alone. There are innumerable other worlds."

Countless glistening stars sprang to life, their lights stretching into thin white streaks as they rushed past. A tiny ball emerged in the distance, only growing larger as the three of them traveled toward it. Then everything froze; they were once again suspended in space.

"Is that"—Jag squinted—"Rixxon?"

Elama beamed. "Your instincts do not betray you. Yes, this is the view of your home from space!"

"I see it!" Sixxis celebrated with a hop. "The jungle, the Great River, and the mountains!" He wrinkled his mouth. "I think I missed something, though. Are you from up there?"

Jag's eyes didn't leave the floating planet. "Elama's from a different world. She says I am, too."

"Indeed," she said with a nod. "Yours is one of many life-sustaining worlds. There are a multitude of societies across the stars, all at varying levels of development." She tapped her arm once more, then again, and again. Each tap transported them to a new environment:

A vast body of cerulean water, its waves rolling in and out of each other;

A barren, sandy wasteland, with dunes reaching for the burning sunlight;

A snow-coated landscape, its details obscured by a chilling shroud of white;

A rolling green meadow, without even a single tree on the horizon;

Finally, a bustling marketplace, its grassy streets and wooden stands littered with people of all shapes, sizes, and colors. They scurried about the square, talking amongst themselves, trading goods and services.

Towering white buildings shot upward on all sides, reflecting a radiant light from the bright sun hanging in the soft blue sky. The crowd's faint murmur faded into the scene, beneath Elama's voice as she continued.

"Between these diverse societies exists a complex yet fragile framework. The people live, work, and play—even make love together. Still..." She tapped her arm.

And a desolate, war-torn image of the same market replaced the festive image.

"Their peace is tenuous. World leaders strive to maintain this delicate balance, but they are often limited by political ambitions or galactic restrictions."

A booming explosion thundered from above, halfway up one of the buildings. Debris scattered and plunged toward the ground. Jag and Sixxis dropped down and covered their heads—but everything washed away before the wreckage reached them.

They were in space once again.

"This is why my people act. We arbitrate galactic peace, setting in motion what others cannot."

Eyeing the nonexistent ground, Jag took a hesitant step toward her. "Where is it that *I* come from?"

Elama grimaced, then lifted her eyebrows. "I'm sorry, Jag." She rubbed her hands together. "Although we know quite a bit about you, we do not know where it is you came from."

Seriously? Even with this whole display?

"How's that possible!?" He said with a more confident step. "You know so much!"

"Whoa!" Sixxis hopped to his brother's side. "Take it easy!"

"If I may," said Elama, "perhaps if you agree to my request, you'll find these answers yourself." She tapped her arm a final time, returning them to the sanctuary.

"I don't think you've made your request yet." Sixxis placed a hand on Jag's shoulder. "Let's hear her out."

Was it confusion, suspicion, frustration—maybe all three? Completely lost on how to handle it all, Jag glanced between Sixxis and Elama as he stumbled back into a newly materialized bed and dropped to a seat.

"I come to you now because my people can no longer accomplish our goals without intervening. A powerful organization known as the Prospectors' Guild—or as most refer to it, the Guild—has increased its activity of late."

Prospectors? Guild? What was this about?

"Though it claims to be a federation of miners and explorers, the Guild has long been using its excavation projects as cover for criminal acts. What's more, the latest leadership prides itself in sapping environments of all valuable resources before abandoning dig sites and moving to other sources. We've been able to indirectly sabotage their operations and rescue worlds from material exhaustion, but our ability to do so decreases with each installation. Making matters worse, operations have only grown more frequent as time has drawn on." She shook her head. "We've been forced to abandon aid to all non-inhabited planets."

Jag's sense of justice welled inside him. "So they come to people's homes, take everything, and leave their planet lifeless? What's to stop them from coming here?"

"I'm afraid they've already come here."

"The men from the village!"

She nodded. "But I have not yet determined why."

Jag's heart pounded in his chest. His mind raced back in time, repeating over and over his mother's words.

Grand purpose.

"Maybe that?" said Sixxis, gesturing toward his machete propped up against the far bunkpost. "They took it from me, along with other stuff made of the same metal."

Briefly, Elama's eyes widened, then relaxed. "Perhaps." She rubbed her hands together. "What is special about that? Where did you get it?"

"My father gave it to me."

"I see."

"What can we do to keep them from coming back?" Jag said.

Elama sighed. "Unfortunately, the Legislature is too easily bought. Others are thoroughly intimidated. We are the only ones who can stop the Guild at this juncture."

She paused.

"This is what I ask of you, Jag: help us." She stepped closer. "Help us take down the Guild and dismantle its leadership. The organization simply cannot be permitted to operate any longer. It's no exaggeration to say that yours is one of many worlds in danger of its treachery." She smiled. "Of course, I do not expect you to do this alone; we will support you as we can."

"But what can I do?"

"You're capable of more than you know. And at the base of it all, I can tell you are driven by deep senses of justice and integrity."

Sixxis shoved his hands into Jag's armpits and hoisted him up. "He's not going anywhere without me!"

"I wouldn't dream of splitting you up," Elama replied with a laugh. "The two of you seem to bring out the best in each other."

"You've got that right!" Sixxis almost yelled.

"How can you be so excited?" Jag pushed away from his brother. "Do you even understand what she's asking?"

"Uhh, she wants us to help her and hopefully also find out more about you." He shrugged. "Feels like a win for everyone."

Leave it to Sixxis to boil such a complicated situation down to a simple phrase. How could he so easily commit to leaving the only home they'd ever known—especially after everything that'd happened throughout the course of day? These events would change their people forever. Perhaps for the first time in their lives, Jag and Sixxis were needed by someone other than each other.

"I can't," Jag said, short of breath.

Sixxis clapped him on the back. "That's the—wait, what?"

"I can't go, Six. Too much has happened here. They're going to need our help."

Sixxis scowled. "You don't have any responsibility to them. You only met them a few hours ago! And besides, we did our part—we trapped that monster in the mine!"

Jag's wish for information was granted, but this was beyond anything he could've imagined. Why him? He'd always been nobody, with no real expectations set on him. Why was *he* suddenly the one everyone was counting on? And who really was Elama? What was an Arbiter? And did she say destiny? Like this was all some sort of predetermined plan?

It was too much.

"If I may," interjected the outsider disguised as a Rixxonian, "it is likely that your greatest utility to your people lies above. They may take care of things here, but they can only do so much. You have the power to protect them in ways they won't even understand."

Sixxis stepped in beside Elama. "She's right, Jag. Whatever's going on, it's clearly bigger than all of us."

"I..." Jag looked to Elama, then to Sixxis, then past them.

Did his parents... did they know about this? That he was from a different world?

"Elama, I'm sorry. I can't leave." Jag fled the sanctuary, all but running through the passageway.

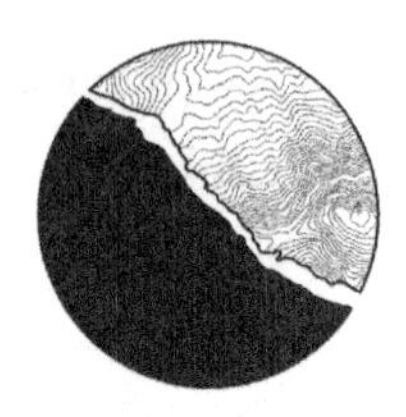

Chapter 9

Tearing into the villa, Jag rushed past the few folks scattered about the banquet hall, flew through the other rooms, and broke into the village square, completely failing to notice Adira, Kithara, and Jade by the door.

"Jag!" Adira shouted, running after him. "Where are you going?"

"Home." He didn't break stride. "I think I've stayed here long enough."

"What's going on? Where's Sixxis?"

"Inside."

"You can't go," she said, grabbing and whirling him to a stop. "I need to talk to you."

"I'm sorry, Adira. I—"

Sixxis appeared in the doorway behind her.

"I'm not one for big celebrations," Jag said. "I'll see you back in the jungle."

"But—"

Jag whipped around and darted down the avenue. While he felt bad leaving Elama the way he did, he felt worse deserting Adira; she definitely deserved better. Maybe he could explain it to her sometime—but would she understand?

"Seriously?" Sixxis said several paces behind him "Are you really going to make me chase you?"

Jag kept moving. "Do what you want. I'll see you at home."

Sixxis must've decided to stay, because Jag couldn't hear his footsteps anymore. But just to be safe, he didn't slow down as he traversed through the market, crossed a few catwalks and platforms, and came to the final bridge—the town's exit. There, he stopped.

A cool breeze blew past, chilling his bare skin as he gazed up at the sky. The storm had dissolved, the clouds dissipated. Alone, isolated on the dark-blue canvas, floated the moon.

The moon...

Did people live there, too? If Elama knew so much, why didn't she know anything about where Jag came from? And how much did mother know? When his parents left to sacrifice themselves, did they take this secret with them?

Racing as quickly as his thoughts, Jag's heart almost exploded from his chest.

Who were his *real* parents? What happened to them?

...did they abandon him?

"Jag."

He jumped. In all his distraction, he hadn't heard Sixxis coming up behind him.

"I can't do it, Six."

"You *can* do it." He stepped up beside his brother. "Especially with me by your side."

Jag squeezed his eyes shut. "I can't expect you to understand. I just—"

"Then help me understand!" said Sixxis, vaulting in front of him and grabbing his shoulders. "I know you have more to say than, 'I can't.' Let me into that thick head of yours!"

"I..."

"Let me guess: you can't."

Why was he being so aggressive about this? Since when did Sixxis have such a strong opinion of what Jag did? Where was his easygoing brother?

"Six—"

"You're being crazy. What happened to your confidence?"

Easy for *him* to say. Sixxis was the most confident person—probably on the entire planet! He never backed down from a challenge. And rubbing it in, he always kept that stupid grin on his face.

"You're the fearless one," Jag said, pushing past and starting across the bridge.

"Am I?"

Jag stopped dead in his tracks. "Are you serious?" He whipped around. "Keeping up with your ego has been a constant battle for me! You're *always* getting us into these situations, and I *always* bail us out! This whole thing is no different!"

"*You* always bail us out?" Sixxis stormed toward him and came right up to his face. "Don't you get it? We succeed because we're together! When have we faced a challenge we couldn't overcome?"

"It's a little different this time," Jag shouted back. "And I won't do it! I won't let you talk me into—"

"You're full of it. You told Elama you couldn't go because the people need you. Now you're leaving them, too." Sixxis folded his arms. "And you're leaving me."

"I just... I want to be alone."

"Fine!" Sixxis shoved him. "Go then!" He turned and started for the village, waving a hand over his shoulder. "I'll see you when I see you."

Jag didn't move. He just stood there as Sixxis gave him what he wanted.

He was alone.

The regret was immediate—but too late. He finished crossing the bridge and entered the gorge with a head of steam.

The trek between the towering cliffs was a somber one. With no one else's feet kicking the rocks, the only sounds echoing through the space were Jag's own steps. It wasn't quiet, though—not to him. Despite the outward calm of the canyon, his head was louder than ever.

Thoughts turned over in his mind at quickening speeds. Before, all he contended with was fear, his reluctance to accept Elama's revelation that deep down, he knew all along. Now he worried that he hurt his brother and caused irreparable damage. They'd never fought—not like that. Jag definitely let himself get impatient and frustrated when things were loud, but he'd never lashed out at his brother—not like that.

Now he had presumably four dead family members and one who was mad at him.

On top of it all, Jag felt small—not in stature, but in his overall place in the grand scheme of things. They'd broken far beyond the confines of normal life, making their way through the jungle, to the Forbidden Village, and into the mountains—all in just one day.

Then Elama told him of the countless worlds out there.

Before he knew it, Jag's feet mindlessly brought him to a cliff's edge, the same ledge he pulled himself onto after their climb out of the pastures. As he stood—gazing down at the faded grass line, past the abandoned farm, and into the jungle whose tall and mighty treetops didn't even come close to reaching his height—the full weight of Elama's request came down on him.

This place—this entire planet was in danger.

"Are you going to tell me what's going on?"

Sixxis stopped a few paces ahead of Adira in the gorge. With everything that'd happened, he wasn't thrilled about the massive, tunneling walls closing in on him from both sides—but he needed to catch up with Jag. "Just a little further, and I'll explain everything."

"This isn't like you two. I don't think I've ever seen you fight."

"He's just… he's got a lot on his mind."

That was an understatement.

Adira ran a tender hand down his arm. "Are you all right?"

Tears welled in Sixxis' eyes—because he was *not* all right. Jag's mental state had always impacted him, so he was sharing in the spiral. And on top of that, he was scared. For the first time maybe ever, he was scared.

"Sixxis?" she said, stepping in front of him. "Are you… crying?"

"Yeah," he said, running an arm under his nose. "Guess I am."

"That's another thing I've never seen."

"I'm an emotional guy, you know." He flashed a grin through his tears. "You should give me a chance."

"I think I've given you far more than a chance," she replied, pressing her forehead into his. "What's going on?" She pulled away. "Talk to me."

Sixxis gazed into her eyes. He thought he was in love with her before they left home, but everything since had made it clear he had no idea what love even *was* before that day.

Skies. Why did this have to be so difficult?

"Sixxis?"

"You know how I have this problem where I don't think before I say things?" he said.

"You don't think before you do much of anything. Sometimes it gets you into trouble, and sometimes"—her mouth tilted into a half-smile—"it's when you're at your most charming."

"Heh—well, I have a lot to say, and I want to think it through before I do."

"Okay."

"I'll explain everything once we reach the other side."

"Okay; I'll be quiet."

A wave of warmth surged through Sixxis' body as Adira slid her hand into his and laced their fingers.

"But first"—she kissed his cheek—"I never thanked you for saving my life."

"I, uhh"—Sixxis' entire face flushed a deep shade of red—"it was—"

"Didn't you say you needed to think?" She pulled his hand and started to walk.

Stumbling forward, Sixxis kept his eyes on Adira as her strong determination drew them on. He'd only met a handful of people in his life, but somehow he'd ended up with the best brother he could ask for *and* caught the attention of the most incredible woman on the planet.

Wait—now there were more planets.

Correction: he'd caught the attention of the most incredible woman in the—what word did Elama use? Galaxy?

The galaxy...

He'd meant what he said about this being bigger than them, but his motives were much deeper than that. In a way, he'd been waiting for this moment all his life.

Just before they parted ways, his mother said one final thing to him: "One day, your brother will need you more than ever. When that time comes, stay by his side."

Sixxis had always wondered what she meant. But now as he pondered her words, Elama's presentation, and the journal in his pocket—that dispelled any doubt as to whether their parents knew Jag was from another world—it was obvious: that time had come.

And it had him *terrified*.

Sixxis seemed confident, but he drew it all from his brother. Sure, he knew his abilities and constantly tested his limits, but he only took chances because he had Jag. He felt safe with his brother—safe from anything that could possibly harm him. Because no matter where they went, Jag was his home. Maybe that's why he could so easily commit to leaving Rixxon.

But then there was Adira. How much could he tell her?

They came hand in hand to the cliffside, their hooked toes curling over the edge.

Sixxis couldn't help himself. "Jag wasn't born on Rixxon."

"I know."

"W—what?" he sputtered. "How?"

Adira pulled her hand away and lifted her brow. "After everything I've seen today"—she shrugged—"it's obvious."

"So you figured it out on your own?"

"Trees can't predict the winds and the rains," she replied, throwing her eyes out over the expanse. "Keep your mind open, Sixxis. Jag coming from another world—along with those men—it's the only logical explanation."

Skies, she was smart.

"I guess I should give you more credit," he said with a grin.

"Is that what this is about?"

Sixxis stepped in beside her and blew out a big breath. "A woman just told us a bunch of stuff and asked for our help."

"A Rixxonian woman?"

"No—well, yes. Uhh..." He scratched at the back of his head. "It's a bit complicated. Something on her wrist changed what she looked like."

"I see."

How could she see? This shit was wild—way beyond *his* imagination.

"What did she ask your help with?" Adira asked.

"Well"—Sixxis slipped his arm around her waist—"there's apparently this big, bad organization—the one that sent those guys, actually. It's been stealing resources from different planets, and she wants our help stopping it."

"That would explain why they were looking for that metal."

Sixxis nodded.

"So, are you leaving?" Adira leaned her head on his shoulder. "I assume if Jag goes, you go, too."

"I don't want to—not now." He sighed. "But you're right: if he goes, I have no choice."

"He has to," she said, burrowing her nose into his arm.

Sixxis placed a gentle hand under her chin and lifted it up. "He does—for our sakes and for his own."

"And for Rixxon." Now Adira was the one tearing up.

"Hey now!" said Sixxis, warmth exuding from his smile. "This isn't goodbye. I'll be back!"

"You'd better be." Adira grabbed at the clothes on his chest, pulled his face in close, and kissed him.

Without hesitation, Sixxis wrapped his arms around her and returned the affection she so enthusiastically gave him. Passion surged through his body as he acted on a love he'd held for so long but only that day fully realized. And for a few blissful moments, the Rixxonians shared in the moment, knowing it would be their last for a while.

Adira dropped to a seat when they broke apart, dangling her legs over the edge. "I'll be busy while you're gone."

Sixxis sat down beside her. "What do you mean?"

"Kithara, Jade, and I have been talking," she said, leaning her head on his shoulder and kicking her feet. "There are clearly threats greater than our inter-regional struggles, something this news only makes clearer. It's time to unite the people of Rixxon under one banner." She closed her eyes and fell still. "It's time for me to finish what my father started—to find our people who have been scattered throughout the jungle."

"You're talking like you have to do this alone."

"The mountain folk have enough to repair from this tragedy. Besides, they don't know the jungle the way I do; they'll just slow me down." She burrowed into him again. "I was going to ask you to help, but I understand that you can't."

"I'm sorry."

"Don't be sorry. You have a responsibility to Jag."

"Just you wait," he said, leaning his head on hers. "I'll see this through, then I'll help unite our people."

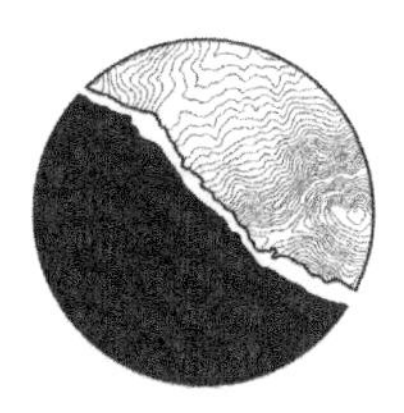

Chapter 10

Jag stood before the chasm. The rushing of the Great River below soothed his mind, as did the jungle's vibrant green across the way.

He'd missed the sun and its warming light.

The lonely walk down the pass had given him plenty of time to wade through most of his thoughts, but that didn't mean things were any less *loud.* Because even now, back here by the jungle, Jag was still out of place.

How much did his mother know? And what happened to his *birth* mother?

Sixxis stepped up beside him. "Hey, brother."

Jag had heard the two of them talking as they came down the hill, so he wasn't surprised. He didn't even look. "Sorry I blew up back there."

"I'm sorry, too."

"And Adira—I feel bad about how I treated you."

"Don't worry about it," she said. "It's been an... emotional day."

"You know, I came back here to go home," Jag said, "but when I got here, I realized I didn't have the rope; I couldn't cross." He started to turn. "And even if I could, I'd be leaving you two be"—his eyes widened.

Resting her head on Sixxis' back, arms wrapped around his body, Adira smiled.

Jag lifted an eyebrow. "Did I miss something?"

"You could say that," she replied.

"Long time coming, if you ask me."

Sixxis snickered.

"I hear you'll be... traveling soon," she said.

"So he told you." Jag took a deep breath in through his nose, held it for a moment, then let it out through his mouth. "I don't know if I can do it."

Despite wondering why he was different all his life, Jag had never really questioned who he was. But with that now *thrown* into question, it was almost like he was losing himself.

"It doesn't matter if you can do it, Jag; sometimes we don't have much choice." Adira squeezed Sixxis. "Your sense of duty is too strong. You'll go."

"Besides," added Sixxis with his signature grin, "we all know you left the rope on purpose. You never had any *real* intention of going home."

Maybe Jag *did* leave the rope on purpose. Maybe deep down—beneath all that instant overwhelm—he knew he was going to help Elama.

"You're a lot like me," Adira said. "You go where you're needed most. It's the reason we went on this journey together in the first place."

"I know it worked out," Jag said, "but this all happened here—a place we know. Out there, who knows what—?"

"Say it."

"What?"

Adira squeezed Sixxis tighter.

"...we stand tall as trees," Jag said.

"You can never know what will happen," she replied with a nod. "All you can do is try to shape it."

"I'm not nearly as strong as you."

"Strength comes in many forms, and yours will play well in the unknown. You're smart, resourceful, quick-witted. After all, Rixxon is plenty dangerous." She released Sixxis and took a step back. "You've managed to not only survive"—she smacked him across the head.

"Ow!"

"You've kept this bonehead alive, too!"

"Hah!" Sixxis rubbed at his head. "Probably deserved that."

"I'm glad to see you two aren't bickering anymore," Jag said with a smile.

"Oh, give it time." Sixxis gave Adira a light kick, then met her gaze. "Hey—would you give us a minute?"

"Sure; take all the time you need. I'll be up ahead."

"Wait!" Jag dropped his quiver and unloaded the special arrows. "You should take these."

"Are you sure?" she asked, head atilt.

"Yeah. I can't imagine a few arrows will help where we're going."

She took one in hand and turned it over. "They truly are beautiful."

"Better hope you don't run into the Thakk again, though," Sixxis quipped. "He's probably still got one"—he pointed to his eye.

Adira rolled *her* eyes. "Thank you, Jag," she said, bowing her head. "I'll leave you boys to talk." She rounded the nearest building and left their view.

"I'm happy for you," Jag said.

"Thanks, brother. It was... unexpected."

"Not to me."

Sixxis lifted his head to the sky. "It's been some ride, hasn't it?"

Some ride was right.

"And it's only getting started." He stepped toward the edge. "I've never told you this, but that night, mother said there would come a day when you needed me more than ever—and that I should stand by your side."

Jag staggered back. "What?"

"I always thought it was silly," Sixxis said with a shrug. He smiled over his shoulder—not his normal, mischievous smile, but one brimming with love and sincerity. "Because I'll always stand by your side."

Grand purpose...

"I don't understand," Jag said. "Mother knew?"

Sixxis nodded, then pulled a small, leather book from his pocket. "Here," he said, holding it for Jag behind his back. "I found this back in our bungalow."

Jag fanned through several pages and found one folded over. "Is this—"

"Mother's journal. I marked a page for you."

Wazzaru took me there today, to the place where he found him. It's odd, a sort of metal orb. We told the chief about it, and a party is being sent to excavate what they can from the wreckage.

It's strange. I felt a severe sense of cold from the orb, yet I feel nothing but warmth from the child who has come to be my son. I can already tell he will grow to be strong and kind. He just has that energy about him. I wonder if it comes from his true mother.

Wazzaru told me about her today.

He hadn't mentioned anything about the woman until he brought me to the orb. Maybe he couldn't bring himself to say anything, maybe he was worried I wouldn't take the boy in if there was another mother.

It's strange. Knowing she's here, buried in the jungle, I feel that much more connected to her... and to Jag.

Yes, Jag. That's what Wazzaru says we must call him.

"My mother is here?" Jag's looked up. "Our parents knew?"

"I guess," Sixxis replied. "There's more if you read on. Apparently father found you in her arms, but she was dead."

"So he buried her and brought me home?"

"See for yourself. The journal's yours."

Jag closed and glanced down at the book. "Do you think—"

A shriek echoed from the center of the farm—shooting their eyes at each other.

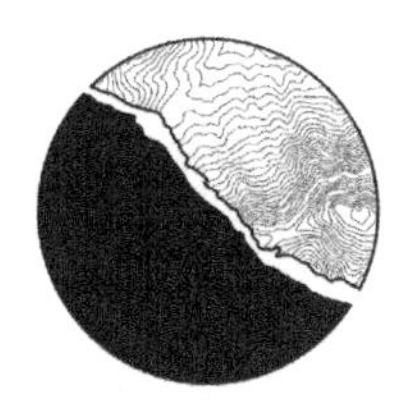

Chapter 11

Jag fell in behind Sixxis as they charged the barn and peeked around its corner.

On her knees, hands in the air, Adira faced away from them. And as Jag leaned out for a wider look, another person came into view, stepping over the pile of special arrows in the grass.

It was the yellow man! But how?

Jag grabbed Sixxis—before he launched forward—and pulled him back behind the barn.

"I don't know how that guy's still alive," Sixxis whispered, revving his fists, "but he won't be for long!"

"They did some serious damage in the village," Jag said. "We've got to be careful."

"If he so much as touches her, I'll—"

"Where are your friends?" said the yellow man.

"No friends," Adira replied. "I'm alone."

"Ah—but there... you *lie.*"

BOOP BOOP.

"Scanner readings indicate one more piece of precious metal, just beyond that building."

Sixxis hopped toward the corner. "Guess that's our cue!"

"Wait!" Jag said. "We need a—"

"We'll figure it out!" With a double pump of his eyebrows, grin stretched wide across his face, Sixxis turned and walked out, hands in the air.

Skies. Jag should've known he had no hope of slowing Sixxis down—not with Adira in trouble. He tucked it in and jogged to the barn's other side.

"Ah, there we are!" The man pointed his weapon at Sixxis. "And who is this—her boyfriend?"

"Yes, actually." Sixxis winked at Adira.

"I've got to hand it to you two," the man said. "You're primitive beings, yet you managed to best me *and* steal from me—but that's where you made your mistake. You were so easy to track."

"We took you down once." Sixxis reached for his machete. "We can do it again."

The man snapped his weapon toward Adira. "Let's not do anything hasty."

Sixxis' fingers splayed and rested on the handle.

"That blade belongs to me," continued the man, nodding to the arrow pile. "Why don't you toss it with the rest of my things?"

"This doesn't belong to you. It's—"

"Come now." He walked forward and pressed his weapon into Adira's forehead. "We must play nicely."

"Okay okay." Sixxis kept one hand up as he slowly unsheathed his machete. "Just don't hurt her." He tossed it across the grass, clanging it into the other metal.

"Wonderful!" said the man, spinning and stowing the weapon on his belt. "Perhaps now we can have a *civilized* conversation."

Sixxis folded his arms. "Can't say I have much to say to you."

"I could just kill you now," he said, kneeling and bringing his face level with Adira's. "But that would be such a waste." He floated a hand up to stroke her face—only it wasn't yellow like the rest of him. It looked to be metal, not as lustrous as the special metal—but clearly *not* a normal hand.

"Such strong, agile creatures," he said. "I would love to have one of you on my side."

Adira spat. "Don't touch me."

"Heh." The man stood and took a few meandering steps away from her. "The way I see it, you have three choices. One: you die, here and now." He glanced over his shoulder. "Two: you come with me, and I give you new life, new purpose as members of my personal regiment—my *appendages*—with knowledge and power you've never even dreamt of. Three?" He turned and lifted his head to the mountains. "The beast takes care of you."

"So it *was* you who released the Thakk," said Adira.

"*Thakk*?" The man whirled around. "I *like* that! It's the perfect name for something that will end a civilization."

Skies. What were they going to do? Jag couldn't load up without giving away his position, *and* he gave all the metal arrows to Adira. Nothing he had would pierce the man's armor.

"Well, you're out of luck," said Sixxis, slotting a foot back. "We sealed it up in the mountain."

"*Really*?" The man dropped his hands and slapped his hips. "You people are impressive—but unfortunately, that eliminates one of your options."

"Why are you here?" Adira asked. "Why would you release such a monster?"

The man's neck cracked as he rolled his head around. "Tell me," he said, stepping toward the arrow pile, "how did you come by these?"

Slowly, silently, Adira lowered a hand toward her ankle scabbard. "My father told me this metal was a gift from above," she said, drawing a dagger. "And it is *above* that you must go!" She sprang to her feet and slashed at the back of his neck.

The man hopped forward, *narrowly* avoiding getting cut open. He threw his right hand behind him with a grunt and knocked the blade from Adira's hand.

With the commotion, Jag dropped the front of his crossbow and scrambled to load up.

"I've had about enough of you." Having recovered his machete, Sixxis launched into attack mode. He sliced down at the man—but the man sidestepped the strike and laughed.

"I promise," he said, "you can't possibly beat me."

"We'll see about that," Adira replied, drawing her other dagger.

The man gestured to his weapon. "You do understand that I can blow you away with—"

Jag's arrow ripped across the farm and flung the weapon from his hand.

"Nice shot!" Sixxis yelled as he slashed down again.

The man brought his metal hand up to block the attack—and the blade went right through it. "Agh!" He ripped the machete from Sixxis with his remaining hand and threw it across the grass. "How *dare*—"

Adira lunged, but the man hopped to the side and dodged—then plunged his foot into her stomach. Recoiling, staggering back, she dropped her weapon.

"That's better," he said, dropping to a crouch, swaying side to side. "Shall we begin?"

"You're the *worst*!" Sixxis launched at him and threw a punch. Then—when the man ducked and heaved an uppercut at his jaw—Sixxis bobbed his head back, surged into a backflip, and kicked him square in the chin.

The man clutched his face and stumbled back—only to get upended by Adira's sweeping leg. He crashed into the ground.

Finally reloaded, Jag took aim and fired—this time at the man's face—but the arrow splintered on impact.

What? A direct hit, dead center of the forehead. And this after he fell off the top platform back in the village. How was this guy still alive? Were all Lommorians this strong?

Wait—there were other Lommorians in the village. What about—

"You really are a *nuisance*," said the man, lunging for his fallen weapon. Without looking, he fired at Jag.

Explosions of light erupted across the farm as Jag dropped his crossbow and rolled from harm. Its wooden frame exploded into pieces behind him.

Still grounded, the man shot at Sixxis and Adira, sending them running for their lives. "Hello?" With them cleared out, he pressed to his feet, turned, and fired round after round at the barn. "Where's our third friend?"

Just like the crossbow and the hut back in the village, the weapon burst the barn into pieces. Doing his best to dodge flying debris, Jag hustled away and kept out of view.

As the light-and-sound barrage dissipated, the man stood out in the open between a handful of buildings. "Oh come now. Are we scared?" He stretched his arm forward and started to rotate, firing repeatedly in all directions.

Jag dropped to his stomach and shielded his neck.

No good. All the cover would be gone at this rate; the three of them would be dead in minutes. Jag needed to do something.

Still spinning, the man let out a maniacal laugh.

Jag waited for the perfect moment—then bounced up, sprinted at him, and slid feet first.

The man hit the ground hard—but not for long. With the greatest of ease, he rolled his legs over his body, sprang to his feet, and pressed his weapon into Jag's face.

Sprawled out in the grass, Jag scrambled backward with no hope of defending himself—then the man lowered his weapon.

"You..."

His head jolted to the side.

"You are..."

It jolted again.

"Who... agh!" His head lurched back as a blade came bursting through his chest, sparks popping all around it.

Sixxis brought his head over the man's shoulder. "Nice knowing you." He stepped back and kicked forward, and the man fell limp. Dead.

Again.

Sixxis heaved the body onto his shoulder and started to walk.

Finally comprehending what had happened, Jag shook his head out. "Where are you—"

"I'm making sure he doesn't come back again."

"What?"

"He's going in the river." Sixxis hobbled off. "Say bye-bye!"

"Wait!"

"Nope!"

Jag flopped backward, pressed his head into the soft grass, and closed his eyes, letting the sun warm his face. He'd survived everything so far—barely—but every passing event filled him with more questions. And with the sudden quiet, the worries compounded.

What was that about? Had the man... recognized him? There's no way. And why was his head all twitchy?

Jag needed answers. But the man was gone—for good this time.

"You all right?"

He creaked an eye open to find Adira approaching. "Yeah. I'm okay."

"This has been some day, hasn't it?" she said, offering her hand.

Jag eyed the impressive Rixxonian before taking her hand. Just above her radiant smile, her tight bun was still intact, not even a single hair out of place. How could she keep such composure?

He popped to his feet with Adira's help. "I couldn't have predicted any of this when—"

A loud whirring droned into the area, consuming the momentary quiet.

"What now?" yelled Adira, drawing her longbow and nocking an arrow.

The whirring swelled in intensity, like it was approaching from the sky. All around, blades of grass flickered under an intense wind that swept through the space. But still—there was nothing there.

There was nothing anywhere!

"We need to go," Jag said, grabbing Adira's hand. "Now!"

They ran off toward the river, snaking around broken buildings until they came to those untouched by the man's weapon. There, they ducked into a doorway, pressed their bodies up against the wall, and waited for the whirring to stop.

Adira slumped to a crouch as silence overtook the farm. "What in the name of—"

"Jag?" a voice called out. "Are you okay?"

It was Elama!

"Someone's..." Adira glanced up at him. "...calling you?"

Jag let out an enormous sigh of relief. "Yeah, it's safe," he said. "She's... a friend."

Finally—something convenient had happened!

"Is this the woman Sixxis told me about?" Adira's brow wrinkled as she took Jag's hand and pulled herself upright. "The one who's Rixxonian but not really?"

Skies, Six—how much did he tell her? Oh well; she'd have probably figured it out on her own by now.

"Yeah, that's her—come on." Jag stepped out into the open. "Elama?"

Searching the wreckage across the way, Elama hopped a bit, clearly startled when he called her name. "We heard what could have only been advanced weaponry and came as quickly as we could!"

"Don't worry about me," said Sixxis, appearing from behind a building to Jag's left, a wild grin on his face. "I'm fine, too!"

Elama strode across piles of debris as she hustled toward Jag. "What happened here? And"—she smiled at Adira—"oh, hello. I don't believe we've met."

"This is Adira," Jag said, placing a hand on his friend's back. "She knows everything."

"I... see."

Sixxis approached with one hand behind his head. "That one's on me. Sorry—I needed to talk to someone."

"I suppose it's all right—so long as you told no one else."

"In his defense, ma'am," Adira said with a subtle bow, "I figured much of it out on my own. These men, the Thakk, and now this encounter... there's only one explanation, really."

"You're quite intuitive", Elama replied, her expression relaxing. "Yes, I suppose having experienced every... *odd* happening on this day, there's only one conclusion you could draw." Her eyes swept across the three of them. "And you're the only ones to have seen it all. Tell me: what happened to the Guild operative?"

Sixxis lifted a hand into the air and whistled as he brought his finger down, imitating a splashing sound when he reached his waist. "But not before I stabbed him."

Elama gasped. "I must say—I'm impressed! That could not have been an easy battle."

"We *almost* lost," Adira added, "and I would've died without these two."

"Don't worry, m'lady." Sixxis whirled his hand and offered an exaggerated bow. "We had it all under control."

Did they have it under control? It sure didn't seem that way to Jag—they didn't have *anything* under control.

Skies. What was he getting himself into?

"Elama," he said, taking a strong step forward, "I'm coming with you."

"Ah!" She clapped her hands together. "You've decided! What changed your mind?"

Learning his parents knew he was from another world, the man's reaction when they came face to face, all the death and destruction—Jag had a lot of reasons. But nothing drew him on more than one simple thing: the truth. He'd never find his answers here. If they were to be found at all, they'd be out there.

Up there—beyond the skies.

"It's just clear Rixxon isn't safe," Jag said, keeping the rest to himself. He smiled at Adira and echoed her words from earlier. "I can't stand by—not while I know I can help."

"There's my Jag!" said Sixxis, clapping him on the back. "Too bad it took almost getting blown up to convince you of your destiny!"

Grand purpose...

Everything had happened so fast. And looking back on it now, Jag wasn't sure how much choice he had in each step. *Was* this destiny? Was it all... *supposed* to happen?

A pit rose in his stomach; his body started to ache.

Jag *couldn't* believe he had no power over what was coming. It went against everything he was—though he didn't know much about *that* anymore either.

Too much to think about. He just needed to keep moving.

"I'm not sure about that," he said.

"I wouldn't write off the notion of fate so quickly," replied Elama, bringing her wrist to her face. "Torin, it's time."

"Roger that, commander," crackled a thin, deep voice.

"My friends, you have seen many things you cannot explain today. I'm afraid you're about to see one more."

Jag's jaw dropped, as an enormous, metal structure trickled into view behind Elama, its dark-gray body shimmering in the soft sunlight. Quite a bit taller than the farm buildings, it had rounded edges and two cylindrical shafts sticking out toward them. Jag couldn't tell how long it was.

Air hissed from below the shafts as a portion of the metal lowered to the ground, forming a ramp to the interior. A man—another "Rixxonian" in strange clothing—walked out, stopping as his feet touched the grass.

"Amazing..." Jag wandered forward a step. "How'd you do that?"

Elama smiled. "It's called a cloaking mechanism. Think of it as a sort of camouflage. It hides our ship from view." She gestured toward the ramp.

"'Ship?'" Sixxis repeated. "Will this thing take us up?"

Elama chuckled and started toward it. "Yes, this spacecraft will be our ride to other planets. Her name is *Pioneer.*"

"Her?" Jag wondered aloud.

Elama stopped beside the man and smiled. "You have much to learn. But first, allow me to introduce Torin, my second."

"Pleased to meet you sirs," he said, tipping his close-cropped head toward Jag and Sixxis. "Ma'am." He bowed to Adira, then looked up at Elama. "Commander, I have plotted a course to Korrignolan. We are ready to leave at any time."

"Thank you, dear friend."

Torin nodded, then walked back up the ramp.

"This..." Adira—who'd been lagging behind the pack—meandered forward, almost as if she'd teeter to the side and fall over at any moment. "...it's incredible."

"You may join us, if you wish," Elama offered. "I sense great strength and determination in you. I'm sure these two would benefit from your presence."

"I appreciate it," Adira replied with a bow, "but I must stay behind. Besides, it would look very strange if all three of us disappeared. Jag, Sixxis, I'll go back to the mountain village for the celebration and tell them you went on to the jungle to prepare."

"Prepare?" Jag said. "For what?"

Warmth radiated from her smile. "Kithara, Jade, and I aim to unite the people of Rixxon. These events have made it clear just how small our past troubles are."

"Yeah!" Sixxis ran and took his place by her side. "Adira's going to comb the jungle and find our scattered people!"

Jag's mouth wrinkled. "I wish I could stay and help."

"You *are* helping," said Adira, shaking her head, "in a way none of us can." She smiled at Sixxis. "You two make sure our people are safe out there, and I'll do the same here."

Jag let out a big breath. "This is making it harder."

"If I may," Elama interjected, "this is certainly not a forever goodbye. You will see each other again." She paused and eyed the three companions. "At any rate, I will leave you to each other. Jag, Sixxis, I'll see you onboard." She turned and ascended the ramp.

"Well, boys," said Adira, "be careful, all right? Don't die." She looked up at Sixxis again. "If you do, I'll find you and kill you again."

Sixxis bent down, whispered something in her ear, and kissed her on the cheek. She responded by flinging her arms around him and holding him close.

When Adira broke from his body, she approached Jag and gave him a less emphatic but still passionate hug. "Stick together, okay?" Her face stretched into a Sixxis-style grin. "Without each other, you're both"—she shrugged—"average."

"Hey!" said Sixxis, tossing his shoulder at her. "Don't look down on us, oh mighty queen of the jungle!"

Adira's grin faded. "I'll miss you." She turned to Jag. "You, too. Never forget where you come from. Though there is no Rixxonian blood running through you, your mark has been left on this world. It won't be the same without you."

No doubt things would've been easier with Adira along. Jag couldn't help but feel alone at times as he did everything he could to keep himself and his reckless brother alive. Would that change on this journey?

"Hello?" Sixxis knocked on Jag's head. "Still with us?"

"Oh—uhh—sorry." He nodded. "Thanks, Adira. Stay safe."

"That's it?" Sixxis folded his arms and cocked a foot back. "I think you owe her a little more than that."

Skies—he really did.

"Sorry. There's..." His mouth wrinkled. "There's a lot on my mind."

Adira stood tall. "Through the winds of change..."

"We stand tall as trees." Jag finished.

"You can never know what will happen," she said again with a smile. "All you can do is try to shape it."

Never know what will happen—today made *that* clear.

Jag smiled back. "Take care of yourself."

"You know I will."

After a long look and a final hand squeeze, Sixxis turned from Adira, threw his arm around Jag, and walked them up the ramp.

"Everything's about to change, isn't it?" Jag asked.

"Not everything," Sixxis replied. "We still have each other."

Warmth surged through Jag's chest. "I'm glad to have you with me, Six."

"Like I said—you always will."

Making it to the top of the ramp, they turned and looked down at the one they were leaving behind.

"See you soon!" Sixxis shouted with a wave—as a loud *KERCHUNK* shook the floor and swung the ramp up in front of them.

"What'd you whisper to her?" Jag asked, elbowing his brother.

Sixxis double-pumped his eyebrows. "Wouldn't *you* like to know?"

ACT II

Part One

The Team for the Task

Chapter 12

"Welcome aboard *Pioneer,*" Torin said with a bow. "If you would please follow me, I will show you to the bridge." He rotated his pale-green, Rixxonian frame and started up the narrow corridor.

"Thank you." Jag's boots clomped on the hard flooring as he fell in behind him.

It was all so sudden.

The moment the ramp closed them off from Rixxon, they were transported to another world. The ship's interior was simple, dark, cold—nothing like the vibrant warmth Jag was used to. A dull metal coated every surface of the cramped hallway, illuminated only by mellow blue lighting that hummed from its edges.

"I guess 'bridge' means something different now?" Sixxis said into his ear.

"No idea."

"My apologies," offered Torin without turning. "The bridge is the room in which we control the ship. The commander awaits you there to brief you on your first mission." He gestured to a recessed door on his left. "This is the bunkroom. You may rest here once you have finished speaking with the commander." He indicated the next door in the line. "And here, you will find the intelligence interface prepared to instruct you on the basics of galactic civilization; the commander will explain that as well."

Torin continued on, approaching the end of the short corridor—and the far wall whooshed to the left. Stepping through the new doorway, he extended his arm toward two high-backed chairs. "Please take a seat."

Elama stood on the room's other side, staring through the massive front glass. She turned to face the Rixxonians as they entered. "Welcome, my friends! What do you think of *Pioneer?* Not much to speak of as far as appearances go—and not very big—but she's a special ship."

Jag's head moved in a wide arc as he took in the bridge. An intricate array of lights, buttons, and knobs lined the walls on both sides, wrapping down onto different tiers of raised metal structures facing the front glass. And through that front glass, he could tell they were level with the tip of the tallest farm building.

"This..." he muttered. "...isn't big?"

Elama smiled at Torin. "No, I'm afraid not. You will see bigger before long."

The front station featured two large chairs, much like the ones Torin had indicated in the back. Between them and the glass, a collection of handles and levers joined two big screens, calling Jag's mind back to the yellow man's device.

"Huh." He slumped into his seat as Sixxis took the other. "So what do we do first?"

Elama withdrew a small, glass tube from her pocket and held it up for them.

Jag's mouth wrinkled as he inspected the pink liquid inside. "What's that?"

"You're about to be exposed to many things you've never even imagined," she said with a smile. "Consider this a sort of primer for your mind."

"What does it do?"

"It contains a compound that—once I drop it into your eyes—will seep into your neural network. Among other things, you will understand the major languages in this region of space, and you will comprehend galactic standard time."

"I... see," Jag lied. What was she even talking about?

"Sounds neat!" said Sixxis, tilting his head back. "Ready!"

With a chuckle, Elama shuffled over to Sixxis' seat, squeezed out a drop in each eye, then turned and smiled at Jag.

With no reason not to trust her, Jag leaned back as the cool liquid buzzed through his eyes and into his brain—and its impact was instantaneous. Hard to say *what* impact, exactly—he still felt the same—but it was definitely doing *something*.

"Wonderful!" Elama stowed the tube and took her place in a lone, raised chair in front of them. "Now, I suggest you buckle your restraints. Your first warp jump will be jarring."

Self-conscious at all the questions he'd already asked, Jag just nodded. He reached a hand across his body and pulled a stretch of webbing over his shoulders, then did the same on his other side. And once he latched them at his chest, he looked over at his brother.

Sixxis was all tangled up in the webbing, clearly struggling. "OH!" He wriggled free and mirrored Jag. "Got it!"

With a nod to Torin, Elama rotated her seat and faced forward.

Torin touched the rear wall at her command, zipping the door shut. He then brushed past them, dropped into the front, leftmost chair, and began tapping away at the deck in front of him.

The ship jolted and banged to life.

Focusing forward, Jag refused to take his eyes off the farm as the ship veered skyward. Soon, all that shone through the window was the cerulean expanse.

This might just be the last time he'd see it.

"This is unbelievable!" said Sixxis, leaning forward in his seat. "Jag, did you ever think we'd leave home like this?"

"No, I..."

The sky's coloring deepened, darkened, then faded into a vast sea of black. The sheer emptiness took all speech from Jag. Squinting—struggling to make sense of the immense void before him—he fell short of breath.

A wave of cold washed over him.

"Torin," said Elama, "why don't you give these gentlemen a look at their beautiful planet?"

Jag swore the ship didn't move, but before he knew it, the two-toned image painted itself on the black canvas, radiating far more beauty than it did during Elama's presentation in the mountain sanctuary.

Sitting there, it all seemed impossible.

Half the orb gleamed a vivid green; deep, dark gray shrouded the other half; and the Great River's brilliant blue peppered the planet's midsection.

"Elama," Jag said, "Why is it that the mountains never see the sun?"

"It is one of the most astounding things I've ever seen—and it makes Rixxon Prime completely unique!"

"I'm sorry—did you say Rixxon... *Prime*?"

"Indeed! Your world is just one of a planetary triptych. And since it supports sentient life—unlike its partners—it is considered the primary body."

Jag blinked; his mouth wrinkled.

"Look into the distance on either side of your homeworld," she continued, pointing through the glass. "Most planets are parts of a system, one that revolves around its own star. Yours is no different; however, these two side bodies are large enough that their gravities battle against each other, ultimately holding Rixxon Prime in place as all three planets revolve together."

"But what about the moon?"

"It revolves around this cluster of three, which is why both hemispheres of your home only see it for short periods across the span of many hours. When it can't be seen, it is simply hiding behind your neighboring planets."

"This is wild," said Sixxis, head darting side to side.

Elama let out a chuckle. "Sixxis, I think you in particular might like this next part." She sat up straight and pressed her back into the seat. "Torin, let's head out."

"Roger that."

The entrancing view of Jag's lifetime home—the only place he'd ever known—was swept away, again invading his perception with black. But it wasn't as overwhelming this time. And as his mind further adjusted, a sea of small, bright lights filled his eyes.

"Ready to jump," Torin reported.

Elama waved a hand over her shoulder. "I would suggest holding your head flush with the seatback."

Just as Jag took her advice, an unbelievable force pressed him back. The far-off, stationary lights sprang to life, whizzing past the window in streaks of white as the startling power of the ship's motion held him paralyzed. He couldn't move anything but his eyes, but that was fine.

He had plenty to look at.

Torin flicked a few switches. "Stabilizing the cabin in three... two... one..."

And just like that, Jag could move again. "What just happened?"

"Well done, my friends!" said Elama, rotating to face the brothers. "You have just made your first warp jump."

Sixxis' grin hadn't left his face. "I like the sound of that! What's it mean?"

"It means we are now traveling significantly faster than the speed of light!"

Torin tilted his head back. "Estimated arrival at Korrignolan: ten hours."

"Ten..." Sixxis' eyes popped open. "*Hours*? We just sit here until then?"

"My, you're a hasty fellow, aren't you?" Elama laughed, bigger and longer than any time previous, then wiped a tear from her eye. "I apologize; I have awaited this moment for a long time."

"You've been waiting for this?" Jag said.

She nodded. "I don't mean to pressure you, but I feel I can be forthright now that you're here: there is a lot riding on the success of your mission."

"Like what?"

"Aside from the fate of many systems that may fall victim to the Guild's resource-draining operations, it's no exaggeration to say that the *truth* is at stake."

"The truth? About what?"

"For starters, your origins." She smiled. "I know it sounded like a secondary concern when we first spoke, but I do hope we can help you find the answers you seek."

An indescribable kindness exuded from Elama as she spoke. Jag couldn't help but believe her—and believe *in* her.

She pulled a small disc from her pocket, held it in her palm, and clicked its side with her thumb. An image appeared, floating over top of it—some sort of lizard man. "This is a holoimage of Pert Gubora," she said, "a Laktilian, and the current leader of the Prospectors' Guild."

"Laktilian?" Sixxis repeated.

She nodded. "A lizard being from the planet Laktilia. You will need to quickly become used to seeing creatures unlike yourselves."

Pert Gubora's red, scaly skin blazed through the hologram. Much like Sixxis, large, uncovered feet set his foundation, with extra leg joints that lifted him off the ground. Matte black armor reached from above his feet to his collar, leaving nothing but his impressive tail uncovered. And his long neck seemed small next to his even longer snout.

"We can do that," Jag said.

"As I mentioned in the cavern, the Guild has recently upped its activity. Per bylaws set by the Galactic Legislature, the organization is not to operate on inhabited planets unless given express permission by their occupants. This occurs most often when there is need for Guild supplies. In exchange for its various commodities, the Guild takes a sum of money and a plot of land on which it may begin excavating."

Sixxis shrugged. "Seems fair."

"It was—for a time. For many years, the leadership of the Guild forged contracts with governments, stipulating a specific time frame during which it could operate and promising a percentage of their harvested resources to the planets' citizens."

"We didn't give them permission to come to *our* planet," Jag said, eyes fixed on the lizard man.

"Yes; that is a troubling development, indeed. Class V primitive planets—that is, inhabited worlds whose people have yet to make contact with another planetary species—are by all accounts off-limits to Guild personnel."

"Why's that?" Sixxis asked.

"It is of the Legislature's belief that worlds should be left to develop until they are ready to enter greater society. There are a number of things civilizations come to find in their own due time. The government merely hopes to not stunt the growth, so to speak, of any set of people."

Sixxis sat back. "Guess we got a bit of a head start. Makes you wonder how long it would've taken us to get here if those goons"—his eyes widened—"uhh, not you, of course! Erm—sorry. I'll shut up now."

"No need to apologize," she said with a laugh. "I'm actually quite impressed at how well you've handled this."

"We stand tall as trees," Jag recited.

Elama beamed. "You Rixxonians are impressive people."

"I just wing it," Sixxis added with a grin.

"So what changed with the Guild?" Jag asked, eyeing Pert Gubora.

"Recent intel suggests that the organization has been misrepresenting its findings. Disappointed with the reported yields, political leaders frequently elect to extend excavation timelines. If they don't, the Guild simply refuses to leave; they continue mining until there is almost nothing left, then abandon the sites."

"Did this start when this man took control?"

She nodded. "It was approximately two years ago. Eight planets have since been sapped of virtually all valuable resources."

"So if we take out this Gubora guy"—Sixxis folded his arms—"things might go back to normal?"

"I'm afraid not." Elama clicked the disc, and a different image replaced Pert Gubora's. Covered in a similar matte black armor, this person—another man—had a build and proportions similar to Jag's. Maroon streaks and symbols adorned his plated covering, which ran the length of his body below the neck.

Jag undid his restraints and leaned in closer.

"Joining galactic civilization will be quite a shift for you two," Elama said. "You see, more beings will resemble you, Jag. Sixxis will be the one to stand out." She smiled. "Rixxonian DNA is incredibly unique."

The very sight of the onyx suit shot fear down Jag's spine. But despite his unease, he felt somewhat drawn to the image.

"We do not know this man's true name," she continued. "He is known simply as 'The Advocate.' Gubora tends to manage the business and political sides of things, while he deals with outreach, brokering, and execution."

Jag pointed to a strip of metal on the Advocate's head. "What's that?" Starting below his right eye, it looped up in line with his nose and stretched over top of his head, wrapping down and around his neck.

"No one knows for sure. Most believe he so equipped himself because of the dangerous nature of his position; it is not uncommon for people to take such precautions. And he has a brilliant mind, one in which he takes great pride."

"What do *you* believe?"

"I..."

She paused, almost like she was thinking, then nodded to herself.

"It is widely known that Pert Gubora was banished from his homeworld years ago for experimentation on fusing organic and synthetic matter—that is, combining man and machine. Such acts are forbidden by the Legislature except in medical situations. It's conjecture, but I believe the Advocate is a product of these experiments."

Jag's eyes shifted as he remembered the sparks flying from the yellow man. Was *he* part machine? That would've explained the metal hand.

"Weird," said Sixxis. "So what's this Advocate guy's deal?"

"Six months ago, he was elevated and labeled Gubora's right hand. When we heard of his promotion, we began intercepting a number of encrypted transmissions that—"

"Sorry," Jag interrupted. "Encrypted?"

"I apologize—an encrypted message is one that is heavily disguised. To that point, we'd been able to understand all Guild transmissions. These new messages—coming through what we call the 'Dark Relay'—we have yet to decipher."

"So they started sending a bunch of secret messages." Sixxis shrugged. "What's the big deal?"

"Shortly after we found evidence of these encrypted communications, anomalies began popping up across the far reaches of space."

"What kinds of anomalies?" Jag asked.

"Heightened aggression. Violent acts. Sudden wars on worlds with long, peaceful histories—and it's likely no coincidence that the Guild had recently increased its weapons production tenfold. Finding themselves in abrupt need, many planets signed new contracts."

"And you think this has something to do with this"—Jag squinted at the figure floating above the disc—"Advocate?"

She nodded. "Each of the new contracts was negotiated by him personally."

"So we can't just take out Gubora," Jag said. "With him gone, the Advocate would take over, and things might get worse?"

"Precisely."

"What more do you know about him?"

Elama rubbed her hands together. "Unfortunately not much. We know he and Gubora are very close, and that Gubora has taught him everything he knows. But our fragmented information only goes back so far; we have yet to find anything about him beyond eighteen galactic standard years ago."

Jag's head tilted. "Galactic—"

"Give it just a moment," Elama said with a smile. "The serum should help."

...galactic standard years. Jag had never heard it before, but it somehow felt familiar. Maybe the stuff was working already.

"So how do we figure out what's in the messages?" he said.

"Yeah," added Sixxis, "how are we supposed to do that?"

"Not alone," she replied. "We have identified two individuals that may help in that endeavor, and we are on our way to one of them now."

Elama clicked the disc once more, and a new image appeared, this one a woman with sapphire skin. Other than her blue-tinted body, she was physically similar to Jag. Projected there in her simple black pants, sleeveless white shirt, and black vest, she seemed small, though it was hard to tell in the hologram. Jet black hair hung down one side of her head. The other side was completely shaved.

"She's... beautiful," Jag said.

"Ohoho!" Sixxis reached across and shoved him. "Someone have a little crush?"

"This is Miss Remy Troyer," continued Elama. "She is a Guild engineer. As a child, she and her twin sister were taken in by the organization when their home was destroyed."

Jag sat back and looked up at Elama. "So we have to convince her to leave the Guild *and* help us undermine its operations?"

Sixxis snickered. "Nice one, Jag. We have to *undermine* the *mining* group."

Well, at least *he* was having fun with all this.

"Yes," Elama replied. "Only I suspect it will not prove difficult. We have information that should sway her to our cause."

"What kind of information?" Jag asked.

"Miss Troyer is on bereavement leave from her duties. Last week, her twin sister, Omeka, drowned when an auxiliary shaft flooded on Polt. Miraculously, she was the only one to perish in the accident—because it was no accident."

"Yikes," said Sixxis.

"Our intelligence proves that Omeka was murdered by the Guild. What's more, the explosion that destroyed their childhood home years ago was actually caused by gaseous byproducts of an unlawful Guild depository."

Jag's eyes leapt back to Remy's projection. "So she's spent her whole life working for an organization that destroyed her home, basically abducted her, and killed her sister?"

"Quite accurately summarized! We are en route to the planet Korrignolan now. We only have a rough idea of where she lives, so you'll need to ask around." Elama withdrew a small, rectangular object from her pocket. "Give this to her. Implore her to look through its contents; that should do the trick."

"Thank you," Jag said, taking the object.

"Once she joins the cause, you will have a wealth of knowledge regarding the Guild's inner workings at your disposal. You will also have a brilliant engineer capable of astounding technological feats." She clicked her disc.

Another person appeared, a hairless man with horns hooking from his cheeks round his chin. He wore a body-length white frock, with an umber belt matching his complexion.

"This is Ferris Bilanthia," Elama said, "a doctor-turned-politician who openly challenges the Guild. Once you recruit Miss Troyer, we will take you to the galactic capital to speak with him about joining the team."

Sixxis leaned in close. "Look at those *feet*!"

Like Sixxis', they were bare. Unlike Sixxis', they looked more like hands than feet.

"Imagine the shit I could do with those!"

Elama clicked her disc a final time, stowing the image. "It will be a while before we arrive," she said. "I suggest you use this time to rest up and review what we've prepared in our intelligence interface."

"Ah, yes," Jag said, standing up. "Torin mentioned those."

"The chambers are soundproof, and the computers inside are programmed to recognize you. The modules will help acquaint you with galactic civilization."

Unbuckling, Sixxis hopped up and gave Jag a shove. "Sounds like you've got some learning to do!"

"Me?" Jag's face scrunched. "*Just* me?"

"Yeah—*just* you. You're the thinker. And besides, I have a date with one of those bunks." He stretched his arms up and let out an exaggerated yawn. "I'm beat!"

"Great," Jag sighed, voice dripping with sarcasm. "Glad to know you trust me so much." Having already been inundated with so much new information, he wasn't sure how much room was left in his brain. But he didn't have much choice. "Thanks for everything, Elama."

With a kind smile, the Arbiter nodded. "Just down the hall, you'll find everything you need. I'll stay up here; I have things I must discuss with Torin."

Jag turned and led Sixxis back down the corridor, stopping in front of the first door as it whizzed upward. "Are you really not going to do these?"

"Maybe later," Sixxis replied, waving a hand over his shoulder as he continued on toward the bunkroom. "So many beds!"

Rolling his eyes, Jag entered the dark room. A faint, amber light faded into the space as the door shut behind him, followed by a voice.

"Analyzing."

Startled, Jag jumped.

"Confirmed. Welcome, Jag! Elama has instructed me to educate you on the basics of galactic civilization, including but not limited to: galactic organization, common world structures, monetary systems, and basic technological concepts."

Jag drew a deep breath. "That sounds like a lot."

"Don't worry," laughed the voice. "You dictate the pace of our session, and we don't have to complete it all now. Are you ready to begin?"

Chapter 13

Standing beneath an awning, the final covered portion between the Silineese Palace and his ship, the Advocate stretched his arm forward—and cursed the miserable, *wet* planet.

"Damn this place," he mumbled to himself—though he could have screamed. Nobody would have heard anything over the static rush of the deluge. "And I thought I hated it before." He charged toward *Superior*.

The moment his full frame broke into the open, the rain consumed him. The surrounding curtain made it near impossible to see anything as it pelted his entire body, rattling on his armor and metallic plating. Running blindly, he continued forward.

Best to get there sooner. Then he could leave Sileen—*forever*.

The moment *Superior's* rounded back end phased into view, he tapped his wrist, tucked his head, and picked up his pace. He pressed his mad dash up the narrow entrance ramp, through the still-opening door, and into the rear workshop—where he slammed into a gurney and threw it aside.

Because the weather on Sileen was not the *only* thing angering him.

The Advocate was just about to enter the king's court when his link to the operative on Rixxon Prime went dark. He admittedly got a bit hasty once planetary scans located the metal, but it was still to be a simple in and out. The beast's heat signature all but leapt from those cold caverns, and they hardly found any resistance. But the resistance they *did* find clearly bested them.

He came to a full stop as the gurney slammed into the far wall, its contents spraying out and banging on every surface. Behind him, the ramp retracted; the door closed.

"Rotten *pests.*" His gravelly voice drifted into the now-quiet workshop, as his gaze drifted to the glint of his tensed fist in the dim space. Feeling the brilliance of the orgo-steel alloy, he ran his other hand through his fingers, across his wrist, and up to where it met the armor on his shoulder.

That special metal...

It more than belonged to the Advocate—it was a *part* of him, lining both the inner and outer workings of his body. For years he'd been scouring the galaxy for traces of it, a search made more necessary when he gained his current position. Now he'd spent months brokering deals with planetary officials and making close assessments of all substances native to their worlds. Until the other day, he'd failed to find any sources outside his being.

Now, he *had* found it—on Rixxon Prime. He finally had more. He could be *better*.

But what about that man?

The ringing comm terminal beside the fallen gurney broke his trance. He crossed the room, accepted the call, and dropped to a stool, as Pert Gubora's holographic bust appeared above the side table.

"Ah, old friend! How go things on Sileen?" The Laktilian lowered his snout, bringing a beady eye closer to the Advocate. "I trust negotiations were fruitful yet unsuccessful?"

The Advocate sighed. "I got thrown a bit just before the meeting, so it happened a little fast." Eyes closed, he leaned forward and rubbed at his temples. "But the meeting was never the real show here; everything is going according to plan." He sat up, a devious smirk stretched across his face. "Tonight, the outcasts receive their 'gift.' I suspect we'll be hearing from the king before the night is through."

"Exsssellent!" hissed Gubora, spitting his tongue out and around his mouth as he lingered too long on the sound.

The Advocate shuddered. "You know I hate when you do that."

"Ah, but the exsssitement you create brings it out of me, old friend!"

Old friend was right—only friend, more like it. Gubora was the only person the Advocate had ever really known. And despite his continued use of the word *creation*—the Advocate had become *far* more than Gubora could ever understand—the two had developed a strong bond. What's more, their unique blend of skills—Gubora's intelligence, vision, and silky tongue, and the Advocate's ruthless, do-whatever-it-takes attitude—had elevated the Guild to unprecedented heights. Together, they had seen operations triple.

But the Advocate still knew better than to put his full trust in the Laktilian.

"If I am not mistaken, this marks your quickest success yet," said Gubora. "If you truly are off your game as you say—which this performance does *not* suggest, I might add—perhapsss you should take some time for yourself."

The Advocate leaned back. "It *is* pretty hard being in so many places at once."

"Heh—it certainly does ssseem like that, old friend. I don't know how you do it."

"Maybe I'll tell you someday," he said with a grin. "But for now, I think you're right: Some time off would be good. I actually have something I need to look into."

Gubora's head tilted. "A personal errand? How rare for you."

And just like that, the Advocate grew irritated. "I have a life, thank you. There's a lot more to me than there was when you were in my head all the time."

"Ah—I did not mean anything by that, of course! You are and always will be my greatest creation—"

There it was.

"—but I acknowledge that you have developed and grown into something far beyond what I imagined all those years ago."

At least he had *that* right.

"What isss it you are doing?"

The Advocate folded his arms. "I'm looking into something."

"Sssо much detail, as per usual," Gubora replied with a chuckle. "I will leave you to it, then. Talk soon, old friend." His image zipped upward and disappeared.

Were he being honest, the Advocate would have said he was looking into *two* things. There was the metal, yes—that precious, impenetrable substance that existed seemingly nowhere but on his body and on Rixxon Prime of all places.

But there was also that *man*.

It was strange. Rixxon Prime was a Class V planet, likely thousands of years from first contact, so the presence of offworlders was forbidden by the Galactic Legislature. That obviously hadn't prevented the Advocate's plans, but the chances of running into someone *else* from offworld were infinitesimal. Not only that, but something about the man gave the Advocate pause, like he'd *seen* him before. Perhaps the man and the metal were linked, and perhaps the Advocate to them both.

Had he finally found evidence of his existence beyond what Pert Gubora had told him?

Spinning his stool, the Advocate let his eyes rest on the still-standing, undisturbed gurney. He rolled over and placed a hand on the white cloth covering his latest project. "Soon you will see the sun."

The man's identity did not betray the significance of the day: After years of no trace whatsoever, the Advocate had *finally* found the substance he was searching for. And the timing couldn't have been better! He'd been growing more and more tired splitting his attention across operations in multiple star systems. He needed something—some*one* he could rely on to help shoulder the load. Now, he merely needed to excavate the source on Rixxon Prime, and he would have plenty of metal for the operation.

He clenched the cloth. "You will be my greatest appendage yet."

Chapter 14

Cross-legged on the bottom bunk, Jag shut his mother's journal.

It'd been a restless "night." With everything slowed down, the cold quiet of space was unnerving, leaving far too much space for his swirling thoughts. So he distracted himself: he studied the intelligence interface until he couldn't stay awake. But even after stumbling down the hall and collapsing onto a bunk, he only managed to drift off for a short while. And when he woke up, his mind continued to churn.

Then he remembered the journal.

He hadn't forgotten it, exactly. But its words seemed inconsequential after everything he'd learned from Elama. His parents obviously knew some of who he was and where he came from, but his mother sure as skies didn't write anything about it in the journal. Jag hadn't found anything about his grand purpose—just stories about him and Sixxis as kids.

It all seemed so... small.

Jag wasn't sure if he was irritated with the lack of information or confused over the secrecy. Either way, it was uncomfortable. He closed his eyes and drew deep breaths, searching for inner quiet—but it was no use. As it had all night, his brain betrayed his efforts and fixated on the hologram of the Advocate.

Sixxis, of course, slept soundly in the bed above him.

"Jag, Sixxis," emanated Torin's voice from the room's perimeter, "we will be arriving at Korrignolan soon. Your presence is requested on the bridge."

Sixxis' long, green toes stretched beyond the base of the top bunk. "Guess that's our cue."

"I don't know how you slept after all that," Jag said, swinging his feet to the ground.

"I don't know how you *didn't* sleep," Sixxis replied as he thudded onto the metal floor. "*Skies* it's cold out here."

"Did you even touch the interface?"

"Yes, actually." He grimaced. "But I got hung up on the demolitions section."

Jag tilted his head.

"I learned about how to blow stuff up."

Great—just what Jag needed. The fireball had awakened some dangerous fascination in his foolhardy brother.

"Well," he said, "I guess we should get going." He led Sixxis out of the bunkroom, up the corridor, through the whooshing door, and onto the bridge.

Elama welcomed them with outstretched arms. "Ah, gentlemen—I trust you were comfortable?"

"Nice and cozy, thanks!" Sixxis returned with a smile.

"Wonderful! We will be exiting warp in a few minutes—enough time for you to suit up." She approached and placed her hand on a tall cabinet at the rear of the bridge. Its doors flew open to reveal two gray-armored suits.

"We made these in anticipation of you joining us," she said, stepping to the side. "Each is built to your physical specifications, with a retractable helmet that will assist you in breathing on toxic planets." She smiled. "I think you will find them to be quite functional."

"Ooh!" Sixxis let out with a hop. Scurrying over to the cabinet, he pulled out the taller suit and fiddled with it. "How's it work?"

"Just..." Elama flicked a switch on its upper arm. Its front opened and retracted—dropping Sixxis' jaw. "Step right in!"

Sixxis slammed his mouth shut, shoved himself into the half-suit, and jabbed at the arm switch. The sleek alloy folded over him, covering most of his green body.

Oh, Six. First the space travel, then the lessons on explosives, and now a new toy. This was all so exciting for him.

With a laugh, Jag tapped the shoulder of his own suit. Unlike his brother, he elected to admire it before jumping in, running a hand along its interior. It was soft to the touch—maybe a sort of insulation.

"Korrignolan can be dangerous," Elama said, placing a hand on his shoulder. "I'm only sorry I don't have weapons for you—yet."

Jag lifted an eyebrow. "Yet?"

"Once you recruit your companions, I will have you come to our base, where I'll have more supplies for you." She smiled. "I'm quite excited to show you what I've designed!"

Jag returned her smile, but only momentarily; Sixxis was jumping up and down behind her. "Six, what are you—"

"This stuff is super light," he said, lifting his left hand to inspect a button on the suit's wrist. "I wonder what—"

A helmet zipped over his head, constructing itself from the material behind his neck. He gasped for air, gripping wildly at his covered face.

It took everything Jag had to not fall over laughing. "Elama, didn't you say the helmets were supposed to *help* us breathe?"

"Oh." Sixxis stopped moving, dropped his arms, and after a few swigs of fresh, filtered air, pressed the button again to stow the helmet in his collar. "Yup, you're right."

Elama laughed, this time more heartily than ever. "Yours in particular was a challenge, Sixxis. We designed it to support your unique joint formation. Your armor has quite a bit more flex than Jag's, and you'll notice it doesn't stretch over your feet."

"Yup—thanks for that! I don't like caging my toes."

"I suspect not! From what I've seen of your people, your phalanges are quite critical to your abilities."

Jag stripped down to his undergarments as they bantered, then stepped into his armor. The soft, warm interior folded over him, hugging his body until he too was covered, from the curled collar down through the attached sturdy boots. The armor was a bit stiffer than what he was used to, but much lighter. "Thank you, Elama."

"My pleasure," she said with a bow. "Now, if you each wouldn't mind taking a—"

BOOP!

"Go ahead, Dom," said Torin from the pilot's seat.

A high-pitched, reedy voice buzzed into the room. "Torin, commander, one of my contacts just informed me that a sudden insurrection began last night on Sileen. The planet's king has entered into a contract with the Guild for weapons to combat the rebels."

Elama strode forward and leaned her hands on the terminal. "Do you have any more information?"

"Negative."

"Very well; thank you, Dom. Please prepare the workshop beside the hangar. I expect we'll arrive in twelve hours."

"Yes, ma'am!"

BOOP!

"This is troubling news," Elama sighed, sinking into her chair. "I have little doubt the Guild supplied both sides of this war."

Jag took his seat. "I guess that means we've got no time to waste."

"Indeed we do not. I trust you are ready?"

Ready as he could've been.

"Good timing," Torin said as he pulled back a lever. The whizzing stars fell still, leaving before them a massive—and massively dreary—gray planet. "Welcome to Korrignolan."

"I'm afraid that's the only welcome you'll get," said Elama, facing forward. "We'll drop you at the spaceport and wait for you to return with Miss Troyer."

As *Pioneer* entered the dismal planet's atmosphere, a deep-crimson horizon faded onto the bridge. Lofty metallic structures littered the sprawling cityscape. While they were tremendous in size, most looked to be falling apart.

"A red sky..." Sixxis mumbled. "Creepy."

"It is an accurate omen." Torin pressed into the controls, veering the ship left. "More of a waystation than a planet, Korrignolan is objectively unsafe. This main city is infested with members of the Prospectors' Guild, the Korrig Collective, and formerly the Marauder Faction."

"Formerly?" Jag said, as the city's endless run-down scaffolding raced past the window.

"The Marauder Faction is a band of pirates and smugglers. Most of them resided here until six months ago."

"What happened six months ago?"

"They all left the planet within the span of a week."

"Huh." Sixxis took his seat. "Where'd they go?"

"We have yet to figure that out," said Elama, "adding to the already strange nature of their departure."

"What was so strange?" Jag asked.

"It is not odd for a group to change its home base," she replied, "but it *is* odd for it to happen so quickly. That said, it's not unlike the Marauders to undergo rapid shifts in operations. I suspect the reason will make itself known in time."

"What about the Collective?" Jag said.

"The Korrig Collective is a small yet powerful organization." Torin altered course, toward a large, domed structure in the distance. "It operates a system of underground banks and provides questionless loans to interested parties. Agreements are fraught with high interest rates, authoritarian conditions, and hidden provisional clauses. Although the Legislature has yet to prove any foul play, it is widely known that borrowers often disappear when they do not uphold their contracts."

"That doesn't sound good."

Torin shook his head. "Perhaps you should review the 'Criminal Organizations' module when you return."

"Not a bad idea," Jag muttered, undoing his restraints and drifting forward for a better look.

A sea of people milled about the avenues below, traveling almost in lanes as they bustled between the broken-down buildings. Seedy characters lined the street edges. Jag swore they were throwing things into the crowd, and then a group of them surrounded and grabbed somebody.

Unsafe was right.

The mob thickened as they made their way closer to the dome. With that and all the soaring structures closing in around them, Jag felt cramped even on *Pioneer*.

"Shuttle," hummed a disembodied voice in the ship, "please identify yourself."

Torin held down a button. "Shuttle one-zero-one-two-five, Sigma Class, requesting dock permission for refuel and resupply."

"Please hold."

DING!

"You're cleared. Please proceed to docking bay ninety-four."

"Thank you."

A round hole appeared on the enormous dome as they approached. Torin piloted the ship inside, washing the beige coloring of its interior over the red sky.

It was astounding! Spread throughout the dim port, zipping past the window were countless ships of all shapes and sizes.

Pioneer continued on at Torin's controls, lowering gradually toward the ground. Pulling above and alongside a long walkway, she proceeded straight.

"Here we are," he said. "Bay ninety-four."

In quick, concurrent motions, *Pioneer* surged forward, tilted backward, rotated, and came to a gentle, hissing rest on the circular platform.

"This is where you get off!" said Elama. "We'll await you here. Just remember: bay ninety-four. Oh, and take these!" She offered Jag a handful of coins. "You'll need to ask around to find Miss Troyer."

Jag took the coins with a nod. "We'll look for a pub. The interface said those are good places for information."

"If I'm not mistaken, there should be one near the main spaceport entrance."

"Got it!"

THUMP! Sixxis stood up fast and banged his head into the ceiling. "Ow!"

"I apologize," said Torin. "I should have warned you: Gravitational forces will vary planet to planet, and Rixxon Prime's is roughly double the galactic average. You will feel lighter most places you go."

Sixxis rubbed the top of his head. "Maybe I should slow down."

"I'm not sure that's possible," Jag said with a grin.

The brothers exited the bridge and returned to the bunkroom. There, Sixxis trotted across to fetch and equip his machete, then jogged back to Jag and held out his arm.

Jag tapped their forearms. "I guess the mission starts now."

"Nah," said Sixxis, tossing an arm around his shoulder and starting them down the corridor. "The mission started when we followed those goons in the jungle. It's just been one thing after the next since then."

Jag stopped. "Thanks for being here with me, Six. I'm not sure I could do this without you."

"You couldn't," he replied, waving over his shoulder.

Jag grinned to himself and jogged forward, overtaking his brother as they descended the ramp. And together, they stepped onto the concrete—onto this new world.

The platform stretched away from them until it reached a walkway, the same they flew alongside as they entered. And all around them, people scurried about, entering and exiting ships parked at the docks.

It was incredible! Red, blue, yellow, brown; tall, short, thin, round—every person was different, a far cry from Rixxon Prime where everyone other than Jag was the same emerald hue with the same orange hair. Except the mountain folk, of course. But they were all so similar, too.

Jag might actually *succeed* at blending in

They continued on as the walkway passed through a massive, soaring archway and into a grand hall. Before, the distinct voices of the passersby all but evaporated into the spaceport. Here, all that noise blended into an overwhelming cacophony, echoing and bouncing about the barriers of the cavernous, domed ceiling.

"This must be the central station," Jag guessed. Ornate but tarnished decorative fixtures hung about, swaying in the stale air. The place was likely beautiful long ago. Now it was run down, just something to pass through.

Sixxis shrugged. "Sure."

Gazing over the crowd of people—who didn't even look up as they pushed past and bumped into each other—Jag pointed to another archway opposite them. "I bet that's the main entrance."

"Lead the way!"

Doing his best to avoid collisions, Jag proceeded through the congested station with his brother in tow. The poor air quality combined with an odd stench amidst the crowd; he quickened his pace to escape it, caring less who he nudged. Things thankfully quieted and slowed—and *smelled better*—on the other side of the arch.

As they set out on the dilapidated foot highway, people on both sides tried to get their attention. Jag kept his focus forward, searching for something that might look like the pub—which was *ridiculous* given that he'd never seen a pub before.

But after a few minutes, he gestured to a dingy building at the base of some jagged scaffolding. "Look."

JARNUK'S

BEST SCREECHERS THIS SIDE OF THE

BERABULUS NEBULA!

Sixxis raised an eyebrow. "What's a screecher?"

"No idea—but maybe this is the pub." It was the only thing so far that looked even *remotely* like what Jag had imagined. He clutched the curved handle, pushed the door open, and stepped inside.

Calm music permeated the room, singing in symphony with the tinkling of glasses. It seemed like the right place!

"Let's talk to the bartender," Jag said, starting across the room. They weaved between a collection of round, wooden tables, half of which were occupied, and came to the empty bar.

Sixxis looked around, confusion evident in his twisted expression. "Where's the—"

"Ah, hold 'yer schmigworts," replied a gruff, gravelly voice.

An exceptionally small, gray hand shot up, clasping the edge of a platform running the length of the bar's backside. Another hand followed, then a cloven, rounded foot. Up climbed a man who couldn't have been more than a third of Jag's height.

"What'll ya have?" Drawing a rag from the pocket of his greasy, white apron, he wiped the sizable horn protruding from his face, then similarly cleaned the smaller horn between his beady, black eyes.

Jag offered a timid smile. "Jarnuk, I presume?"

The man's ears—which stuck straight up—flickered. "Depends."

Sixxis held in a laugh.

"Depends on what exactly?" Jag asked.

"On what 'ye want, a course!"

"We're looking for someone."

"I see—okay then! Jarnuk's m'name." His ears flopped about as he spoke. "This here be mah 'istablishment."

Sixxis let out a snort, and Jag threw his body between them to block Jarnuk's view. "Pleased to meet you." He kicked back, nailing his brother in the shin.

"Yer awfully polite," Jarnuk said with a rasp in his voice. "Don'tchu think for a second you can con me inta tellin' you whatever it is you wanna know! I been 'round this place fer a looong time. I seent the folk who come through."

Sixxis turned and pressed his back into Jag's, laughter all but bursting from his clamped lips.

"No cons," said Jag, waving his hands in front of him. "Like I said, we're just looking for someone. Her name's Remy Troyer."

"Y'lookin for Remy?" Jarnuk hopped onto the bar and—with one eye closed—came right up to Jag's face. His brow furrowed as he pressed a stubby finger into his chest. "She's a good gal, but I don't know you. If ya think I'm just gonna tell you where ta find her, you got something else goin' in that brain a' yers."

"Please," Jag said, taking a step back. "We're... old friends. I heard about her sister and—"

"Ah, Omeka." Jarnuk's arms fell to his sides. "She was a good gal, too. Inseparable, those two." He cocked his head to the side and peered over his horn, squinting his glistening, black eyes.

Jag shifted under the miniature barkeep's gaze. "Please, sir. I would very much like to see her."

Jarnuk turned and hopped to his platform, keeping his back to Jag. "Ya know, I pride m'self in bein' an outstanding judge a' character." He grinned over his shoulder. "I can tell you mean 'er no harm. Sure 'nuff, I can help you!" He pointed at the door. "Head out there, take a right, then count three alleyways b'fore takin' a hard left. Remy's in Unit 303. That's on the third floor."

"Thank you!" Jag started to turn.

"Hold it!"

He stopped, rotating once again to face the tiny man.

"Ain't such a thing here as free information. You gotta buy a drink!" He took a glass in one hand and flipped it through the air to his other. "What'll ya have?"

"Give me a moment, please, Master Jarnuk."

"Master Jarnuk? You talk funny, but I like the sound'a that!"

Jag spun to Sixxis and ushered him forward a few paces. "He told me where the engineer lives; I'm going to go check it out. He's demanding that we order a drink in exchange for the information, though. Maybe you should stay here and keep an eye out for her."

"So you're going to do all the work while I sit and drink?" Sixxis' face spread into his signature grin. "Works for me!"

Jag returned to the bar with a smile. "Thank you again, sir. I'm going to go talk to Remy. My brother here will take that drink."

"Brother, eh?" Jarnuk eyed the travelers. "Don't see much resemblance."

"It's a long story," Jag said.

"Hmm..." Jarnuk spun the glass in his hand. "Well, if I hear somethin' bad come'a Remy, I'ma send out fer you!"

"I promise," Jag said with a bow, "you won't hear anything like that." With a nod toward Sixxis, he zigzagged through the tables and exited the pub.

"Well?" Jarnuk leaned back and started tapping his hoof. "What'll ya have?"

Sixxis thought back to the sign. "What's a screecher?"

"Ah, ye've never had a screecher?" Jarnuk whisked about his platform, whipped up a small, sapphire cocktail, and handed it to Sixxis. "And since it's yer first time, you'll prolly want this." He flipped another glass through the air and pressed it into a knob. Amber liquid flowed from the nozzle above.

Who knew Sixxis would get the chance to kick back on this mission? He took the drinks and offered a few of Elama's coins.

"Uhh," Jarnuk said, "I think ye've overpaid."

Sixxis waved him off. "Don't worry about it."

"Much obliged, m'friend!" Jarnuk scuttled away with a hop in his thick-footed step,

After turning and choosing a booth in the corner, Sixxis crossed the room and got comfortable. He had an unobstructed view of the entire pub—as the front door flew open. In stepped a massive man wearing a navy-blue trench coat and burnt-orange pants.

"Barkeep!" he said. "I'll take a screecher!"

"Comin' up!" Jarnuk replied.

What an entrance!

The man's close-cropped, silvery hair shimmered in the gloomy pub, contrasting his dark face as he walked with a swagger toward the bar. "Thank you, sir!" He reached a thick arm forward and grabbed the glass.

The two of them next to each other—talk about hilarious. The guy could've probably squeezed the life out of Jarnuk with just two fingers!

"Hey, Borum!" called a man sitting at the bar. "You owe me thirty DGs!"

This was going to be interesting.

The big guy set his drink on the bar before turning to the man. He walked slowly, his black, calf-height boots pounding the paces between them. "It's pronounced Bo-RAM!"

And with that, he *rammed* his fist into the man's face.

"You tell your boss I already paid his fee!" He shifted to face the rest of the pub, all eyes on him. "Anyone else got a debt to settle?"

Bam! That was one way to handle things. While the others averted their eyes and resumed what they were doing, Sixxis all but blurted out a cheer. And that caught the man's attention—they locked eyes.

Uh oh.

Sixxis looked down and took a sip of the amber stuff, but kept one eye up.

Grinning a mischievous grin, the man shot an arm to his left and held up two fingers. "I'll take two more of those screechers, Jarnuk." Now with three drinks in hand, he approached the corner booth.

Skies. Why did Jag leave? It took almost no time for Sixxis to piss someone off.

"Well hello there! I've never seen anyone quite like *you* before." The man winked. "What's a beautiful creature like you doing all alone? Mind if I join you?"

"Sure," Sixxis replied with a genuine smile. Should he have been scared? The guy didn't *seem* all that bad—not if you didn't make him mad, anyway.

"The name's Bo-Ram Chinosin—ace pilot." He slid into the booth and rested his arm on a ledge behind Sixxis' head. "I've got a beautiful ship, you know. She's docked not far from here if you'd like to see her." As he spoke, his other hand unbuttoned his trench coat, revealing a second set of arms—equally as massive as the first—folded beneath it.

Sixxis' eyes widened. "I think I got your name from your—let's say conversation—with *that* guy."

As the man stumbled to his feet and glanced toward them, the four-armed Bo-Ram bucked his head—spooking and sending him running—then burst into a rowdy bout of laughter. "You can call me Bo," he said as he calmed down. "And contrary to what I've shown so far, I'm a lover"—he pumped his brows—"not a fighter."

Sixxis offered a grin of his own. "All right—Bo, then. I'm Sixxis. How about I pass on seeing the ship, but we have a drink? I've never tried a screecher."

"D'you know why they call it a screecher?" Bo unfolded his second set of arms and handed Sixxis the blue beverage that sat undisturbed on the table. Lifting his own, he clinked their glasses, and they tossed their drinks back.

"Yeeeooow!" Sixxis hollered, scrambling for his other drink.

"Bahaha—that's why!" Without another word, he offered Sixxis one of the remaining screechers.

Once again, they took the plunge. Sixxis managed to keep in his screech his time.

"A fast learner, I see." Bo inched closer.

"So, Bo—"

Sixxis snickered at the rhyme.

"—tell me about yourself."

Jag came to his third flight of open-air stairs and started to climb. The whole structure felt unstable; his bounding steps rattled both his ears and the steps themselves. But he probably should've expected that from everything he'd seen on the planet so far.

Maybe it wasn't the best idea to split up the first time they visited a new world. Sixxis was pretty good at getting into trouble when Jag wasn't around. It would've been great if Adira came to help keep an eye on him.

Reaching the top step, Jag found the number displayed on the first door: 301. He counted two more doors and found it: 303.

He knocked.

Maybe he was overreacting. After all, Sixxis was stronger than him; he'd probably be fine. Plus Jag had already found the engineer's house, so it wouldn't be long—if she was home, of course.

Skies. Jag had been so caught up in everything that he hadn't even considered how to *talk* to Remy. It's not like he had much experience meeting new people. Kithara and Jade were his first in who knows how long, and Adira was the only woman he'd ever known around his age. Forget fighting the Thakk—what do you say to someone whose sister was just murdered?

He knocked again.

"Yes?" came a smooth, even-toned voice from inside.

A lump rose in Jag's throat. "Miss Remy Troyer?"

"Who is asking?"

Just try not to say anything stupid.

"My name is Jag. I have information about your sister."

The door swung inward, and Jag was met by the stunning, azure woman—even more stunning than in Elama's projection. Despite being a fair bit smaller than him, she had a similar body shape. The neutral, dim tones of her clothing accentuated her dark facial features.

"Jag is a strange name," she said, zipping a black vest over her white, sleeveless top. "Yes, I am Remy Troyer. What information do you have?"

Jag's mouth wrinkled. "I'm sorry to hear about her," he said, shuffling his feet. "I've lost someone before, too. I—"

"I do not need your condolences."

That caught him off guard. "Umm... I have intelligence that proves your sister's death wasn't an accident."

Remy squinted. "That is impossible."

"Impossible? From what I—"

"It is impossible for you to have this information," she interrupted without a single shift on her blank face. "Guild incident reports are not public record. They are not even shared with members of their corresponding dig sites."

Skies. Even if Jag *had* thought about this conversation ahead of time, it wouldn't have made much difference; he couldn't seem to get his footing. "I also have information about the explosion that destroyed your childhood home."

She scowled. "How do you know about that?"

Sensing his opportunity, Jag ignored her question. "It was caused by gasses from a nearby Guild installation."

"Also impossible. Even if your assertion is true, it is likely that all existing evidence would have been destroyed by the Guild years ago." Remy grabbed the door. "Whoever you are, whatever your goals are, you may leave now." She started to shut him out—and he crammed his foot in the way.

"Please, Miss Troyer. The Guild is up to something, and it spells death and destruction across the galaxy. I'm putting a team together to stop it."

"Remove your foot. And do not call me Miss Troyer."

Jag pulled the object from his pocket, which he'd learned from the interface was called a data drive. "Here." He shoved it into her hand. "Look through this."

Remy glanced at the drive, at Jag's plaintive expression, then back at the drive. "Very well." She kicked his foot out of the way and slammed the door.

Chapter 15

Remy stumbled back a step, flopping into her chair and rolling away from the computer.

The evidence this Jag had presented was irrefutable: her sister had been murdered, making the subsequent revelation that her parents and childhood home were incinerated by the Guild's carelessness of far lesser circumstance.

The chair knocked into a large, black duffle, stuffed to the brim. Dropping her feet to the floor, Remy clutched and lowered her head.

Omeka was her home, the only safe haven in her life, one she defended with all her strength. A week ago, that home was removed from existence, washed away in what was publicly known as an "accidental flood." Remy had yet to process it—and she now knew it was no accident.

It was beyond question: the Guild must feel the repercussions of its actions.

A burning sensation swelled near the top of her stomach. Was it... anger?

Remy zipped up her second duffle. It was clear she had no plan when she began packing. She was simply leaving: leaving Korriginolan, leaving the Guild—leaving it at all. Then, the moment she finished preparations, her mind consumed her and dwelt on one simple fact: she could not live without Omeka. And so she stayed, sitting in that understanding, contemplating possible... actions—until her mind went blank.

The next thing she knew, a knock at the door drew her back to reality. Two hours had passed—*two hours* without conscious thought or even awareness of her existence.

She needed a way out, an enormous ask for a guildsman. And now this Jag... perhaps a way out had presented itself.

The heat radiated up her body, spreading through her chest before rising into her throat. Confirmed: it *was* anger, something she had not felt in quite some time—and she was grateful for it.

Since Omeka's death, Remy's entire mind had been a haze. Despite possessing little to no motivation, she attempted to carry on throughout the week, but seemingly zero percent of her faculties functioned at optimal capacity. Given how much she prized and relied on her intelligence, this was disconcerting.

Now imbued with rage, she felt her drive returning.

Jag's data merely revealed that the flood was triggered manually—a process too complex to be executed without intention—but there was no doubt the Advocate was behind her sister's murder. Nothing happened on that planet without his knowledge. More accurately, nothing happened on that planet unless he ordered it so.

Remy's hand folded into a tight fist, darkening her sapphire skin as it shook.

Attacking the Guild was illogical, impractical to her survival. Yet she had every intention of ensuring its utter destruction.

And she would see *personally* to the Advocate's demise.

A knock at the door beckoned her once again: it was time.

Remy rose to her feet. She hoisted a bag over her shoulder, carried it across the room, and dropped it by the entrance before returning for another. Then with one bag in hand, she pulled the door open.

"Good—you are still here," she said, blank faced. "Your intelligence is legitimate; I will help you. Take these." She thrust a bag into Jag's unwitting arms, pushed the other out with her foot, then slammed the door and crossed the room for her backpack. Sliding her arms through its straps, she pulled it up and fastened the hip and chest belts.

"One more," she said, eyeing the apartment for the last time. Years of memories with her sister flooded her mind—vanishing after but a moment as she turned her attention to the matter at hand. She threw the final duffle's straps over her head and pressed the bag into her chest, then returned to the door and pulled it open.

Jag stumbled into the apartment.

Imbecile.

"What are you doing?" she said, scowling.

"I was—uhh—listening to see where you'd—"

"It is rude to spy on people. Are you ready?

Jag blinked. "Y—yes."

Remy hustled past, bumping into him in the process. "Let us depart," she said halfway to the stairwell. And when he had yet to move, she halted and turned sharply. "Are you coming? This matter is highly urgent; I would think you might understand that."

"Ahh—yep!" Jag sprang upright and jogged to catch up. "You just—uhh—surprised me."

Remy turned and started down the stairs with him scrambling after her. "I am a woman of reason," she said. "I cannot argue with factual information. The Prospectors' Guild has lied to me. It murdered my sister and poses a threat to many others. I will not allow lives like mine to be destroyed, and I will not allow more people to be unknowingly forced into indentured servitude."

"Just like that?"

Remy froze. "I am..." She looked down at her trembling hand, at the anger flowing from her fingers. "I must make things right."

Jag dropped one of the bags and moved to put a hand on her shoulder. "If we work together, we'll—"

"I know what to do," she said, bursting off down the stairs and sending him stumbling. "And surely you do, too. To dismantle the Guild, we must remove Pert Gubora and the Advocate. They must cease to exist."

Once again, Jag ran after her. "But that's a little easier said than done, don't you—"

"All beings can perish." She did not break stride. "Pert Gubora is flesh and blood, just like you and me. The Advocate is—well, I am not entirely sure *what* he is. We simply must find his weakness and exploit it."

He could be defeated. It was a simple fact.

"I suppose you're right, Miss Troyer."

Remy stopped and rotated to face him. "Please, call me Remy."

"Okay." Jag smiled. "Remy."

She eyed him, then turned and jogged off.

"Sorry," he offered as they rounded out of the alleyway and onto the main road. "What's in these bags?"

"Supplies: tools, computers, weapons. Where are we going? I presume you are not from here. Are you docked at the spaceport?"

"Yeah, but we have to grab my brother from the pub first."

Bo reared his head back, body booming with laughter. "Sixxis, you sure are something! I don't think I've had this good a time in *ages!*"

Sixxis lifted his forehead off the table and flopped over, laughing just as hard. It'd been a *thrilling* couple hours listening to stories of Bo's travels. This must have been what living was *really* like!

Bo put an arm around him and scooted closer. "I've talked too much. How's about *you* tell a story now?"

Snickering, Sixxis put way more effort than should've been necessary into figuring out what he could tell the enormous, four-armed man. Then as he opened his mouth to speak, Bo pressed a finger into his lips.

"Why don't we go back to my ship? You can tell me everything there."

Skies. What a *bummer!*

Sixxis cleared his throat, teetering side to side as the screechers sent him spinning. "Shit, Bo. I'm really sorry—and flattered." He leaned back and threw an arm into the air. "But I'm in love!" he trumpeted—then collapsed onto the table in another fit of laughter.

Would Sixxis ever catch up with all this excitement? Not long ago, he was just doing the same old thing. Now he felt so *alive*—and he'd made a new friend!

A hiccup lurched his head up. "She's incredible," he said, bringing his eyes level with Bo's as a tear ran down his cheek. "I just—"

Bo placed his finger back on his lips. "No need t'pologize. Love is a powerful force, and I know *true* love when I see it." He slapped Sixxis on the back. "You been caught by it!"

Sixxis grimaced with one eye closed. "You can tell?"

"We Quadmalians pride ourselves in bein' very perceptive," said Bo, interlacing his fingers and stretching them out in front of him. "I can tell you're sincere." He pressed a palm into Sixxis' chest. "Your heart is elsewhere."

"*Phew.*" Sixxis looked down at Bo's big hand as it swirled about. "I'm glad you understand. I wouldn't want to make you mad—not like that one guy!" He clutched Bo's arm and all but doubled over.

"Tell me about her, friend," said Bo, sliding a glass of water his way.

Sixxis gulped some down and started talking with a full mouth. "Her name's Adira." He swallowed. "She's back home on Rixxon Prime."

"Rixxon Prime, eh? Haven't heard'a that place."

Uh oh—probably shouldn't have said that.

"Yeah, it's... uhh—"

"Six?"

Sixxis turned to find Jag striding across the pub.

"Brother!" he yelled, hopping to his wobbly feet, only to fall back into Bo's arms. "Sit—have a drink!" He tossed a finger over his shoulder. "This is my new friend, Bo!"

"Well, hello there!" Bo propped Sixxis up. "And the excitement just keeps coming! You're just as beautiful as your—did you say brother?" He tilted his head. "You don't exactly look like brothers."

"It's a long story," said Jag. "It's nice to meet you, but we need to—"

"Hah!" Sixxis roared. "Long story is right!" He exploded to his feet, almost knocking the table over. "Brothers—til' the end!" He thrust his fist into the air so hard that he teetered back and fell laughing onto the seat cushion.

"Too many screechers," said Bo with a grin. "Here—lemme help." He stood, pushed the table aside, and scooped Sixxis up, cradling him with all four arms. "Where we headed?"

Jag nodded and led them out to the street.

"What are you doing?" Asked a tiny blue woman standing between four huge bags—must've been Remy. "It is impossible that either of these men is your brother."

"It's a long story," Jag repeated.

"I'm the brother!" Sixxis hollered from Bo's comfortable cradle, with a sudden movement that would've probably made him fall if his carrier only had two arms.

Remy's face showed nothing, but she was clearly unimpressed. "I would calculate that our chance of success just dropped at least fifty percent."

"Success at what?" Bo asked.

"Nothing," Jag replied.

Remy shot Jag a glare. "We have business with the Guild's leadership."

Bo's humongously thick eyebrows bounced upward, like they were dancing on his face. "Ooh, that sounds exhilarating—and *dangerous*! I'm a great pilot, you know. If you need a ship, I'm your guy!"

"Come on," Jag said, ushering them forward, "let's head to the spaceport."

The party—now consisting of four—entered the grand archway and proceeded through the station. Sixxis had the time of his life being carried.

"I'm parked this way," said Bo, gesturing through a smaller gate. "200 block"

"We don't need a ship—sorry." Jag continued down the walkway. "I appreciate your help, though."

"Who are you, anyway?" Remy asked.

"The name's Bo-Ram Chinosin—ace pilot. I'm no friend of the Guild, either." He paused. "Don't have many friends, really. I do my own thing mostly: go job to job, make enough to live and pay off my"—his face lit up—"Heeeyyy, I owe *a lot* of money to the Collective. I bet messing with the Guild could absolve my debt!"

"That seems probable," said Remy, picking up her pace. "Where are we parked?"

"Ninety-four," Jag replied, falling in step with her.

Sixxis got confused when they made it to the dock. He recognized the ship, sure, but the man outside—he was blue! "I think those screechers are messing with my head."

"Welcome back," said the man, inspecting Sixxis in Bo's imposing arms. "Is everything all right?"

"I'm sorry," said Jag. "Who are you?"

"Torin," he replied.

Remy examined him with a puzzled look on her face. "Im..." She squinted. "...proba ble. It is highly unlikely that you are Phyatoraen. I have met very few of my kind since my home was destroyed."

"It is a visual alteration, Miss Troyer. I change my form to perhaps make you feel more comfortable."

Remy's expression stayed dry. "It is not working—and please call me Remy."

Torin bowed. "My apologies." He turned to Bo and Sixxis. "It appears our friend has had too much to drink," he said, removing a small, gun-shaped object from his pocket. He pressed it into Sixxis' forehead and clicked a button.

Sixxis' eyes shot open, then crossed as countless beads of moisture exited through the pores on his forehead and floated toward the whirring device—like someone was pulling his brains out.

And then literally everything changed.

"What?" He brought his head around in a wide circle. "What happened?"

"Too many screechers," Bo repeated.

"I have removed the alcohol from your system," said Torin, stowing the device. "It is likely you will have a headache." He turned and ascended the ramp.

"Finally—someone civilized." Remy followed him into the ship.

"Headache feels like an understatement," Sixxis said, rubbing at his temples as Bo released his feet to the ground. "Thanks for the assist, big guy."

"Certainly, my new friend! Looks like this is where we part ways." He slapped Sixxis on the back, shoving him forward. "If you need me again, you know where to find me."

"Thanks, Bo." Jag turned to Sixxis. "Can you walk?"

"Oh yeah—my feet are fine. It's my head," he replied. "I think I need to lie down."

"Bahaha—Sixxis, you're a riot! I truly hope I see you again." The big man looked to Jag, offering two eyebrow pumps. "And you, too, my handsome friend."

"Hah!" Sixxis blurted. "You're too much!"

Bo shrugged a massive shrug. "What can I say? There's a lot of beauty in this galaxy." He placed a hand on Jag's shoulder. "You got 'em from here?"

"We'll be fine," he said with a nod. "Thanks again!" Jag threw an arm around his brother's waist and hobbled them onto *Pioneer*. He helped Sixxis all the way to the bunkroom, where he flopped him onto one of the beds.

With the screechers sucked out of him, Sixxis couldn't help but feel guilty. Here was yet another situation his carelessness hassled Jag. First it was the fireball—the *grenade*—then it was the whole battle with the Thakk. Now their first stop on a new world, and he'd gotten drunk.

Elama—*blue* Elama—entered the bunkroom. "Welcome back, my friends! I see you were successful."

"Yes!" said Jag. "And Sixxis had too much to drink."

She chuckled. "I must say, I'm envious you were able to let loose after everything that's happened lately."

"I've always been good at blowing off steam," said Sixxis, laying back. "Sorry, Jag."

"I just hope you let off enough steam for both of us."

"Probably did!" He winced and squeezed his eyes shut. "And I'll pay for it."

"Well," said Elama, "it'll be a few hours before we reach our next destination. Perhaps this is a good time for you to rest."

What a *marvelous* idea!

"Where's Remy?" Jag asked.

"Torin set her up in one of the other chambers. She's getting right to work on decoding the messages."

"Great! And where are we going next?"

"The galactic capital, Palatia. We have time, if you'd like to review more information with the interface. Perhaps galactic governance would be a suitable topic."

Jag nodded. "And I want to look into the criminal groups, like Torin suggested." He followed her out of the room

Sixxis leaned back and sucked in a deep yawn. All *he* wanted to do was sleep.

Chapter 16

Damned humidity. Why were all these planets so *wet?*

The Advocate spent the entirety of his trip between Sileen and Rixxon Prime doing the only thing that could quiet his mind when it was stretched thin: tinkering, working with his hands. But now that he was here—slopping through mud and muck, wading through an insufferable mess of brush and brambles—all calm had left him.

Despite incredible rage over his operative's defeat, the Advocate thought it best to leave the Rixxonians alone for now. Instead, he headed for the larger reading—presumably the metal's source. Later, once he'd determined how it came to the planet, he would return to excavate. And so as to not underestimate the green folk again, he would bring support.

The jungle did him no favors in his quest, offering no clean landing zone within a two-hour walk of the signal. Then as he followed his scanner north, the thicket only grew denser. So with every laboring step that pressed into the soft ground, he pressed further into his fury.

But also his curiosity.

The Advocate's memory banks contained files stemming back eighteen years, with nothing dated prior to the moment he awoke on Pert Gubora's operating table. Evidently because "the neural fusion process proved more complex than anticipated," the lizard was unable to save his memories.

The story he'd been told was that Gubora found him nearly dead, lying alone in an alley on Korrignolan, and that the power of his sheer will to survive made him a perfect candidate for "the operation." And as a result of that operation, he became the first full-mind-and-body fusion of organic and synthetic matter.

The first of his kind. The advocate of a new race.

Many assumed his name to be a title granted by Pert Gubora when he was elevated to his new role, but it had been there since day one. Given galactic restrictions, he couldn't widely publish this fact, but that didn't stop him from leaning into his identity. And so for eighteen years, he'd continued his constant quest—his insatiable thirst for betterment. With his recent creation of the Intelligence, progress to that end had grown exponentially; every day his influence expanded. This metal would take that to unimaginable levels. It would change everything.

But what about the man?

A branch cut the Advocate's face, bringing him to a halt. Distracted, he'd lost awareness of his surroundings and failed to realize the magnitude of the all-encompassing jungle about him.

"Can't see a thing," he groaned, "just like the damned rain." Constant animal noises invaded his ears; the perpetual smell of growing plants and rushing waters flooded his nostrils; he could even *taste* the air, it was so thick.

Truly, the Advocate stood in the middle of nowhere, with not a single marker or even break in the brush to suggest there was anything of significance nearby. He checked his scanner to verify he was still on the right track.

"Dammit!" he yelled, whipping the falchion from his belt and clicking the button on its hilt. A faint buzzing joined the creatures' continuous drone as a jagged, blue electrical band jumped from the blade's edges.

The Advocate slotted into a run, cutting crosswise in front of his body to clear the way, slashing out his frustration. But it was impossible to remove *everything* from his path; the branches nicked and scratched at his face, just as intrusive thoughts nicked and scratched at his mind.

Some offworlder had come to Rixxon Prime. Was *he* the source of the metal, or had he also scanned the planet? And why was he familiar? Confusion compounded with the Advocate's anger and frustration—until he burst into a small clearing and stumbled to a stop.

A thin sunbeam warmed his face as he regained his balance, shining through a hole in the canopy ceiling. With its light, a gentle calm washed away his anger, leaving him fully present—comfortable.

It was... yes, it was another familiar feeling, one whose previous origin he couldn't place. That was now two in a short while: first the man, now this.

He only ever knew of one such peculiar feeling, one that almost might connect him to his past self: overlooking Polt's astounding, crated cliffs from his open-air workshop. Gazing down through the canyons, across the strokes of rusted red and orange that painted the landscape, he found tremendous calm. He found that same calm here in this small glade, only it was accompanied by inexplicable warmth.

After basking in it for a moment, the Advocate stepped aside and allowed the light past him, where it fell on a patch of vibrant grass. Something about the patch drew him in; before he realized, he knelt and pressed an open palm into it.

Feeling a sudden urge, he closed his eyes.

An image appeared in his mind—a woman, only her back was to him. As her amber hair waved across the black frame of his consciousness, he felt something—a name perhaps—on the tip of his tongue. But he couldn't make it out for the life of him. And then she vanished, leaving nothing but the darkness of his eyelids.

His eyes fluttered open.

"What is this place?" he said, craning his neck to inspect the curious clearing, an impossible cutout in the overwhelming brush. He felt a desire to linger in the space, perhaps so he could see the woman again. There was... something about her. He knew it—even though he couldn't see her face.

As the Advocate knelt, allowing himself to experience the warmth, his eyes fell on a dirt trail surrounded by a tunneled entanglement of branches. He didn't need to check the scanner to know it was the way forward; that same warmth emanated from the path. It drew him on more than his desire to see the woman kept him.

It was a peculiar thing, this place. Just a few steps into the tunnel, it became clear the trail had been traveled before. It was well marked, almost like a sort of entrance from the impossible-to-find clearing. It felt both a part of the jungle and very much removed from it.

Curiosity quickened the Advocate's footsteps. The light about him dimmed as he worked down the constricting hill, and the tunnel's density muffled the jungle noise. Before long, his path broadened into a recessed, covered glen.

He stopped.

Gone were the sounds of the creatures and trickling creeks. Faint sunlight accompanied a quiet stillness, diffused many times over during its trip through the layers above. Root systems twisted and turned beneath his feet, snaking about each other toward the glen's opposite side. And there, embedded in the surrounding plant life, sat a small, spherical vessel.

It was open. The front portion dug into the ground, a tongue sticking from its mouth.

Inside sat a single, red seat.

So... this is where the man had stowed his ship. No doubt, this was the metal's source—at least on Rixxon Prime. But where did it *truly* come from?

Buoyed by the glen's warmth, the Advocate took a strong step forward. His boots knocked in soft cadence with his accelerating heartbeat.

Though the vessel had been picked over inside and out, he knew from his scan that there was *plenty* of special metal remaining on its frame. And this ship couldn't have been anything more than an escape pod. Perhaps he could track it back to its launch point—to *more* metal.

Grinning to himself, the Advocate placed a hand on the pod—and all calm swept from him. It left him empty, cold, like he was drifting alone in space.

He delayed but a moment.

"Let's see where you come from," he said, ducking to enter the pod—and the cold swelled to terrible fear the moment he touched the seat. Alone in this tremendous jungle, seated in this diminutive ball, the Advocate was consumed by absolute dread. His heart raced, threatening to burst from his tritonic-steel chest.

Tritonic steel... yes, that's what it was called. But why had he just remembered? Why now?

At a sudden urge, the Advocate screamed. Agony and anguish overtook his body as he yearned for the peace he'd felt just before. There was something about the vessel, something dire—something he needed to *escape.*

Summoning all his courage, he shoved his head down and flicked open the panel beneath the seat, then drew a few tools from his belt and tinkered with the wiring.

To his right, a small touchscreen hummed to life.

"Now..." he muttered, tapping away. "Where do you come from?"

A group of coordinates appeared on the screen, indicating the pod's point of origin to be an impossible distance away. This wholly unhelpful information only surged the Advocate's discomfort.

Thinking quickly, he searched the ship's memory banks for its point of launch.

There it was—not far.

Chapter 17

Pioneer exited warp, greeting the travelers with a sight far more appealing than Korrignolan.

This trip was no less unnerving than the last. Still unable to quiet his mind when the silence set in, Jag spent most of the short journey sifting through information on galactic governance. And when he finished with that, the interface helped him scour the galaxy map for species similar to him—even though it was pointless. If Elama didn't know, he wouldn't have found anything.

At least they were here now, onto the next thing.

A glowing cerulean filled Jag's eyes as they entered the stunning planet's atmosphere. "Is all of that"—he leaned forward—"water?" It was like the Rixxonian sky: blue, endless.

"Palatia is a relatively small planet," said Torin, once again projected as a Rixxonian. "Approximately eighty-five percent of the surface is covered by a vast ocean. A majority of its land masses are moderately sized islands, all interconnected by a light-rail system."

Surrounded by the blue expanse, pristine, white roadways weaved between each other, raised and supported by equally pristine columns that plunged into the sea.

"Just think of what people back home would say about all this water," Jag said.

Sixxis sat with one eye pinched. "I don't think I'm in the headspace to do much thinking."

"We will take you to the largest land mass." Torin steered *Pioneer* toward a towering, white structure in the distance. "The main island is approximately three times the size of the Rixxonian mountain settlement."

Sixxis cupped his face with both hands and bent forward, blocking the radiant sunlight shining through the window.

Jag unbuckled and walked forward. "The governance module said the Galactic Legislature is on the main island. What else is there?"

"Many things: the spaceport, markets, housing, assorted businesses."

"And the ambassadors from the most advanced and influential planets meet there quarterly to discuss issues and draw up laws?"

Torin nodded. "Although the ambassadors meet only four times a year, each planet's consular lives here and does most of the actual political work. Logically speaking, this planet provides the optimal layout for this purpose. Its organization and subsequent construction were quite ingenious, especially given how long ago the government was established."

Shade overtook the bridge as the structure's enormous, alabaster wall blocked the sun. Jag's eyes drifted up its massive frame. "Where do we find Doctor Bilanthia?"

The rear door zipped aside.

"Each consulate resides on its own island," said Elama, striding toward them and stopping behind Jag. "From the spaceport, you will travel through the market and to the railway station. There, you'll board a train to the Horranite Consulate."

"That sounds simple enough. Should we come back here when we're done?"

"No," she replied. "We would like you to meet us by Hurrash, the fourth moon of the sixth planet in the Horranite system."

"You're going to leave us here?" Sixxis mumbled, head still in his hands. "What if he doesn't want to help?"

"With almost nothing to show for it," said Torin, "Doctor Bilanthia has been fighting against the Guild for years. He will recognize the gravity of—and opportunity presented by—Remy's defection, so much so that I would calculate the odds of him denying you at one percent."

Pioneer joined a queue line. She proceeded through a square cutout on the wall, into the galactic capital's Monumental Spaceport.

Sixxis creaked an eye open—and jolted back in his seat. "Whoa!"

A dazzling array of colors flashed to and fro, flowing from the seemingly endless stream of ships flying about, striking Jag speechless. Up, down, left, right—he couldn't even find the boundaries of the structure.

The Korrignolan spaceport was incredible—this was a whole other level.

"Pretty amazing nobody crashes," said Sixxis.

"The traffic is quite well directed," Torin replied, as their queue line approached a large, floating platform.

They pulled up beside the metal terrace before long, and Elama placed a hand on Jag's shoulder. "Hop out, locate the doctor, and meet us by Hurrash."

"On it," Jag said, finally tearing himself from the view. He made for the rear door, pulling Sixxis up on his way. And as they progressed down the hall, one of the side doors whizzed upward.

Remy walked out, looking at a flat device in her hand.

"Hi, Remy," Jag said. "How's it—""Well, thank you," she replied without looking up.

"Sure you don't want to come with us?" Sixxis asked.

This time, she *did* look up. "No; I have work to do. Good luck." She dropped her head, crossed the hall, and entered the opposite room.

Sixxis shrugged. "She's something."

"For sure," Jag replied, continuing down the corridor.

She really *was* something. Remy was unlike anyone Jag had ever met. Then again, that was becoming a bit of a trend. He'd been introduced to a lot of new things lately.

Despite her cold presentation, Jag was drawn to Remy. Maybe he felt connected to her because they'd both lost family sooner than they should have, maybe he was just attracted to her. He honestly wasn't sure; Adira was about the only woman he'd ever talked to at length.

When the Rixxonians' feet hit the platform, *Pioneer* flew away, leaving them alone amidst a massive and diverse crowd of people.

"Well"—Sixxis scrunched his broad shoulders together—"this is uncomfortable."

"There doesn't seem to be any exit," Jag said, stretching up onto his toes. His head swiveled side to side as the final two ships deposited their passengers. "Maybe we—"

VRMM! The almost-full floor vibrated to life, startling Jag as it began to drift downward.

"We're moving!" he celebrated.

"And we seem to be the only ones surprised by that."

High above, far below, and all around, ships whizzed past every which way, blowing a constant wind about. But despite all the commotion, the crowd's thick murmur swallowed all sound until—*KERCHUNK*—the platform latched itself onto a larger walkway, and the people streamed out in all directions.

After waiting for things to thin out, Jag and Sixxis proceeded toward a lengthy, horizontal light in the distance. The light swelled up as they drew closer, revealing a huge opening that spanned the structure's width.

"*Skies*—sun's back." Sixxis blocked the penetrating rays with his hands—then his face lit up. He pressed the button and deployed his helmet, sighing, "Muuuch better!" as the dark visor shaded him from the sun

"Maybe next time I leave you alone," Jag said with a grin, "you'll think twice before getting drunk with a stranger."

The brothers followed the crowd out of the spaceport and into the marketplace.

"I feel like I've been here before," said Sixxis, as their feet pressed into the soft, green grass.

He was right. The place seemed familiar.

As Jag moved through the marketplace, weaving between the wooden stands and ignoring their vendors' pitches, that feeling only grew stronger—so he stopped. He craned his neck, gazing up the soaring, shining white buildings surrounding the space—and his jaw dropped.

"Six, look up," he said, tugging at his brother's arm.

Sixxis' head floated backward. "These buildings are so big." He wobbled. "They're making me dizzy—or maybe that's just the screechers."

"We *have* been here before! This is what Elama showed us back in the sanctuary. Don't you recognize it? First it looked like this, then—"

"The building fell on us!"

"Incredible..." Jag's eyes drifted to a small post a few paces away. He jogged toward the sign, then turned and pointed at a big, golden gate in the distance. "Looks like the railway station is that way."

As the brothers meandered through the marketplace, people tried to shove things into their hands. Sixxis failed to react quickly enough one of those times, and the vendor—claiming he'd purchased the item by touching it—demanded payment. Luckily, Elama had given them plenty of coins.

The stands eventually thinned out, leaving nothing but brilliant, flawless grass between them and the open-air entrance. They continued on, squishing their feet into the soft ground, then stepping onto a luminous, white roadway. And as they approached the clear space beneath the tremendous archway, a voice startled them to a stop.

"No pass detected," it said. "Where would you like to go today?"

"Umm, Horranite Consulate?" Jag said.

"Horranite Consulate," the voice repeated. "How many passengers?"

"Two."

"Thirty, please." A small, gray tube shot up from the ground.

Jag looked at Sixxis, shrugged, then dropped in a few coins.

"Thank you. Please proceed to track twelve. To reach the Horranite Consulate, transfer at the entertainment district: exit the car and proceed to track one." A glass wall—that Jag didn't notice before—zipped into the ground in front of them. "Have a brilliant day!"

"Huh," said Sixxis, walking forward to inspect the near-invisible barrier. "Would've definitely walked right into that."

Jag brushed past and crossed under the arch, stepping back into the open. The roadway stretched on and branched out into fifteen perfectly lined rows of trains.

"Brilliant is right," said Sixxis, coming to his side. "The sun here's even brighter than back home." He gripped at his head. "All this white stuff doesn't help."

"It's all so... big," Jag muttered. "Way bigger than it looked from the air."

"Shit's wild, Jag."

Jag turned and took in the great white buildings a final time, then looked forward, gazing out at the even greater ocean.

They were a long way from Rixxon Prime.

Chapter 18

"Finally." Remy reached over the holotable, grabbed the newly unlocked file folder, and pulled it close.

Upon boarding *Pioneer*, Torin escorted her to the ship's workshop—a small, simple room off the main corridor with a waist-high bench stretching round its perimeter. A handheld touchscreen and connector cable sat on the center holotable when she walked in. According to Torin, they were left for her by someone named Elama.

Plugging the device into the table, it took Remy mere hours to discover the pattern in the encrypted messages. Her success was, of course, due to her expansive knowledge of Guild procedures, tactics, and tendencies, but the speed at which she solved it was facilitated largely by the sophistication of the Arbiters' tech. Then, delving deeper into the capabilities of the handheld, she was able to calibrate, boost, and target its signal receptor with a pre-programmed decryption key—all before they made it to Palatia.

The device was *exceptional*. Its systems and simulations were simply unparalleled.

Intrigued, and seeing how well her request to remain alone and undisturbed had been honored, Remy took advantage of her time and access to the Arbiter network to do some digging. At every turn, she was met with blocks in the system. This would not have been a problem under normal circumstances—she had yet to meet a firewall she could not bypass—but this was no standard network.

It was near impenetrable. Every door in and out of the data was far more intricate than any security system she had previously contended with.

Despite hours of effort, this was the first repository she had succeeded in unlocking. "Let us see your contents," she said, exploding her hands outward to open the folder.

PERSONNEL FILES

Remy leaned forward and pressed her hands into the table. All that time, and she had managed to find nothing more than dossiers on herself and her new "companions."

With a sigh, she opened her own file and scanned it. Once satisfied with its accuracy and completeness, she tossed it aside. Having gleaned all she needed to know about Sixxis upon their first meeting—regardless of his capabilities, he would have clearly never survived without his brother's watchful eye, a relationship dynamic Remy knew all too well—she turned her attention to another file.

JAG

Nineteen years old—just like Remy. And from Rixxon Prime?

It was staggering, the juxtaposition. Remy had been recruited by someone from a Class V planet—still in its second echelon of technological discovery—and brought onboard *Pioneer*, a ship whose capabilities surpassed those originating from advanced civilizations such as Laktilia, Horran, or even old Quadmalia.

Jag's file was extensive, housing information that stemmed back to when he was six months old. But for all the content, the absurdly detailed information on every facet of his life, the most basic entry read:

PLANET OF ORIGIN: UNKNOWN

"I trust the space and equipment are meeting your needs?" hummed a voice into the workshop—presumably Elama's.

Remy's focus shot to the door. "Affirmative."

Meeting her needs—a vast understatement. Nothing Remy had ever encountered operated at such capacity, even after ten years in the Guild. It simply did not add up. Who were these Arbiters, and how did their tech far exceed anything that—to Remy's profound knowledge—existed anywhere in the galaxy?

"Good," said Elama. "I must apologize that we have yet to speak. I've had a few things to take care of."

"It is all right," Remy replied, eyes still fixed on the door.

"Would now be a good time? I'm sure you have many questions."

Many questions indeed.

"Yes; you may come in." Remy swiped the projection from the table, then tapped at the handheld to remove all evidence of her investigation. If these Arbiters truly were this advanced, they were inherently dangerous. Best to keep her exploration under the radar.

The entrance flew upward. In stepped a Lomorrian woman.

"Oh dear," she said. "There's nowhere to sit."

"I work more efficiently on my feet," Remy replied, placing the handheld on the center table. "Elama, I presume?"

The woman nodded. "Torin informed me of your discomfort with the Phyatoraen projection. Given your time in the Guild, I thought this would perhaps be more familiar for you."

"Your... projection. How exactly does it work?"

Elama beamed. "I was hoping you might ask! Explaining it to the others was, well, a bit lackluster." She held up her left arm and gestured to the metal bracelet hooking round it. "It is a device of my own design, able to detect and rewrite those pieces of an individual's genetic code pertaining to physical characteristics."

Remy opened her mouth to speak, then closed it again. She motioned for Elama's wrist. "May I?"

"Why, of course!" said Elama, presenting the device.

Remy turned the yellow-scaled, Lommorian arm over in her hand, inspecting the bracelet. "So simple in both design and concept, yet I imagine exceedingly complex in execution."

"You certainly have *that* right,“ Elama said. "As I'm sure is the case for you, trial and error are close friends of mine. This is design Mark IV." She laughed. "You would not believe the outcomes of its first iterations!"

It was... disarming, the way Elama spoke to Remy. Despite her suspicions, she could not help but be drawn to her. That said, Remy was a careful, logical person. She had learned long ago that appearances and airs were simply masks people put on themselves—literally, in Elama's case.

"To most, this technology is unfathomable. How did you go about creating it?"

Elama chuckled. "Let's just say I've been studying genetics for a very long time."

A perfectly crafted nonanswer.

"Where is it you come from?"

"Far beyond the confines of this galaxy, I'm afraid."

Another nonanswer.

Remy squinted, eyeing the woman projected as a Lommorian. "May I see your natural form?"

"Another time, perhaps," Elama said with a smile. "For now, I would love to answer any questions you might have about the mission."

Remy had no questions about the mission. Their goals were clear: Destroy the Advocate and Pert Gubora. Disband the Guild. Wipe every trace from existence.

No, her curiosity was of another nature, one she was sure Elama would continue to evade. But that did not stop her.

"I know the job to be done," she said. "My questions pertain to your level of technological advancement."

Elama rubbed her hands together. "What is it you'd like to know?"

"I simply wish to know *how*—how is it that you have accomplished so much on this relatively small ship? To my knowledge, no mainframe on a vessel this size can sustain such efficiencies within its systems, especially while at warp."

Elama's smile stretched wide across her face. "I presume you have decrypted the transmissions?"

Remy nodded. "Quite quickly. And I have this"—she swept to the handheld—"set to detect, intercept, and decrypt any future messages."

"Ah, I'm glad you like that!" Elama said, smile stretching even wider. "You may keep it."

Remy opened her mouth to speak, then closed it again. She would certainly make great use of such a powerful device.

"I designed it *for* you. It's why the interface is similar to what you are accustomed to."

Remy looked down at the device resting on the table, as with it, the encounter grew even stranger. But even this kind, confusing gesture did not mitigate her suspicions—because it did not betray the potential danger these Arbiters posed.

Whatever was happening, it was far more complicated than she could have predicted whilst leading Jag away from her apartment.

"Elama," she said, matching the mysterious woman's gaze, "my question."

"Ah, yes!" Her ridged browline lifted into a kind expression. "You asked how it is we are so advanced, technologically speaking?"

Remy nodded.

"Time is a powerful construct," Elama said, turning and pressing her palm into the wall. "With enough of it, we can accomplish virtually anything. But with too much"—her head drooped, lowering her eyes to the floor—"or a lack of control over what time we *do* have, we can lose ourselves."

A moment passed, as Remy had no idea how to respond. Then, "How old *are*—"

"Commander," hummed Torin's voice, "we will arrive at base in three minutes."

Elama's gaze snapped back to Remy. "This has been quite enjoyable! I would very much like to continue our discussion another time."

"...very well," said Remy, narrowing her eyes.

"I'll meet you on the bridge." With a bow, Elama exited the room.

Another nonanswer—more detailed yet less informative than the last—then a complete bailout by her second-in-command.

Clearly, Elama was hiding something.

Chapter 19

"Horranite Consulate," dinged a voice into the train, as the double doors on either side split open. "This is the end of the line. All passengers not wishing to return to the entertainment district must exit."

Jag grabbed one of the many vertical bars in the empty car and pulled to his feet. It'd been quite the ride, simultaneously zipping across the water at blistering speeds and not moving at all. It somehow felt different from traveling at warp, maybe because landmarks were visible through the windows.

Sixxis hopped up from his seat. "I can't *believe* how quiet and relaxing that was—I feel better already!" He bounded for the open door with another hop.

Less quickly—but just as eager—Jag followed him out.

"This place is wild," Sixxis said, walking with his hands behind his head.

Jag stood and watched as the train zoomed off. Land masses peppered the horizon, the only things signaling the break between water and sky. It was a nice shift from Korrignolan; even with all his hesitations, Jag had been excited to see new worlds and people, but their first stop left something to be desired. Palatia, though—absolutely beautiful!

Much smaller than the previous two, this station featured just one track shooting out over the ocean from a lone, white platform. The island itself was similarly small; contrasting with where they'd started the day, it couldn't have been any bigger than the Forbidden Village square. A short path led across to a rectangular building embedded in a large rock face. And like everything else they'd encountered so far, it glimmered a bright white in the sunlight.

"How do they keep everything so shiny?" Sixxis asked as they came to a large set of double doors.

"Beats me." Jag pressed them open and stepped into the consulate. Aside from a small, crescent-shaped counter opposite them, its vaulted foyer was empty.

"Nobody's home?" said Sixxis.

With a shrug, Jag started across the space, his boots tapping the tiled floor as he made his way to the counter. There sat a raised, square surface with an adjacent sign:

PRESS BUTTON FOR SERVICE.

He gave the button a push.

"Greetings." A purple, holographic bust materialized over top of the square. She had enormous, darkened eyes, and dull, hooked horns reaching down over her chin from her cheeks. "I am the Automated Entrance Liaison—AMEL. How may I assist you today?"

Jag tilted his head and inspected the hologram. Sixxis poked at it, scattering its pixels.

"Please refrain from disrupting my display," requested the projection as it reformed into a solid image. "And I invite you to adhere to consulate regulations by removing your facial covering unless correlated to a health restriction or religious practice."

Sixxis' head jerked backward. He stowed his helmet.

"We're hoping to see Doctor Ferris Bilanthia," Jag said.

"Consular Bilanthia's office is located on the second floor in room 220. Do you require any other assistance?"

Jag tossed his head side to side; there wasn't an obvious way up. "How do we get to the second floor?"

"There is an elevator in the wall to my right."

Jag nodded. "Thank you."

"I am glad to have been of service," said AMEL, bowing her head. "Have a brilliant day!" Her light zipped inward and disappeared.

Sixxis bent over and squinted at the empty space left by the projection. "That was weird."

Mouth wrinkled, Jag led them to the far wall. Finding a button where AMEL said the elevator would be, he pressed it—and *DING!* A door opened to reveal a small room.

"Guess this is it," he said, walking in and pressing the button marked "2" on the wall panel. The door closed in front of them.

"Floor two," sounded AMEL's voice as the room lurched to life.

Jag held his face up to the button panel. "How long do you—"

DING! The doors opened again.

"I guess that long," Sixxis said with a shrug.

Together, the brothers started down a tall, slender hallway. Vibrant wood paneling covered every surface, save the padded, narrow rug running beneath their feet. In almost no time at all, they found a plaque beside a gap in the left wall.

"220," Jag read. "This must be it."

They turned to find another crescent counter. Beyond the empty desk, two doors reached for the ceiling, one open.

"Hello?" Jag said, creeping toward the open door. "Doctor Bilanthia?"

"Yes?" replied a light, silvery voice from inside. "Come in."

Jag beamed at Sixxis and stepped into the office, shielding his eyes as intense sunlight blazed through the wall-sized window opposite them. Bookcases spanned floor to ceiling on both sides of the glass. And in the middle of it all, Doctor Ferris Bilanthia stood with his back to them, gazing out at the sea, his beige body covered in a loose, white frock.

He started to turn. "Hello, how may I—"

His glistening, black eyes reflected Sixxis' emerald-green frame.

"My my—what are *you*?"

"I'm sorry?" Sixxis glanced at Jag.

"My apologies," offered Bilanthia, rubbing his enormous hands together. "I may be a doctor and a politician, but in my heart, I am fascinated by people. And I have *never* seen anyone quite like *you* before!" With quick steps, he shuffled around the desk separating them. "Where are you from?"

Jag turned and shut the door, then nodded to his brother.

"Rixxon Prime," Sixxis answered.

Bilanthia's big eyes grew even bigger. "Rixxon Prime, you say? How is that possible? To my knowledge, Rixxon Prime is a Class V planet millennia away from space travel."

"You know of Rixxon Prime?" Jag said.

"I do!" Bilanthia leaned back and half-sat on his desk. "It is a rather fascinating celestial phenomenon. I don't know of any other inhabitable planets with no sense of planetary revolution. I presume you live in the jungle?"

"Yup!" Sixxis tossed his orange hair to the side. "I'm Therulin through and through."

"Ah, that must be one of the tribes—splendid!" He looked to Jag. "Where do you call home?"

"I grew up on Rixxon Prime, but I'm from elsewhere."

"You *don't* say." Bilanthia looked down and drew a hand across his ridged browline. "So not only do I have *two* Rixxonians in my office, one is from offworld—and *both* speak the common tongue. Fascinating!"

Jag's eyes shifted to Sixxis.

"Oh dear me—I am so sorry! Where are my manners?" He scrambled to his feet and shepherded his visitors to a pair of maroon armchairs. "My name is Doctor Ferris Bilanthia, Representative of the Planetary Parliament of Horran, Consular of the Peoples of Merutan." With a bow, he rounded his desk and took a seat. "It is an honor to receive such distinguished guests." A smile pressed onto his cracked lips as he gazed up at the ceiling. "I'm probably the first person in this quadrant to host a Rixxonian!"

The warm reception struck Jag. In all his years on Rixxon Prime, no one had ever treated him with such respect or fascination—other than his parents, of course.

"My name's Jag," he said. "This is my brother, Sixxis."

"Brothers?" Bilanthia leaned forward. "This continues to intrigue me."

"We're here to ask for your help."

Tilting his head, one arm folded, Bilanthia ran a thumb down his right cheek horn and a long, spindled finger down the other. "You have traveled far, so I can only assume this is important. Please, go on."

"We've recently come across information that suggests the Guild is meddling in planetary affairs, causing disturbances and all but forcing governments to sign contracts."

Bilanthia's smile sank. "This is not surprising. I myself have noticed a correlation, but nothing more than that." He sighed. "I fear I have no proof."

Encouraged, Jag continued. "They released a monster on our people. Thankfully, we were able to trap it in our mines before it took too many lives." He glanced at Sixxis. "We left shortly after that."

"I'm truly sorry to hear that." Bilanthia sank back and swiveled in his chair. "The Guild's presence on your planet was unequivocally illegal, but unfortunately, your word will not be enough."

"We have more," said Sixxis. "Or we will soon."

"What do you mean?"

"The Guild's been sending encrypted transmissions through a dark relay," Jag said, "and we think they're related to the disturbances."

Bilanthia froze, hand still on his face. "Go on."

"We're assembling a team to stop whatever the Guild is planning."

"Your intentions are honorable—but why are you telling *me* this?"

"We believe you can help."

"Oh, my friend," he said with a chuckle, dropping his hand to his frock. "I'm sorry, but it is difficult for a man of my status to drop everything and help strangers on a hunch."

But Jag wasn't about to give in. "We've recruited a Guild engineer. She's currently investigating the transmissions to find their source."

"Guildsmen are not easily persuaded to betray the organization. Once they do, they are instantly marked for death. Who is this person?"

"Remy Troyer," Jag replied.

"Remy Troyer..." Bilanthia leaned back and stroked his horns. "Where do I know that—aha!" He jolted upright and tapped at the desk, whisking his fingers about the lights on its surface.

Jag wrinkled his mouth at Sixxis. "Sir?"

"As I thought!" Bilanthia slammed his hands down and rocketed to his feet. "Remy Troyer is one of the best the Guild has! How did you convince her to help you?"

Jag grinned. "Does that matter?"

"I suppose not," he replied, plopping back into his chair. "So... a Rixxonian, a Rixxonian offworlder, and a Phyatoraen Guildsman want to stop the Guild." He brushed at his horns again. "But why would they ask *me* for help?"

Jag shot a puzzled look at his brother. "Your connections and medical skills?"

"I left medicine years ago to put political holds on the Guild's dark dealings, but I have long feared I am limited here." Bilanthia rotated his chair and gazed out the window. "Too many of my colleagues have other motives."

"Then come with us!" Jag said, scooting forward in his seat. "We just want to do the right thing."

"The right thing... You do know how to get to my heart, my boy." Bilanthia's head lifted. "Perhaps this is my chance to change things once and for all." With a nod, he spun and offered a wide smile. "Very well—I will help you!"

Jag all but leapt from his seat. "Excellent!"

"We need a ship, too," Sixxis added.

"Ah," Bilanthia exhaled. "I'm afraid that might be a bit complicated. My medical liner was recently destroyed, and all I have left is my personal vessel. It's a zippy little thing, but merely a puddle jumper. It can fit three with little room for much else." He sighed. "Battling the Guild certainly has its consequences."

Jag and Sixxis shared an awkward glance—then Sixxis' eyebrows jumped.

"That's all right," he said, "we have a backup plan. Can you give us a second?" Hopping to his feet, he wrestled Jag from his chair and rushed to the room's back corner.

"What do you mean 'backup plan?'" Jag whispered, glancing over his shoulder.

Bilanthia stretched out his long neck, a curious look on his face.

"What about Bo?" Sixxis grinned. "He's got a ship, and he seemed excited to help out!"

"That guy from Jarnuk's? I don't know; I'm nervous to include anyone Elama didn't recommend. We're supposed to keep this a secret, remember?"

"Yeah... about that."

Jag's brow furrowed. "What'd you tell him?"

"Nothing specific! Just our names, some things about Adira..." Sixxis paused, shifted his feet. "...aaand I might have said I'm from Rixxon Prime."

"Six!"

Guess Jag was right—he shouldn't have left him alone.

Peeking over his shoulder, he returned his voice to a whisper. "If something goes wrong, and the Guild finds him, they might—"

"I know, I know," said Sixxis, waving his hands in front of his body. "I messed up. But I think we can fix it! If he's with us, then there's no harm done!"

Jag's expression didn't change.

"It's not just damage control!" Sixxis continued, faster. "He's got ship, he says he's an ace pilot, and if you didn't notice, he's huge! I bet he'd be a big help!"

Jag sighed. All things considered, it really was the best course of action. "Okay. We go back to Korrignolan—but you've got to be more careful!"

Sixxis' eyes fell to the ground. "I know." He brought them level with Jag's. "But you know, brother, sometimes you're *too* careful. I think we'll need to take some risks out here."

He was probably right. They were *already* in over their heads.

With a nod, Jag returned to the doctor's desk. "Sorry about that. We *do* have a backup plan; we were just discussing it."

"Rather heatedly, it seems," Bilanthia said with a chuckle.

"We need to get to Korrignolan. Can we take your—what did you call it?" Sixxis' face scrunched. "'Puddle jumper?'"

"Korrignolan? Why ever would you want to go there?"

"Our backup plan."

Squinting his huge eyes, the doctor inspected the Rixxonian. "Yes, I can get us there."

"Let's get going, then," Jag said. "We've no time to waste."

Bilanthia nodded. "Wait here." He scurried to his office door and opened it.

In stumbled another Horranite man.

"Burl?" said Bilanthia, cocking his head back. "What are you doing?"

"Ah, um—sorry, consular." Burl held up a rag. "I was polishing the door handle."

"Thank you for that, actually. Things have been feeling a bit dusty lately." He smiled. "I'm taking a leave of absence. Please redirect my calls to Consular Skiff."

Burl snapped upright. "Yes, sir!"

"You know what?" added the doctor. "Why don't you take a vacation? Some time away would do you good." He ushered Burl out and shut the door, then pressed a button on a wall console beside it—and one of the side bookcases lowered into the floor.

Sixxis jumped in place. "Whoa!"

"Being a politician certainly has its perks," said Bilanthia, as the now-bare wall split open. "Down this elevator, we'll find a private hangar with my sporty little thing, *Unity*." He stepped inside. "Shall we?"

Without a word, the brothers hustled to join him on the elevator. The lift shot downward when Bilanthia entered his code. And moments later, the doors opened to reveal a low-ceiling hangar, with a small, diamond-shaped spacecraft.

"It's beautiful," Sixxis admired, running his hand along the ship's purple and white body.

"*She* is beautiful," corrected Bilanthia, curling a hand and hand-like foot around the ladder rungs that ascended toward the raised glass cover. "Hop in boys—we're Korrignolan bound!"

Chapter 20

The Advocate pulled back the lever to dial down *Superior's* warp drive. The pod's launch point wasn't far from Rixxon Prime, so it hadn't been a long trip. And now, he was here.

...not much else was.

Peering through the front glass, the Advocate was greeted by nothing more than floating debris. If this was where the pod came from, it really *was* an escape pod. And from the looks of things, it *barely* escaped.

The hours since the downed pod had been perhaps the longest of the Advocate's life. His project all set, ready to receive her new materials, he had nothing to keep his mind at bay. And so he sat, lost in thought, unmoving in the cockpit. He'd shaken the fear by now—but not the thought of it. That overpowering, incomprehensible fear was both completely foreign and oddly familiar to him, like the warmth in the glen and the man's face.

With every step further on this odd sort of quest, he felt himself drawing closer to something—something important. A deep determination to get to the bottom of it drew him on, ejecting all other matters from his mind.

A collection of larger pieces signaled a clear center to the wreckage. Around them, the deserted debris expanded outward.

His ship would only get him so far; he'd have to go out himself.

Steering carefully, the Advocate brought *Superior* as far as she could fit, then turned and descended the ladder to his workspace. There, he donned a propulsion oversuit, stepped into the airlock, and initiated the sequence.

Air hissed about him, washing away the ship's gentle whir. He remained still for a moment, taking in the silent scene.

Abandoned wreckage had always made him feel off, like he could *feel* the space between life and death it left behind. Here, that barrier seemed even thinner, as whoever wanted this ship destroyed *really* wanted it so; it had been torn to shreds, metallic slivers drifting in this lonely region of space.

But the Advocate had come too far to stop now.

Rejecting his hesitations, he hopped into the void, toward the largest mass of abandoned metal. Unmistakable hunks of tritonic steel shimmered in the black as he drifted, their lustrous coating illuminated by the far-off stars.

The wreckage was *brimming* with the stuff!

His curiosity regarding the truth behind these emotions—and perhaps his identity—had taken the metal from his mind. Now he'd come away with both answers *and* healthy amounts of it!

The Advocate grinned to himself. And after a few soundless moments and soft redirects with his thrusters, he came to an exposed platform. Pulling himself close to its charred edges, he found marks—left irrefutably by a Guild mining laser.

So... not only was he somehow connected to this ship, but so was the Guild. The further he progressed on this discovery mission, the more it seemed Gubora had been lying to him all these years.

More than before, he hungered for the truth.

Making his way up the long platform, he located a terminal. It was obviously dead—but to the Advocate, no machine was truly dead. He would soon have whatever secrets it held.

"Let's see what ails you." He drew his sword and engaged its electrical band. After cutting the terminal free, he positioned himself behind it and pushed back toward *Superior.*

HISS! Air rushed through the interior door's edges as the ship's gravity regulated. Drifting to the ground, eyes locked on the blank screen, the Advocate removed his helmet, popped open the lower panel, and got right to work.

The circuitry was quite simple. After mixing and matching the frayed, disarrayed wiring, he grabbed a battery pack and attached it in several places. The screen faded to life.

"Ah—now that wasn't so hard." He closed the panel and stood facing the screen.

SHURIKEN

CREW LOGIN

Without even a single thought, the Advocate put his fingers on the keyboard and entered information into the username and password fields.

Verifying...

Confirmed.

Activating visual scan.

A visual scan? That might—

Confirmed.

Welcome back, Garrison.

...Garrison?

A series of dates filled the screen.

How had he logged in so easily? Was it... muscle memory, long forgotten by his waking mind?

The Advocate selected a date, and his face—his *own face*—appeared. He was talking, but there was no sound.

"Dammit!" He pounded the terminal with both fists, then closed the silent video and clicked another date. His face appeared again.

"Impossible." He tried a third. And this time he wasn't alone in the video that came on screen: With him was an amber-haired woman. The two of them laughed together.

Ever so gently, he pressed a hand into the screen. "Ash—"

His body convulsed, as uncontrollable guilt invaded his neural network.

Was this... *his* ship?

The Advocate dropped to a knee and stuck his head beneath the terminal. Locating the physical databanks, he drew a connector from his belt and plugged in one end. And when he ripped back to his feet with the other in hand, he paused, questioning his impending decision. Because whatever he was to learn from this terminal, it would change the fabric of his life and alter the course of his destiny.

Destiny... He often dreamt of such a word. He knew himself to be one of great destiny—always had—and it was this knowledge that completed his resolve.

Drawing a deep breath, the Advocate inserted the connector into a port behind his left ear—and instantly lurched to the ground, pounding his knee and fist into the airlock as the terminal's contents flooded his storage system.

This *was* his ship. This was his *life*. And someone in the Guild was responsible for destroying it.

He scanned his newly acquired files to locate the latest entry. First, he would eject the terminal back into the wreckage and scavenge for enough tritonic steel to complete his latest appendage. Then, he would search Guild records for all information regarding that date and speak with those responsible.

Because this last surviving terminal was merely a video-diary station. For all his newfound knowledge, he still had no idea what happened.

Chapter 21

Jag swept ahead, leading his companions through the deserted streets. "Jarnuk's should be right up here."

The trip to Korrignolan proved to be his best travel experience so far. Crammed into *Unity,* the three of them had no choice but to talk. And Bilanthia proved to be excellent for conversation! The kind, inquisitive man was *very* interested in life back on Rixxon Prime.

"This place gives me the creeps at night," said Sixxis. He'd finally recovered from his screechers after another inflight nap.

"We'd best move quickly," Bilanthia advised. "These roads are not safe after dark."

Sixxis bent forward and let out a loud cough. "And I thought the air was gross before."

"Ferris," Jag said, "do you—"

"Please." Bilanthia shuddered. "My father gave me that name, and I shy away from it when possible."

"Bilanthia then. Do you know why the sky is red?"

"Years of pollution," he replied. "The last of the natural plant life died years ago, stripping the ozone of fresh air."

"You gotta admit, Jag," said Sixxis, "really makes you miss home."

"I imagine the air on Rixxon Prime is quite immaculate!" said Bilanthia.

Sixxis smiled. "Crisp is what I like to call it—really cleans you out."

"There it is," said Jag, pointing at Jarnuk's. "I'll be right back." He hustled across the street and swung open the door. Calm, soft music crawled out.

"'Ey there!" sand Jarnuk's voice across the empty pub. "Did ya find Remy?"

"I did!" The door closed behind Jag as he stepped inside. "Thank you."

"Glad ta hear it," said Jarnuk, wiping a rag down his horn. "That gal don't deserve many'a the things that've happened t'her." He blew his nose.

"Have you seen the big man, Bo?"

"Aye—left with some Lommorian gal a while back. I'm closin' up now."

"Okay." Jag reached back for the handle. "Thanks for the information. You've been a great help."

"I like you. You'll always be welcome at mah 'istablishment." Jarnuk smiled as much as his horned face would allow. "You take care now, y'hear?"

"I will," Jag said, returning the smile. "You do the same." He exited the bar and rejoined his companions.

"Well?" said Sixxis, leaning against some scaffolding, arms folded.

"He apparently left with a Lommorian woman a while back."

"Ah, Lommoria," Bilanthia sighed. "The Guild's been poaching its people for decades."

"Lommorian..." Sixxis' head tilted. "Those are the yellow, scaly folks, right? Beak mouths?"

Bilanthia chuckled. "Indeed, my verdant friend. Lommoria doesn't have much for valuable resources or opportunities, so many citizens join the Guild's ranks at a young age." He shook his head. "It's about the only thing that will get them off the streets."

"I bet they don't know what's coming for them when they join," Jag said. He glanced at his brother. "You talked to Bo most. Any idea where he'd go?"

Sixxis shrugged. "His ship?"

"200 block," Jag recalled with a nod. He started back for the spaceport with a hop in his step.

"It's a bit more complicated than that," continued Bilanthia, jogging to catch up. "As horrible as Guildsmen's actions can be, a majority are just following orders. Lower-level prospectors often have no knowledge of what goes on above them."

As Jag swept into the towering hall, a stale draft twinkled the rusted fixtures overhead. "Not telling people what they're really doing; seems like a crime in itself."

"Ah, but this is where the complexity lies. You see, many of the workers *choose* ignorance. They want the comfort of knowing they're doing honest work—which on the surface, of course, they are—because to them, their positions with the Guild are alternatives to having nothing."

Jag's heart hammered his chest, bringing him to a sudden stop as the others treaded past. "So if we stop the Guild, we'll be taking lives away from good people?"

Bilanthia turned, his mouth crooked beneath his hooked horns. "I'm afraid so. But I've had a plan in the back of my mind for some time now. My—"

"Fellas," Sixxis interrupted, "maybe we shouldn't get ahead of ourselves."

That was unexpected. Sixxis suggesting they slow down?

"You're right," Jag said, drawing two deep breaths. "We don't even have a plan yet."

Bilanthia tilted his brow. "...you don't have a plan?"

Damn right they didn't have a plan. What was Jag even thinking? This was *way* more complicated than a giant monster killing everybody. There were normal people—*good* people that were going to get hurt if they succeeded. How could he make the right plan?

Was there a right plan?

Too much had happened in such a short time. In a way, it was good; it kept him moving. But now that it was all coming back, Jag was in over his head. What was he—

"Don't worry!" said Sixxis, flashing his signature grin. "Figuring it out as we go is one of our—err—*Jag's* specialties." He clapped his brother on the back. "One step at a time, right?"

"Through the winds of change..." Jag muttered to himself, taking in two more breaths to refocus. He nodded. "One step at a time."

Bilanthia pressed a hand into his chest. "Please do not misunderstand! I am here and ready to do my part. You Rixxonians intrigue me, and I cannot help but trust you already." He let out another chuckle. "Perhaps we were fated to meet."

Fate... there was that word again.

Elama had already advised Jag not to write off the idea, and now Bilanthia was talking about it. Was there such a thing? Was all of this destined to happen? How could he fulfill his *grand purpose* if he didn't even know who he was?

Sixxis stretched his arms up and brought them to rest behind his head. "I don't know about the whole fate thing. Even if it's real, it's not like we can control it, ya know?" He tossed his hips at Jag. "We just do what we can."

Easy for Sixxis to say. He didn't have several people suddenly watching him—counting on him.

Jag shook his head out, then lifted it toward the numbering on the wall. "200 block," he said, charging forward and leaving his thoughts behind.

Identical to their previous dock, the 200 block was just as still as the deserted nighttime streets. A constant mechanical thrumming blanketed their steps as they rushed down the stone walkway, searching for any signs of the enormous man.

"Did he say anything about what his ship looked like?" Jag asked.

"Nah," Sixxis replied. "He just—"

Their heads jerked toward the platform on their right, where a series of loud bangs and clangs resonated from inside a navy-blue ship.

"Gunfire!" Bilanthia whispered, his wide eyes growing wider.

Jag ducked behind a stack of crates on the platform. "Over here!"

Just what they needed—to get in the middle of some thug fight. This was supposed to be a quick in-and-out.

Heart pounding yet again, Jag peeked around the rightmost box as the ship's back end jolted to life. A yellow body shot out from the opening and crashed onto the dock before the ramp made it to the ground.

"You got about five seconds"—a shirtless Bo stormed out, throwing a mess of clothes at the ground—"to get the *HELL* outta here!"

After a few seconds, as the woman scrambled to her feet and scurried away, Sixxis skipped into the open, arms outstretched. "Bo!"

Bo—who'd just turned his back and started up the ramp—whipped around and pointed two pistols at him.

"Whoa whoa whoa!" Sixxis threw his hands up. "It's me!"

Bo lowered his weapons. "Sixxis!"

"Jag's here, too!"

"It's good to see you beautiful men!" Bo exclaimed, twirling and holstered his weapons. "Boy did things take a turn when you left. I headed back to Jarnuk's for more drinks and got talking to *that* scum. Pittin' harpy tried to rob me when we got back to my ship." He pointed to his eye with a wild grin. "I gave her a mark to remember me by, though."

Bilanthia inched his head above the crate stack. "Are you—"

Bo spun, drew a sidearm, and aimed its barrel at him.

"Wait!" Jag said, racing over to try and force Bo's arm down. "He's with us!"

Bo lifted a single, silvery eyebrow. "Y'might think twice before startling a guy, sir." He stowed his weapon.

"Sir?" Sixxis exploded, doubling over in laughter. "Since when were *you* the polite type?"

Bo placed his lower arms on his hips and shrugged with his upper. "What? He looks important—definitely not a regular here on Korrignolan."

"I'm sorry to surprise you," Bilanthia said as he crept from behind his cover, "but I am simply *astounded*." His steps quickened as he approached. "Are you a *real* Quadmalian?"

"As real as yer britches!" Bo's expression flattened. "Er, y'know what I mean. I see you're not wearing pants."

"It is an honor to meet you!" Bilanthia rushed the colossal man and crossed his arms.

Bo responded by forming an X with his lower arms. Still crossed, the two men shook hands and bowed to each other.

"A true gentleman!" Bo exclaimed as he lifted his head. "I haven't done the traditional greeting in ages. Not many recognize our customs—hell, not many *know* our customs!"

"This is Doctor Bilanthia," Jag said.

"Pleased to meet ya, Doc. Name's Bo-Ram Chinosin, ace pilot—you can call me Bo."

"A likewise pleasure, Bo." Bilanthia beamed at Jag. "A Rixxonian, a Rixxonian off-worlder, a Phyatoraen, a Horranite—and now, a *Quadmalian*." He clapped his hands together. "This is more of a diplomatic endeavor than virtually *any* of my efforts on Palatia!"

"Palatia, huh? So you're a politician?" Bo winked at Sixxis. "Better watch myself."

"Oh no no no my marvelous friend—you have nothing to fear from me! I am a doctor and a diplomat by profession, but galactic ethnography is my *true* passion."

Sixxis leaned to the side and scrunched his face. "What's that?"

"I am *fascinated* by the breadth of existence—half the reason I came with you in the first place. It's not every day you're visited by beings from a Class V planet who seem to know their way around technology and civilization!"

"Eh, Jag gets that stuff. I just go with the flow."

Bo's deep, belly laughter echoed down the block. "And that's why I like you, Sixxis—you're as real as they come!" He wiped a tear from his eye. "So what brings y'all back?"

"We decided to take you up on your offer," Jag said, "if it still stands."

"So..." Bo pumped his brows. "You *do* find yourself in need of an ace pilot." He let out an exaggerated sigh. "You know, I felt rather spurned when you left with that *alluring* blue woman. Thought I might never see you again."

"Hah!" Sixxis slapped his leg. "You only have one setting, don't you?"

"What can I say?" Bo replied with a shrug. "I told you: I'm a lover, not a fighter. Man, woman, Rixxonian, Phyatoraen, Horranite—they're all just labels. I see artistry and beauty in all creatures, and I can't help but act on it." His lips formed a wry smile as he tilted his head and winked. "And I assure you, my 'acting' skills are *exceptional.*"

"So will you join us?" Jag asked. "We're taking on the Prospectors' Guild."

"It's about time someone did something about those villains. I won't lie—it's nice to think of a galaxy without them." Bo grinned. "If you beautiful beings and that little blue lady will be along for the ride, count me in!"

"Great!" Jag couldn't help but bounce a bit. "That's the whole team!"

"All aboard!" Bo shouted.

"I'll hop in *Unity* and meet you all in orbit," said Bilanthia, scuttling off.

Jag fell in line as Bo led him and Sixxis up the entrance. Their feet clanked as they stepped up the ramp, across a small hangar, and into an elevator flanked by two open doorways.

"This is *Zara,*" said Bo, tapping the wall console. "She's my special gal."

The elevator brought them up a level, where they exited and proceeded down a long, narrow hallway, not unlike the one on *Pioneer.* This one, however, was stained dark blue, and it didn't lead to a single door. At its other end, the cabin expanded into a big, open space. Opposite them sat an exposed lift platform, again flanked by two open doorways.

"The bridge is up here," said Bo, leading them onto the lift. It brought them to the raised bridge deck, where six big chairs faced forward, and an even bigger chair faced back.

Jag walked toward the larger, raised seat—probably belonging to the ship's enormous pilot. The deck stopped at its base; another seat rested in the open space below.

Three planets, three spaceships, three new companions—each unique and different from the last. He'd broadened his horizons *far* beyond Rixxon Prime, and that didn't even account for everything he'd learned from the interface on *Pioneer.* It'd been thrilling to see it all, to take in the contrast of these worlds—especially after being the single point of contrast in the entire jungle—but it sure seemed like the fun was about to end. Soon, all eyes would be on Jag.

And with everything Bilanthia had said, it was all a lot more complicated than he could've ever predicted.

"Where we headed?" Bo asked, smacking his gigantic hand on Jag's shoulder.

"Hurrash—that's the fourth moon of the sixth planet in the Horranite system."

"Solid memory," said Sixxis, hopping into a chair.

Bo dropped into his seat and punched some buttons on the right-side panel. "All keyed in! Take a seat 'n get comfortable." He folded his lower arms as the chair rotated, elevating itself in the spacious bridge area.

Jag chose the chair beside Sixxis and buckled in—and he was suddenly back on Rixxon Prime, staring down the gorge, about to enter this unknown path riddled with guaranteed but unseeable danger. And just like then, there was no sense going back.

"We stand tall as trees..."

"What's that?" Bo called over his shoulder.

Jag shook his head out. "Nothing." He glanced at Sixxis, who offered a supportive smile.

"I'm by your side, brother," he said.

Jag returned the smile, then returned his attention forward. And before he knew it, they were out of the spaceport and rising into the atmosphere—onto his grand purpose.

Chapter 22

The Advocate placed his tools on a gurney and stepped toward the edge of his exposed, cliffside workshop. After the long, somewhat confusing flight from the launch point, with so much new information flooding his neural network, his emotional circuitry was running haywire. And so he stood, staring down at Polt's auburn expanse, searching for answers.

It was odd—uncomfortable even. It was clearly the Advocate in the diary footage, and the files even dated back nineteen years, beyond his working memory banks. But something still held him back from full understanding, some... disconnect between himself and the recorded memories.

Perhaps because they were not his own; they were files from a computer.

This was all he knew, this half-man, half-machine existence. He took supreme ownership of his role in the galaxy all those years ago when he was born in Pert Gubora's laboratory: the first successful fusion of organic and synthetic matter, the only of his kind, the advocate of a new race.

But did he have a life before this?

He'd sifted through all incident reports on and around the pod's launch date. There was nothing—absolutely nothing that indicated something had happened there that day—which was impossible. The Guild required that all violent incidents be reported.

He drew a deep breath, hoping the space would soothe him as it normally did.

For some unbeknownst reason, Polt's landscape filled him with a deep sense of comfort. It was the first of his inexplicable feelings, of which he'd now experienced three more. Here, standing at the extended edge, overlooking the vast valley that glowed burgundy in the setting sun, he'd come up with his greatest schemes.

It was here he experienced the mental breakthrough that led to his most treasured invention—one he had yet to share with Pert Gubora. Something held him back, something he couldn't place until recently. But these discoveries had confirmed his decision: despite their history, Gubora could not be trusted.

It was just as well; he'd been growing more and more irritated with the Laktilian.

The Guild's recent efforts had required the Advocate's presence in too many places at once. He grew weary—exhausted from splitting his attention across star systems. But things could be different. His Intelligence had computed countless measures to increase their operational efficiencies, and devised simple tasks to execute them. If Gubora would simply allow him to proceed, Guild productivity and profitability would skyrocket, lessening his burden.

"At least my newest operative will be ready soon." Nodding to himself, the Advocate turned to face the workshop interior. A blinking light across the space caught his eye: a waiting message from Burl, his contact in the Horranite consulate.

Time to see what the good doctor was up to.

The Advocate engaged the message; Burl's holographic bust materialized before him.

"Greetings, Advocate. I am making contact to inform you that Consular Bilanthia has taken a sudden leave of absence. He fielded two visitors prior to my arrival at the consulate today. I unfortunately did not see them, but I *did* manage to overhear some things, particularly the word 'Guild' a few times. I thought it pertinent to bring to your attention. I hope my conveyance of this information is evidence of my loyalty to you."

Greedy bastard. The man obviously wanted more compensation—and he would get it. This was vital information indeed.

The Advocate minimized Burl's recording and opened a holochannel to Gubora.

"Hello, old friend," echoed the Laktilian's voice. "I've heard news of an uprising on Sileen. It ssseems things have gone as planned." He licked and lingered on each successive hissing sound.

"The king contacted me just hours ago: the contract is set."

Gubora smiled a wide, vicious smile. "You've outdone yourself."

"Thank you," the Advocate replied, feigning true appreciation.

"Do you have any ideas for your next target?"

"That's actually the reason I called. I've just received a message from Burl."

"Burl..." Gubora's tongue slithered from his mouth. "Your contact in the Horranite Consulate?"

He shuddered at the lizard's vile thinking face. "Correct."

"What is our friend Doctor Bilanthia up to?"

"Two men visited the consulate yesterday, and he took an immediate leave of absence."

"Interesting. What could this mean?"

"I don't know," the Advocate replied, shaking his head. "But Bilanthia has proven to be a real nuisance. This is just another instance of him meddling where he shouldn't."

"I concur; however, our operations are airtight. Whatever he has, I cannot imagine it's serious."

"We should have silenced him a long time ago."

"Patienssse, old friend. We cannot openly assassinate a politician, especially one who so publicly works against us."

Coward, soft—probably due to his past with the doctor.

"Ssstill," Gubora continued, "this is troubling. I propose we interrupt his actions. Perhaps it's time we put operationsss into place in the Horranite System?"

"An interesting idea," said the Advocate, accessing his databanks. "There are fourteen planets in the Horranite System, nine of which are inhabited. Horran is the center of the region, both politically and astrogeographically. Seven small planets are home to outreach colonies established by the Central Horranite Authority. The remaining body is populated by a lower species that manages its own governmental dealings."

"I am pleased to see your consciousness operating at such outssstanding capacity. Your time away must have given you what you needed." The Laktilian lifted his head. "I trust you recognize the weak link in this chain of planets?"

"Given Bilanthia's firm stance against us, Horran and its colonies are untouchable, but we can immediately act on Merutan."

"It *isss* his consularship, after all. He'll have no choice but to come out of hiding." Gubora's snout stretched into a sly smile. "Make it so, old friend. The Merutanians are easy prey."

The Advocate nodded. "I'll check in once I've given the order."

Uncontrollable rage overcame the Advocate the moment the call disconnected. He swiped his arms across the crowded gurney behind him, throwing all its miscellaneous mechanical bits to the ground.

He *hated* Bilanthia. At seemingly every turn, the man did everything possible to hinder Guild operations—but that wasn't the source of the Advocate's anger, not this time. No, this time it dwelt on that *asinine* lizard. Gubora wasn't just hiding the truth—he was holding him back!

Slowly, the Advocate removed his gloves.

Holding his two hands beside each other—one of flesh, the other a fusion of flesh, tritonic steel, and bionic compounds—he gazed deeply at the stunning amalgamation that lined his skeleton as it glimmered in the far-off sun. Thinking back to the first iterations of his engineered body, he saw no comparison to today. Today, he was *magnificent.*

How could Gubora not see his superiority—and trust in it?

He placed a hand on his latest creation, her body encased in pristine, white armor identical to his own black. "*You* shall be magnificent."

As much as he wanted to continue his search for truth, this latest news on Bilanthia's movements required his immediate attention. He would set things in motion, then he would find and speak with Jag.

Yes... *Jag.*

There was an infant in the footage, one the people onboard *Shuriken* called Jag. No doubt this Rixxonian man and the child were one in the same, not after it was clear the escape pod had been in that glen for years. The most likely scenario was that the pod escaped and crashed onto Rixxon Prime, so this Jag would have information on the whereabouts of the other crew members. Perhaps they were on Rixxon Prime as well.

Perhaps the Advocate would soon find... *her.*

But first—Bilanthia.

"The time has come." He picked up the final piece to his latest project: a glowing, white helmet to go with her brilliant white armor. While functional, they were merely precautions; tritonic steel lined her frame, including portions of her insides. She was truly beautiful, a work of art second only to the Advocate himself.

"Wake up, my new appendage. I have a mission for you."

ACT II

Part Two

The Dark Relay

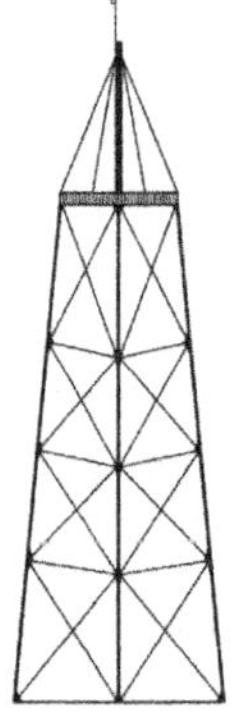

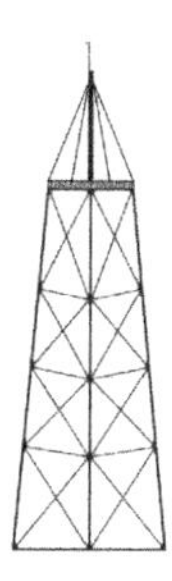

Chapter 23

Jag slid a hand forward and peeked at one of the three facedown cards in front of him.

Insisting they kill time on the way to Hurrash, Bo had convinced everyone to play—not that convincing them was difficult. Bilanthia seemed to jump at the idea, and Sixxis was always up for anything. Jag wasn't going to be the only one to refuse.

But unfortunately, the game hadn't proved much of an effective distraction. Things were as loud as ever as they sped through space.

Jag shifted in his seat, one of eight surrounding the circular table at the center of the open-spaced crew mess. An orange counter lined the long, dark-blue wall behind Bo, with various fixtures spread throughout and a row of cabinets beneath. A long metal shelf ran just below the ceiling; handles of assorted pots and pans stuck out from their assigned places.

"Round five," said Bo, nodding to Jag as he dealt the last card.

Jag inspected the line of five facedown cards at the table's center and chose two to turn two over. Still nothing close to an expert on the nuances of gambling, he pushed two chits toward the line.

"This sure brings back memories," Bilanthia sighed, calling Jag's bet. "I played a lot of Thrush in my younger years—had a fair bit of success, too!" He shook his head. "But in all my days, I've never come across anyone as good as you, Bo."

"We Quadmalians pride ourselves in bein' very perceptive." Bo added his two pieces to the pot. After Sixxis did the same, Bilanthia turned over another of the five cards.

Jag placed a reserved bet.

Bilanthia called.

"You can tell a lot about a person by the way they Thrush," said Bo, upping the bet. "Sixxis, you're a gambler at heart."

"No risk, no reward." Sixxis dropped a handful onto the table, raising the stakes further.

"Jag, your moves are calculated. I can tell you put a lot of thought into them."

Oh, Jag was thinking all right—but about more than just the game. He took several seconds before calling the bet.

"You're a little harder to read, Doc."

"It sure doesn't seem that way," said Bilanthia, sliding his hand across the table. "If I'm not careful, I may lose everything I own to you!"

Bo scratched at his chin, then turned over a fourth card—and it set Jag up nicely! Holding back a smirk, he tossed eight chits forward.

"Ohoho!" Bo threw eight of his own into the pot. "Something's got Jag excited!"

Sixxis joined in. "Let's ride!"

"Back to your hands," Bo said, reminding them of the gameplay.

As each of the remaining players inspected his second card, Jag's enthusiasm all but sank. Deflated, he tapped the table and nodded to Bo.

Likewise, Bo tapped the table.

"Hmm..." With a finger on his lips, Sixxis tilted his head. "Like I said—no risk, no reward!" He popped up, lifted his entire stash, and dropped it onto the pile. "Thirty-seven!"

"Skies," Jag said, tossing his cards. "I'm out."

Bo closed one eye and peered at Sixxis. "What're you hiding my foolhardy friend? Aw, hell with it!" He counted thirty-seven chits and threw them in. The players then each flipped over two hand cards, leaving the third facedown.

"Here we go!" Bo turned the fifth and final center card, then fanned the rest of the deck for Sixxis.

Twinkling his fingers, Sixxis ran his hand across the fan, pulled out a card, and placed it faceup next to the center line.

"Aha! A Quad-Thrush for the Quadmalian. Looks like another round for me!"

"It's not over yet!" Sixxis flipped his third hand card—and his shoulders sank.

The table's focus rested on Bo as he rotated his final card. "What!?" He launched upward, almost forcing the table over.

The black hole—Jag still wasn't sure of all the rules, but *that* card wasn't good for the big man. It meant instant loss in a player's hand.

"Yes!" Sixxis celebrated, cradling the funds at the center of the table. "I love that you're never safe in this game!"

Bo transitioned between a few faces—before his head reared back in roaring laughter. "One in 256 were my odds, and a'course—I pulled the black hole!" He winked at Sixxis. "Good thing we're not playin' for real money, right?"

"Yeah," Sixxis replied, "since I have none!"

The big man roared out again. "You *kill* me, Sixxis. I—"

BOODOODOOP!

"Looks like we're about there," Bo said, wiping a tear from his eye. "Excellent game, all." He hopped to his feet and lumbered out of the mess.

"Perhaps we should clean up." Bilanthia gathered the scattered cards and organized them into two neat stacks, then crossed to the booth sticking out from the wall opposite the counter. Flanked by padded benches, the rectangular table featured a wall-mounted storage spot for the game pieces, identical in shape to the booth itself.

With Sixxis' help, Jag collected the chits and dumped them into the black bucket between the two card stacks. "We'd better get up there, too." He exited the room, took a hard left, and stepped onto the lift.

"I must say"—Bilanthia joined him and Sixxis on the platform—"it certainly is nice to be off the grid."

The lift started to rise.

"Off... the grid?" Jag wondered aloud.

Bilanthia nodded. "Nobody knows where I am. It's quite freeing." Humming a little tune, he strolled onto the bridge and took a seat.

Sixxis looked at Jag and shrugged. "Nobody *ever* knows where we are."

With a grin, Jag walked forward and elected to stand, holding onto a seatback and staring forward as the ship exited warp.

Other than a large, orange moon, the void was empty.

"You sure they said Hurrash?" Bo called over his shoulder,

"Give it a second." Thinking back to *Pioneer*'s camouflage, Jag kept his focus forward. He had no intention of missing it.

"But there's—"

"Hello, my friends," Elama's voice hummed through the intercom—as bit by bit, a colossal, metallic body materialized before them.

"Fascinating!" Bilanthia blared, almost bursting through his restraints.

Jag's jaw dropped as the fullness of the elongated vessel trickled into reality. It was astounding, far beyond anything he could've imagined! A slender, cylindrical shaft connected its two ends: a towering, jagged front and a bulbous rear.

"Welcome to *Assurance,*" said Elama.

Fastened by four broad cables, a circular platform separated from the underbelly of the ship's back end and lowered into space.

"Well pits," said Bo. "This sure is something."

Zara flew forward, coming to a stable hover over the platform's center. And without a sound, the metal circle caught her as it rose into the ship.

Assurance held Jag speechless as her metal innards replaced the black of space. His eyes entangled themselves in the intricate array of pipes and wires lining the shaft, as a torrent of impossibilities invaded his mind.

"This has been a scholar's dream!" said Bilanthia, throwing off his restraints and running forward. Soft lighting and sparks glistened in his beady eyes, as the boom of the shutting airlock echoed around them.

"Pretty high tech." Bo reclined in his seat and stared straight up. "Guess I'll power down."

The shaft opened outward, bringing the platform to rest in an enormous, open hangar. Two Horranites worked in the room's corners.

"What *is* this place?" Bilanthia marveled.

"It's your people, Doc," Bo replied as his seat lowered to join the bridge deck. "Shouldn't you know?"

Bilanthia maintained his focus on the mysterious workers. "I'm not aware of any installations by Hurrash. And to my knowledge, no civilization has mastered cloaking technology on this grand a scale."

"It'll make sense when I introduce you to Elama," Jag said.

Bo unbuckled himself and pressed to his feet. "That the lady who just talked to us?"

"That's her!" Sixxis bounded straight from his seat, past the lift, and—

THUD!

"Skies! Sorry, Elama."

"It's quite all right."

Jag hustled to the edge of the bridge deck. "What happened?"

"I kinda plowed her over," said Sixxis, scrambling to help Elama—now projected as a hairless Horranite—to her feet.

Elama splayed her fingers and wiped them on her tunic. "As I said, it is no problem. Where is Doctor Bilanthia?"

"I am Ferris Bilanthia," he announced, coming to Jag's side. "To what organization does this ship belong? I've never heard of *Assurance.*"

Elama offered a respectful bow. "I am Elama Singh, commander of this vessel. My people and I are not Horranites; we project ourselves as a race you recognize to perhaps make you feel more comfortable."

"Fascinating... And who are you?"

She smiled. "All in due time, Doctor."

"Project yerself?" Bo plodded forward and dropped to a seat, dangling his legs into the lower area. "Sounds fancy."

Elama's eyes widened. "Indeed. Welcome to you as well—erm—who are you?"

"Bo-Ram Chinosin," he said with a wave of his hand and a courteous nod.

"Bo-Ram." Elama bowed again, then shot a glance at Jag. "Might I have a word?"

Jag rode the lift down and walked with Elama until they were several paces away from the group. A touch nervous—but not questioning himself—he waited for her to speak.

"You've returned with the doctor," she whispered, "but you brought another who was not cleared by us."

"We met Bo on Korrignolan when we were looking for Remy. He actually offered to help after Six..." Jag's eyes shifted. "...*vetted* him—but we turned him down. Then Bilanthia told us his bigger ship had been destroyed by the Guild, so we had to make a quick call."

"I see."

"Sixxis trusts him." Jag nodded. "And I trust Sixxis."

Elama glanced over Jag's shoulder, then looked back at him. "And what kind of relationship would this be if *I* didn't trust *you*?" She smiled. "Gentlemen, please follow me; we have much to get you up to speed on." She swept down the corridor, leading them onto the elevator.

"It'll be a squeeze with all of us," Bo said, stopping behind them. "You folks okay gettin' cozy?"

Sixxis shoved him forward. "In you go, big boy."

"Hey—watch it, you lanky son of a bitch!" Bo caught his eye, and the two erupted with laughter.

Elama pressed the wall button. "Quite a bit of character in this group."

"Should keep things interesting, I guess," Jag said.

The elevator doors opened at the bottom floor. Down two small steps, *Unity* rested in the main cargo area, right where Bilanthia parked her. Jag admired her pristine, purple-and-white body as they proceeded past. "She's a beautiful ship."

"We've been through a lot together, she and I," said Bilanthia. "She's the only one to have stood by me through it all."

"A man after my own heart, Doc!" Bo replied.

As they exited and rounded the ship, Jag got a much fuller view of *Zara* than he did in the dim Korrignolan spaceport. The vessel—like its pilot—was *huge*, clad in dark blue and burnt orange. "Do you dress like your ship on purpose, Bo?"

"My bond with *Zara* is *deep*."

"*Zara*?" Bilanthia pricked himself on one of three cylindrical shafts forming semi-circular boundaries around each of the ship's dual thrusters. "What a beautiful name."

Bo ran a hand across her dark-blue frame. "Beautiful name for a beautiful lady."

"You two talk like your ships are alive," said Sixxis, lacing his fingers behind his head.

Remy appeared from around the corner. "It is not uncommon for pilots to grow attached to their vessels."

"Hi, Remy," Jag said. "This is Doctor Bilanthia, and you've already met—"

"Bo-Ram Chinosin," declared the Quadmalian. "Bo, to you."

"Yes, hello; you may call me Remy."

"I heard you would be here!" said Bilanthia, rushing toward her. "Whatever brought you to join this cause, I cannot be more thrilled to work with you. It is an absolute pleasure!"

"I cannot say the same," she replied, expressionless. "I do not mix well with politicians."

Bilanthia chuckled. "I'm afraid I can't blame you there. I do, however, take pride in being unlike my colleagues. I hope you will warm to me in time."

"We will see."

"Remy has been hard at work since we left Korrignolan," said Elama, coming to their side. "All, please follow me. We will proceed to the briefing room as my crew adds a few upgrades to Master Chinosin's ship."

Bo's boisterous laughter filled the hangar. "Master Chinosin? Ain't nobody *ever* called me *that!*" He wiped a tear from his eye. "And whattya mean, upgrade? My baby's perfect!"

"I do not doubt that! We have many advanced systems, however; I feel you will be impressed with our work."

Bo narrowed his eyes.

"We will not remove anything, nor will we alter any functions. We'll simply boost her equipment's capabilities and add a few things." Elama bowed with just her head. "I assure you: no harm will come to *Zara*."

Bo wobbled a bit, then nodded. He turned and pressed a palm into *Zara's* exterior. "Keep an eye on 'em, 'kay girl?"

Elama smiled. "Now if you would please follow me."

"I will run ahead," said Remy, catching Jag's eye.

As Jag motioned to follow, Sixxis grabbed and yanked him backward. "What's up?" he asked, rubbing at his arm.

"I want to talk to you before we kick this off."

"What is it?"

Sixxis looked him right in the eye. "This is *your* mission, Jag. The Arbiters came to *you.* The rest of us are here to help where we can, but *you* need to take charge, just like you did with the zerns, with the Thakk, in the mountains—all of it."

What? Where was *this* coming from?

"I know you better than anyone, so I know I'm right on this: You're composed, confident, and brilliant under pressure. Away from that pressure, you're less certain."

It sure seemed like Sixxis was reading his mind. Jag had no idea what he was doing.

"But the others are—"

"They're not *leaders,* Jag. Experts, sure. Remy's brilliant—that's obvious. Bilanthia is connected and powerful. Bo's—well—the *other* kind of powerful." He paused. "They may not know it yet, but they need you just as much as you need them. You just have to show them—and you have to start now."

The Arbiters *had* chosen Jag—but why? Elama said a little about it, but she just seemed interested in helping him. Did she know more than she was letting on?

Grand purpose...

"Jag," said Sixxis, interrupting his thoughts. "I need you, too. And I have unbending faith that you'll keep me level."

At this, Jag had no choice—just like he had no choice but to leave Rixxon Prime. It didn't matter what he knew or didn't know. Duty brought him here, and duty would carry him forward.

"We stand tall as trees," Jag said with a nod. He put his hands on Sixxis' shoulders and pressed their foreheads together. "Thank you, brother—for everything."

They embraced.

"Now come on," Sixxis said as he pulled away. "Something tells me Remy doesn't like to be kept waiting." He turned—and jumped. "Whoa! Torin, how long have you been standing there?"

"Not long." He stepped back and gestured around *Zara*. "Your new weapons are ready. If you would please follow me, I will take you to them while the commander speaks to the others."

Sixxis grinned at Jag—of course. More new toys.

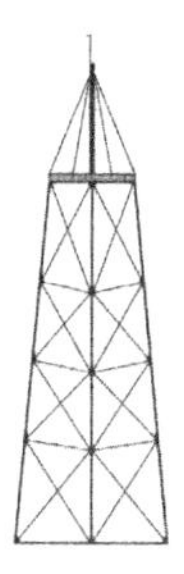

Chapter 24

Jag tossed his new quiver over his shoulder and stepped into the briefing room. Across a large, glass table, Remy fiddled with a handheld device while Bo and Bilanthia chatted.

"Ah!" said Elama, just inside the doorway. "How do you like your new equipment?"

Jag lifted the boxy weapon and clicked a button on its side. Two of its upper limbs shot out, forming a semicircle joined by two cables.

Sixxis whistled behind him. "So cool."

"It is a pulse-rifle-crossbow hybrid," Elama explained, "fashioned after your weapon of choice. I'm quite proud of the design!"

Jag flicked at the cables. "Aren't bows and arrows a little—I don't know—*primitive* for this mission? The interface talked all about weapon systems, and—"

"You'll find this bow is *far* from primitive," Elama said with a smile. "You have at your disposal three kinds of arrows. Those with gray tips are designed to pierce armor, those with red will trigger an explosion, and the purple arrow is affixed to a strong cord wound tightly through the base of your quiver."

"Right." Jag nodded. "Torin explained all that."

"Did he mention that you could load up to five arrows at a time?"

"...five?" That was a *big* upgrade from his old, slow-loading bow. "He didn't."

"Loving this over here," said Sixxis, holding up his new machete. "Perfectly balanced with what I've already got!"

Remy's voice cut through the conversation. "Now that we are all here, I would like to begin." She tapped her handheld, dimming the lights in the room as everyone gathered round the table's blue glow

"I have triangulated a number of known signal receptors and compared them to Guild installation blueprints and diagnostics. In doing so, I have located the physical source of the encrypted transmissions."

"The dark relay," Jag said.

"Correct. The messages are being sent from a station on Polt." She tapped her device, and an orange, ringed planet appeared above the holotable.

Jag connected the dots. "Is that—"

"Yes," said Remy, glowering at the image. "It is no coincidence that the relay is located on the same planet on which my sister was murdered."

"Feels like we should've seen that coming," Sixxis said with a shrug.

Remy squinted at Elama. "The Arbiters have tried multiple times to locate the source, but they have failed because each transmission divides and reflects itself across a multitude of 'dummy relays' before being disseminated to those for whom it was intended."

"So," said Bilanthia, folding his arms, stroking at his horns, "the message starts on Polt and splits?"

"Precisely. Each message dissolves into a minimum of eight encoded segments before traveling through the dummies. These segments are then sent to their original destination, at which point they are reassembled to deliver the transmission content."

"Can you figure out what they say?" Jag asked.

Remy's expression flattened even further—if that was possible. "That is why we are here. An encrypted transmission was sent just hours ago. The Guild means to initiate operations on Merutan."

"Merutan!" Bilanthia strode forward, illuminating his face in the table's glow. "I suppose it's a good thing we're already so close!"

"You know of Merutan?" Jag said.

"Merutan is a Class IV planet under diplomatic protection of my people. Its developmental stage would normally label it Class V and deem it untouchable, but its status is complicated by the fact that it neighbors Horran." He looked to Remy. "What does the Guild intend to do?"

"The transmission references a 'holy war.'"

Bilanthia's tan complexion faded. "It can't be..."

"What's got you so spooked, Doc?" Bo asked from his spot, propped against the wall.

"The Dutans—one of the societies on the planet—are a deeply religious people. At the center of their sacred temple sits an idol they revere above life itself, believed to have been given to them by the gods."

Jag folded his arms. "So this idol—what if something happened to it?"

"I see two possible scenarios. In one, the Dutans assume the idol was taken by the Merus—the other society—and a planetary conflict ensues—a 'holy war.' The Dutans are not well enough equipped for warfare, so they would undoubtedly reach out to the Guild for aid."

"And the other scenario?"

Bilanthia sighed. "Dutan society crumbles and descends into barbarism. The Merus would have no choice but to take up arms and defend themselves. In this scenario, *they* would be the ones seeking Guild assistance."

"Seriously?" said Bo. "All this over an idol?"

"Religion is a powerful construct," Bilanthia replied. "Belief drives many, especially on lower-developed planets." He shook his head. "Civilizations have fallen by lesser means."

"Then we just need to make sure nothing happens to the idol," Jag concluded. "Where do the Dutans keep it?"

"In the forests of their territory. The temple is guarded at all times, and a popular destination for the citizens; it's likely to be crowded."

"So what's the plan?" Sixxis asked, nudging his brother.

Jag ran his tongue along his bottom lip. He saw enough mass suffering on Rixxon Prime, so he wasn't about to let these people get hurt. And besides, all his time spent hunting showed him that creatures got less observant when they felt alone and safe—so they'd keep an element of surprise by isolating the Guild.

"Step one will be to clear out the temple," he said. "Is there an easy way to do that?"

Bilanthia's brow twisted—then his eyes lit up. "Yes! If a Horranite diplomat visits, it is customary that all citizens—Meru and Dutan alike—gather at the steps of the Capitol Building in Meru Plaza. That would leave the temple vacated aside from the guards!"

"Perfect—we'll need you to gather the people."

"But it takes time for people to congregate."

"What if we do something extra to draw their attention? Get them moving faster?"

"Extra? Like what?"

Jag turned to Bo. "Ace pilot, think you can handle that?"

"You bet yer third armpit I do!" he replied, grinning a savage grin as he shoved off the wall. "I'll get the whole *planet's* attention."

"You said the temple was in a forest, right?" Jag said.

Bilanthia nodded.

"Should be no problem for you, Six."

"Leave it to me!" said his brother, shooting an arm into the air.

"The spaceport is located by Meru Plaza," Bilanthia continued. "Anyone wishing to depart the planet must come back through there."

Jag wrinkled his mouth. "Remy, can you—"

"Affirmative." She swiped a finger across the handheld, wiping the projection from the table. Another image appeared after a few taps.

A large building with columns lining its exterior sat atop an impressive set of marbled stairs. The stairs led down to an open square with tables and chairs situated on both sides. And a collection of canopied tents gathered opposite the building.

Jag placed his hands on the table's edge and leaned in. "Bilanthia, What can you tell us about the Plaza?"

"It is a beautiful, communal space at the foot of the Capitol steps. There is a bustling, outdoor market at its south end, so it's almost always crowded. With so much commotion, it will be difficult to spot anything suspicious."

"What about the route to the temple?"

"There is a single path through the forest, running due west."

"Remy, can—"

The plaza's image shrank; a bushy, multicolored forest materialized at its borders.

Bilanthia pointed to a break in the trees. "There."

"Okay," Jag said. "While Bilanthia meets with the people, I'll sit here on the western side and keep an eye on the path. Sixxis, you'll be at the temple. Bo, Remy, could you mill about the market? Look for anything suspicious?"

"Sure thing." Bo pounded a fist into his chest. "I can—"

"I will also watch the path," Remy interrupted. "I am rather adept with a sniper rifle; I can remove anyone suspicious with a single shot."

"Really now?" said Bo. "You're full of surprises, little one."

"Please do not call me that."

"That's a good plan," Jag said with a nod. "Two sets of eyes are better than one."

Remy zoomed in on a water tower on the plaza's eastern side. "I will lay up here."

"That's the plan then!" Jag said. "Bo will get everyone's attention, then head to the market while Sixxis moves for the temple and Remy and I watch the path. Bilanthia, you'll... talk to them?"

The doctor smiled. "Oh, I can always think of something to say."

"Very well." Remy tapped her handheld, deactivating the table and turning on the lights. She then snaked between her companions and handed each a small, rubbery ball. "These are inner-ear communication devices, provided by Elama." She placed one in her ear. "They will coordinate with your neurons. If your brain intends for us to listen to something you say or hear, it will be transmitted."

"Incredible..." Jag muttered.

"We've taken the liberty of upgrading the interior systems of Master Chinosin's vessel," Elama added, "building in an advanced medical bay and a holotable compatible with Remy's tablet, as well as furnishing a liveable crew quarters and stocking the ship with food. We also cleared the clutter in the engine compartment; I thought Remy might like that space as her workshop."

"Thanks for that." Bo scratched at his side. "Been meanin' t'clean it myself for a bit now."

"I believe that's everything!" Elama finished with a slight hop. "Remember all: you must tell no one of our involvement."

Remy narrowed her eyes. "I will gather my things."

"Right to the point, that one—I like her!" Bo lumbered out of the room after Remy.

"Jag," Elama said, "a moment?"

Sixxis caught Jag's eye, then threw an arm around Bilanthia and started for the door. "*Finally*—a chance to talk with you one on one. I've been dying to know what it's like to have hands as feet."

"This is where we say goodbye for a time," Elama said through a soft smile.

Jag took a step back. "What do you mean?"

"We've done all our mission parameters will allow," she explained. "You are on your own from here. Should you need to contact us, you may use the comm room. We installed a hidden channel that will respond to your genetic code."

"Just like that? You're gone?"

"I'm afraid so," she said, raising her ridged browline and scrunching her mouth. "We have other matters to attend to." She stepped closer and took his shoulders in hand.

Jag shifted under the uncomfortable silence of Elama's piercing gaze. It was almost like she was looking right into his soul, analyzing whether or not he was fit for the task.

Not that she needed to; he was doing it enough himself.

A single tear streamed down the Arbiter's cheek. "Good luck, Jag." With this, she stepped back and gestured for the door.

Luck... Jag had never considered himself to be very lucky. But Elama had confidence in him—for whatever reason—and that buoyed his own confidence. It didn't answer his questions, though, and those questions all converged on the Advocate. Why was he doing all of this? Why did he murder Remy's sister? And why did he send people to Rixxon Prime? The metal couldn't be the only answer—it was too simple.

Was mother right? Was this all tied to Jag's grand purpose?

Caught off guard by the strange interaction, Jag got so lost in thought that he barely registered any of his movements as he walked through the towering hangar, around *Zara's* deep-blue body, and into the cargo area. He took the elevator up, then progressed through the narrow corridor, past the new holotable, and onto the exposed lift.

"Get the lead out, Jag!" yelled Bo from the pilot seat as the platform lowered *Zara* into the shaft.

Shaking his head clear, Jag engaged the lift, rode it to the bridge, and took his seat. Much like the walk up, the trip down the shaft was a blur; before he knew it, the vastness of space sat undisturbed before them.

"Errybody ready?" Bo called over his shoulder.

Was Jag ready?

Everything had happened so fast, he'd barely had time to think. Then again, maybe that was good. It kept things from getting too *loud.*

"Through the winds of change..." He looked to his brother, by his side like always. And after an affirming nod, he turned his head forward. "Let's do this."

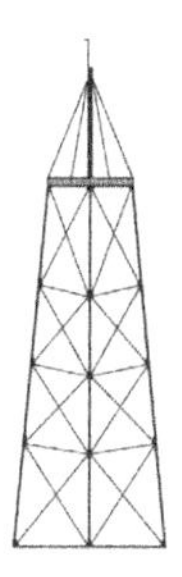

Chapter 25

What a show!

High in a tree by the temple path, Sixxis sat on a branch kicking his legs. Masses of people flooded into the plaza below, coming from all directions after Bo and *Zara's* big demonstration—at least that's what Sixxis assumed. The sun reflected off the white steps and almost blinded him every time he looked down.

That's okay, though. He had a *great* time looking up.

It'd been *incredible* watching Bo's fancy flying—and talk about style. Flips and spins, rolls and turns—he did it all! He even skipped the spaceport and parked atop the capitol steps.

Imagine how it would've felt to be inside during all of that! Too bad Sixxis missed the fun ride; Remy flew him and Jag to the surface in *Unity*. Still, he had to give the big guy some credit.

"That sure was something, Bo!"

"Hah—that wasn't even *half* of what *Zara* can do! Jag, we're parked; I'm en route to the market."

"Got it," Jag said. "I'm in position."

"I am also in position," Remy reported. "Sixxis, can you see me?"

The water tower sat undisturbed across the way. There wasn't even a ladder, so how she got up there was beyond Sixxis. "Nope!"

"You should get moving," Jag said.

"On it!" Sixxis wrapped his hands around the branch, dropped down a level, and turned west. A sea of red, orange, yellow, green, and purple leaves shrouded his path into the forest. "These barely look like trees," he said, bobbing up and down. "Such flimsy branches."

"You are wasting time," said Remy.

With a shrug, Sixxis took off through the limbs at a light jog. He couldn't move as quickly as back home, but he didn't have much trouble. Before long, he'd—

SNAP!

"Wh—whoa!" He stumbled as a branch broke under his weight—but falling was one of his specialties. He swung back onto his feet before long.

"Don't worry everyone; almost fell, but I'm good."

"Imbecile."

"Aww, thanks, Rem!"

Sixxis couldn't help but laugh to himself as Remy sighed into his earpiece. That girl; she took everything too seriously, just like Jag. She needed Sixxis to lighten things up.

Good thing that was his specialty, too!

He took off again, moving slower and watching each step; better not risk falling for real and alerting any Guild thugs.

Even though the leaves were all different colors—which really threw him off—being back in the trees, back on a planet with crisp, fresh air felt like home. Sixxis savored the wood's texture on his bare feet. It beat the skies out of the cold, metal flooring of those spaceships.

The crowd chatter from the square dissolved as he made his way west, leaving just the sounds of his rustling and the few folks walking below. He was eager to prove his worth to his new teammates, and Jag couldn't have set him up any better: go through the forest, find the temple, get an eye on the operative.

Easy!

The trees in front of him disappeared before long, revealing a circular clearing with a giant, gold pyramid at its center.

"Whoa!" he said. "This place is incredible!"

An obelisk spanned the height of the temple at each corner, with another sticking up from its pinnacle. Two soldiers stood guard at the double doors, each holding a large spear.

"How's it look?" Jag asked.

"Nothing weird—wait."

"What is it!?"

"Do..." Sixxis squinted. "...do the Dutans have two heads? Bet that makes standing guard easier!"

Remy's deep sigh again filled his earpiece. "You have been on this planet for three hours now," she said. "Did you just notice?"

"Six, don't scare me like that."

Skies. Jag was probably nervous enough already. Better not make things worse.

"Sorry."

Sixxis would be fine; he could handle this. No prob—

A black figure zipped out from the treeline, wearing the same armor as the goon from the riverside farm. *This* goon dashed across the clearing, dropped to a crouch by the temple, and crept along until he made it to the corner.

"Team, I've got eyes on the bad guy."

"Good," Jag said. "Don't let him out of your sight."

Prowling around the corner, the operative approached the temple entrance—where he popped up, slit the guard's left throat, spun around his back, slit the right throat, and pressed himself against the recessed doorway without a single sound.

THUMP! The limp body hit the ground, startling the remaining guard. She tiptoed toward her dead friend.

This wasn't going to end well.

The operative sprang from the door and flew through the same series of moves, killing her just as brutally and quickly. Neither guard stood a chance.

"Skies—two down already." Sixxis scrunched his nose. "Or four. I don't totally get the two heads thing."

"Don't take him on yourself," Jag said. "Try to—"

"But he's gonna *kill* everyone*!*"

With a dagger in each hand, the operative kicked the doors open and exploded into the sanctuary.

"I've got to get down there!" Sixxis sprang into action, skipping down his tree and into the field.

"Be careful!" Jag called out.

"Do *not* ruin this mission!" added Remy.

Ruin? More like get it off on the right foot! There was no *way* that goon would see him coming.

Sixxis darted into the entryway and peeked through the open door—to find another guard dead on the golden, stone floor. Crouched low, the operative swayed side to side, facing down his sole-surviving obstacle.

"What is this?" demanded the guard's right head.

"How dare you defile this sacred place!" added the other.

"Sacred is a rather relative term," the operative taunted, flourishing his blades. "Don't you think?"

Sixxis snuck into the temple, positioning himself several paces behind the operative and drawing his machetes.

"We are protectors of that which is holy!" The guard twisted her double-edged spear and pulled it apart into two shorter halves. Twirling one in each hand, she cocked back into a defensive stance. "You will come no further!"

"I don't have time for this." The operative lunged at the guard, slashing his daggers down at her. And as she parried the attacks, Sixxis found his opening: he leapt forward, spun, and swept his powerful legs at the operative's feet.

The operative hit the ground hard. "*You* again?" he said, windmilling his legs and popping to his feet. "How did you get off Rixxon Prime?"

Sixxis took a step back. "How did you—"

"You must *both* leave this place!" interrupted the guard, launching a flurry of attacks. But the operative ducked, dodged, and parried everything she threw at him—then thrust a foot into her chest. She stumbled backward.

Sixxis jumped in next, coming up behind the operative and slicing down—but again, the operative was ready. He hopped to the side and swung his leg back. And when Sixxis jumped to avoid the hit, he grabbed him by the leg, spun, and hurled his body across the sanctuary.

Sixxis rebounded off the wall, pounding into the ground.

The guard then lunged—and in subsequent motions, the operative dodged the attack and severed her right hand. She toppled to the floor, calling out in agony.

"A pitiful attempt," said the Guildsman, circling his prey.

"I am placed here by the divine," the guard proclaimed. "I cannot—"

The operative threw a hard kick into her ribcage. "Six down, two to go." Rearing his daggers overhead, he moved to stab her in the back—but Sixxis redirected the blow and saved her life.

"How do you know where I'm from?"

"I have eyes *everywhere*," laughed the operative.

Sixxis dove at him and slashed down at successive diagonals. The operative ducked side to side, avoiding two blows, then dropped to a crouch and held his daggers above his head.

CLANG-CRACK! The machete split both blades in two.

"How *dare* you!" said the operative. He jumped up, planted a hand into the ground, and threw both feet at Sixxis' chest.

Disoriented, stumbling back, Sixxis completely missed the next attack; both his weapons flew to the floor as his body slammed into the wall.

"This..." The operative knelt and picked up a machete. "It belongs to—agh!"

From her place on the ground, the guard had thrown her spear end and impaled him through the shoulder.

"You are a *nuisance!*" Bounding side to side, he leapt up and brought his attack down—decapitating her—then raced for the pedestal at the room's center. He grabbed the idol, turned toward the entrance, and broke into a sprint.

Weaponless, dizzy, Sixxis threw himself in front of the door—but the operative just tossed him aside as he dashed past and took off into the clearing.

"Uhh, guys," said Sixxis, panting, wheezing, stumbling to the door, "we've got a problem. Eight guards down over here, and he's headed your way."

Idiots.

Remy's new companions were inadequate at best. Clearly, she was the only one capable of getting anything done.

No matter. She would neutralize the operative herself.

From her prone position atop the water tower, she had a full, unobstructed view of the area through her sniper scope. The crowd gathered below, listening to Doctor Bilanthia as he rambled about interplanetary relationships, news from the Legislature, and the lovely summer weather on Merutan.

Politicians.

Remy turned her attention to the western treeline. Based on the distance to the temple, the operative would arrive any minute. And given the open space, picking him off would require little effort.

"Sixxis, describe the target."

"He had a spear sticking through his shoulder last I saw him."

How surprisingly helpful.

Remy ran a hand along the barrel of her rifle. Despite her newfound issues with the organization, the Guild had offered her all the combat education she could ask for. Sniper training was the logical route; such a technical weapon, usage defined by precision and skill. And Remy had mastered it, just as she did everything else.

"Jag," she said, "call it out if you see him. I will do the same."

"You got it!"

At least they listened. This would be much more difficult if they did not respect her intelligence or expertise.

On a different occasion, looking out over this kaleidoscopic forest may have stirred memories in Remy, deep memories of her home on Phyator—of a time when there was more to life than surviving.

Especially with Omeka gone, Remy did not have much beyond herself.

"Remy," Jag said, "black armor, north of the path."

Pivoting, she zeroed in on the target. It was an easy shot, and with such distance from the plaza, it would not draw attention.

"I have him in my sights."

"This is very exciting," said Bo, "but don't you think this might be a bit risky with so many people around? I thought the sniper was a backup—ooh!"

"I will not make a sound," Remy assured.

"Awright; I'll just keep shoppin'. Just found somethin' real nice!"

"I'll head for the path and turn toward the forest," Jag said.

At least *one* of the others was focused on the mission.

"Affirmative." Remy drew a slow, deep breath. "Firing in three... two..."

Her round zipped through the operative's chest. He stumbled back and dropped to a knee, hunching forward.

"Direct hit," she reported.

Slowly, the operative lifted his head toward her. He scowled as he stood, then turned south and sprinted away.

"Impossible! Jag, he is still alive—coming your direction!"

"Got it." Jag rounded north as he breached the treeline and broke into a jog. "I see him."

"Keep moving," Remy directed, following the man's motion. "I will bring him into your arms."

"What's that going on back there?" Sixxis quipped.

"Now is not the time!"

Remy ran a finger down the trigger; the operative continued south; Jag weaved north through the trees.

"Three..." This time, Remy would aim for the head.

"Two..." Once more, she drew a deep, controlled breath.

Just as the operative reared his head back—having seen Jag coming toward him—his body lurched to the side, momentum carrying him directly into Jag's arms.

As promised.

Jag dropped to a knee and laid him on the ground. "Skies, Remy—that was incredible!"

"Is he dead? Is the idol secure?"

Jag searched a small satchel on the operative's hip before holding up a small, stone statue. "Got it!"

Good. They were successful.

"You must return it to the temple at—"

Remy whipped her sights southward.

"Jag, watch out!"

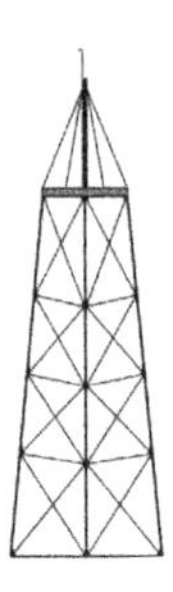

Chapter 26

Jag whirled around. With just a split second to react, he dropped the idol and dove to the side—as a humming dagger struck deep into the tree behind him.

He rolled and popped to his feet.

"This is actually quite convenient," buzzed his assailant's thin, mechanically altered voice. She released the blade, leaving it embedded in the tree as she turned and crept her small frame toward him. "I was going to have to come find you." Sunlight glinted off her sleek, white-armored casing as she cracked her neck to the side. "But it appears you've saved me a trip!" She broke into a sprint and threw a punch.

Jag ducked and brought his own punch rounding up toward her kidney—but *SLAP!* She caught his fist with one hand. Then gripping it with both hands, she whirled him about and smashed his back into a tree.

"Guys," he said, wincing at the immense pain, "I need a hand!"

"I'm coming, brother!" Sixxis yelled.

"What?" Bo said. "What's going on?"

"Need a hand, you say?" The operative hoisted him over her head. "I can give you that!" She bent at the knees and lobbed him out past the treeline.

Jag hurtled into the clearing between the forest and the capitol steps, rolling until his momentum stopped. And as he pressed to his hands and knees, the operative pulled the dagger from the tree.

"Such beautiful steel," she said, turning it over. "Still perfect."

Jag had seen that steel before. "Why—"

"You shouldn't meddle in things you don't understand," she said, sheathing her weapon.

Jag wasn't quick enough as she rushed him, plunging her foot into his stomach so hard it might've gone right through him were he not wearing armor. He flew through the air, thudding into the grass a few paces from the crowd's perimeter—setting everyone into a panic.

"I hoped to not cause a scene," said the operative, continuing toward him amidst the chaos, "but you've really pissed me off lately."

Jag pushed to his feet and drew his rifle—but it was no good; there were too many people. What if he accidentally used an explosive arrow? What if someone bumped him and threw his aim somewhere dangerous?

No. Too many innocent people would already be hurt. He couldn't add to that.

Stowing his weapon, Jag held both hands in front of him as the woman threw another punch. And his strength *barely* proved enough; he wrapped his hands around her fist and slowed the momentum of her attack—but all it did was distract him.

Without pause, she brought a left hook into his side.

Jag's ribs shattered as the excruciating blow lifted his body from the ground and slammed it onto the capitol steps, further scattering the frantic masses. With the wind knocked out of him, he lay still, staring up at the sun, blindly awaiting his fate.

CLANG!

Jag recaptured his breath and shielded his eyes—finding Sixxis between him and the operative.

"Get up!" he called over his shoulder, holding her dagger in place with both machetes.

Arm trembling, the operative pressed the blades downward. "I grow weary of you."

"Pretty sure we haven't met," Sixxis replied, spinning and sweeping his legs at her feet, upending and crashing her onto the marble. "You must be mistaking me for some *other* handsome green guy."

Jag composed himself and popped up. With the woman lying on the ground just past Sixxis and the crowd about them thinning, he chanced his weapon—but not fast enough.

The operative pressed her hands into the ground, kicked over her head, and launched to her feet. She knocked Jag's rifle from his grasp with a powerful, backhanded strike, then spun and brought a fist at his face.

Jag ducked, then threw an uppercut with all he had, striking her helmeted chin. She stammered back into Sixxis, who clasped his arms tight and lifted her from the ground.

"Careful, Six! She's—"

The operative threw her head back—smashing it into Sixxis' face—then kicked her legs and flipped him forward over her shoulder.

"OUTTA MY WAY!" boomed Bo's voice over the cacophony of hysterical voices. A swath cut through the crowd as the enormous Quadmalian pushed his way toward them. "Remy, you prolly can't get a shot in the crowd, can you?"

"Negative," she replied.

Jag lowered his shoulder and barreled into the operative—knocking her to the ground—then dove sideways for his rifle. Weapon in hand, he loaded an armor-piercing arrow and waited for his opportunity.

Behind him, Sixxis sprang to his feet, picked up his fallen blades, and lunged. But the operative was ready: she rolled to the side, rolled back over her head, and pushed to her feet, kicking him in the chin as she flipped up.

She then drew her blade and pounced.

Her incredible speed made it impossible for Jag to find his opening. Even though she had just one weapon, Sixxis couldn't do anything but backpedal as he parried hits with both machetes. But then an opportunity came—and Jag's arrow embedded itself into the operative's chest.

But it didn't seem to phase her.

Enraged, she threw Sixxis aside and turned toward Jag, clicking something on her weapon. A blue-electrical band zipped around the blade—as she pulled the arrow from her flesh and snapped it in two.

"This being is not entirely organic—like the last one," said Remy. "We cannot defeat it in hand-to-hand combat. I will retrieve *Unity* and provide assistance."

"What can I do?" asked Bilanthia.

"Doc, you get *Zara* fired up for a quick getaway," Bo replied.

"On it!"

Jag fired another arrow, this one at the operative's helmet—but she dodged it with an effortless cock of the head. She then charged, lifted her blade overhead, and brought it slashing down.

Dropping his rifle, Jag slotted a foot back, crossed his arms over his head, and caught her forearm, holding her back with all he had.

Skies—she was too strong!

"Don't worry," she taunted as the blade inched toward his forehead, the electrical field humming hot near his skin. "I have no intention of killing you. I have too much to—"

Her body lurched backward.

Bo had finally arrived, and with the full vigor of his four arms, he lifted her over his head, spun, and flung her deep into the field.

Jag scrambled to recover his rifle and launched an explosive arrow. It erupted on impact, its burst engulfing the operative and everything around her.

"That oughtta do it," said Sixxis, panting as he came to his brother's side. "Nice one."

"You were just in time," Jag wheezed. "Both of—"

"I wouldn't get too comfortable," said Bo.

Enveloped by the settling dust, a bent-over silhouette drifted upright—and the operative shot out from the dispersing smoke an instant later.

What in the skies!?

How was it possible? Nobody could take a beating like that—let alone get blown up—and be just fine. What were they dealing with? Was every Guild operative like this? How could they possibly succeed?

There wasn't time.

Jag pushed out three quick breaths, then stowed his weapon and swept his companions behind him. "Form a triangle behind me!"

Sixxis stepped forward. "What are you—"

"Just trust me!"

Sixxis scrunched his face and hopped back to form his tip of the triangle.

"Leave some for me," said Bo, taking his place.

It was just like on Rixxon Prime—with the zern in the jungle—right?

Mouth open, tongue out, Jag darted at the operative, lunged, and slid feet-first at her legs. She leapt over his body with a grunt, tucked into a roll, and bounced back to her feet.

Just like on Rixxon Prime.

"Nice move," said Sixxis, closing in on the surrounded operative.

Jag drifted to his feet and joined the shrinking triangle. "Who are you?"

"Me? Hah! Who are *you*?" All the fighting had cracked a small hole in her white helmet; a tuft of black hair spilled out. "Do you even know?"

"Did the Advocate send you?"

"In a manner of speaking."

"Why are you here?"

"Isn't it obvious?" she buzzed. "To sow *chaos.*"

"Well, we're here to stop you!

"*You* are nothing," she said, lowering to a crouch. "*I*... am everything!" She launched at the ground and whirled her lower body, knocking both Jag and Bo to the ground.

Ever agile, Sixxis was quick enough: he hopped over her attack, came down slashing—and didn't stop. But dipping and ducking, the operative dodged each attempt in the onslaught—until he *finally* landed a strike, slicing her inner thigh.

Yellow blood oozed from the gash, driving her into a fit of fury. She grabbed Sixxis with remarkable rapidity and threw him aside.

Back on his feet, Bo cracked his neck and threw four mighty hooks, one after the other. The operative blocked them right in order—forearm, forearm, shin, shin—then backflip-kicked him in the jaw.

He stumbled back a step.

"You'll regret that." Shrugging off his coat, Bo drew a hand across the deep, red gash on his chin. "I'm usually a nice guy," he said, winding his arms, "but sometimes nice doesn't cut it."

At breakneck speeds, Bo barraged the operative with fists and feet. After failing to block most of the blows raining down on her, she curled into a ball and knocked side to side, taking everything in the body.

It was insane. Four arms, two legs—how could anybody withstand *that*?

A hard hook cracked open her balled body, giving Bo an opening to land a hit square in her stomach. The operative doubled over for just a moment, then exploded into another backflip kick, this one knocking the winded Quadmalian onto his back—and *she* didn't even look tired! Her fractured armor was about the only thing showing signs of battle.

Skies!

Jag notched three arrows in his crossbow and fired them at one of the cracks. At such close range, they all pierced her side.

Roaring out, the operative dropped to her knees. And when the echo of her cry dispersed, a new, much louder sound filled the space—followed by a bevy of flashing lights.

It was *Unity!*

"Get to the ship—now!" said Remy. "I will—"

Gunfire erupted from the ground, the last known position of the operative.

"Damn!"

"Get out of here, Remy," Jag barked, "you'll be shot down!"

"Affirmative." *Unity* veered up and into the atmosphere—but then all firing stopped.

Had Remy managed to hit the operative?

"Bo," Jag said, "get in there and toss her one more time."

"With pleasure." Bo charged forward and took hold of the injured operative. Spinning, swinging her around, he lobbed her into the field once again.

Jag notched four explosive arrows. "Now get to *Zara*," he said, loading the final, purple-tipped arrow. "Both of you!"

Sixxis shook his head. "Not without—"

"I'll be right behind you!"

"Come on, Sixxis!" Bo yelled, plodding ahead. "We gotta go!"

As Sixxis ran off, Jag turned his eyes on the woman. Back on her feet, she removed the arrows from her side and sprayed something on the wound.

"Bo," Jag said, "can you take off with the back entrance open?"

"Sure—but why?"

"Just do it!"

"You got it! Errybody—hustle up and strap in!"

Zara's engines roared through the plaza as she lifted from the ground.

Resuming her assault, the operative sprinted toward Jag. He fired red-tipped arrow after red-tipped arrow, littering the area with explosions, forcing her to repeatedly redirect her path—and in turn slowing her down.

"Now or never," he whispered to himself, hoping the magnet arrow was as simple as Torin described. He whipped around and fired at the ceiling of *Zara's* cargo bay. As his shot cleared the opening, he smashed a button on his quiver to engage the magnet, then another button to pull himself in. And *just* before the operative reached him, it whisked him from her grasp.

As he flew off, quickly rising with the fleeing *Zara*, Jag finally caught his breath. The operative kicked at the grass below, turned, and ran off toward the treeline.

They made it!

Jag brought himself into the hangar and hung on tight until *Zara* stopped moving, at which point *Unity* flew in and stabilized herself beneath him.

The glass opened upward, and Remy popped from her seat. "We must go to the bridge."

"Right!" Jag hit the release button and dropped to *Unity's* metal body as the cargo door shut behind them.

"Hang on," Bo's voice boomed into the bay. "We're gettin' outta here, and we're doin' it fast!"

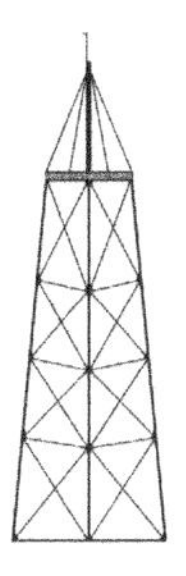

Chapter 27

Dammit!

Seated in his open-air workshop, the Advocate leaned back.

There was no longer any question: Jag and that Rixxonian *pest* were the visitors Bilanthia left with. They'd meddled in his operations three times—and now they apparently had a Quadmalian on their side.

And the *sniper!* Did he hear the name Remy? Had Remy Troyer defected?

Five in all—and they were clearly expecting him on Merutan, a fact all but confirming Remy's involvement. It was highly unlikely those Rixxonians or Bilanthia could have decoded the encryption. It was far too sophisticated.

Perhaps this was good timing. More and more as things unfolded, the Advocate wanted to speak with Jag. Now, at least he knew he was listening.

It couldn't be coincidence: Jag, the downed escape pod, the coordinates, the files, the Rixxonians' mysterious departure from that backwater planet. There were obvious connections between them all, and that didn't even account for the Advocate's inexplicable feelings. Something was at work, something stemming beyond him and his past.

His head jerked to the side.

What was happening?

What... *happened?*

It would help if he could... *feel* the things his former self felt in the video files. That was the most troubling part. Because they weren't his memories, he could only see and hear—not feel. But it was no doubt him in the footage.

So what happened to his memories?

Ashley...

Yes, she appeared in several of the files—a woman identical to the one he saw in his mind's eye in that Rixxonian glen. If Jag could only help him find her, she could help him understand. She could—

The comm station signaled an incoming call.

"Old friend," hissed Gubora's voice, "we must talk."

"If this is about Merutan"—he glanced over his shoulder—"I'm aware of what happened."

"First the fiasco on Rixxon Prime, and now this mess. Your operatives are slipping, old friend."

The Advocate waved a hand over his head. "You worry about your end, I'll worry about mine."

"I'm afraid you underestimate both the sssevерity of our situation and the densssity of the damage control I must now manage."

"You'll be fine. You always are."

Irksome lizard. Where did he get off talking to the Advocate like this?

"I have other"—Gubora's tongue shot out of his mouth—"information."

"Must you keep doing that?"

"One of my watchers on Korrignolan informed me that Remy Troyer met with the same man from the Meru Plaza incident. We've been unable to confirm that she is indeed off the grid, but regardlessss, this news is not good for us."

So... Remy Troyer *had* defected.

"That would explain the sniper fire," said the Advocate, "and the fact that they were there in the first place." His hand formed a fist. "How *dare* she use our training against us." The anger burning inside him sent a tremor up his body. "We *made* her what she is."

"That may be true," Gubora replied, "but if she has indeed turned on us, we have a major problem on our hands. She knowsss too much."

"It doesn't matter how much she knows—she has no proof. And besides, I already have a plan."

Gubora's snout tilted into a half-smile. "And thisss is why we are a good team! I will do what I can with the Legislature." His smile faded. "You must be more careful."

Careful? What a joke. There's a difference between careful and cowardly. Gubora was unequivocally the latter.

"Bilanthia is with them, too," added the Advocate. "Every day that passes, I'm more sure we should have removed him from the equation years ago." He spat. "You have a soft spot for him."

Many times, Gubora had regaled the Advocate of his time spent working with Bilanthia on advanced prosthetics. It was their work together that launched both men's success, but their relationship took a turn when Gubora wanted to research the interweaving of organic and synthetic minds. The good doctor couldn't bring himself to work against galactic regulations.

Gubora squinted. "You give me too little credit, old friend. He is nothing to me; this is merely the careful way to do things. As I have said many times, we cannot openly assassinate a politician, especially one as influential as Bilanthia."

There was that word again—*careful.*

"Whatever," the Advocate grunted, brushing him off. "Do what you must; I'll do the same."

"Be careful, old friend. I'll see you soon." The hologram zipped upward and disappeared.

Old friend... pah!

If that half-witted Laktilian truly *was* the Advocate's friend, he would never have been subjected to all this discomfort and confusion of late. The lizard was hiding something—that much was obvious. For some reason, he didn't want the Advocate to know his past. But why?

In all his experiments, did Gubora *steal* the Advocate's memories? So he could control him as his... pet?

Gubora may have had rank over the Advocate in title, but that's where it stopped. They were equal in role. Their operations spanned different arenas and almost never crossed, and it had been years since the Advocate fielded any real command from his "superior." But now—now that things were going wrong—Gubora had tightened his grip, like in the early days.

It was *outrageous.*

No living being in the galaxy compared to the Advocate. His insatiable need for betterment had driven him to heights never before fathomed by organic *or* synthetic existence! And yet Gubora still cautioned him, telling him repeatedly to be *careful.*

He didn't need to be careful. He merely needed to take care of business—and the incident on Merutan made it evident his enemies were no match for him. They weren't even a match for *one* of him.

Tipping the scales would eliminate any resistance whatsoever.

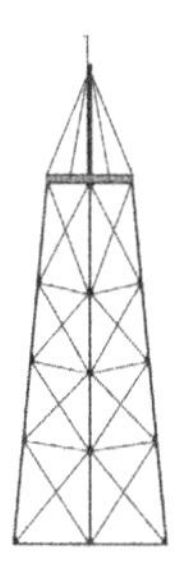

Chapter 28

Jag's eyes creaked open. Soft, whirring medical instruments murmured into his ears.

How long had he been asleep?

After the escape from Merutan, Bo claimed he knew exactly where to go to "lay low for a while." The adrenaline wore off once they hit warp; Jag doubled over in pain, almost *hearing* his ribs crack again. Thankfully, Bilanthia made quick work of his injuries.

Jag swung his legs over the edge of the operating table. Distant clinks echoed in to accompany the med bay's whir. *Zara* was otherwise still and silent.

The next eclipse hadn't even set in back home, and Jag had already been to three separate worlds. It'd been exciting, really. New planets, new people—and since he'd distracted himself through the quiet times, cramming his brain to prepare for what lay ahead, he'd barely stopped moving since they left.

But every successive blow from that operative knocked the reality of the situation back into him. He *wasn't* prepared—and he was clearly missing something.

First, the yellow man seemed to recognize him. Then the operative on Merutan said she was going to have to "come find him." And when Jag asked who she was, she laughed and flipped the question back—like she was mocking him. Did the Guild know something he didn't?

...or was it the Arbiters?

Back on Rixxon Prime, he was sure all the events were connected. Even now, with everything expanded beyond his own planet and frame of reference, that feeling was growing—and the clash on Merutan only made it stronger.

Because it sure as skies felt like some sort of twisted setup.

Aching all over, Jag put weight on his bare feet and felt an immediate twinge in his chest—again when he stretched his arms up.

What was he doing out here?

Grand purpose... fate... Elama definitely knew more than she was letting on. He needed to talk to her. He needed to know more.

Jag gripped the table's edge and stretched his legs back, marveling at the thin, white device arching over its metallic surface. This thing had somehow repaired his bones in almost no time at all.

It was incredible.

There was still so much he didn't know about the galaxy, about technology—about himself. How could he hope to make any difference? How could he possibly stop the Guild? He hadn't even met the Advocate yet, and he'd almost died *three times*. He was lucky to come out with just a few broken bones.

Wait. That operative said she had no intention of killing him. She said she had too much to... to what?

What was going on?

"We stand tall as trees," Jag recited to himself—but even that didn't work. His heart drubbed at his chest as the loudness clamored into *Zara's* quiet calm.

He needed answers.

Jag made for the open doorway. He'd barely given himself time to explore the ship, so stepping into the blue-tinted corridor felt foreign even though he'd walked up and down it a few times. He pressed a palm into the wall, focusing on the cool feeling against his skin.

Comm room—just down the hall. Treading lightly to avoid the pain in his ribs, he came to another open doorway.

Something startled him as he moved to step inside.

...laughter. It was just laughter. Sounded like Sixxis and Bo were having a good time up on the bridge.

"I really need to relax," Jag muttered, entering the comm room. He crossed a small, narrow bridge connected to a tiered, circular platform. Lowering himself carefully down each level, he descended the step-like rings until he came to a pedestal at the room's center. A thick, white line drew a hand on its glass surface.

Fingers splayed, he placed his hand inside the lines.

"Hello, Jag," emanated a warm voice.

He ripped his hand from the glass.

"...seriously," he sighed, touching the pedestal again. "What's wrong with me?"

"Hello, Jag. To whom would you like to place your call?"

"Elama."

"Very well, I will attempt to contact Elama Singh. One moment, please."

The door hummed shut behind him, cutting out all sound. Soft, indigo lighting illuminated the chamber.

Unsure what to do, Jag left his hand on the display and waited. Time passed, nothing happened. And just as he was about to say something, the voice returned.

"I'm sorry, Jag. Elama is unavailable at this time. Would you like to leave a message?"

Of *course* she was unavailable.

"Yes," he said.

"Begin speaking in three... two..."

BOOP!

"Wait—uhh." Jag cleared his throat. "Hi, Elama. We went to Merutan to head off the Guild, but they sent more than one operative and caught us off guard. We caused a real scene, but I'm the only one who got hurt as far as I know."

He paused.

"The operative talked like she knew me, or at least like she knew who I was. Do you have any idea how that's possible?"

Skies, Jag. He came into this all fired up and ready to set Elama straight, then had no idea what to say when it came down to it. She'd been nothing but kind and supportive so far. For all his suspicion and fear, he still couldn't help but trust her.

"I'm just a little confused," he said. "I was hoping you might have more information."

Jag lifted his hand from the glass. The lights extinguished, and the door opened.

How could Elama just turn him loose on this? He didn't stand a chance against that operative, even though she was way smaller than him. How do you beat somebody who's part machine? And how do you even *become* part machine?

"Surprised to see you up and about already."

Jag turned to find Sixxis leaning against the doorframe. "Oh—hey, Six. Yeah, I feel a lot better already." His mouth wrinkled. "I guess it's a good thing Elama found us a doctor. She probably knew something would happen."

"Something was bound to happen at some point." Sixxis crossed the bridge and hopped down to the central platform. "What's this room's deal?"

"It's the comm room. I just tried to contact Elama."

"Whoa—you can do that?"

"That what she said, but she didn't answer. I left a message."

Sixxis kicked at the pedestal. "Shit's wild, Jag."

This brought a smile to Jag's face—*exactly* what he needed. He could always count on his brother to lighten things up a bit. But that lightness faded quickly.

"Six," he said, "you've got to be more careful."

"What?"

"I..." Jag drifted around, turning away. "I thought I might lose you back there."

"Don't worry," said Sixxis, setting a hand on his shoulder, "it worked out, right?"

Jag shrugged his hand off. "It may have been that simple back home, but not out here. These people we're facing... they're way past us."

"If we stick to—"

"Just promise me, Six." He turned and locked eyes with his brother. "Promise me you'll slow down—that you'll *think* before you do things."

"I..." Sixxis shut his mouth and eyed his brother's face, then nodded.

"Thank you," Jag said, half-smiling.

Sixxis half-smiled back. "Soooo... how do your broken bones feel?"

"They're apparently not broken anymore, but they don't *feel* normal." Jag rubbed at his chest. "I can tell which ones are new. They feel... I don't know—young?"

"Young?" Sixxis repeated, lifting one of his fiery eyebrows.

"Like they're more sensitive—more fragile."

"Huh." He slotted a foot back and folded his arms. "Guess you'll have to be careful, too."

"Don't worry," said Bilanthia from the doorway, drawing the brothers' attention. "Your injuries are minimal—relatively speaking, of course. I will ensure you make a full recovery."

"Thanks," Jag replied with a smile. "Not sure what I'd do without you."

"Well you don't have to worry about that, do you?" Bilanthia returned the smile, then clapped his enormous hands together. "Anyway, I think it's high time we all got to know each other better. The Arbiters were wonderful enough to stock our mess with all manner of foods for the journey." He stepped back and gestured into the hallway. "If you would please join me, I've prepared a meal for us!

"Thank—"

Jag's gratitude was cut off by a series of resounding *THUMPS*: Sixxis' feet hitting the ground as he leapt up each level, one–two–three. "Yes you did! I'll go get Remy!" He tore off down the hall. "Bo! The doc made food!"

Bilanthia snickered. "It's like he's a child wrapped in the body of an intergalactic athlete."

"You don't know the half of it," Jag replied.

With another smile, Bilanthia again gestured into the hall. "Shall we?"

Jag climbed up the platforms and followed Bilanthia down the corridor. An intoxicating blend of smells seeped into his nostrils as they passed the holotable and entered the mess, where a collection of wide-bodied bowls littered the circular table. Thin, brown liquid bubbled up from a few; a thicker, yellow liquid filled a few others; and mounds of produce piled out of the rest in a wide array of colors.

"It is by no means extravagant," said Bilanthia, crossing to the counter and picking up a bowl of thorny fruit, "but it will help us recover from this first mission—and it will give us a chance to talk."

Not extravagant? Jag couldn't even begin to count the number of eclipses it'd been since he had such a feast. His mouth watered just *looking* at all of it—even though he had no idea what any of it was.

"Doc!" Bo said as he appeared in the doorway. "You shouldn't have!" He slammed into the largest seat and pulled a bowl toward him.

"But of course I did!" Bilanthia replied. "News from Merutan has hit the airwaves: The Dutans have secured the idol, and nobody was injured. So we have cause for celebration!"

Sixxis popped in next. "Don't eat it all without me, Bo!" He plopped himself beside the Quadmalian and dug right in.

Eager to eat, curious to learn more about his companions, Jag took a seat by Sixxis, as Remy arrived. She'd been alone in the engine room since they left *Assurance*. As far as he knew, this was the first time she'd even come up the elevator.

"Hi, Remy," he said.

"Hello." She stood still, clearly taking in the scene.

"How are you?"

"Fine, thank you." Leaving space between herself and the others, she chose the seat closest to the door.

"Everything you see is traditional Horranite cuisine," explained Bilanthia, leaning against the counter behind Jag. "Soups are widely eaten on Horran; they are crucial to replenishing body moisture in our dry climate."

"Don't take offense if I don't touch the yellow stuff," said Bo. "I've never been one for cold soup. Freaks me out a bit, honestly."

"Cold soup!" Sixxis scrambled for a bowl. "Just like home!"

"This looks great," said Jag, reaching for a round, purple fruit. "Thanks for—"

Sixxis belched. "Sorry," he said, grimacing, eyes shifting between his companions.

"I'm glad you like it, friend," Bilanthia said under a chuckle, his long, spindled fingers wrapped around the bowl in his hands. His expression then faded as he looked at Remy. "Will you not eat?"

"I do not care for soup—hot or cold."

"There's fruits and vegetables, too!" Bo rumbled through a full mouth.

"Fine," she said, grabbing a purple fruit.

Jag took his first bite—and *skies* was it incredible. "Bilanthia, do you miss your homeworld?"

"At times, yes. Horran is a beautiful place full of wonderful people." He placed his bowl on the table and sat down. "My home is not Horran, though—not really."

"What do you mean?"

"My home is and has always been my work. For some time, this work held me on Horran. I was the foremost authority on tissue regeneration and accelerated bone repair—as *you* now know firsthand—as well as advanced prosthetics, an exceedingly complex discipline given its strict galactic legislation."

"Strict legislation?"

"Combining organic and synthetic matter is a touchy subject for the Legislature. Limbs and the like are just fine—it's the mind where restrictions come into play. Basic artificial intelligence is one thing, but merging it with live thinking patterns is fully frowned upon."

"I have read of your work in prosthetics," Remy said as she eyed a wedge of bright-green fruit in her hand. "It is quite ingenious."

Bilanthia beamed. "Coming from you, that is perhaps the ultimate compliment! Eventually however, my work became able to automate itself. My days of helping people on my home planet were coming to an end." He stared forward, past Bo on the table's other side.

"Then a good friend of mine told me of wretched acts done by the Guild, and my path was laid before me. I abandoned medicine for politics."

"So Palatia became your home?" Jag said.

"Weren't you listening?" Bo ran an arm across his mouth. "He said his *work* is his home. Home don't gotta be a place! Take me, for instance: I ain't been back to Quadmal in almost fifteen years. I drifted from planet to planet until I came across my baby here." He bent back and stroked the floor. "Now home is wherever I want it to be—because home is *Zara*."

"Where *did* you get this magnificent ship, Bo?" Bilanthia asked, scooting forward in his seat.

"Found her in a junkyard on Korrignolan—pitted fools were gonna sell her for scraps! I pulled a loan from the Korrig Collective right away: enough to buy her, fix her up, and make her spaceworthy again."

Sixxis swapped his bowl for another on the table. "How much was your loan?"

"You let me worry about that," replied the Quadmalian with a wink. "Besides, I'm hopin' we take out the Guild, and the Collective just"—he snapped his fingers—"acts like nothin' happened."

"What about you, Jag? Sixxis?" Bilanthia scooted forward even more. "I'm eager to hear about your experience."

Remy—whose head was down—ran a hand through her hair and looked up at Jag. "I too would like to know more. I understand you hail from a Class V planet?"

Jag nodded. "We're from Rixxon Prime. Our parents died defending our village from invaders when we were kids. We escaped, but our people were scattered. We've been living on our own in the jungle ever since."

"Ah—hate t'hear that," said Bo. "Prolly tough to lose your parents and your people in one swing."

Sixxis gulped some soup, then slurped the leftover broth from his face. "It sounds all doom and gloom, but life on Rixxon Prime was pretty great! Clean air, beautiful trees—and Jag's the best brother I could ask for. I think I'm pretty good at a lot of things, but wherever I fall short, he picks up the slack." He grinned. "And then of course, there's Adira."

"Ohoho, *Adira*!" Bo repeated with a full mouth, leaning back, swinging his body around, and rocking forward. "You told me 'bout her." He swallowed. "Sounds like a quality gal. No *wonder* you were able to resist me so easily the other day."

"You're a beautiful man, Bo"—Sixxis pumped his brows—"but my heart is elsewhere. Adira, Jag, and me actually fought this legendary monster called the Thakk right before we left. It was epic!" He paused, then squinted. "Thakk," he said again. "Thakk."

"Six," Jag laughed, "are you broken?"

"You know," he said, "now that it's not a huge beastie trying to eat me, it's a really cool word. Super fun to say!"

"Hah!" Bo pounded the table, sending everything into the air for a moment. "Sounds like some sorta curse! Thakk this; thakk that."

"This is thakkin' great!" Sixxis joined Bo in laughter.

"You two just feed off of each other, don't you?" Jag said.

"Instant buds, we were," Bo replied, slapping him on. the back.

Bilanthia cleared his throat. "I would like to hear more about the monster."

"Oh *thakk*—it was awesome!" said Sixxis. "There were four of us, and Jag thought up this big plan right before we fought it. Then I almost died, but I was saved by this badass lady, Jade, and then we—"

"Six"—Jag gave him a shove—"breathe!"

With full, dramatic flair, Sixxis sucked in some air and let out a cleansing sigh. "Why don't you take it from there?"

Jag rolled his eyes. "We trapped the beast in a mine. Then when we got back to our people, Elama showed up disguised as one of us. She told me I'm from another world and that she'd been watching me for years."

"Intrigue!" said Bo. "What happened next?"

"She asked me to help her stop the Guild, which was responsible for setting the monster loose in the first place."

"That sounds too simple," said Remy. "Rixxon Prime is nowhere near any civilized region of space. Why would she watch you for so long? What is it that sets you apart?"

"Trust me: I've been asking myself the same thing."

Remy's brow furrowed. "Where is your homeworld?"

With a wrinkled mouth, Jag let a breath out through his nose. "I only know what I've just told you."

"So you have no idea where it is you come from?" Bilanthia clarified.

Jag shook his head. "All I know is that I've never met anyone like me."

"What about you, Remy?" Bo asked. "Where do you call home? Surely not Korrig—"

"I have no home." Remy burst to her feet and blew out of the mess.

"Welp." Sixxis belched again. "*That* was uncomfortable."

Bo's mouth twisted. "You talkin' 'bout the burp—or the Remy of it all?"

"Both?"

Their eyes met—and they exploded. Sharing in a raucous bout of laughter that echoed through *Zara's* metal corridors, they walked arm in arm out of the room.

Jag sat back.

What in the skies just happened? Was Remy okay? Maybe he should go check on her. It'd probably be good for them to talk anyway. He'd been wanting to—

"Home is a complicated thing," Bilanthia muttered, snapping Jag to the present. "I hope you find yours someday—before something happens to it."

"...before something happens to it?"

"Do you know why it is so rare to come across a Quadmalian?"

Jag shook his head.

"It is one of the most tragic events in the history of this galaxy," he said, raising his ridged browline. "But it is not my story to tell. You should ask Bo about it sometime."

"I... see."

Beaming horn to horn, Bilanthia clapped his hands together. "I'm glad we did this! It seems that whatever our reasons, we all hold nothing in this galaxy more important than this mission—and I am therefore confident we will hold true to each other and have the courage to succeed."

"I hope you're right," Jag said through a smile.

Bilanthia stretched out his limbs, splaying each of his fingers and toes. "Well, I think I'll lie down for a while.

"Not a bad—"

Remy appeared in the doorway. "I have intercepted another transmission," she said, locking eyes with Jag. "It calls you by name."

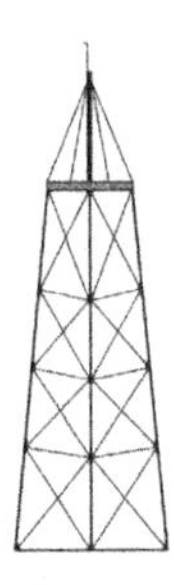

Chapter 29

"Hello, Jag. You've certainly piqued my interest.

"I would like to speak with you—and since I know you're listening, I cordially invite you to Polt. You may land in the valley just south of the main communications array. It's about the only structure on the planet visible from space, so it won't be hard to find.

"I merely wish to talk, so you are to come alone and unarmed.

"Don't dawdle, now. I would hate to see what happens to your green friends if you deny my invitation."

Jag teetered forward and propped himself on the holotable as Remy finished reading the message. "He wants me alone? And how does he know my name?"

"The Advocate is a true villain," said Bilanthia. "You cannot go alone."

"He's probably stronger than that Merutan gal, too," Sixxis added from the far wall. "I don't like the idea of you taking him on by yourself."

It was true. Jag got the shit kicked out of him just hours ago. Things would be even worse against the Advocate.

"If I may," Remy interjected, "perhaps this affords us an opportunity."

"What do you mean?" Jag asked.

"Your presence may distract the Advocate, allowing me to upload a virus through the dark relay."

"Oh thakk!" Sixxis bounced from the wall. "I totally forgot the dark relay was on Polt! Is that the communications thingy the message talked about?"

"Affirmative." Remy tapped her handheld, and the orange, ringed planet appeared above the holotable. "Under normal circumstances, it would be impossible to evade the planetary radar, reach the surface, perform the operation, and depart without detection. With you diverting his attention—and likely that of his planetside operatives—we may have the window of opportunity we need."

Bilanthia's ridged browline furrowed. "I'm not sure I like your use of the word 'may.'"

"With the virus uploaded into the network, all Guild communications will be sent into disarray."

"Really?" Jag asked. "Just like that?"

"Affirmative. It is quite simple."

"How do we do it?"

"*We* do not do anything. *I* simply need to access the tower's upper portion. There is a panel onto which I can plant a bug, through which I can upload the virus." She tapped her handheld, and the planet's image was replaced by a tower, its steel girders rising and tapering to a point above two flanking mountains. "The sole caveat is that Guild personnel will be able to reverse the virus should they find the physical location of the bug."

"So..." Sixxis tapped his fingers on the table. "If they find it, they can fix it?"

"Affirmative."

"What if we"—he brought his hands together, then made an exploding sound as he burst them apart—"blow the place when we're done?"

"That is..." Remy tilted her head. "Actually, that is a spectacular idea."

Sixxis leaned in and cupped his ear. "What's that you said?"

"Do not test me."

"Ah, leave 'er alone ya lunk!" said Bo, clapping him on the back.

"Once the virus is uploaded," she continued, "it will need approximately twenty minutes to infect the network."

Jag shook his head. "But he specifically said to come *alone.* He'll know if we show up together. I also have no idea how to fly."

"*Unity* has an excellent pre-programmable auto-pilot function," Bilanthia offered. "She can take you to the surface with the press of a button."

"What about that planetary radar?" Jag said. "Wouldn't it notice if *Zara* flew down there?"

Remy nodded. "That is our current obstacle. We must get to the surface undetected. Otherwise, the Advocate will likely kill you."

Yeah—Jag would've liked to avoid that.

He turned to Bo. "Any ideas, ace pilot?"

A corner of the Quadmalian's mouth curved into a wicked, sideways grin. "I've got a few tricks up my sleeve."

"Which one?" Sixxis asked.

Bo caught his eye and shrugged. "All of 'em?" And they erupted with laughter.

"Imbeciles," said a narrow-eyed Remy.

"What sorts of tricks are you referring to?" Bilanthia clapped his hands together. "I'm eager to see what *Zara* can do!"

"You'd prolly try to talk me out of it if I told you," Bo replied with a wink. He glanced at Remy. "You especially, little one."

"Please do not call me that."

How could they joke around so much? This was by no means a fun trip—couldn't they see that? After the fight on Merutan and how they left the plaza, there wasn't any room for error.

It was all devolving too quickly. Jag needed to get a hold of things before they got out of hand. He had to bring everyone together.

"Okay, Bo," he said, "keep the plan to yourself; we trust you. Remy, what's on the other side of these mountains? Can you pull the picture back?"

Remy nodded; as the tower shrank, more of the surrounding landscape materialized.

"How do you have all this stuff, Rem?" Sixxis asked.

"My Guild clearance gives me access to schematics of most active installations, as well as topographical maps of their planetary areas—or rather, it *did*. I downloaded everything I could when I arrived on *Pioneer*. It is likely the Guild will deactivate my logins once it learns of my defection."

"Pits," said Bo. "You think of everything, don't you?"

"Yes."

"Bahaha!" Bo all but fell over, clutching at his chest as his head reared back. "And brutally honest! Your whole deal really brings me back. I love it!"

Jag ran a finger along a narrow valley parallel to the one housing the tower. "Bo, could you get everyone here?"

"Looks like a smooth enough runway." Bo wiped a tear and pounded his chest. "You can count on me 'n *Zara!*" He looked at Bilanthia. "I'll need a copilot, Doc. Interested?"

He bowed. "I would be honored to get to know *Zara.*"

At least Bilanthia was easy; he was ready to help any way he could.

"Great," Jag said. "So Bo will get you all down, then you just need to scale the mountain and cross to the tower." He looked to Sixxis. "Up for a climb?"

Sixxis stepped up beside and mirrored Bo, pounding his chest. "Always!"

"I am quite able," said Remy, "but I am unsure how effectively I will—"

"Don't worry." Jag grinned at his brother. "He may not seem like the smartest, most capable guy, but he really knows how to climb."

"I'll make sure you get up there," said Sixxis, returning the grin. "No problem!"

"Very well." Remy nodded. "Jag, you seem to have a plan. What is it? I will not resist so long as I get where I must."

Sure, Jag had a plan—but it hinged on putting himself in probably his most dangerous situation yet. If the Advocate really was as unpredictable as everyone said, chances of getting out unscathed were pretty small. Still, Jag felt drawn to the man. He had since seeing Elama's first projection.

If the Arbiters couldn't give him answers, maybe the Advocate could.

Arms folded, he ran his tongue along his bottom lip. "I should limit my time on the surface—just in case. Bilanthia, could you get the autopilot set up and leave me behind? Would that work?"

"Absolutely!"

With a tap, Remy zoomed out until Polt and its surrounding bodies appeared. "We could leave you on this adjacent moon."

"Perfect! Then Bo will get you to the surface, and Sixxis will get you up the mountain. Let me know when you're there, and I'll fly down. Once the Advocate is distracted, you can use my cable arrow to get across to the tower."

"How do we blow the place?" Sixxis asked with a bounce in his heels.

"Plastic explosives," Remy replied.

"I'm in. Do we have some?"

"Yes."

"Do we have enough?"

"No."

"Can we make more?"

"Yes."

"Can I help? I'm pretty good with my hands. You'll just have to tell me exactly what to do—because I have no idea what I'm doing."

Remy glared at Jag, then let out an enormous sigh *dripping* with irritation. "Fine. But—"

"Yes!" Sixxis yelled, throwing a fist into the air. "I'll meet you downstairs." He tore off running down the hall.

Remy tapped her handheld, removing the images and bringing the lights back up. "It is as if he is an infant wrapped in the body of a capable athlete."

"Hah!" Jag doubled over. "That's *exactly* what Bilanthia said a bit ago!"

"Well, it is true." She walked off.

"I can't get a full read on her," Bo said as she left, "but I'm a big fan."

"Jag," said Bilanthia, "there's something about this that doesn't sit well with me."

"What's that?"

"To be blunt, I wish to know *why*—why has the Guild gone to such lengths to sow chaos? And how do they justify putting such operations in place on Class V planets?" He shook his head. "While the organization has hardly ever been reputable, this is a sharp redirect. Pert Gubora has never been one to take such risks as to interfere on lower-developed worlds."

"Could it be the Advocate?"

"Perhaps." Bilanthia rubbed at his cheek horns. "But things are seldom as shallow as they seem..."

He had *that* right. Jag was still racing to keep up with all of it. "I guess this is just one more answer I'll need to get out of him."

"Well"—Bo clapped Jag on the back—"Polt's not exactly close, so we'd better get moving. We'll need to go in and outta warp a couple times."

"In and out of warp?" Jag lifted an eyebrow. "Why?"

"Hah—you don't wanna fly into a planet, do you?"

"I'm sorry?"

"Traveling at high speeds is dangerous and must be done carefully," Bilanthia explained. "If we don't plot a specific course, we run the risk of hitting any number of objects in space."

"That makes sense," Jag said.

"And when there is no straight-line route that can get us somewhere, we must execute multiple jumps—again, to avoid hitting anything."

"Got it."

"We'll have time to kill while we're gettin' there," said Bo, again clapping Jag on the back. "I saw you on Merutan; let's just say you've got room to grow in the hand-to-hand combat area if you're goin' toe-to-toe with the Advocate." He laced and stretched his fingers forward, cracking probably all twenty knuckles. "I'd be happy to spar with you—give you a few tips."

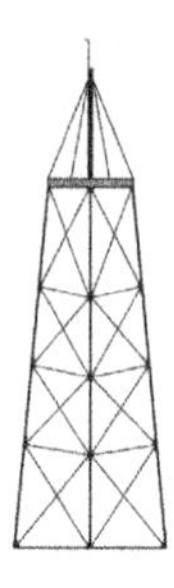

Chapter 30

Jag rocked to the left and threw up a forearm.

Combat wasn't exactly his strong suit. He was plenty athletic and strong, but back in the jungle, all he needed to do was hunt and climb. And even though he and Sixxis had trained at times—mostly when they were bored—he'd done more fighting recently than he had his entire life.

He got pretty lucky back on Merutan—that much was obvious. He needed to improve if he was going to survive.

At the doctor's orders, Jag spent their first warp jump resting, recovering from his injuries. The whirring med-bay arm helped him sleep, much needed help given his mind's rapid, spinning anticipation of meeting the Advocate. As they made the second jump, he got up and moving. He tried Elama again—she of course didn't answer—then stretched out every muscle he could, eager to get to his practice. And with the third jump, they got started. They'd been sparring in the cargo bay since.

"Aha—nice block!" Bo flicked a thumb across his nose. "Let's see if you've really learned." He threw a series of quick punches.

Right, left, left, right, Jag blocked four blows and ducked a fifth before—

"Gotcha!" Bo froze, fist inches away from Jag's injured ribs. He stepped back, pulled a towel from his waistband, and wiped it across his brow. "Prolly enough for this session."

"Thanks, big guy," Jag said, doubled over, hands propped on his knees.

Bo clapped him on the back and sent him stumbling. "Don't mention it! With any luck, we'll keep you alive a few more days. Bahaha!"

"Do be careful, please!" said Bilanthia, pushing himself from the wall beside the elevator. "We don't want any reinjuries."

"I'm okay," Jag assured. "Bo managed to avoid hitting me where it hurts."

"I'm here to *help*"—he slammed onto the metal floor—"not *hurt*."

Jag rubbed at his new arm bruises. "You didn't exactly pull your punches."

"Oh, I didn't?" Bo leaned back on his upper arms, folded his lower, and winked. "Hah—a'course I did! You're not ready for the full strength of a Quadmalian. It's legendary stuff!"

Bilanthia caught Jag's eye as he shuffled forward and sat on the steps. "With everything that's happened, I'm glad you so proudly represent your race."

"Bo," Jag said, also taking a seat, "I'd love to hear more about your homeworld—if you're willing to talk about it, of course."

The big man lifted an eyebrow. "Why the sudden interest?"

"Well, I've heard the history is..." His mouth wrinkled. "Tragic."

"Ah, so yuh've heard." Bo sighed. "Yeah, it's not the happiest of tales. The biggest bummer is that Quadmal was an outstanding place one day. Now it's nothin' more than a toxic wasteland."

"Toxic?"

He nodded. "Ain't nothin' been able to survive on that planet since it all went down."

"What happened?"

Bo squinted and eyed Jag, like he was inspecting him.

"Is something wrong?" Jag asked.

"Nah—just confirmin' something. Sure you wanna hear the story? It's a real downer."

"I'd like to get to know you, Bo." He smiled. "It sounds like we might have some similarities."

"Hah—did someone just decide one day that your mere existence was too much of a threat and then poison your planet?"

"No, but people *did* attack my village in the dead of night when I was a kid."

"Ah—I didn't mean no harm by that." Bo scratched his head. "I don't really handle tough conversations well; never have."

"You don't have to tell me anything you don't want to," Jag said.

Bo waved him aside. "Nah, I'm okay. Somethin' 'bout you made me comfortable real fast, and we Quadmalians—"

"Pride yourselves in being very perceptive?" Jag lifted a single eyebrow, drawing a grin from the big guy.

Bilanthia flexed his spindly fingers on the floor and started to stand. "I can leave, if—"

"Nah, you're good, Doc. The way you greeted me when we first met... it meant a lot. Ain't a lotta people who care to respect our customs."

Bilanthia smiled. "If there were sides to choose—or rather, had I been with the Legislature when there *was* a side to choose—I would have fought for your people 'til the end."

"I know you would've," Bo said, grin returning. "You know, it's a big deal I let you touch *Zara's* controls back on Merutan, even in that crazy situation. I don't trust many people with my baby."

"I'm honored," Bilanthia replied with a kind nod, "and I cannot wait to get to know her further."

"Anyway, back to Quadmal—sorry, Jag."

"No problem." Jag leaned back and mimicked the big man's sitting position.

"So, we had it all: Our people were innovating, our planet was thriving, and it'd been some twenty years since the last planetside conflict. More and more every day, the biggest brainiacs of my kind were growing our tech leaps and bounds."

"What sorts of things were they doing?"

"Building stuff, mostly—like *Zara* here." He caressed the floor. "She's a Quadmalian build."

"I knew it!" Bilanthia's eyes widened. "My apologies; please continue."

Bo winked at him. "It wasn't all sunshine, though. Remember how I said it'd been twenty years since the last planetside conflict? Well, we'd been feuding with the folks next door for five. Then everything changed—forever."

Jag tilted his head. "What happened?"

"We signed an armistice. The war was over."

"That sounds good!"

"It was—until it wasn't."

Bo pounded his fist into the floor.

"After five years, the fighting stopped—and just five days later, those *criminals* broke the truce." His fist started to tremble. "I remember like it was yesterday. I was out and about, doing a little a' this and a little a' that, when a ship popped into the atmosphere above the capital. Next thing I know, a weird gas starts filling the place; everyone starts coughing."

Jag gasped.

"Everyone panicked. Then I saw someone drop dead, so *I* panicked. Those who could flooded the spaceport and got out of there. I didn't have a ship, so I hopped on a freighter."

"Did you ever go back?"

Bo shook his head. "No point. Errybody was either gone or dead."

"I have seen analyses," added Bilanthia, squeezing his big eyes shut. "Some of the gas lingered close to the surface. Whatever drifted higher into the atmosphere liquified, rained back down, and seeped into the ground. In just hours, not only was the air virulent, the soil was completely desolate."

"What about your family?" Jag asked.

"Never saw 'em again. After a while, I could only assume they were dead. And then..." Bo flopped onto his back, letting out an enormous sigh. "I don't know all the details of the rest of the story. Doc, maybe you can fill him in?"

"The consularship of Klyshal—that's the neighboring planet—appealed to the Legislature. They told tales of the war, painting the Quadmalians as savages through stories that have since been debunked."

"That doesn't seem fair," Jag said.

Bilanthia nodded. "And it was made worse by the fact that—due to the scattering—there were no Quadmalians present to submit their side."

"So what happened?"

"At the close of their appeal, the Klyshalians claimed that due to the combination of these 'aggressive tendencies' and its clear physical, intellectual, emotional, and mental advantages, the Quadmalian race was too dangerous to be kept intact. The Legislature voted in favor, and no aid was given to the scattered people. The Quadmalians were thus doomed to wander the stars, scattered with no hope of returning to their homeworld."

"Just like that?"

Bo pounded another fist. "Damn right, just like that! And now everywhere I go, people are scared a' me before they even meet me! S'why I cover my arms when I'm out and about."

Jag's mouth wrinkled. "But I thought the stories were debunked?"

"And there," said Bilanthia, standing and brushing his hands down his frock, "we see the issue of information in this galaxy. Despite being refuted by scholars, historians, and ethnographers alike, the Klyshalian claims were far too detailed and incendiary. They spread like wildfire—a wildfire that has yet to be put out."

One of the engine room doors whooshed aside. "No," said Remy, walking out.

Sixxis came out after her. "Pleeaaase?"

She grunted. "Will one of you *please* tell this *infant* that we cannot test an explosive while on board the ship, let alone at warp speed?"

Bo's body seized inward. "You try'na kill us, Sixxis?" He rocked side to side, roaring with laughter.

"Fine," sighed Sixxis, looking down and kicking a foot. "I'll wait."

"Good." Remy looked to Jag. "We have created enough explosives to destroy the tower."

There it was—the task at hand. Entranced by Bo's story, Jag had almost forgotten they were headed to Polt. He'd almost forgotten that he'd soon face the Advocate.

Alone.

BOOP BOOP.

"Guess we're about there," said Bo, sitting up.

Sixxis offered a hand. "Up you go, big guy."

"Remy," Jag said, "are you ready? Do you feel nervous?"

"Negative."

"Really?"

She nodded. "While this is certainly a stressful circumstance, I find my comfort in factual information."

Jag's mouth wrinkled.

"The Advocate murdered my sister and continues to wreak havoc across the galaxy," she said, looking him dead in the eye. "He must be stopped—it is fact—and I..." She paused. "*We* are the only ones who can do that." She turned and headed for the elevator.

Facts. What were the facts?

The Advocate sent people to Rixxon Prime. They released a horrifying monster that feasted on the mountain folk. And when the operative at the farm saw Jag, he paused—like he *recognized* him.

On Merutan, the first operative killed several people without thinking twice. The second picked a fight with Jag, Bo, and Sixxis in broad daylight, in the middle of a crowd of people, with no hesitation or regard for life.

She too acted like she knew Jag—and like he didn't know himself.

"Ready, brother?" Sixxis put a hand on his shoulder.

Jag's gaze floated up from the ground, to his brother. "Ready."

Ready to get to the bottom of this.

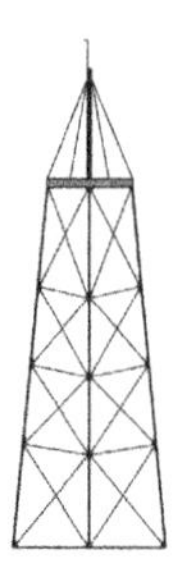

Chapter 31

Remy sat back in her seat, focus fixed forward through *Zara's* front glass. Jag was in position, the autopilot programmed, and the explosives packed, ready for placement. All that remained was the descent, which Remy felt apprehensive about until moments ago.

Now, staring at the orange planet floating before them, she felt... nothing. Sheer emptiness invaded her being, like the fog she had not experienced since Jag provided the truth behind Omeka's death. Even the anger—which consumed her perception and defined every moment thus far on this voyage—was gone.

Then something trickled in: fear.

She feared the blackout, the full departure from consciousness that occurred the moment she finished packing up her apartment. In essence, she feared herself, the absence of reality her mind might create without her consent.

"Here we go," said Bo, pressing *Zara*'s thrusters forward, directing her toward the planet's ring.

Sixxis sprang forward and grabbed the underside of the pilot's seat. "Why are we going into that stuff?"

"All part of the plan," replied Bo, fist in the air. "You'll prolly wanna buckle up."

Sixxis backpedaled as *Zara* dipped into the floating dust. "What is all this?" he asked, crumpling into the chair beside Remy.

"Rock, ice, and dust, mainly," she replied, eyes glued forward—the only direction that promised reprieve. "As you can see, the particles range in size, from microscopic bits to those as large as mountains."

"And we just needa find—ah, that'll do!" Pressing into the controls, Bo steered toward a larger space rock in the distance. "Doc, it's time," he said, pointing below him. "Hop down in that chair and do as I say."

Bilanthia hustled down the side staircase and took his place with eager haste. "Ready for instruction!"

The doctor had an air about him, one much different from any politician Remy had ever encountered. It was surprising, despite his immediate claims of being unlike his colleagues. He in fact seemed quite sincere, much like Sixxis, like Jag, even Bo.

These men... they were kind, respectful, decent—divergent from most people Remy had met in her life. Even Sixxis—a manchild who seemingly never stopped moving or speaking—acquiesced to her request and kept silent for the duration of their work on the explosives.

"Jag," Bo said, carefully maneuvering through the belt, "still good over there?"

"Good over here!" Jag replied.

"Okay errybody"—Bo laced his fingers, stretched all four arms forward, and cracked what must have been every joint in his hands—"hold on to something."

Remy gripped her armrests. "What exactly are—"

"Just trust me, my blunt, blue friend." He flicked a switch. "Doc, I'm activating the radar. Keep an eye; make sure I don't hit anything."

Sixxis pressed back into his chair with a grin. "I'm excited to see the show, Bo!" he said as *Zara* drifted forward, narrowly avoiding the floating debris. "I don't know how you—"

BANG! Something struck *Zara* as she came to rest before a rock twice her size.

"Gah! Oh well; we're here now." Bo pressed a button on the panel above his head. Two cylindrical fixtures raised up from either side of his feet, buzzing and humming until they stopped beside his torso. "Keep her steady, Doc." He inserted his hands into the cylinders, then called over his shoulder, "Sixxis, you're gonna love this."

The ship shook, as *Zara's* lower front sides jolted from her metallic frame. And as Bo raised his arms perpendicular to his body, she mirrored his movements.

"Whoa!" Sixxis hollered. "This is wild!"

Bo lifted his arms overhead and waved them side to side. "Pretty cool, huh?"

"Pretty cool!? It's like she's dancing!"

"I've heard of Quadmalian technology," said Bilanthia, "but this beats any story!"

"She's a special lady," Bo replied, bringing his arms down.

As the front end of each metallic arm split apart, *Zara's* clawed fingers splayed out. Open-palmed, she pressed her hands toward the massive space rock.

"Pop!"

Zara kicked back, blasting hunks of rock in all directions.

"Okay, commentary time's over." Bo cracked his neck to one side. "Gotta focus."

Her claws balled into fists as the last of the loose rock scattered. Slowly, they floated forward into the two holes left behind.

"Keep an eye on the map, Doc; use the side exhaust thrusters to position us so we land five clicks east of the relay."

"Ten-four," Bilanthia replied.

"Incredible..." Remy muttered.

"What was that?" Bo called over his shoulder, a savage grin stretched across his face. "Did I manage to impress our smarty-pants engineer?"

"Trajectory set," Bilanthia reported.

"Awright, I'm gonna engage the rear engines here in a sec. Things are gonna get wonky, Doc; just keep track of our heading and make whatever adjustments you can." He cocked his head back to the two observing passengers. "Try not to puke when we hit the atmosphere, 'kay?"

Sixxis' grin matched Bo's.

"When I give you the signal, Doc, engage the lift mechanism. Got it?"

"Keep our direction consistent and wait for the signal." Bilanthia nodded. "Ready!"

"Here we go!" Bo bent his lower arms at the elbows, and *Zara* did the same. He then increased the engine power with his upper arms. And together, he and *Zara* began pushing the rock toward the planet.

"What's he doing?" Sixxis asked Remy.

"The planetary radar detects all objects entering the atmosphere, but it is likely to ignore a falling meteorite; it is not uncommon for such objects to crash into the planet's surface."

"Won't they know we're there when we get closer?"

Remy's back pressed harder into the seat as *Zara* picked up speed. "Negative. Given the mountainous terrain of the region, their systems will be unable to detect our presence so long as we stay low to the ground."

"My thoughts exactly!" Bo called back. "Now hold on!"

He snapped up at the elbows as *Zara* broke the atmospheric shield: her back end swung under them until it pressed into the falling rock.

"Hah!" Sixxis bounced in his seat. "Now I get why you said something about puking!"

Bo pulled a handle toward his body. "Powering down just enough to keep us flush."

The further they fell, the faster they flew. Gleaming in hazy sunlight through *Zara*'s front glass, the planet's features multiplied and grew on the horizon.

"This is thakkin' great!"

"Bahaha!" Despite his focus, Bo's head reared back. "Sixxis, you kill me with that thakk thing!"

"Impact in fifteen seconds," relayed Bilanthia, tapping at his screen.

Bo rolled his head around. "On my count. Three... two... one... NOW!" He threw his arms forward. Outside, *Zara's* limbs did the same.

They pushed off the meteorite and flipped backward.

"Engaging the lift!" Bilanthia said as he jabbed at buttons and pulled back a lever.

"Crunch time!" Bo ripped his arms free and put all four hands to work. "Starting the engines—hang on!"

Remy's body rattled side to side as the red-rock canyons twisted and turned in front of them: *Zara* barrel-rolled until she was upright, flying away as the meteorite pounded into the ground behind them.

"Pull up!" Bo yelled, yanking the controls toward him. "Sending power your way, Doc!"

An immense force crunched Remy's body into the chair.

"Roger that!"

She popped up, then squished into the seat again.

"Ahahahaha!" Sixxis hollered beside her. "This is a blast!"

Another pop.

"What are ya doin, Doc?" said Bo.

"Short bursts! I'm not convinced she can handle sustained redirection!"

Remy bumped about in her seat as the lift mechanism boosted them upright. And as everything stabilized, they slowed to a manageable speed.

"Yeeaaaah!" Sixxis trumpeted. "*Thakk*, that was incredible!"

"I now understand why you insist your vessel is more than a ship," Remy said behind a slight smile. "That was quite impressive."

"If my count's right"—Bo threw up two fingers—"that's *two* compliments from you in a short time. I'm on a roll!"

"Do not get used to it."

"Hah—never would!"

Stripes of red, orange, white, and tan soared by both sides of the window as they progressed through the pass—Remy's first time on the lonely planet in what felt like a lifetime.

A lifetime without Omeka.

"We will arrive at the eastern base of the mountain adjacent to the relay shortly," Bilanthia reported.

Zara flew forward a ways, then slowed to a stop and lowered to the ground. *Hiss!* Exhaust flew out from her body, spewing orange dust everywhere.

"Here we are: Polt." Bo's seat rotated and lowered, depositing him onto the main platform. "Thank you for joining us today on Bo-Ram Spacelines. I hope you enjoyed your ride!"

"That was incredible!" Sixxis threw off his restraints and rocketed to his feet. "How many times have you pulled that off?"

"Well..." Bo winked. "That was the first time I tried it."

"What!?" Bilanthia spouted as he scurried up the steps.

"I told you it was crazy—and that you'd try to talk me out of it! Besides, I knew it'd be fine with a co-pilot." Bo clapped Bilanthia hard on the shoulder, throwing him forward. "And you were brilliant, Doc!"

These pleasantries and celebrations notwithstanding, they had work to do. And the longer Remy sat, the less likely she was to stand under the weight of the expectations she had set for herself: she would see to the Guild's destruction, to the Advocate's demise.

It all started with the relay.

"Let us go." Rising to her feet, she turned for the lift platform.

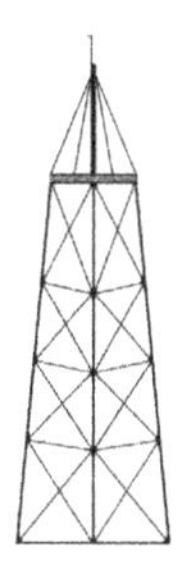

Chapter 32

Zara's cargo ramp lowered, kicking up dust and bringing Polt's quiet surface into full view. Its terraced, flat-topped mountains were unlike anything Sixxis had ever seen—but that was no surprise; he'd only ever seen the pointed peaks of Rixxon Prime.

Skies, he hadn't seen much of anything, really—but after what *Zara* just did, he bet nothing would ever surprise him again!

"This place is beautiful," he said.

"Not to me." Remy hoisted a bag over her shoulder, clomped down the ramp, and started for the mountain across the way. "This is merely the location of my sister's murder."

"Uhh, right."

Thakk.

That wasn't how Sixxis wanted to start this. He'd been looking forward to the climb, to some one-on-one chat time with Remy—especially after the silent hours they spent working on the explosives. It took everything he had to keep quiet.

The mountains loomed overhead as he jogged after her. Squatty, pale-green bushes peppered their path up a dusty slope, toward the first vertical face. And a series of plateaus showed the way from there, their rusted colors extending into the burnt-orange sky.

This was going to be an easier climb than Sixxis thought!

"I can get us up this stretch real quick," he said, stopping. "I'll take your bag." He took and pressed it to his chest, then stepped in front of Remy, crouched, and pointed to his back.

"Excuse me?" she said.

"Hop up and hang on tight!"

"Oh man, this I gotta see," said Bo.

Sixxis rotated to find their two crewmates standing on *Zara's* ramp, watching. "No time to lose, Rem," he teased.

With a sigh, Remy clasped her arms around his neck. "Is this really the best—"

Before she could finish, Sixxis charged up the slope's soft dirt, bounded from the ground, and touched down on the first terrace. "The gravity's even lighter here! This'll be *fun!*"

Remy clutched him tight. "I request a warning next—"

He danced up another level, then another. With the next a ways ahead, across a field of small boulders and gnarled trees, he crouched to let her off. "Sorry; thought I'd just get that out of the way."

"We should get moving," Remy said as she dropped to the ground. "I will take my things."

"I don't mind carrying. It's already—"

"I will take my things."

"Seriously, Rem, it's fine—I don't mind helping. You've... you've been through a lot." He bent down and ran a finger through the dust. "I bet it's not easy being here."

"I am fine."

Squinting at her, Sixxis brushed past and started across the plateau, waving a hand over his shoulder. "I don't believe you."

"Wh—what?" she said, stumbling on both her feet and words.

"Bo and I've been talking; we're worried about you." And that was *before.* Sixxis had noticed an *extra* bad energy coming from Remy since they dropped off Jag.

Her pain—it was *palpable!*

"It's just gonna be you and me for a while, so there's no sense hiding it."

"I—"

"It's okay, Rem—I get it." His feet scraped to a stop. "You and your sister were on your own for a long time, and you feel alone now that she's gone." His head lifted up the cliff ahead. "I don't know what I'd do if I lost Jag..."

He turned to her and smiled. "You're not alone, though—not anymore."

"You cannot begin to under—"

"Try me."

Stuck in the middle of a word, Remy's mouth was open. She shut it slowly. And even more slowly, she brought her eyes up and down Sixxis' tall, lean frame.

"You like what you see?" he asked with a grin.

"No," she scrambled, shaking her head. "I—"

"Oh lighten up!" He gave her a shove. "We're fine. I know I'm not your type."

"No." *Finally*—she smiled! "You are not."

"So," he said, starting again for the cliff, "tell me about your sister." He stopped after a few steps, when he realized Remy hadn't moved. "Are you coming?"

"Yes; I apologize." She walked toward him. "I... have been meaning to thank you."

"For what?"

"For being respectful when I asked for silence."

"Oh." Sixxis waved her off. "I get it. Jag needs quiet to concentrate sometimes, too." He turned and walked beside her. "You two are pretty alike, you know."

"How so? I do not see it."

"Well for starters, you're both terrible at asking for help. You act like you're the only ones who can do this and that. Sure, sometimes it's true, with you especially—you're thakkin' brilliant—but you could *definitely* stand to rely on us more."

Remy kept her focus forward and didn't respond—but this was nothing new for Sixxis. He'd learned years ago when to give Jag the space he needed to think. She clearly needed that right now.

After five minutes, they came to another cliff. "This one's too high to jump," Sixxis said, craning his neck up the towering crag. "I'll have to climb."

Remy nodded.

"Gimme just a couple minutes!" Bending at the knees, he sprang up onto the wall and grabbed hold. The weaker gravity made the ascent easy from there. Still, Sixxis knew there wasn't much room for error on this mission—and he sure as skies wasn't going to be the one to blow things, not after his conversation with Jag about Merutan—so he was intentional with every move. Hand, hand, foot, foot—in a few minutes, he pulled himself up onto a ledge.

Phew!

Turning, he basked in the beautiful expanse. Distant craters dipped into the earth, their red colors accentuated by green and blue tufts scattered across the landscape. Already *Zara* looked so small.

It was wild. Rixxon Prime, Korrignolan, Palatia, Merutan, Polt—he'd been to five worlds now, and they were all so different. But nothing came close to home.

Home...

Really, Jag was his home; that'd always been the case. But now that they were away from Rixxon Prime, he missed it more than he thought he would—probably thanks to Adira.

Hopefully she was okay.

"Sixxis," said Remy.

Whoops—back to it!

He dropped the pack and rooted around until he found Jag's rifle and quiver. Loading the cable arrow, he aimed straight down. "Coming your way!"

Remy sidestepped as his shot almost hit her.

"Sorry."

"It is fine." She wrapped the cable around her wrists and put her feet on the wall. "Ready."

"Comin' up!" Sixxis cocked a foot back to stabilize himself, then clicked the button. And as Remy came whizzing up over the cliff's edge, he grabbed her hand to help her up. "Easy!"

"Yes," she said, brushing dust from her thighs. "Well done."

"Shall we—"

"I learned long ago that people let you down. Omeka is the only person I've ever truly relied on."

"Well, from what I know about you—which isn't much—you haven't been around many great folks in your life, have you?"

"I suppose not."

"I'm pretty great."

Remy scowled, but then her face twisted into a half-smile. "You are a child."

"Shit's more fun that way," Sixxis said with a shrug, turning his back on the dropoff. "Oh look—there's a bit of a trail, and it's not too steep. We can do the next stretch on foot."

She nodded. "Lead the way."

"You got it!" Slinging the quiver and rifle onto his back, bag onto his chest, Sixxis started up again. "Ready to talk about your sister?"

"What would you like to know?" she asked, falling in behind him.

"What was she like?"

"She was the opposite of me in many ways. In many others, we were the same."

"Sounds like Jag and me. How were you opposites?"

"Almost to a fault, she was kind, and she exuded warmth. She..." Remy sighed. "I would not be alive were it not for her, and I can never tell her that."

"She knew."

"Sorry?"

"Just trust me: she knew."

"I do not—"

"You don't really get how emotions work, do you?"

"In the Guild, emotions only get you into trouble. I saw it time and time again with Omeka. She would express herself, get taken advantage of, and I would need to protect her."

Well that explained a lot—and *oof* did it sound familiar.

Sixxis skidded to a stop. "You gotta let yourself feel, Rem. All that stuff just sits in your body—I'm convinced of it." He started to walk again. "It's probably why you're so tense all the time."

"I am not tense."

"Yes you are," he doubled down, waving a hand over his shoulder. "Just like Jag."

"Jag is tense?" Remy jogged to catch up. "I do not see it."

"He internalizes a lot, but I know what's really going on. He's about to go see the Advocate—and *thakk* is he terrified! But he'll never say anything. Like you, when he knows what needs to be done, he'll *always* do it."

"I... see."

Their conversation died down again, this time for ten minutes or so—long enough to reach the next face.

"It's creepily quiet here," said Sixxis, breaking the silence. This one looked like a harder climb—definitely longer. "You mind hanging onto the bag?"

"No."

"I'll pull you up in a bit," he said, dropping the pack.

"Very well." Remy folded her arms and leaned against the jagged cliff. "Do not fall."

"Was that a joke?" Sixxis asked with a grin.

She threaded two fingers through her hair and flicked it to the side. "Perhaps."

"Hah!" Planting his foot on a deep ledge, Sixxis began to climb.

So Remy was *finally* opening up! Good thing—because the more Sixxis learned about her, the more similarities he saw between her and Jag. The two of them could *definitely* help each other in ways Sixxis couldn't. If he could just get them to—

His foot slipped.

"Wh—whoa!" He squeezed his holds to keep from falling.

That was thakkin' close!

Turning his brain off—he needed to be more careful—Sixxis continued his climb. He pulled himself onto the next-and-final ledge several minutes later.

A ways ahead, beyond the massive dropoff on the plateau's other side, the tip of the relay tower rose above him.

Guess it was time.

"Jag," he said, "we're up."

"Got it! Heading down."

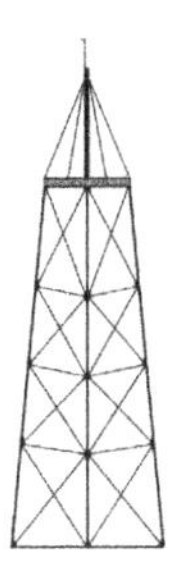

Chapter 33

Remy grabbed Sixxis' helping hand as the cable brought her over the cliff's lip. "Thank you," she said, stabilizing herself and striding across the plateau.

Before her stood the tower.

It was almost... familiar, the way Sixxis had been talking to her. Only one other in her life had ever communicated with such candor: Omeka. Perhaps this distinction, this similarity was the driving force behind what she was now thinking—what she was now *feeling.*

Was it?

Yes... Remy felt *comfortable,* a sensation she all but renounced the moment she learned of her sister's death. But now she somehow did not doubt Sixxis' claims that she could rely on him. And she somehow felt closer to Jag.

Jag...

She had taken him for granted thus far in their voyage, that much was certain. It was quite impressive that such a being—one who just recently had his entire identity turned on its head—could be as effective as he had on the galactic stage. Not only that, but he remained *excruciatingly* kind and accommodating at every turn despite Remy's hardened exterior.

That exterior drew itself from her time in the Guild, memories her return to Polt had dredged to the surface. It was a time when nothing mattered but survival—a time she spent constantly alert, always honing her capabilities so as to keep her sister alive as well as herself. And so she developed her mind, playing into her natural gifts as she furthered innovation for the organization she now despised with every fiber of her being.

She placed a foot close to the edge and leaned out over the gap. It was a sizable drop to the surface; one false step would surely kill them. She would need to keep an eye on Sixxis.

Did she... *care* for him?

"So Rem," he said, dropping to a seat on a nearby boulder, "I just realized that after spending hours with you building these things, I have no idea how they work."

"They are made of a malleable substance that acts as a strong adhesive: It will stick to virtually any surface with little effort on your part. You merely need to disperse them evenly about the tower"—she pointed downward—"especially on the lower sections."

"Easy enough. How do we make them"—he exploded his fingers and puffed his cheeks.

"I have detonators for each; however, if you space them efficiently, we need only trigger a chain reaction."

He flopped backward. "Sounds like a lot of pressure. Can I just shoot Jag's explodey arrows at them?"

"I suppose that would work fine."

In a way, Sixxis astounded Remy. He was... easy; overwhelming at first—but easy.

The unmistakable sound of *Unity* bursting through the atmosphere disrupted the dusty scene's calm. Her white-purple frame flickered on the burgundy backdrop as she swooped down the mountain range, looped around, and came to a gentle hover at the valley's far end. There, she descended in place, pressing into the dirt with a delicate bounce.

"If I may." Remy lifted the crossbow-rifle from the ground and fired across the gap, fastening the cable to the tower's metal frame.

"Nice shot!" said Sixxis. "Jag, we're crossin' over. You good down there?"

"Yeah, I'm fine."

"Do you see any movement?" asked Remy.

"No, not—wait. Someone's coming out the front door."

Remy whipped the compressed sniper rifle from her lower back, clicked the extender button, and zoomed in on the front door. It did not take long to confirm Jag's report: leagues below, the Advocate approached *Unity,* the white-armored operative at his side.

"Jag," she muttered, "that is him."

Just then, more people emerged from the building, these ones wearing traditional black armor. They marched forward in a perfect double line behind the Advocate and his operative.

Fear re-entered Remy's consciousness, this time not for herself—but for Jag.

"I already count nine operatives," she said. "I do not know what he is planning, but I would advise staying in *Unity* as long as you can."

"Good idea."

She turned to Sixxis. "We must make haste"

"Haste is what I'm best at!" Sixxis shot up and coiled the cable around his boulder, then approached the cliff and dropped to a seat. "See you over there!" Grabbing the wire, he lowered himself to a hang, wrapped his legs around, and proceeded across.

He truly *was* a child wrapped in the body of a capable athlete. It was impressive how fluidly he moved when one minute mistake might spell his demise. He was quite fearless.

Remy's intelligence was far too exceptional to advance across the gap in such rudimentary fashion. After stowing her rifle, donning a waist harness, and grabbing two powered ascenders, she heaved the bag onto her back and returned to the precipice. There, she fastened to the cable and lowered herself off the edge, then attached and activated her ascenders.

Effortlessly, she whizzed across.

"That was neat," Sixxis said as she dropped to a beam.

"Indeed." She bent over and clicked a button on her boots, humming them to life.

"There's twenty down there now."

"Then we have no time to lose," Remy said, handing him the pack. "I will upload the virus; you plant the explosives." She crossed the metal girder, then placed her foot on the connecting vertical beam and walked up it.

Sixxis scratched his head. "Uhh—what?"

"I am sorry?" Now upside down, Remy came to a stop. Her black hair dangled and drifted in a subtle wind. "I thought you would enjoy planting the explosives."

"Oh, I'm *thrilled* about that. I just don't get how you're doing... *that*."

"Doing what?"

He bent to the side, tilting his head until it too was upside down.

"Oh." Remy approached him. "My boots are magnetized, much like the arrow tip. Now please hold still." She reached into the pack for her handheld. "I will meet you back here in twenty-five minutes."

"You got it!" With the utmost grace, Sixxis bounded down three levels of girders.

Remy drew a deep breath and turned her attention upward. The tower's steel frame surged into the sky, to its pointed apex. From that apex, a thick rod protruded downward—her target.

Her magnetized boots made the ascent rather easy; she reached the horizontal beam adjacent to the rod's base before long. Crouching, she disengaged the magnetization, stowed her handheld, and drew another deep breath—then launched herself, rotated midair, and engaged her boots to stick safely to the central rod.

"Thakk, Rem—that was incredible!"

"Please maintain your focus." A series of red, blue, and yellow lights blinked at varying speeds above her. "Jag, I will begin uploading shortly. We will need at least forty-five minutes."

"Forty-five minutes—I can do that."

Could Jag do that? It felt like a tall order given the circumstances.

The Advocate had come to a stop a ways ahead, his metallic dome glinting through the swirling dust. The Merutan operative stood tall in her small frame just behind him, as the double line filed out from her position to form a wide arc.

"Six, any chance you've got an updated count?"

"I'm getting Fifty—plus the Advocate and the gal in white."

Fifty!?

Jag shifted in his seat, courage sapped away. If the Advocate really just wanted to talk, why bring fifty troops? What was this about?

What had Jag gotten himself into?

As the operative lines stopped moving, the Advocate's deep, commanding voice boomed, "Jag? I know that's you in there. Are you coming out?"

Heart racing, Jag ran through the quick button sequence Bilanthia showed him to verify the programmed return trip. "We stand tall as trees..." he mumbled to himself, eyes closed, running his hands along his thighs. He tried drawing deep, controlled breaths to slow things down—but it was no use.

"I'm sure this is a bit outside what you expected." The Advocate stepped forward and gestured to the arc behind him. "I know what it looks like, but this is in no way a threat. Think of it as a grand reception!"

Grand reception? Yeah, these people *definitely* knew Jag.

Now or never.

Flipping a switch, he stood with *Unity's* opening glass, then swung his legs onto the ladder lowering from her side. With hesitation in every step, he counted the rungs until he pressed a foot into the ground.

Would he get off this planet alive?

"Welcome to Polt!" said the Advocate, throwing his arms up and wide. "It's not much as far as planets go, but it has its beauties."

Jag approached the black-armored villain slowly, but confidently. He was in no way ready for this, but that didn't matter: He had a job to do. He needed the conversation to last as long as possible.

And he wanted answers.

The Advocate clapped his hands together. "I'm excited to finally get to know you."

Finally get to know him? What did *that* mean?

"Oh, lighten up!" he said, hands dropping to his waist. "No harm will come to you here."

Dust settled around Jag's feet as he stopped. "I don't buy that, given that she"—he nodded to the white-armored operative—"tried to kill me a few hours ago."

"*There* you are! I was beginning to think you weren't going to talk." The Advocate tossed a hand to the side. "And didn't you hear? We had no intention of killing you."

Jag narrowed his eyes. "Why did you call me here?"

"Did you even *listen* to the message?"

"Yes."

"Then you know I just want to talk!"

"I just... find that hard to believe."

"Ah." A smirk stretched across the Advocate's lips. "I think you'll soon find it hard to believe many things."

Jag's mouth wrinkled. Where was this going?

"All in due time," continued the Advocate, turning away. "And if talking doesn't interest you, perhaps we can call it something else: an information exchange"

"Information... exchange?"

"Yes. As in, I tell you something, you tell me something." He glared over his shoulder. "As in, this *can't* be a one-sided conversation."

Jag folded his arms. "What sort of information could you possibly want from me?"

"Oh, I assure you: we have quite a bit to gain from each other."

Well—*that* statement all but confirmed the Advocate knew Jag somehow. And it was clear the guy *loved* to talk. Maybe Jag's job wouldn't be so hard after all; just keep him going.

And maybe he'd finally get some answers.

"Who are you?"

"The answer to that question became a tad complicated recently, which leads me to what I wish to share with you. But first"—the Advocate spun to face him—"who are *you*?"

There was that question again.

"Jag."

"And where do you come from?"

A soft breeze swirled a mess of red and brown into the air.

"Oh come now, no reason to be difficult! How about this: I promise to answer your questions truthfully, and you do the same. *We* promise to always be honest with each other."

"Sounds fair." If Jag could trust him.

"Excellent! Now, where do you come from?"

"Rixxon Prime."

"Lie!"

Jag tilted his head, inspecting the curious-but-menacing man. This was far from what he expected. It almost seemed like the Advocate was leading him on to something—like he was guiding the conversation.

"Interesting..." said the Advocate. "So you really *don't* know."

"Why do you talk like you know me?"

"Because I do—or rather, I *did*." Again, the Advocate turned his back. "You see, you and I come from the same place, millions of light years away from here." His head drifted up and off into the distance.

"What place is that?"

"Earth, Jag. You and I are from a planet called Earth. And we—or rather *you*—are *human.*"

The information hit Jag with all the force of his first warp jump. "How do you know that?"

"It's astounding, I know," replied the Advocate, splaying and stretching his fingers toward the sky. "I just learned this myself." He made a fist and brought it close. "You see, I was once a human named Garrison Trapp, sent from Earth on a lifelong mission to make contact with other sentient species."

"What do you mean you just learned this yourself?"

"Hmmm..."

"Well?"

"I suppose I *did* promise honesty. It will feel good to say it out loud anyway." He cleared his throat. "My memories go back eighteen years. Thanks to my robust filing system, I know the precise date my existence began."

"...filing system?" Jag repeated.

"Don't play dumb with me!" shouted the Advocate, whipping around. "I know your new friend, *Remy Troyer*, has deduced by now that my appendages and I are partly synthetic beings."

Jag's eyes widened. "I don't know who that is."

"Tsk tsk tsk," clicked the Advocate, shaking his head. "You promised to be honest—"

The white-armored operative snapped her sidearm and pointed it at Jag.

"—and you're a terrible liar. I'll give you one more chance to play by the rules."

"Jag," said Remy, "it is all right."

Hesitating a moment, Jag nodded.

"*Thank you!* Anyway, I recently came in possession of some video files created before my databanks—video files of *me.*"

"Where did you get them?"

"When you caught me off guard during the fight at the farm, you triggered something in me—something deep. I'd... seen you before. You were clearly from offworld, so I went looking for information."

"Hang on," Jag said, waving his hands in front of his chest. "I'm confused. I didn't fight you at the farm."

The Advocate grinned. "As a matter of fact, you *did*—just like you fought me on Merutan."

"You're not making any sense. We've never met."

The Advocate placed a hand on his hip and eyed Jag up and down.

Was he... waiting? Waiting to be asked?

"Well?" Jag grunted. "Are you going to tell me what you're talking about?"

"To put it simply," said the Advocate, turning his back again, "I have transcended common existence." He lifted his hand to the sky—his other hand this time. Its steel shell glistened in the hazed sunlight.

It shone the same as the metal from Rixxon Prime.

"I have become more than *myself.*"

Jag's eyes held fast to the steel hand. "What do you mean?"

"It'll be easier to show you." The hand balled into a quick fist—and every operative in the arc dropped to a knee, drew a weapon, and pointed it at Jag.

He jumped back and threw his hands in the air. "What the—"

The Advocate's laughter roared through the valley. "I am them," he declared, turning to Jag.

The operatives snapped upright.

"And *they* are *me*."

"Impossible..." Remy muttered.

Jag shook his head. "I don't understand."

"Collective consciousness, shared intelligence—call it what you will."

"A hive mind," Remy concluded.

"What does that mean?" Jag asked, staring straight into the Advocate's eyes.

"It means we share the same neural network. It means *we* are *one.*" He threw his arms into the air. "Oh, it feels *incredible* to tell this to someone! For too long has my genius gone unrecognized!"

"You've never told anyone?"

"Most minds cannot hope to comprehend what I've become."

Jag surveyed the arc, giving brief pause to each operative. "Are they..." He continued sweeping his eyes down the line. "...alive?"

"In a manner of speaking. They retain their individuality and are technically alive, but their minds lie within my Intelligence."

People—they were *people*!

"Don't worry. All were either volunteers or near death."

Near death...

A pit rose in Jag's stomach as his gaze fixed on the shortest operative—the one with a tuft of black hair sticking through a crack in her white helmet. "Who was she?"

"Aha—you really are sharp! *She* is my greatest appendage, second only to me." The Advocate turned and placed a hand on her shoulder. "It's a shame Remy isn't here to see how great you've become—isn't it, Omeka?"

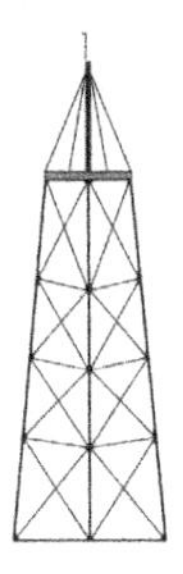

Chapter 34

Something snapped inside Remy.

Like his operatives, the Advocate was partly machine—that much was no surprise. But to learn that he had developed a functioning hive mind… it was unfathomable. Such technology was theoretical at best, and that only pertained to synthetic neurological fusion across short distances. The monster had mastered this, *and* integrated it with his own *living* mind. What's more, he had taken the minds of many others.

Including Omeka.

Without hesitation, Remy swung around the rod, drew her rifle, and zoomed in on the surface. A seemingly impossible distance away—on a different world entirely—the operative removed her helmet to reveal a sapphire-blue head. Metal plating covered one side, messy black hair the other.

"Skies, Rem," said Sixxis, "is that really her?"

"Yes." There was no mistaking it. "Or rather it *was* her. I do not know *what* it is now."

It was *vile.*

"What do you mean? She's got to still be in there, right?"

"I… do not know."

"Hang on," said Bo. "Did Remy just say she don't know?"

"If it's anything like the theories," added Bilanthia, "this is not good."

"What is it?" Sixxis asked.

Remy kept her scope glued on the Advocate. He stood there, gazing lovingly at Omeka as if she was his child—as if he *loved* her.

It was *revolting*.

"To my knowledge, hive mind technology exists only in theories—like the doctor said. Essentially, all parts act on behalf of the singular, central mind." She shuddered. "I now understand why the Advocate refers to his operatives as '*appendages.*'"

"I don't like that one bit," Bo said.

A burning rage began to rise from the tips of Remy's toes. "The Advocate has enslaved these people." The fire rose up through her stomach, spread past her chest, and flowed down her arms. "He did not just murder my sister; he turned her into his *pet.*"

The fury seeped into her trigger finger.

"I will *kill* him."

"Whoa, Rem!" Sixxis hopped beam to beam, quickly rising toward her. "Jag's down there. You gotta cool it!"

Cool it—she could not do that. The fire was too hot.

"Plus they'll know we're up here once they kill Jag—and we're not exactly set for a quick getaway."

Slowly, she began to squeeze

"What are the facts?" Jag asked.

The facts...

The Advocate murdered Remy's sister. He turned her into an abomination and took control of her mind. He also did this to at least fifty others, and he has been the direct source of pain and suffering across a multitude of star systems.

Remy's finger began to relax.

Because there were fifty-one other instances of him, shooting him now would accomplish nothing. He would survive, and they would surely be killed.

She closed her eyes.

They were the only ones capable of stopping him, and their best chance was to upload the virus and detonate the tower. If she fired, it would result in catastrophe for that goal and for all of them.

With a deep breath, Remy stowed her rifle.

Even from afar, staring down the Advocate—having *just* learned of his true origins—Jag had shown compassion to Remy. His active attention rested on her despite his own perilous situation.

Sixxis... Jag... it had been some time since Remy felt so... *cared for.*

DING!

Remy took in another deep breath. “Thank you, Jag. The upload has finished. The network will be infected in approximately twenty minutes.”

Twenty minutes.

“The facts?” laughed the Advocate.

“Y—yes,” Jag stuttered, hesitating, distracted by Remy’s state of mind. “The facts. How is it that you were human, but now you’re... this?”

“Ah—*this* is where the exchange happens.“ The Advocate pulled his hand from Omeka’s shoulder and rushed toward Jag. “I was hoping *you* might help *me* answer that question!”

Jag took a step back. “Me?”

With an enthusiastic nod, the Advocate put an arm around him and started walking. “I traced my metalloid scanner to a downed escape pod buried in that sticky mess of a jungle you call home. That pod’s launch point brought me to a set of coordinates, where I found video files of—“

He stopped.

”—*Garrison.*”

“So?”

Dropping his arms, the Advocate drifted forward without Jag. “It’s... disconcerting to see images of yourself and not remember.” He lowered to a knee and pressed a hand into the dirt. “I see what’s happening, and I hear what’s being said—but I don’t *remember.*” His fingers scraped through the sand. “I don’t *feel* what I must have felt.”

“I still don’t get how I can help.”

“Ashley.” The Advocate flipped his hand, tossing sand aside as he popped to his feet. “Garrison speaks highly of Ashley.” He looked Jag dead in the eye. “Tell me, where is she? Where is Ashley? I...” His gaze fell; his steel hand trembled. “I would very much like to see her. I think she can help me understand—help me fill in some gaps.”

Jag’s eyes narrowed. “I don’t know who or what you’re talking about.”

“Ashley?” He took a step forward. “Your mother?” Another step. “I know you both made it to Rixxon Prime. That escape pod was yours, and there’s no way you survived on your own!”

"My mother's name is Mara. She died defending my village."

"*Ashley.*" The Advocate's head twitched. "Your *human* mother." His tone swelled with intensity. "*Where* is she?"

Jag shrugged.

"You," he grunted. "You aren't making this very easy." His fingers tensed, balling into fists. "*Quit withholding information*. You *must* contribute to the exchange."

Jag couldn't stall any longer. "She's dead. I don't remember anything about her."

"She's... dead? Ah!" The Advocate doubled over and collapsed to a knee, pounding a fist into the ground. "How is that possible?"

Feigning disinterest, Jag shrugged again. "All I know about her, I read in a journal."

"And what *do* you know?"

"She's buried somewhere on Rixxon Prime."

The Advocate's head lurched up. "The clearing! I suppose I'll have to head back to that overgrown planet regardless of what happens here today."

"What do you mean?"

"It all rests on you, Jag," said the Advocate, floating upright. "Don't you want to know the truth behind your past? Where you came from?"

Of course he did—it was *all* he wanted.

"I can help you, and you can help me."

Right—as if the Advocate wouldn't kill him when he wasn't useful anymore.

"If you would just... let me in. Let me unlock your subconscious and find the memories buried deep inside you. Together, *we* can discover what happened."

"What happened?" Jag repeated. "You mean you don't know?"

"My files are merely video journals. They don't explain anything beyond what Garrison chose to share, always looking over his shoulder, worried others were listening. You and I—the only humans for 2.5 million light years—*we* can learn the truth."

Humans... *They* were humans.

What were the odds that Jag's one enemy was the only other of his species he'd met—that he'd probably *ever* meet?

"I've seen it in the videos, Jag. You were born on the ship—on *Shuriken*." The Advocate's head twitched. "In merging our minds, you'll have access to all that footage. You can know them as I once did."

Jag's... family. His *real* family.

The possibilities flooded his mind. He'd finally found what he'd been looking for: The truth behind his identity. He wasn't Rixxonian. He was *human*—from Earth. And from what it sounded, his mother was—

Wait.

"Are you my father?"

"No. Garrison made it clear he was not your father." The Advocate gripped at his forehead as his head twitched again. "In fact, his mood soured quite a bit when you were born."

His mood... soured?

Jag stood tall. "What happened to my parents?"

"I don't know."

"What happened to my parents?" he repeated with more intensity.

"I told you: I don't *remember*."

"Well, you say you don't remember. But the way I see it, you're the only one who survived—and you turned out to be a murderer." Jag tore forward and shoved the Advocate. "How do I know you didn't murder *them?*" He shoved him again. "What happened?" Again. "What happened to my parents?"

"I *told* you..." Face in hands, the Advocate shuffled backward—then threw his head to the sky, screamed, "I DON'T REMEMBER!" and buried his bionic fist into the sand.

The earth trembled beneath Jag's feet, as a profound silence descended upon the valley.

Then came the Advocate's deep, heavy breathing. "This is your last chance," he said—as every operative in the arc snapped to attention. "Join me—*help* me—and I won't just gift you with capabilities beyond your wildest dreams—I'll leave your precious Rixxonians alone."

"Radar indicates multiple ships exiting the rear of the relay," Bilanthia reported.

"You're lying!" Jag said with a scowl.

The Advocate exploded from his position. "You insubordinate, insignificant piece of shit!" He grabbed Jag by the arm, whirled him about, and tossed him aside.

Crashing into the solid, unforgiving ground knocked reality back into Jag. Making the Advocate angry wasn't the best tactic—skies, it was probably the *worst* thing he could've done.

"I don't need your consent," the Advocate muttered.

There it was—the catch. He never had any intention of letting Jag go.

"We'll settle this cleanly," he continued, drawing his sword and dropping it in the dirt. "No weapons, no tricks. Just you and me."

He laughed.

"I'm going to enjoy this. You meddled in my affairs on Rixxon Prime, disabled two of my operatives, *and* caused a scene on Merutan. That last one in particular is making things rather difficult for me."

"I'd say sorry"—Jag pushed to his feet—"but that would be a lie."

"Hah—a backbone. More for me to shatter!" He charged.

Diving from harm's way, Jag rolled and sprang to a ready stance.

"Good," said the Advocate. "You *are* better than you showed on Merutan."

Jag prepared himself as the Advocate lunged and threw a hook at his cheek. He blocked and absorbed some of the blow's strength—but it pushed his arm into his head and bent him sideways. Whirling around to redirect, he flailed at the back of his assailant's knee.

The Advocate buckled forward, then swung at Jag's thigh—but Jag had already followed the momentum of his attack, landing in the dust a safe distance away.

"Impressive," muttered the villain, circling him. "It seems that jungle has made you quite capable. I'm sure it was difficult keeping up with those *fascinating* Rixxonians." He grinned. "They'll make *perfect* additions to my regiment—*especially* the one from the farm!"

"No no NO is he talking about Adira!" Sixxis hollered.

"Leave Rixxon Prime alone!"

"Do not let him get to you, Jag," said Remy. "We need five more minutes."

Jag took a deep breath.

"I am *exceptional*—I will do what I please!" Bounding side to side, the Advocate leapt into the air and brought his shining, steel arm hammering down. The bionic fist sunk deep into the sand, just missing Jag as he jumped to the side.

Jag then clamped and crashed his hands down—but *BONNNGGG!* The Advocate's metallic neck covering sent a throbbing pain up his arm.

So much for that.

Scrambling, he kicked the Advocate in the face. The force shot the villain upright—just so he could cock his fist back, bring it squarely into Jag's chest, and send him flying backward.

"Don't you see?" The Advocate stood tall, cracking his neck to both sides. "You can't win."

Jag recovered quickly enough to land standing—but not quickly enough to dodge the next attack: He regained his balance only to be swept off his feet—and *THUD!* His back slammed into the ground. Then the glaring sun dulled as another strike plunged toward him; he rolled out of the way. Two more blows rained down, and he just managed to avoid them.

Then—noticing a window of opportunity—Jag heaved his foot into the Advocate's crotch.

He took a staggering step back.

"So," Jag said, stumbling to his feet, "you *do* still feel pain in some places."

"*That* was a mistake."

As the Advocate launched a barrage of punches, Jag crossed his arms, covered his face, and balled his upper body to try the trick he learned from the Merutan operative: with one leg slotted behind him, he swayed side to side, taking each hit and looking for an opening in the attack pattern.

And he found it!

Pivoting, he drove his foot into the Advocate's kidneys—just like Bo taught him—and found more soft tissue!

But the Advocate caught Jag's leg after just a moment of recoil. "You!" He torqued it hard to the side, sending him spinning through the air and crashing into the ground. "You've made my life very difficult, and—"

His head twitched, freezing him in place.

Then he drifted upright, lifting his gaze into the distance. His breathing grew heavier, pushing out his chest with every inhalation. "Your existence..."

He nodded slowly, then faster.

"It *bothers* me." The Advocate yanked Jag from the ground, tossed him overhead, and caught him in a wide-arm spread. "So I will end it!" His maniacal laughter echoed through the valley, joining with Jag's agonized screams as he bent him in all the wrong ways—almost pulling him apart—then crouched and heaved him forward.

His strength all but gone, Jag rolled a ways and flopped to a stop. There he lay, motionless.

"Jag," Sixxis muttered, "you okay?"

"Yeah—just buying time," he whispered, holding in a cough. "I don't know how long I—"

"What's that you say?" The Advocate cupped his ear and leaned in. "You'll have to speak up."

"Two minutes," said Remy. "We will detonate as soon as we can. That should draw his eye enough for you to escape."

The Advocate's boots stomped a cloud of dirt into Jag's face. "Taking a break?" He kicked him in the stomach. "Get up!"

Hacking and wheezing, Jag squeezed himself into a tight ball. After another moment—still buying time—he stretched back out and staggered to his feet. "There's one thing I don't get."

"What's that?"

"If you really *were* human, how did you become... this?"

"My earliest memory is of Pert Gubora going on and on about how incredible I am, how I'm the advocate of a new race—one that for the first time in history combines man and machine to perfection." A wild grin flashed across his face. "And as you know—"

Each operative in the arc took a commanding step forward.

"I have expanded my existence. I have become *better*, and I am no longer alone!" He threw a right hook.

Jag ducked the first punch. With another flying toward him, he ducked again. And when the third came in, he whisked to the side, grabbed hold of the Advocate's outstretched arm, and tried to whip underneath—but he was fading fast.

And his opponent wasn't even winded.

With seemingly no effort, the Advocate pulled his arm in and threw Jag to the ground. "This is all humanity can muster?" he said, clapping in slow, sarcastic applause. "Pitiful."

"I'm—"

The Advocate's foot plunged into his stomach. "*You* are done talking."

Flat on his back, energy depleted, Jag couldn't do much as his attacker straddled and wailed on him. He managed to block a few hits, but it wasn't long before his strength gave out. He took several hard blows to the face—until with what felt like his last effort, he caught the Advocate's fist

"Still some fight left in you?" A smug expression buzzed over the villain's menacing, metallic face. "We can't have that!" He brought his steel hand down onto Jag's left wrist—and *CRACK*—snapped it in two.

Jag hollered out in agony.

"I have a shot." Remy rotated the rifle's focus, sights locked on the Advocate.

In the valley below, the biomechanical monstrosity pounded Jag into the ground. The indoctrinated behind them were not watching—because they *were* him. They simply stood there, lifeless husks of their former selves.

It was *sickening*.

Sixxis heaved the bag onto his back. "What if you miss? You might hit Jag, then he'll know we're here."

"That will not be a problem." Remy had no intention of shooting the Advocate himself. At this point, removing any of the operatives would cause him the same pain—that is, any but *her*.

One minute.

Yes... Remy would do it. It was what needed to be done. And it would send a message—a message that she was coming for him.

Closing her eyes, she took a deep breath and redirected her aim.

Forty-five seconds.

Jag would not last forty-five seconds. She would need to fire early to divert the Advocate's attention, but not so early that he would have the chance to turn back and kill him.

"Sixxis, are you ready? I will buy extra time."

"Yup!" he confirmed, holding up the crossbow-rifle, explosive arrow loaded.

Remy drew another deep, controlled breath—and pulled the trigger.

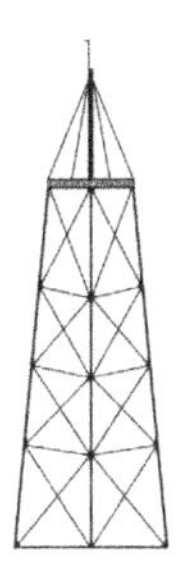

Chapter 35

One second, Jag was sure he'd die. The next, the Advocate was gone.

Rolling onto his side—his body pressed into its newly created ditch—he creaked an eye open and spit out a mouthful of blood.

"No!" On his knees across the dirt, the Advocate lifted Omeka's head from the ground.

What... happened?

"You were my greatest work." He squeezed her arm, as a tremor surged up his own. Soon his entire body convulsed.

...did Remy shoot her sister?

"You!" The Advocate whipped his head toward Jag and leapt to his feet. "You didn't—"

A cracking explosion echoed through the valley, engulfing the tower in a cloud of fire, shooting its pieces in all directions.

Everything was happening too fast. Jag couldn't comprehend it all.

"Remy," said Sixxis, "how do we—"

"Parachute."

"What?"

"Jump and press the new button on your collar!"

"What the—whoa!"

Sixxis, Remy... they were all right. The Advocate—where was he?

Jag blinked as hunks of metal rained down from the sky, almost in slow motion. The operative arc had disappeared—no, that wasn't right. It'd collapsed onto the Advocate's position.

Were they... protecting him?

"Jag, get outta there!"

Sixxis?

Jag rolled onto his back.

Sixxis... he was right. Jag needed to—

A steel girder came screaming toward him.

"Skies!" Brimming with sudden adrenaline, Jag rolled to the side—as the girder slammed into his ditch.

Too close.

He planted his hand in the dirt, pushed himself up, and limped for *Unity,* moving as fast as his broken body could—as *CRASH! BANG! THUD!* Debris smashed into the ground around him.

Not far now. Just a little—

He stopped.

Omeka... he couldn't leave her.

Jag turned and picked up his pace with a painful grunt. All but dragging himself, he hobbled past the huddled mass of operatives and came to a stop beside Omeka's body, where he dropped to a knee and threw her over his shoulder with his non-broken hand. Then he shuffled off with wreckage falling all around him.

In what felt like an eternity—but couldn't have been more than a minute—Jag made it to *Unity's* ladder and started his labored climb. Rocking back and forth, contending with Omeka's jostling body every time he released and grabbed the next rung, it took everything he had to make it to the top. And when he did, he flopped her into the backseat and tumbled in after her, then clamped a hand on the pilot chair, pulled himself up, smashed the autopilot button, and collapsed back.

ACT II

Part Three

The Race to Rixxon Prime

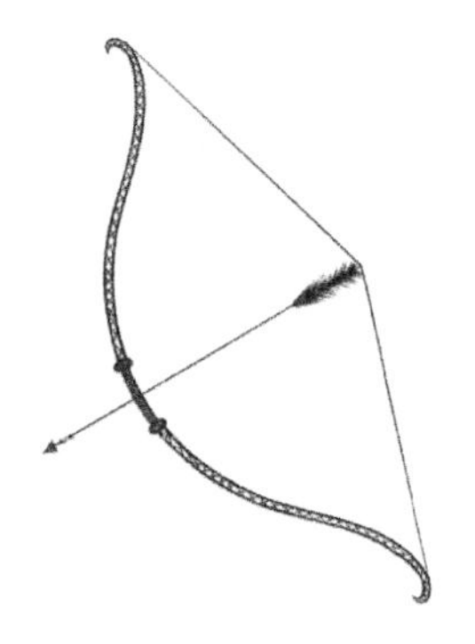

Chapter 36

Unity's interior hissed as she lowered to a soft bounce on the moon—at least that's where Jag *assumed* they were.

The moment *Unity*'s glass shut, the violent dissonance faded to muted thuds, giving way to the frail sounds of his labored breathing. In, out, in, out—every motion pained his body as they fled the dusty canyon. So he just lay there, heaped on Omeka as black consumed the orange sky, its endless void swallowing everything he thought he knew.

He'd left it all—not that he ever had much—to come out here in search of the truth behind who he was: his identity. Now he'd found it, but it'd left him broken and more alone than ever.

Earth...

What if there really *was* no hope of ever seeing it? What's worse, not knowing where your home is, or knowing it's completely inaccessible?

...or what if the Advocate was lying?

It's not like he had a real reason to be honest with Jag. It was probably just some elaborate trick.

No, that couldn't be it. There was something about him—something about the way he was during the conversation. It almost seemed like he snapped, like something broke loose inside him. And he knew things nobody else knew.

Jag shut his eyes again, washing his internal black over the black of space.

That downed pod must have been the orb from his mother's journal. Had the Advocate gone there? Was it him, or was it one of his... *appendages*?

"Jag." Like a far-off, unattainable comfort, Bilanthia's voice waded through the shroud of his perception. "Can you activate your breathing apparatus?"

Did any of this matter? The biggest thing here was that Jag and the Advocate were the same: they were both *human.*

"Jag," Bilanthia repeated.

Blinking awake, Jag found the doctor's covered face above him, on the glass' other side.

"Your helmet," he said.

With a nod—and without moving otherwise—Jag engaged his helmet. As the glass then swung open, Bilanthia climbed over the lip, leaned on the seat, and pressed some device into his forehead—then gasped.

"Is that..."

"Yeah."

Bilanthia's brow furrowed. "I see."

"I'm sorry."

"For what?"

"I got a little"—Jag winced at a sharp pain behind his eye—"I didn't get the answers you wanted."

"That's quite all right," Bilanthia replied, pulling the device back and inspecting it. "We should get you to the medical bay immediately." He turned and activated the engines.

"What did you do?" Jag muttered—painfully.

"I detected your injuries from your brain signals."

"How am I looking?"

Bilanthia sighed. "You're concussed. And you have a broken wrist, three cracked ribs—plus rebreaks to the two you injured on Merutan—multiple microfractures in your face, and a sprained knee."

"Hah." Jag coughed. "Is that all?"

Before he knew it, *Zara's* dark-blue interior painted over the black canvas above him. *Unity* came to a gentle landing in the cargo hold.

"Errybody onboard?" Bo said through the comm.

Bilanthia pressed a button on the console. "Yes, we're all here."

"Awright—settin' course for Rixxon Prime!"

"Rixxon Prime!" Jag yelled, shooting up at the waist as the cargo door shut.

"We heard everything." Sixxis bolted from the elevator and jumped up to them, clacking his feet onto *Unity's* metal frame. "It was about as open a threat as he could make."

"And it's a long trip," Bilanthia added. "You will have plenty of time to rest."

"...thakk, Jag." Sixxis pointed below his brother.

Jag nodded and tried to push himself up. Wobble-armed, he didn't make much progress.

"Let me help," offered Bilanthia, swinging his feet onto the ladder. He guided Jag to the side, off Omeka's body.

"I'll—uhh..." Straddling the passenger area, Sixxis pulled Omeka up by the legs and cradled her. "Jag are you"—his head tilted—"why are you looking at me like that?

Remy had emerged from the engine room behind him, her face paled a lighter shade of blue. "...you have brought Omeka."

"I couldn't leave her there," Jag said, smiling as much as he could.

"I..."

"I don't know how you"—Jag shut his eyes, wincing at a twinge in his chest. He breathed in, then out. "Thank you. I'm not sure I would've survived those last few seconds."

"It is..." Remy's voice drifted away, then faded back softly, "...you are welcome."

"You okay, Rem?" Sixxis asked.

"I... am fine."

"Do you think you could learn about that hive thingy through Omeka?"

"Six!" Jag lurched toward his brother—and immediately regretted the sudden movement. "Give her time."

Sixxis walked forward, bent at the knees, and hopped down. "Sorry," he said, presenting Omeka to Remy. "I guess I'm a little nervous about what happens next. I thought if we could get into his head, we could get ahead." He snickered. "Heh—get into his *head* to get *ahead.*"

"You are impossible," Remy said, narrow eyed.

Jag wobbled to his feet with Bilanthia's help. "You don't have to—"

"No," she said, looking past Sixxis. "It is all right. Time is not something we have at the moment. The Advocate is unpredictable, and he will certainly be angry after this encounter." Her longing gaze fell on her sister. "It is our only option."

"Only if you're sure," Jag said.

Remy closed her eyes, then nodded. "Sixxis, please follow me." She turned and reentered the engine room, with Sixxis and Omeka right behind her.

Hopefully she was okay.

Jag's worry for Remy swirled with his already mounting thoughts. He didn't know why, but somehow they were harder to control than ever.

He was human. The Advocate was human. They were the same. How was it possible? What happened all those years ago?

"Hang on, all," boomed Bo's voice. "We're making the jump in three... two..."

Jag gripped hard on the pilot's seat. The hangar shook as *Zara* launched forward.

He'd been deceived. This was all too coincidental—too connected. Did Elama lie to him? Did she know?

Jag loosened his grip and turned to Bilanthia as the ship stabilized. "I need to get to the comm room."

"You need to rest," Bilanthia replied with a raised brow.

Suddenly, the pain all surged at once; Jag doubled over.

How could he keep going? The Advocate was clearly too strong for him—and now there were over *fifty* of him. If this is how Jag fared in a one-on-one battle, what could they hope to accomplish?

Was everything lost?

Sixxis' voice trickled in. "I'll help with Jag."

Help—Jag needed help. He needed to talk to Elama. He needed answers. But he'd already tried contacting her twice; she hadn't answered.

Had she abandoned them?

"Up you go." Sixxis folded an arm around Jag's back, scooped his legs, and stepped up onto the ship's body. "This might hurt a bit." He lowered to a seat and dropped down.

A sharp pain shot into Jag's head as they hit the floor.

His mother—he finally knew her name: Ashley. What happened to her? How was it they both escaped, but only he survived?

None of it made sense.

Sixxis stepped into the elevator. "I can't believe it—*Earth*. We finally know where you come from!"

Bilanthia joined them without a word.

"Who knew the Advocate would be from the same place?" Sixxis continued. "What do you think about that?"

What did Jag think about that?

"I don't know."

The elevator doors shut, trapping them in the tiny box, constricting his reality.

"I hope you're not in your head too much about it."

In his head? Of course he was in his head! What was Sixxis even saying? Jag's entire world had been turned upside down! Everything he knew, everything he was—he'd lost his identity.

It'd been consumed by the Advocate.

"I'm fine."

"You and Remy might be pretending to be fine, but I'm not. Nothing's fine, Jag—and that's okay to admit. Some real shit just went down, and you can't downplay it like you always—"

"Stop."

"We can get through this—we can get through this together!"

Jag's eyes rolled back in his head as seemingly every blood vessel in his body tried to burst from his flesh. His breathing turned shallow; his throat closed up. He was cold—no, he was hot—or maybe both.

Every step he took since their hunt assaulted his brain, fear of his impending doom devouring each one. Had he come this far—all this way—just to lose everything?

The elevator door's sharp edges dulled as they opened. Soon everything was blurry.

He was dying. He had to be dying.

"Jag, you okay?" Sixxis asked, quickening his pace.

Jag's breathing picked up even faster. Each gasp for air felt like his last.

"Hurry!" Bilanthia shouted, rushing into the med bay. "Get him onto the table!"

Sixxis hustled through the door and laid Jag down, as Bilanthia came to his side with a small syringe. "Focus on my voice." He plunged the needle into Jag's neck. "Block everything else out. Just breathe."

Jag's jumping veins calmed instantly. But he couldn't stop his chest from rising, falling, rising, falling. It was too fast—too much. He just wanted it to end.

A knifelike pain pierced his head, contorting his face.

"Breathe," said Bilanthia. "Let yourself rest."

The pain subsided; his face relaxed.

"That's it. You're doing great. Stay focused on my voice."

Blinking wildly, Jag did everything he could to shut out his thoughts and do as the doctor had ordered. His blinking slowed in pace with his breathing, and soon everything faded away.

Chapter 37

Tearing into his workshop, an automated cart trailing his hurried steps, the Advocate took visual stock of the damage his neural network had already assessed.

While the relay was completely demolished, all pieces of the station embedded in the cliff survived. But far worse than the destruction of any structure or Guild resource, no less than seven of his appendages were deactivated—now scattered across the six gurneys before him.

His *greatest* had yet to be found, presumably because Jag *kidnapped* her.

How was it possible? Jag's companions had managed to make the approach to Polt without detection. And then, when the Advocate pulled his operatives forward into the valley—essentially *vacating* the tower for them—they rigged it to explode!

Once again he had underestimated them—or perhaps he had *overestimated* himself.

Yes... despite fusing tritonic steel to Omeka's body and connecting her to the Intelligence—integrating their minds and developing his most intricate connection to date—it wasn't enough. He needed more.

He needed to *be* more.

The Advocate's hand tensed to a fist.

More he would become.

The moment the dust settled, he charged to *Superior* and zipped to *Shuriken*'s wreckage to harvest more steel. He would take everything he learned in his work on Omeka to new heights as he restored his fallen operatives. And while he worked, his others would prepare more specimens for him: Already a regiment raced to Rixxon Prime, another to the fortress. He would soon grow both in strength and numbers.

And yet, there still remained the question of his past.

Speaking with Jag revealed nothing outside what he already suspected: the two were *Shuriken*'s sole survivors—a tragic revelation despite his predictions. He now had no hope of learning anything of his past beyond the first video diary. His only chance at truth was to merge minds with Jag, hoping for even vague memories of what happened to Ashley.

And with this dependence on Jag, a familiar rage swallowed all grief for his lost past.

In the footage, it was clear Jag's birth distressed Garrison. But all he expressed was annoyance over how they didn't have enough rations to take care of a baby on the ship. He griped about how stupid his crewmates were to conceive a child mid mission.

Before meeting with Jag, this was all the Advocate knew. But something clicked while he was beating that poor excuse for a man senseless. It was more—it was *deeper.* He hated Jag's existence with every fiber of his being, just as he understood Garrison did before him—but why?

Gah! Why couldn't he remember!?

In a single motion, the Advocate ripped his falchion from its scabbard and activated the electrical field. Then he slashed and screamed, filling the canyons below with the raucous rhythm of his destruction.

It *had* to be Gubora. That damned lizard must have stolen his memories!

Sparks erupted from his blade as he sliced at each fixture, spewing metal in all directions, dissolving the workshop into a scattered mess of scrap, tools, and spare parts.

Gubora would answer for—

WHOOSH! The entrance flew upward behind him.

How *convenient!*

Gubora's head cocked back. "Old friend... what is happening here?"

The Advocate lowered his blade and looked over his shoulder. "Just working through a few things."

"I... sssee." Gubora stepped over a heap of wrecked parts, his claws clicking on the metal flooring as he tiptoed forward. "I am relieved to see you alive."

The Advocate deactivated and stowed his weapon. "I'm sure you are."

"When the communications grid went down, I came as quickly as I could—and when I saw what remained of the tower, I feared the worst."

"Well," said the Advocate, brushing his hands together, "I'm fine." He cracked his neck to one side, then the other.

"I'm not sure I believe that. Something seemsss..." Gubora's tail swished. "...different."

Different? Could it be that the Advocate had learned of his treachery?

The cretinous monster. How *dare* he pretend to care!

"Like I said"—the Advocate turned and folded his arms—"I'm fine. Now why are you here? I assume you didn't come all this way just to check on me."

"Whatever happened here has invaded every corner of our systems. The entire infrastructure has been corrupted."

So… those idiots had managed to infect the network before blowing the tower. He'd underestimated them more than he thought.

The Advocate narrowed his eyes. "Remy is the only one who could have done this. She's proven to be just as much a nuisance as Bilanthia and the others."

"There's more." Gubora's tongue spat out, hissing as he muttered, "The Legislature has called me to tessstify at a hearing.

"So? You've done that before. You always figure out a way to wiggle out of the mess."

"It's different this time. There are forty-one confirmed witnesses from the events on Merutan, and the preliminary information I've gathered suggests that all but a few have said the 'small, white-armored Guildsman' was the battle's inssstigator."

"Well she's gone now. You can tell them she went rogue."

"…what do you mean she's gone?"

She was *taken* from him.

"I lost her in the explosion."

"What happ—"

"I'm handling it."

Gubora tilted his head, seemingly inspecting his *old friend*. "This debacle has become more than a political issue, I'm afraid. The Buyer is displeased. She's threatened to pull her funding if we do not resolve things soon."

None of this mattered, and the Advocate couldn't get his mind off what *did:* the truth.

He sank into a chair and rolled backward.

"Did you hear me?" said the lizard. "Without the Buyer's support, we may never recover!"

"Where did you find me?"

Gubora took a step back. "I'm sorry?"

"Before I was…" The Advocate looked down at himself. "Before I was *this.* Where did you find me?"

"I've told you many times before, old friend: I found you beaten and bruised in the Korrignolan slums."

Liar.

"And what did you do to me?"

"I brought you to a full recovery, then enhanced you in every way. I helped you *ascend*—to become something more than you were, just like you wanted."

"You say I wanted this?"

"Oh yes, you wanted nothing more than to be *better*. I could see it in your thoughts. A deep hunger for improvement drove every turn of your life."

Perhaps that last part was true. Everything he'd done to this point was in pursuit of growing his strength, his influence, his intelligence—his *capability*.

A dense silence befell the workshop. The Advocate propped his elbows on his legs and stared at Gubora.

"Old friend, what is it?"

He stood.

"Please—talk to me."

For a moment, the Advocate lingered in the silence. Then, "Why can't I remember anything beyond eighteen years ago?"

Gubora stumbled over his words: "As I have told you, there was a... missshap. I couldn't save your memories."

"Liar!" the Advocate screamed, storming toward him and coming within inches of his snout. "My name *was* Garrison Trapp."

"How did you—"

"I found the wreckage, you *swine*. And in it, I found proof of your deception."

"Wha—"

"The Guild destroyed our ship, you took me—and you stole my past!"

"I most certainly did not!"

"Then how else do you explain it!?"

Gubora's eyes danced across the Advocate's face, until taking a step back, he sighed. "Very well." He turned his back. "Yes, the Guild *did* destroy your ship. You were picked up by a scatpilot and delivered to a nearby installation. There, they tortured you but failed to gain any information because they did not speak your language."

Finally—the *truth*.

"I came in and found you all but dead, and *that* is what impressed me so. Your will to live—your sheer determination to survive—it was *immensely* powerful! It made you the perfect candidate for my work, so I brought you back to my laboratory."

"And what of my memories?"

"I cannot—"

"No more avoiding it. Tell me, *now*!"

With another sigh, Gubora rotated back and locked eyes with him. "You asked me to take them out."

Asked him to take them out?

"That doesn't make any sense. Who would want to forget everything about themselves?"

"It surprised me as well, and I fought you on it. I had no interest in ripping your identity from you. On top of that, I was unsure how you would respond to the operation had you lost sense of your prior self."

The Advocate dropped to a knee as the possibilities consumed him. Was it true? Did he really ask for his memories to be removed? And if so, why? Now—more than ever—he desired the truth.

No, he didn't desire it. He *needed* it.

"You were quite adamant that you forget, and so I hid these things as a promise to you."

Why would the Advocate, one who never failed to be sure—one who spent every day assessing who he was and where he'd been so he could improve—why would he choose to lose his past?

Gubora's claws ticked at the metal as he approached. "I'm sorry, old friend."

In an instant, the Advocate's neural network took account of everything he knew about himself, Gubora, and the galaxy, calculating the chances his *old friend* was being truthful.

"No..." He hung his head. "*I'm* sorry."

"You have nothing to—"

The Advocate shot up and grabbed Gubora by the throat with his tritonic steel hand. "I'm sorry you're too much of a coward to tell me the truth!" He squeezed. "And I'm done waiting for you to come clean."

"Please!" Gubora hacked and wheezed, scratching at the steel, struggling for his life. "You must believe me!"

"Believe you? Hah! You haven't hissed an honest word in your entire life!"

"But I've never lied to *you*, other than to keep my promise!" Gubora choked and writhed about, breathing in as much as his tightening airway would allow. "I swear to you: I am... your... friend..."

His body went limp—and the Advocate's vision blacked out.

"Wh—where am I? Why can't I see?"

"Ah, you are awake," hissed the unmistakable voice of Pert Gubora, "but you cannot see. Hmm..."

Metal clanked on metal, as darkness shrouded the scene.

"I am glad to finally meet. You are *outstanding—y*our will to live is unlike anything I've ever seen."

"Who are you? Where am I?"

"My name is Pert Gubora. You are in my laboratory."

"Wait—you can understand me?"

"Yesss," he replied, "or rather *you* can now understand *me*. And so a test: what is your name?"

He swallowed. "Garrison Trapp."

"And where is it you come from?"

"I... umm..."

"There is nothing to fear—not anymore"

TICK TICK TICK.

Garrison tried to move his arms, but they were strapped down. "Why can't I see?"

"That should be fixed momentarily."

"...fixed?"

"Mmhmm. I mussst apologize: the neural fusion process has proven more complex than anticipated."

"Neural fusion process?" Garrison again tried to move his arms, but the wrist restraints kept them in place. "What exactly are you doing to me?"

The sound of rolling wheels accompanied a rhythmic click. "It is deeper than that, my friend. You and I have together accomplished something *extraordinary.*"

"But I haven't done anything."

"Oh but you *have*. You've been through quite a bit, you see, and it motivates you—no, it *fuels* you to survive."

"What do *you* know about what I've been through?"

Gubora sighed. "I mussst apologize again. During fusion, I couldn't help but peer into your past as I converted your memories—but I think you will be *most* impressed with your new storage system!"

"You talk about my memories like they're files on a computer."

CLINK CLINK.

"Neural fusion... new storage system... Did you turn me into a robot?"

"On the contrary, my friend. I have made you into so much more—the first *ever* full-mind-and-body fusion of man and machine. And I couldn't have done it without your grit."

"...so I'm a cyborg?"

"Your plain choice of words truly betrays the significance of this breakthrough," Gubora grunted. "You are one of a kind, the advocate of a new race. You are *exceptional,* and you can only improve!"

TICK TICK.

"Sssee for yourself."

CLICK!

The lab's chrome ceiling zipped into his reality. A soft, blue lighting hummed about the room's edges—as Gubora's red-snouted face slid over top of him.

"Holy shit—you're a lizard!"

"Hah—yesss!" Gubora's tongue slithered out and around his mouth. "I hail from the planet Laktilia, but you know this. Sssearch your network."

"I... yes. Laktilia—in the Herpetian System."

"Marvelous! Outside Palatian records, you won't find a more detailed galactic map than what resides in you."

Garrison traveled the map in his mind, taking in all his new knowledge. "I don't see Earth." A glint on his left hand caught his eye. "Tritonic steel!" he said, wiggling his fingers and flexing his bionic connections.

"Yesss," hissed the lizard man. "You are far from home, but a piece of it will always be with you. It's quite fascinating, actually. I was amazed to learn how you—"

"Home..." Garrison's eyes drifted from his hand, rounded the lab—then snapped to Gubora. "What happened to Ashley? To Jason?"

"Ahh—excellent! I worried your memories were compromised, but it appears they remain intact." Gubora sighed. "I am sorry to tell you, but you are the sole survivor from your ship."

"They're... dead?" An all-consuming dread overcame Garrison—the same dread the Advocate experienced in the downed escape pod on Rixxon Prime.

Gubora nodded. "And to your end, I must apologize yet again: the way you were treated was"—he drew a loud breath—"*unsssivilized.*"

Garrison's neck and shoulders tensed as a tremor surged up his body. "I can't—"

His head jolted to the side; his heart pounded harder than it had at any singular moment in his life.

"No... no!"

BEEP BEEP BEEP, rang a terminal to his left.

"It is all right, my friend," said Gubora, racing to the terminal and tapping away at its keyboard. "As I sssaid before, there is nothing to fear."

Pounding his head into the table, his body trembling and convulsing, Garrison seized about in an attempt to break free—but whether it was the dread or the table he wished to escape, he didn't know.

BEEPBEEPBEEPBEEP, quickened the terminal.

"Please, try to—"

"It's too much!" His back arched from the table—then slammed into it. "Let me die!"

"I'm sorry," replied Gubora, his typing quickening with the beeps, "but if you wanted to die, your body would have given up weeks ago."

Garrison froze. "...weeks?"

"Yesss. This was quite the undertaking."

"Weeks!?" Garrison's back arched, his head rounding with his convulsing body. "It's been weeks!?"

Gubora hopped over and clutched his shoulders. "My friend, you must—"

SLAM! Garrison crashed his body into the table. "Don't you get it?"

SLAM! "Didn't you see?"

"I do get it—you are in pain. And I *did* see. You were sssimply in the wrong place at the wrong time."

"Wrong place at the wrong time!?" Finally breaking free, Garrison ripped his tritonic-steel arm from its restraints and fastened its hand around Gubora's scaled neck. "She's dead because of me!"

"If you would just release me," wheezed the Laktilian, "I could help you!"

"Why would I trust you!? You turned me into this—this monster!"

"I can help!" Gubora gripped at his hand, sputtering, "I swear to you: I am... your... friend..."

"I need"—Garrison released him—"I need to forget. I can't go on knowing what happened."

The Advocate blinked, washing Polt's familiar red glow over the scene.

Was that... a memory? Did Gubora trigger it?

His head drooped over, hanging his eyes on the corpse of the only friend he'd ever known, a man he'd undervalued 'til the final moment. Because It was true; it was all true. The Advocate—no—*Garrison* asked Gubora to take his memories.

So *weak*. How could anyone choose to forget?

Whatever happened, it was clear the Advocate was better off without Garrison. *He* had ascended and become something great—but he still didn't understand.

For whatever reason, this lone memory came with none of the context before it. Yes, the Advocate experienced the pain and anguish Garrison felt on the operating table, but he knew nothing of its origins beyond what was said.

She's dead because of me.

She... Ashley?

"Gah!" The Advocate gripped at his forehead as a sudden pain overcame him.

Jag... he was the reason this was all happening. That was about the only certain thing—Jag and the people who were helping him. The Rixxonian, that turncoat Remy, the Quadmalian—and *Bilanthia*.

Bilanthia!

That damned pest had meddled in their affairs for far too long, and now he'd joined up with Jag. It was unacceptable. The Advocate needed to make it known.

Bilanthia would *pay*.

Chapter 38

Remy's body grew heavier with each step up her three-rung stepladder.

This had always been her escape—tinkering, fixing things. She had thought that simple fact would carry her through the operation, but she was wrong. Making matters worse, her mind was not acting at full capacity; simple mistakes riddled her work.

Stabilizing atop the third step, she pulled a tool from her belt and brought it toward the exposed wiring in Omeka's head—then dropped it and teetered forward, clasping her hands round the gurney's edges. Propped up, she rolled her head in a wide circle and swallowed the cold, quiet space.

This engine room had been a place of solace for Remy. The massive, cylindrical casing above her station glowed a soft blue as it spanned the open chamber, its edges disappearing into a faint red ring as they met the walls—an elegant, mechanical marvel second in beauty only to the gentle whirring that accompanied it.

But solace was far from what she had found there since leaving Polt.

For twelve hours now, Omeka had been strapped to this table, positioned at a sharp enough angle so Remy could operate without looking at her. And for twelve hours, Remy had failed to make any progress toward accessing the hive mind.

The technology was simply beyond her.

It certainly did not help that she could not maintain focus. From the moment she was left alone in the engine room, the fog enveloped her mind. Her thoughts were there, if only for a split second as they drifted across a clouded haze and disappeared.

She would never succeed at this rate.

"Remy, okay if I come in?"

As she cast her attention beyond Omeka's lifeless body, Bo's prodigious frame blurred into her vision. She nodded.

"I just, uhh... how you holdin' up?"

"I am..." She pressed a hand into her forehead. "Tired."

With a crooked smile, Bo ambled across the engine room. "You deserve a break."

"There's no—"

"Y'can't save the galaxy if you're too run down to function." He came up behind her and offered a hand down. "I've got somethin' for ya."

"You have something"—she took his hand—"for me?"

Bo helped her to the ground, stepped back, and dug into his pocket. "Saw this in the market and thought a'you; been meaning to give it to you since Merutan." He revealed a black, teardrop stone attached to a simple chain and placed it in her hand. "It's an onyx."

"You thought of me?" Though Remy had never worn jewelry, she was drawn to it.

"A'course!" he said, propping a hand on his waist. "It reflects the profound yet uncomplicated deepness of twilight—like your eyes."

Nobody had ever given Remy such a gift before. Lost, entranced by the stone's dark simplicity in her blue palm, all she could produce was a simple, "Thank you."

"Black onyx is s'posed to transform negative energy and help with emotional health," he said, closing her hand over it. "Considering"—he nodded to Omeka—"all the craziness going around, I thought you might benefit from a little boost."

"It is impossible for a rock to transform energy." Pausing, Remy looked up at him. "However, I understand and appreciate your intentions."

Bo grinned. "If you find your bunk's uncomfortable later, you're welcome to spend the night in my quarters. I can give you a *different* kind of boost."

Remy's expression flattened. "No thank you."

"Hah—that was a joke, a'course," he said with a smile. "Don't think I could, honestly; it'd be pretty weird. You remind me too much of my own sister."

So she was like Jag... *and* Bo's sister?

"I did not know you had a sister."

"*Had* is the word there. Haven't seen her in fifteen years—ahh." He scratched his head. "Not that this is a contest, a'course. Losin' someone you love is tough no matter the circumstances."

And losing them twice?

"You woulda liked Ko-Ra. She was a brainiac like you. Real quick-witted, too."

"What happened to her?"

Bo sighed. "Like everything else, I lost her in the scattering." He stretched his neck back, basking in the beauty of his ship. "At least I got *Zara.*"

Remy offered a faint smile. "She is magnificent."

Returning the smile, Bo again nodded toward Omeka. "How's it goin' down here?"

"It is not, unfortunately."

His smile twisted. "Sorry to hear that."

There was no doubt: Remy would not accomplish what she set out to do on her own. The intricacies of the tightly woven circuitry were more advanced than anything she had ever seen—aside from in one place.

Despite her complete lack of trust, she had no choice: she needed to speak with Elama.

"Bo-Ram?"

"Hah! I'd hope we're *way* past *that*. But it's been a weird stretch, so I'll let it slide."

"Bo," she said through a smile. "I hear you are very perceptive. What do you think of Elama?"

"Elama, eh?" He shrugged. "Seems fine to me; didn't notice any red flags."

"But what about the technology? Does that not make you suspicious?"

He shrugged again. "Nine times out of ten, my first read's a good one. That said"—he wrapped an arm around her shoulder and ushered her toward the exit—"if you don't trust her for any reason, I'll always keep one eye open."

Could Remy... confide in him?

"It is far too coincidental," she said as they walked. "Elama—a being with unimaginable technology and the ability to travel unseen—asks us for help defeating the Advocate, who we learn has achieved a technological feat that exists only in theories. And he has achieved it with what seems to be limitless range and capacity."

"Hmm, when you say it like that, it *does* sound pretty suspicious." Bo plodded forward a few more paces, leading them into the cargo bay and turning for the elevator. "Okay, I'm with ya: color me wary."

First Sixxis, then Jag, and now Bo. These people; they were so... supportive.

Remy stopped. "How is it that you trust me so much, so quickly?"

"You know how I said nine times out of ten, my first read's a good one?" Stepping onto the elevator, he turned and offered a smile. "My next few are even better."

Chapter 39

Jag's eyes fluttered open. Across the med bay, Sixxis sat with his head against the wall, mouth open wide—snoring.

"Glad you're getting some rest," Jag said.

"Huh—what?" Sixxis snorted back to reality. "Oh thakk, you're awake!" He leaned forward and propped up on his knees. "How are you feeling?"

How *was* Jag feeling? Things seemed normal, or something close to it. He *did* have that same sensation as before—when his ribs felt *new.*

A lot of his body felt new. It was unsettling.

"I'm okay. How long was I out?"

"Fourteen hours."

"Fourteen hours!?" Jag shot up at the waist, banging into that same device that healed him not even a day ago.

"Oh, *do* be careful!" said Bilanthia, scurrying across the room. "We don't want you suffering another concussion!" He placed an open palm on Jag's chest, another on his back, and lowered him down. "Please hold still," he said, clicking buttons on the arm; as it hummed up and down Jag's body, a smaller blue piece rotated around it.

"What's the word, Doc?" Sixxis asked, peeking over his shoulder.

"We've successfully repaired your injuries. As before, you will feel somewhat tender for a time."

Jag blinked a slow blink. "We?"

"But of course!" Bilanthia replied, brushing his spindly fingers across the arcing arm. "The device merely stimulates, supplies, and expedites your body's built-in recovery system. You do the rest." He sighed, but with a smile. "Anatomy is fascinating."

Jag sat up—slowly this time—scooted back to clear the device, and swung his legs off the table. Somehow his mind was quiet. He was entirely present, far from where he was before passing out.

"Did you do anything else to me? I feel..." His face scrunched, then relaxed. "...great, actually."

"You had a panic attack," Bilanthia replied, "and a bad one at that. I injected you with a serum to relieve the anxiety; it should wear off any moment."

Anxiety...

"It was scary," added Sixxis. "You were freaking out more than I've ever seen."

Remy appeared in the doorway. "Anxiety is perhaps my greatest fear."

"That makes sense to me," said Bilanthia. "Someone who relies so heavily on her mind, on what is real and factual—"

BOODOOP.

Bilanthia rushed to check a computer on the far wall. "Oh my..." Without another word, he dashed past Remy, out of the room.

"The very notion of losing command of my thoughts—dwelling on what I do not know, ruminating on what has transpired, or spiraling through a series of potential futures that may never come to pass..." Remy walked in and leaned against the other table. "That imbalance terrifies me."

Spiraling... that sounded like Jag all right.

"It is admirable how well you handle it," she said, head tilted up at him, flowing her hair down past her shoulder. "I am glad you are okay."

Something seemed different in Remy. The tension that'd been there most other times Jag talked to her had vanished.

He smiled. "How are you?"

"I..." Her gaze fell to the floor. "I have been better."

"Understatement for the ages," said Sixxis, plopping onto Jag's table as his companions eyed him. He shrugged. "Probably."

Jag looked back to Remy and hesitated. "Is Omeka—"

"Omeka is dead." Her eyes stayed fixed on the floor. "She has been since the Advocate murdered her."

"But—"

"*That*... that was not Omeka. Nor is the being in the engine room. But still..." She looked back up at Jag. "Thank you for bringing her back. You did not have to—"

"I couldn't leave her behind."

Remy's lip quivered.

"It's okay. I—"

"No." She cleared her throat. "Nothing is okay at the moment. After twelve hours, I have failed to make any progress on accessing the hive mind."

"Really?" said Sixxis. "If *you* can't figure it out, who can?"

"I have seen technology of this caliber only once before." Again, Remy locked eyes with Jag. "We must contact Elama."

Elama... Jag had a few choice words for her, too.

"But we must do so carefully," she continued. "The sophistication of the Arbiters' tech makes them inherently dangerous. Frankly, the very fact that they could *speak* to you on Rixxon Prime—comprehend and communicate in your native tongue—is troubling in itself."

Jag's eyes widened. "They're not the only ones who came to Rixxon Prime and could speak our language."

"Yeah!" said Sixxis. "That operative!"

"Who we now know was the Advocate all along," Jag concluded.

Remy's face flushed a lighter shade of blue. "The technology required to interpret and catalog the nuances of language—without consistent, physical immersion in the culture it upholds—is incomprehensible. This is why the Galactic Linguistics Bureau waits for planets to elevate above Class V before studying them; ethnographers spend time amongst the people learning their ways."

Jag's mouth wrinkled. What did it all mean?

"This..." Remy trailed off. "Along with the hive mind, this places the Advocate on a technological plane adjacent to the Arbiters. And the simple fact that *both* have recently come to light throws everything into question."

There it was again—this sense that it was all too much to be coincidence. Jag already felt set up on Merutan, and the encounter on Polt was even worse. Was Elama orchestrating everything, claiming it to be the will of fate?

Remy sighed. "Unfortunately, we are at an impasse. Though we would be wise not to trust Elama, we cannot proceed without her aid. She is just as much necessary as she is unknown and dangerous."

"I've already tried contacting her," Jag said. "She hasn't answered."

"We must try again."

Frustration seeped into Jag's calm. His heart pounded. His mind raced.

There was no *way* Elama didn't know he was from Earth—or that he and the Advocate were connected. Why else would she have kept track of him and sent him on a mission he had no hope of completing?

Remy flinched as Jag pounded a fist into the table. "Is every—"

"No!" he yelled, bursting to his feet. "It's like you said—*nothing* is okay!"

Sixxis leapt to the ground and raised a hand at his brother. "Jag, calm—"

"*Don't*"—he jumped backward—"don't tell me to calm down!"

Everything, all the fear, the hesitation—the *anxiety*—it was all compounding, all replacing itself with nothing more than anger. Jag was done—done waiting to see what might happen. It was time to act, to get ahead for a—

"Uhh, guys," Bo's voice trickled through the open doorway, "you should prolly come see this!"

"That doesn't sound good." Sixxis ran out of the room, with Remy right behind him.

Feet still wobbly, Jag shuffled after them. A voice grew louder as he made his way down the corridor and turned into the comm room.

"What you're seeing here is the current state of Meru Plaza, the global capital of Merutan in the Horranite system." Across the platform's top ring, a Horranite woman gestured to her right.

"Jag." Bilanthia swept an arm toward the ring's inner edge. "You should sit."

With a nod, Jag planted his hand and sank down.

"Immersion mode," said Bo.

The door zipped shut, the lights dimmed—and the image of Meru Plaza burst through the domed ceiling, stretching to the floor circling the platform.

Only it didn't look the way Jag remembered it.

Char marks littered the capitol steps behind the woman, smoldering and smoking into the otherwise immaculate airspace. Market stands were destroyed, tables flipped and flung all over. And the people were gone, save a few meandering through the scattered marble.

"Just moments ago, two vessels bearing the insignia of the Prospectors' Guild entered the planet's atmosphere above where we stand. In an unprovoked attack, they proceeded to fire, supplanting this peaceful afternoon with frantic screams and flying debris"

Silence filled the space between the woman's lines.

"So far, just three have been confirmed dead."

"Such senseless destruction," said Bilanthia, shaking his head.

"This comes just one day after a brawl involving a Guild operative broke out during a visit by Consular Ferris Bilanthia, one that resulted in multiple explosions and a quick getaway by the consular. Currently, it is not known why the Guild has taken such interest in Merutan. Meanwhile..."

Jag leaned forward as the image shifted to another place he'd been: the Horranite Consulate. But again, it didn't look like he remembered it.

He barely recognized it.

The building was gone, almost entirely destroyed. Those same char marks that littered the Plaza baked into the mountain face behind where it once stood.

"Many systems away, two identical vessels entered Palatian airspace, bypassing atmospheric registration. After shooting down two Planetary Police patrols, they initiated an attack on the Horranite Consulate. The only confirmed casualty is Burl Komassen, administrative assistant to Consular Bilanthia."

"Burl..." Bilanthia muttered. "What a shame."

"While it is not confirmed, the precise orchestration of these concurrent strikes has many believing this was some sort of message for the consular. It is long known that he is no friend of the organization."

"It is time," said Remy, crouching beside Jag. "We cannot delay any longer."

"Minimize." Bo leaned back against the rail, folding his arms as the images disappeared. "Time for what?"

"We must speak with Elama," she said.

Remy was right: it was time. But as much as the fire raged inside him moments ago, Jag felt suddenly deflated, heavy.

"Jag." Sixxis stepped down a level and offered a hand. "It's time to get your answers."

Now *he* was right. When did Sixxis and Remy get on the same page?

Sixxis lifted him up and stabilized him. "I'm right behind you," he said, pressing their foreheads together.

Jag closed his eyes for a moment, savoring his brother's support, then pulled away, lowered to the central platform, and placed a hand on the pedestal.

"Hello, Jag. To whom would you like to place your call?"

His body trembling—unsure if he was angry, nervous, scared, or just overwhelmed—Jag glanced at each of his four companions. "Elama."

"Very well, I will attempt to contact Elama Singh. One moment please." Soft, indigo lighting illuminated the chamber.

A moment passed.

"I'm sorry, Jag. Elama is unavailable at this time. Would you like to leave her a message?"

Again? This was *not* okay. Just like Remy said—*nothing* was.

"You know what?" Jag stood tall. "I would."

Begin speaking in three... two...

"I need to talk to you—*now!* How could you just—"

"I apologize for interrupting, but I have an incoming call from Elama."

Finally.

"Let me speak with her."

A tight row of thin, vertical lines appeared, floating above where the news reporter previously stood. "Hello, Jag," said Elama, the lines jumping in cadence with her voice. "I'm sorry for—"

"I've been trying to contact you for days now. Why haven't you answered?"

"We have been, erm... taking care of a few things on our end."

"Vague, as usual." He folded his arms. "Well, while you've been doing whatever, we've been getting our asses kicked out here."

"Yes; I received your messages. How was the meeting on Polt?"

"The Advocate has realized collective consciousness," said Remy. "He has woven his organic mind with a synthetic intelligence that gives him full dominion over at least fifty others."

A wave passed through the display, then, "A hive mind."

Remy caught Jag's eye.

"This is troubling news indeed." She raised her voice. "Torin?"

"Yes, commander?"

"How far would you calculate this galaxy is from full orgo-synthetic fusion with shared intelligence—ah wait. Jag, was that him on Rixxon Prime?"

"Uhh... yes?"

"And Merutan as well?"

"Both."

The waves once again danced larger as Elama's voice grew louder. "So that's orgo-synthetic fusion and shared intelligence with a reach across multiple systems."

"One moment," Torin replied.

Jag looked to Remy, then to Sixxis; both shrugged, Remy with a glare.

"I would estimate that to be an innovation some 800 years early," said Torin, "although my calculations are muddied by the Legislature's long-standing position on artificial intelligence. Regardless, the odds of him accomplishing such a feat at the current time are infinitesimal."

"Well, it's happened." Hands in fists, Jag revved himself up. "And from what I understand, you're the only one with technology even close to that—so it's time for you to talk."

Elama sighed. "All right."

"What do you know about the Advocate?"

"Only what I told you."

"I don't believe you."

"I'm sorry?"

"No, *I'm* sorry," said Jag. "Sorry it took getting the shit kicked out of me to realize there had to be more to it. Why would you watch me on Rixxon Prime? Why would you ask *me* of all people to come out here?"

"I—"

"The Advocate said—well, let's be honest, he wouldn't *stop* talking. And something tells me you knew everything all along." Jag stomped. "Tell me the truth!"

Another wave passed through the projection, accompanying a beat of silence.

"I'm sorry, Jag. It's true, I have not been completely honest with you. I did not lie; however, I did withhold information."

"So make up for it now."

She sighed. "Nineteen years ago, *Assurance* intercepted a distress signal. As we moved to investigate, our scanners picked up an escape pod fleeing a Guild scatpilot. We were able to defend and recover the pod without detection, but it was too late for the larger ship."

Narrow-eyed, Remy looked up at Jag. "It seems the Guild took *your* family as well."

"What about the pod?" Jag asked.

"We found a woman inside, nearly dead from the attack—slumped over an infant."

He stumbled back. "M—me? My mother?"

"Yes," Elama replied. "Unfortunately, we could not save your mother, but you were found to be in good health. Since you would have no recollection of meeting us, there was no problem; we were able to simply relocate you."

"Rixxon Prime... so you put me there."

"Indeed. We analyzed nearby systems, looking first at which planets' atmospheric makeup would support your physical needs, then examining the demeanor of local populaces. From everything we understood about the Rixxonians, they would both accept you as their own, and accept that they did not know where you came from."

"But why watch me for all those years?"

"When I first answered this question, I chose my words carefully. You truly were out of place—all of you. You were the first of your species we had come to detect in this galaxy."

"But I'm not the only."

Again, Elama sighed. "The Advocate appeared six months later. While we did not know for sure, we theorized that the two of you were connected. So we kept an eye on you both."

"Well you were right. He said I'm from some place called Earth—just like him."

"So..." Another wave passed through the lines. "It's true. And you are—"

"Human, apparently."

"I see. And he is human as well?"

"No." Jag shook his head. "He's something else now."

"Taking over the minds of people like Remy's sister," Sixxis added.

"I'm so sorry, Remy. If only I—"

"Why did you disappear?" Jag said.

"I'm sorry?"

"You pulled us together, gave us a grand sendoff, then disappeared."

"I feared too much action on our part would interfere with fate—the same reason I did not tell you of our suspected link between you and the Advocate."

"Fate? You're still going on about that?"

"Fate turns the wheels of time and drives us all, Jag—and I cannot help but feel it has more in store for you."

What was she saying—that his identity was some predetermined thing?

"You must acknowledge the low probability of this sequence of events," she continued. "We place you on Rixxon Prime, and the Advocate comes onto the scene six months later. Some years after that, he rises to his current rank, and anomalies start appearing across the galaxy—including on Rixxon Prime. You stop him not once, not twice, but *three* times on that planet alone."

A strong argument, one that meshed with Jag's own thoughts. But did that mean he had no power over it? Was he destined to face off against the Advocate?

"It stems beyond the two of you, I'm afraid. You see, we had been waiting for the proper moment to get in closer to the Advocate, to..." The projection fell still.

Jag's brow furowed. "To what?"

"I really do feel terrible about this."

"Out with it."

"The Advocate is a very secretive man. Due to our suspicions, we felt the best way to learn more about him was to bring you together."

"There it is," Jag huffed.

"We knew you would need support, and the moment we learned the truth behind Omeka Troyer's death, we thought Remy would provide it. With her on board, the consular was likely to leave his post."

"She's right there," chuckled Bilanthia. "I was not hard to convince."

"The moment we found sufficient evidence, we went straight to Rixxon Prime, only to find a Guild ship descending to the surface minutes after we arrived."

"And one of the men on board was the Advocate," Jag finished.

"*One* of him," Remy corrected.

And just like that, Jag was powerless.

This was all *way* bigger than him, like he really *did* have no choice. Was he destined to lose? Or was his link to the Advocate so strong that he was destined to join him?

They *were* the same after all—they were both *human*. Jag couldn't deny his identity.

But where did the Arbiters play in?

"I do not believe in fate," Remy interjected, "but the Advocate is an abomination. We must put a stop to his murderous ways."

And just like *that*, Jag found strength in Remy.

"Yes," Bilanthia agreed. "Regardless of what we think and feel—with what we've just witnessed on the news—that must be our first and foremost priority. We must work together."

Bilanthia, too. Maybe they *could* make a difference.

"Affirmative," said Remy. "To that end, Elama, I need your assistance."

"How can I help?"

"I have spent hours attempting to access the hive mind through Omeka's neural network and made zero progress."

Elama gasped. "You have her with you?"

"Yes."

"I see..."

"From your previous interaction with Torin, I gather you are well versed in this field?"

Elama hummed a contented hum. "Quite, actually." Clicking sounds clacked through the transmission. "Do you have a scan of her cranial systems?" The clicking stopped. "Oh no no—I am *so* sorry! Her head. Do you have a scan of her head?"

Remy started to say something, then stopped. Then, "Yes."

"Send it to—"

VOOP! Remy's handheld vibrated in her vest pocket. She pulled it out and tapped the screen a few times. "Sent."

"One moment." The lines disappeared.

"What?" Jag said, eyes shooting up at Bo. "Where'd she go?"

"Put us on hold," Bo replied. "She'll pop back up when she's ready."

"You haven't said much."

Bo shrugged. "Don't have much to say. I'm behind you, whatever ya need to do, Jag." He glanced at Remy. "You, too, little one—ah pits, all a'you. Y'all have given me something I haven't had in a long time."

The lines reappeared, accompanied by more click-clacks. "This is breakthrough circuitry. I am *exceedingly* curious to know how he was able to create something so advanced."

"How do we access the hive mind?" Remy asked, eyes glued on her handheld. "Logically speaking, there must be a way."

"It's not the most graceful solution, but it should do the trick."

A hologram of Omeka's head appeared above the handheld, with a collection of wires highlighted orange.

"If you deliver a large electromagnetic burst to this web, it should activate enough of the circuitry to allow you access."

BOOP BOOP!

"That's my cue," said Bo, turning to Bilanthia. "Ready, copilot?"

Bilanthia snapped to attention and saluted. "Ready to go, captain!"

"Hah! There's a good reason I'm not the captain. Pits, there're a *lot* of 'em." Bo jogged around the top platform. "Open!"

Bilanthia scurried after him as the door whooshed aside.

"Probably my cue, too," added Sixxis, also starting for the exit.

"Wait," Jag said, "where are you going?"

He stopped. "You stay with Remy and figure this out. I..." His posture sank. "I've got to find Adira. I need to know she's okay." He looked Jag in the eye. "This isn't like before. I'm not just—"

"I know," said Jag, half-smiling. "Will you be okay on your own?"

Sixxis pumped his fiery brows. "You know I move faster when I'm alone. Besides"—he turned for the door, waving a hand over his shoulder—"I'm home now. I'll be good."

"So you would like me to... shock her?" Remy clarified.

"Yes," replied Elama, "The probe I left for you should be strong enough."

"How do I extract files?"

"There is a panel beneath her right ear. When she's powered, plug your transfer cable—"

"What do you mean, 'powered?'"

For a moment, Elama didn't respond. With everyone but Jag and Remy gone, an eerie quiet filled the space.

"Elama," Remy said, glaring at the frozen projection.

"I would recommend keeping her restrained," Elama finally said. "While I have seen things *like* this, I haven't yet seen an identical case. I don't know exactly what will happen."

"That's comforting," Jag quipped.

Remy's eyes narrowed even more. "Then what *may* happen?"

"It's hard to say. No two minds are the same, so it's virtually impossible to predict anything about a combination."

"Can you just tell us?" Jag said, folding his arms.

Elama let out a deep sigh. "There is a chance the shock will revive her."

"Wh—what?" Remy took a staggering step back. "Will she be herself?"

"Perhaps. The round in her skull appears to have severed numerous connections. I could tell you more if I was there in person, but that's not possible right now."

Jag turned to Remy. "We should get down there."

"We?" she replied, looking up at him.

"Of course. You think I'm going to let you do this alone?"

Chapter 40

"Remy?"

Her perception opened with the elevator doors, pulling *Zara's* cargo bay into focus.

"Are you okay?" Jag stepped through and turned to face her, a crooked smile and raised brow shaping his concern. "You haven't said anything since the comm room."

Eyes wide, Remy darted her gaze to one elevator corner, then another.

It had happened again—she did not recall getting on. And once more, Jag was the one to wake her.

"I am sorry. I was..." She nodded. "I am ready."

"Right behind you," Jag promised, moving aside.

Remy stepped out of the small compartment, into the expansive cargo area, then turned for the engine room. When she came to it, she stopped perpendicular to the open doorway—hesitant to look inside.

Omeka... she might see her again. Or would it be—

"There is a chance we will bring the Advocate here," she said.

"That's fine," came Jag's voice, just behind her. "She's tied up, right?"

Staring forward, Remy nodded. "Right—and I shot her in the head."

"...right." Jag placed a hand on her shoulder. "Are you sure you can do this?"

Could Remy do this? She was not so sure.

With a broad exhalation, she crossed the threshold. Each successive step grew more difficult as she progressed toward her sister's lifeless body. Even the engine's comforting whir could not overpower her plodding on the metal floor.

The ceiling stretched high above her; all around, the walls expanded.

She was very small.

"I'm right behind you," Jag repeated.

Rounding Omeka's gurney, still unable to look, Remy drew a deep breath, approached her workstation, and picked up the probe rod—then dropped it immediately. With another deep breath, she pressed her hands into the table and attempted to focus on the cold metal's touch.

A futile attempt.

Already unprepared to wake her sleeping sister, Remy hesitated further under the weight of a sudden realization: Not only did Elama understand the Advocate's technology, she knew *exactly* what to do with nothing more than a quick glance at the circuitry. This set an evil undertone to the entire operation.

Because for all they knew, Elama intended for them to bring the Advocate onboard *Zara.*

"Remy?"

Exhaling, she turned and took her final steps to the angled gurney, then up the stepladder behind it. Drawing in one final deep breath, she muttered, "Thank you, Jag," and pressed the rod into the exposed wiring.

A moment passed; no response.

"...did you do anything?" Jag said.

"Yes; it appears not enough." She rolled her thumb across the dial to increase the power. This time, the muted pulse jostled her sister's body.

Another moment passed, with still no response.

"Damn." Remy increased the power even further. "Would you please spot me?"

"Spot you?"

"A jolt this strong will likely have recoil."

"Got it," said Jag, positioning behind her.

"Three... two..."

The burst threw Remy into Jag's arms—but *still* Omeka did not move.

"Damn," she cursed, restabilizing with his help. "It appears—"

"Hello?" buzzed a thin, altered voice.

Though faint, it was familiar.

"Who's there?"

Pressing away from Jag, Remy rounded the fixture and came face to face with the operative, a furrowed brow displaying her disbelief. But that disbelief faded quickly.

"Remy," said the operative, a smile tilting half her mouth.

"Omeka!" Remy raced to undo the restraints, embracing her sister before her feet touched the floor. And for several seconds of warm, delicate silence, they stood arm in arm, entities intertwined as before.

Despite all the uncertainty just moments ago, Remy needed only hear her name—needed only feel her sister's presence. For it was a presence she would never forget.

"I thought I would never be with you again," Omeka muttered into Remy's shoulder. Her eyes then wandered up and across the cylindrical engine casing, pulling her body along with them. "Where are we?"

She walked forward a few paces.

"How did I get here?"

"You were murdered by the Advocate and made an abomination."

Omeka lifted her chin up high. "I know. And I helped him..." Seemingly lost, her head drifted down, its gaze resting on her trembling hands.

"What is the last thing you remember?" Remy asked.

"We were fighting that man."

"Probably me?" Jag said, scratching his arm.

"Ah!" Omeka dropped to the floor, clutching her head and writhing about. "Quick!" she called out between screams, gesturing to a region beneath her head's metal plating. "Sever the orange-ended connection!"

Remy responded only with action: she grabbed her wire cutters and cut the cable, rendering her sister motionless.

After a moment of soundless tension, Omeka sat up.

"What happened?" Remy asked.

"Whoever shot—"

"That was me."

Omeka looked up at her, gratitude evident in her soft smile. "Your bullet managed to clear straight through my secondary processor while avoiding the organic matter left in my brain. The Intelligence—that's what the Advocate calls his network—scattered itself into my auxiliary systems." She winced. "It's trying to retake control."

"How is it that you're..." Jag's mouth wrinkled. "...*alive*, speaking to us?"

"It's a lot more complicated than this, but he essentially inserted himself and his network into my subconscious, then swapped dominance with my main consciousness."

Remy collapsed to a crouch. "You were present the entire time."

Eyes glued on her sister, Omeka nodded. "I was powerless, an observer of my own life. Your shock must have jolted my true consciousness back to the surface."

"So he was telling the truth. All the operatives—or rather, who the operatives once were—they are still alive."

"Yes; some more than others."

"Did cutting that wire stop the Intelligence?"

Omeka shook her head. "Only that avenue of pursuit. It won't be long before it finds another."

Standing, Remy approached and offered her hand. "Can I remove it from your body entirely?"

"No." With her sister's help, Omeka rose to her feet, bringing their gaze level. "I died in that flood, Remy. He replaced my saturated lungs with synthetic respiratory and phonatory systems—which are now both supported by and infected with the Intelligence. What's left of me won't survive without it."

Remy opened her mouth to speak, then closed it again. A moment passed, then, "Why did he kill you?"

"Honestly"—Omeka sighed—"I was in the wrong place at the wrong time."

"Elaborate."

"I was working late in one of the Polt workshops, and I overheard the Advocate saying something about going to Rixxon Prime. I'd never heard of the planet, so I looked it up out of pure curiosity. The next day I was summoned to the shafts; the water came rushing right after I got there."

Remy squinted. "Are you sure that was it?"

"Right when I... woke up, I shared his thoughts. I knew he removed me to make sure no one discovered his plans to disrupt development on a Class V planet."

So she discovered the Advocate's intentions for Jag's planet and was murdered for it. Jag then came to Remy, who in turn went with him because her sister was killed.

Perhaps more fodder for Elama's theory of *fate.*

With a howl, Omeka collapsed to her knees and planted her hands into the floor. Breathing heavily on all fours, she convulsed for a time, then fell still.

"I need to die," she muttered, whispers consuming the trace of pitch in her voice, "for good this time." She looked up at her sister. "I would much rather *you* end it."

The request pounded into Remy's stomach. "I do not—"

"Please." Tears welled in Omeka's eyes. "You have no idea what it's like to witness"—she buried her face in Remy's hand—"to *do* those things and have no power over any of it."

"You are correct," Remy replied, running a finger through her sister's hair. "I do not."

Omeka sniffled and sat back. "I've seen what the Advocate is planning. He must be stopped."

"What is that?"

"Expansion."

"What do you mean?" Jag asked.

"He'll never stop growing his numbers."

Jag's mouth wrinkled. "But I almost died fighting *one* of him. How can we hope to stop him?"

"I think it has everything to do with you, Jag," said Omeka.

His head cocked back. "Me?"

She nodded. "Every time the Advocate sees you, he becomes more and more unstable. There's something about the connection between you; it fills him with rage. And it's odd. You heard him say your existence bothers him?"

"Yeah?"

"That's just it: He doesn't hate *you*. He hates the fact that you *exist*."

"I don't get it."

"It's hard to explain," she admitted with a shrug. "Even *he* doesn't know why. He's changing though, a bit with each passing moment—and the direction he's going is *not* good.

"What do you mean?" said Remy, dropping to a stool.

"He's mostly machine at this point, but it's the organic matter that's running the show. His emotions run high: His rage tendencies are spiraling, only getting accentuated by his combat configurations. I wouldn't be surprised if he soon resorts to widespread destruction."

Jag folded his arms. "We're already there."

"What do you mean?"

"He's already attacked both Meru Plaza and the Horranite Consulate."

"I... see."

Remy leaned forward, elbows on her knees. "Can you access his schematics?"

Omeka sighed. "All details of his physical body are stored only in temporary files located within the Intelligence itself."

That was not going to make things easy. Still, there had to be a solution. There was no way they were walking out of this engine room without the data they needed, not after this.

Not after what Remy must soon do.

"If the Intelligence takes over," she said, again standing and offering her sister a hand, "how long before you are removed from control?"

"I'll likely lose physical control immediately." Omeka pulled herself up. "Mentally, I could hold it off for a bit, but I can't say how long."

Turning away, Remy wandered forward a few paces. "While the Intelligence is wrestling for control, will you have access to its contents?"

"I think so. Our minds should coexist within my neural network for a time."

Remy looked to the ground at her side. "Can you let it take you?"

"I beg your pardon?"

"Yeah," said Jag, "what are you saying?"

"We need information." Releasing perhaps the heaviest sigh of her life, she rotated to face them. "And we are low on options."

Omeka massaged her chin for a moment, then nodded. "I can try to get all the information you want—so long as you make me one promise."

"What is that?"

"Once you see anything other than my head move, you must kill me."

Remy's jaw dropped.

It needed to be done, but that did not make it any less difficult.

Closing her mouth, she nodded back. "Your phrasing does give me pause. You said your minds *should* coexist, and that you *could* hold it off. I do not like those words: *could* and *should*."

"Could and should are about as good as we can hope for right now," said Omeka, brow lifted. Then—as if on cue—her head jerked; her face twitched. "What would you like to know?"

"Jag." Remy turned to him. "I thought we might retrieve the Advocate's schematics so we can identify weak points in his physical structure. And he is likely no longer on Polt, so we should obtain information about where he has gone. What do you think?"

His mouth slightly open, Jag took a moment to respond. "Are you sure about this?"

Was she sure? Likely not. But surety had become a luxury.

"There is no other way."

Jag's expression wrinkled as he looked between the sisters. "Omeka, is there any way we can bring the others back?"

"Well, it can obviously happen," she said, stretching out her arms to indicate herself. "But before me, I don't think the Advocate considered this a possibility, so I don't have a concrete answer for you." She turned to Remy. "Your shot was truly one in a million."

"There must be some way to recreate the shot's effect on your body," Remy said.

In a series of motions identical to her sister's, Omeka opened her mouth to speak, then closed it. And after a moment, she said, "The sudden destruction of my secondary processor sent an energy surge through my body that essentially deactivated the Intelligence."

"So we aim for the head."

"It's not that simple. You recall I said some of us are more alive than others?"

Remy nodded.

"Each of us has a different ratio of organic to synthetic matter, depending on our physical and mental states at the time of fusion. Our central processors are located at varying places, decided by which part of us needed the most assistance—or in my case, needed immediate replacement."

"...so yours is—"

Omeka drew a hand down her throat. "Had you shot me here"—she patted her chest—"my body would have died."

"Energy surge..." Jag's mouth opened, his tongue resting on his lower lip. "Like how we brought you back just now?"

Omeka nodded slowly—then faster. "That might work. A strong enough shock could disable the Intelligence, but only for a time. It needs the body to survive just as the body needs it." Then, with a sort of odd smile, she said, "Remy, I wish you could see it. It's truly beautiful."

"What?"

"Artificial intelligence. It learns over time how to better support you and live in harmony with your body." Her smile sagged. "But that unfortunately means the longer someone is fused, the deeper their dependence becomes."

"You grow together?"

Omeka nodded. "It's life, just like any other life. Quite amazing, really—ah!"

"I'll go grab Bo and Bilanthia," said Jag, bounding for the exit. "Just in case!"

Remy smiled as he left. "He could simply call them down here."

"He wanted to give us a moment together," replied Omeka, smiling an identical smile. "I feel a wonderful energy between you two."

"He is a friend."

Friend... Remy had not yet said that out loud.

"Are you sure it's nothing more?"

Remy scowled, spouted, "Nothing more," then smiled—for Omeka truly *was* back. She launched forward and wrapped around her sister. "When I heard you were gone, I thought I might die myself." She squeezed tighter, burying her face and muffling her voice as she confessed, "I almost saw to it."

Something she had yet to confess to herself.

"Remy." Omeka grabbed and pressed her body forward. Gazing deeply into her eyes, she said, "Losing you would be an enormous disservice to this galaxy."

"I do not know what you mean."

"You were *wasted* on the Guild, Remy. All it ever did was make you forget yourself."

"...forget?"

"It's okay. I see you now. I can *feel* you..." Omeka smiled. "You're remembering."

"Remembering what, exactly?"

"That you *aren't* alone. That your feelings *do* matter, and that they *are* important—both to you and to others."

"I don't understand."

"It's Jag—I can tell. You've finally found another decent, supportive person. And he'll take care of you, just like you'll take care of him." A single tear ran down her cheek. "Like you always took care of me."

A warmth grew in Remy's chest. "He is not my only friend. There are... well, there are two others. I still do not know about the politician."

"Hah!" laughed Omeka, shoving her. "Typical. If he's in this crew, he can't be *that* bad!"

Smiling, Remy shrugged. "I suppose not." Her smile faded. "How is it that you are handling this so well? This is rather uncharacteristic."

Omeka's single tear turned to multiple; they streamed down her face. "Since the moment I woke up, I've worried about you—worried about how you were doing without me. When I heard your name on Merutan—when I knew you'd left the Guild—it was liberating!" Again, they locked eyes. "And waking up as myself here, talking to you and Jag... I know. I know you're going to be okay. And I can die knowing it."

"I would not be so sure," Remy refuted. "We still have to defeat the Advocate."

Omeka sniffled into a half-smile. "You will. You always figure it—ah!" She clutched her head. "We're running out of time." She made for the gurney.

Remy approached the table and took her sister in—one last time.

"I miss you, Omeka. I will always miss you."

"I know you do; I know you will. And that's why I couldn't be happier to see that you've found new family to take care of you. You're incredible, but you can't do it on your own."

"I... have been learning that."

Omeka beamed. "I'm so glad I got to see you again—and that I can help you."

Tears welled in Remy's eyes as she nodded. Silently, she helped her sister onto the table and fastened her restraints. And as she pulled the last strap tight, she said, "I am sorry."

"For what?"

"Murdering you twice."

Omeka shook her head. "You didn't murder me; the Advocate did." She smiled. "You *saved* me, and you're going to save me again."

Chapter 41

Sixxis hopped bough to bough, breezing his way through the Rixxonian jungle—and *thakk* did it feel good to be back!

With the dense tree cover, it wasn't easy to find a good spot to land *Zara*. They didn't want to drop in by the farm either, since the open space as Bo put it, "Left them as exposed as a rathcharian's backside." Sixxis had no idea what that meant, but as was typical with the big man, his delivery was *hilarious*.

After some planetary scans, they found a wide enough clearing to lower into, but it left Sixxis pretty far from anything he knew—with a steep climb out, no less. And to top things off, Guild ships dropped into the atmosphere as he pressed up the basin, toward a massive tree at the hill's crest.

So he may have *felt* good, but things were definitely not *looking* good.

More than most places he'd been in the jungle, the branches here weaved in and out of each other, almost like the trees grew as one giant entity. This made it easy for Sixxis to move quicker—to literally run up and down the giant boughs twisting about—as opposed to his usual method of skipping limb to limb, using vines and smaller branches to guide his momentum.

He came close to the big tree before long. Like an enormous flower in full bloom, its wide trunk stretched above the canopy and unfolded into a collection of thick branches. Charging up one final incline, Sixxis launched at an opening between them.

He whistled to himself as his feet clacked onto the wood. "I think I've found my new favorite place."

Craning his neck, he took in the impressive bough spread, like countless fingers splaying out from where he stood on the tree's palm. Even way up here, the thick foliage kept things dim, dark even. And it was absolutely silent, something Sixxis wasn't sure he'd *ever* found in the jungle. He'd need to bring Adira back sometime.

Adira...

Sixxis hadn't been alone, probably since he left her and Jag to toss the operative—no, the *Advocate*—into the river after the farm fight. How long had he been gone?

Almost a week? Was that really it?

Skies.

There's no way Adira could've even come close to finding all the jungle folk in so short a time. She was *definitely* still searching—so she could've been anywhere. But that wouldn't stop Sixxis. He'd find her. He *had* to find her.

He had to make sure she was safe.

A heavy wind rustled the leaves about him as he sucked in a whiff of crisp, fresh air. If he had to be alone, he was glad it was back here in the jungle—his comfort zone. Because even for Sixxis, one who was no stranger to pushing himself *out* of that comfort zone, everything that had happened was—

"Sixxis," hummed Remy's voice inside his ear, "it would be best if we keep off communications for a time."

"Everything okay back there?"

"...yes."

He propped a hand on his hip. "That's not very convincing."

"Just be careful, Six," added Jag. "I'll let you know when we're clear."

"Okay," he replied, shrugging to himself.

That was weird. What could be—

Suddenly, the wind swelled and surged, rushing past Sixxis as a deep droning invaded his quiet moment. Then things started shaking even more—like something was forcing its way down through the canopy near where he stood.

Not good.

"Until next time." Sixxis saluted the towering branches, then skipped across the palm and grabbed a vine. The packed-in plant life made it impossible for him to slide all the way to the surface; he had to get creative to make his way down. But the continuous drone and rushing wind masked all evidence of his rapid movement.

Then it stopped, moments after he hit the ground. Taking care to keep quiet, he tiptoed around the enormous trunk.

"Report," grunted a gruff, gravelly voice.

Sixxis froze and dropped to a crouch.

"Sir!" replied another person. "We've located a collection of heat signatures east of here."

"Several Rixxonians in one place? Doesn't *that* make things easier! Prepare a squad to head there at once." The gravel man cleared his throat. "What of the source?"

"Scanners have located it. Shall I send a squad there as well?"

"No; we can pick it up on our way out. The people are higher priority, and I want to keep all hands available."

"Yes sir! Anything else?"

"Tell everyone to stay sharp. Don't underestimate the Rixxonians."

Damn straight, don't underestimate them!

The people were coming together, just like Adira wanted. *Thakk,* she was incredible. It hadn't even been a week—not even a single eclipse—and she'd gathered what sounded like a pretty big group! And this meant she might be easier to find than he first thought—because there was only one place she'd bring them: the Forbidden Village.

Problem was, Sixxis didn't know how to get there; they found it by accident last time. His only choice was to follow the Guild goons. He'd just need to—

A hand clasped over his mouth.

Chapter 42

Positioned atop her stepladder, Remy clicked the transfer wire into a slot below her sister's right ear. Bilanthia stood to the gurney's left, pistol drawn. Bo waited to the right, ready to pounce at a moment's notice.

"Once I allow the Intelligence access," said Omeka, lashed tightly to the metallic table, "the Advocate will be here. It might be best to remove my eyes."

"I beg your pardon?" said Bilanthia.

She laughed. "Remove the panel below my left eye and sever the wires behind it. That will deactivate my ocular implants."

Remy did as instructed.

"I've been thinking," said Jag. "I want to talk to him again."

Bo cracked his neck to one side, then the other. "Do what you gotta do. We'll be ready."

"It's not a bad idea," Omeka added. "You'll buy me more time."

"Every second counts," said Remy with a nod. "Perhaps you should wait a few moments; see what happens before you begin."

Jag positioned himself opposite her. "Just give me the signal."

It was time.

Leaning forward, Remy ran her fingers through Omeka's hair. "Are you sure this will work?"

Omeka nodded. "If you jolt my exposed wiring again, it will shut me down for good. Hit me with it the moment you see anything but my head move."

"I love you, sister," Remy whispered.

"I love you, too," Omeka replied, beaming, staring blindly forward. "Okay, I'm lowering my guard. Don't believe anything you hear." Her head succumbed to the room's gravity and sank downward.

An instant later, it lurched upward and jolted side to side—while the rest of her body remained still.

"Clever," she said as her disturbing motions came to a halt. "You've taken my eyes."

The Advocate had arrived, a fact made evident not by Omeka's choice of words, but by the energy settling there the moment her body fell still.

It was... *disquieting*.

"I know you're there, Remy. You're the only one in that band of idiots that could have any chance of reactivating me. Then again, I wasn't sure even *you* would be able to do it. I must say—I'm impressed!"

Without a word, Remy lifted her eyebrows at Jag, who lifted his own in return.

"But I'm also very *angry*. You see, you took a *part of me*. That's something I simply cannot get past. I will forgive, though—if you return her to me *unharmed*."

To Remy's knowledge, forgiveness was not a word in the Advocate's vocabulary.

"Have you ever imagined what we could do if we joined our minds, Remy? Think about it. Your genius combined with my Intelligence? We'd be a force to be reckoned with!"

Clenching her fist, still she said nothing.

"Fine," Omeka sneered. "Your silence is the only answer I need. Wait right there; I'll destroy you and your friends." Her head jolted to the side. "Remy!" she cried out. "Please help me!"

Remy darted her panicked gaze to Jag, whose similar expression met hers as she mouthed, "Not yet."

"Gah, you truly are a nuisance!" Omeka grunted. "You've got a lot of nerve after everything we gave you. How *dare* you betray me!" She spat. "Ending your life will be much more than a necessity—it will be a *pleasure*."

They had waited long enough: Remy caught Jag's eye.

"Remy's not here," he said, standing strong before Omeka's deactivated eyes. "It's just me."

She fell still at his voice. "Jag! How's that wrist feeling?"

"Better, thanks."

"I must say: I underestimated you. And you've certainly made me pay for it. I—"

"Why has the Guild been meddling on lower-developed planets? What do you have to gain?"

"My my." She laughed. "You're not skipping a beat, are you?"

Jag folded his arms. "You really ran that last conversation. I still have questions."

"Hah—very well. Shall we continue our promise?"

"Total honesty," Jag replied with a grin. He glanced at Bilanthia and repeated, "Why has the Guild been meddling on lower-developed planets?"

"Isn't it obvious?"

"You're stockpiling resources—I get that. But why the sudden jump in operations?"

"We recently acquired a new investor, and that investor has many needs. We are simply repaying the interest."

Jag glanced at Bilanthia again. "That seems too simple."

"I don't know what to tell you. It *is* that simple."

"But I—"

"Ah ah!" Omeka's mouth tilted into a devious smile. "Remember, these are information *exchanges*."

"I—"

"How did you make it off Rixxon Prime? It seems unlikely that you would disrupt my plans on that Class V planet and then somehow leave it to join forces with my political nemesis, a defector of my organization, and a Quadmalian."

"I—umm..."

"Remember the rules, Jag: you *must* tell the truth."

After an encouraging—but crooked—smile from Bilanthia, Jag drew a deep breath. "When you threatened our people, someone came and asked me to help stop you for good. She connected us with Remy and Bilanthia."

"I see. So—"

"You said there were three of you on the ship. You, my mother, and—"

"Jason. He was the third."

"So Jason was my father."

"Well if it wasn't me"—her head jolted—"there weren't exactly other choices."

"How long were you three on the ship?" Jag asked.

"Garrison says two years in sleep stasis, then about one and a half awake."

"Seems like a long time to spend with such a self-righteous ass—a *murdering*, self-righteous ass."

"Ohoho—tell me how you really feel!"

Remy gasped inaudibly, glaring at Jag as he continued.

"You and I are the only humans anywhere close to here—well, you're at least *part* human. Anyway, I like to think I'm a good—"

"Really?" Omeka scoffed. "Are you about to bitch and moan about how you're some shining light of a person, I'm a dark scourge on the galaxy, and it's made you all confused about what it means to be human?"

The force of her words propelled Jag back a step. "I—"

"It's a little late in life to be learning this, but I get that your situation has been a bit off—so here's your lesson!" Omeka cleared her throat and altered her voice. "Anyone can be born anywhere and end up being anybody." Though blind, she glared at Jag. "All that shit you're worrying about doesn't matter."

"Well—"

"Did you see Omeka?" she interrupted, cutting the conversation forward.

Remy caught Jag's eye and shook her head. The Advocate could not learn of their discussion with Omeka—that was imperative.

"What do you mean?" Jag said. "I see her right now."

"Just now—did you *speak* with Omeka?"

"No."

"Hmmm..." She squinted, still staring forward. "There's something different about you." She lifted an eyebrow—then reared her head back. "Ahahaha—have you embraced your heritage and become a new man?"

"Something feels different all right."

"You know, you seem quite capable," she said, still laughing. "Hell, you *are* quite capable—but *stars* are you naive. I promise you: the fact that you're human has zero significance."

"It's significant to me."

"Oh please. *You* decide who you are." The corner of her mouth tilted upward. "And sometimes, you *create* it."

"Like Pert Gubora created you?"

"Gubora was..." She trailed off. "I—"

"*Was,*" Bilanthia repeated as he stepped toward her, gun aimed at her head.

"Aha—Bilanthia is here, too! Jag, why didn't you—"

Bilanthia pressed the gun into her temple. "I thought it uncharacteristic of the Guild to resort to such meaningless destruction. What did you do to Gubora?"

Turning to him, a vile smirk stretched across her face, she pressed her forehead into his weapon. "It appears the lizard man's death has struck a nerve in the good doctor! What a nice surprise—though it should've been expected."

"You murdered him."

"He was holding me back—in more ways than one." Her smirk stretched wider. "Like everyone else in this galaxy, he could have never truly appreciated what I've become."

"Because you're a monster," Jag declared, standing tall.

"Gah!" Omeka's head banged into the gurney. "Your lack of understanding *severely* diminishes my phenomenal breakthrough. Why must you—"

Her head twitched.

"Why must you *bother* me so much?"

It twitched again.

"You've *always* bothered me—and that's why I'm going to have a chat with your green friends. They know you best. Perhaps I'll finally learn what makes you so unbearably aggravating!"

A slight twitch in Omeka's finger drew Remy's eye—and she did not hesitate. She dialed the probe's voltage as high as it would go, then leaned into her ear. "Do not get comfortable. I will kill you—personally."

"So Remy *is* here—wonderful!" Her hand formed a fist. "I'm glad I—"

Remy drove the rod into her sister's head. The resulting burst threw her from the stool and slammed her into the hard, metal ground—where she found herself stuck.

She could not move.

Desperately trying to regain command of her limbs, Remy blinked wildly and darted her gaze toward the gurney. There, the hand that had previously been a fist hung limp.

"We gotta get to Sixxis," said Bo, pressing to his feet.

"Right," Jag agreed from his hands and knees.

Regaining control, Remy pulled her legs close and curled into a ball.

"Doc, you should stay with *Zara* on the bridge." Bo rumbled for the exit.

"Roger that!" replied Bilanthia, hustling past Jag.

Omeka was alive, then she was not. She was an abomination, then dead—for the third and final time. It was the most terrible pain Remy had ever felt.

But for just a handful of moments—not even an hour—Omeka was herself again. And she did not hesitate to set her sister straight, for Remy truly *had* forgotten.

She had forgotten that inexplicable feeling of their parents' death, to have everything in one moment and nothing in the next. It was pain—like this—that she never got the chance to process. No, she did not have time for emotion; she spent the next several years keeping herself and Omeka alive. But keep them alive she did, and they grew safe—comfortable as she rose the ranks of the Guild.

"Remy?" Jag said.

Her life only rewarded the retreat from emotion, but there was no doubt: All she'd done was avoid them. And as a result, she hadn't truly lived.

Jag dropped to a knee and put a hand on her back. "It's over."

Omeka, her parents, the other mind-enslaved operatives, the people on Merutan... all these people had lived, only to have their choice in life taken away from them. And Jag. Merely trying to make sense of his life, he was beaten sense*less* for it—yet here he was, with Remy.

A single tear ran down her face. "I am sorry,"

"No," said Jag, scooping her balled body and holding her close. "You have nothing to be sorry for. You lost someone important—*again*. Just let it all out."

And let it out, Remy did.

She wept. For the first time in over ten years, she cried out audibly, inaudibly, even with just her body itself. The grief—the overwhelming loss and suffering she'd held down for so long—it consumed her, just as her screams consumed the hollow of the cavernous room.

But all the while, Jag held her tight, squeezing harder as her cries grew louder.

This went on for a full minute. Then, sniffling, Remy muttered, "Thank you. I..." She leaned away from him, her full smile glistening on her tear-coated face. "I am glad to call you my friend."

Jag smiled back.

"Sixxis!" she said, her face blowing outward. "You must go!"

"Will you be—"

"Yes, I will be fine. Go!"

With a nod, Jag popped to his feet and ran for the door.

Straightway, wiping an arm across her running nose, Remy stood and crossed to the workbench to see what Omeka had found for them. She tapped the handheld's screen to life and was greeted by a first-person video recording. In it, she recognized the landscape of Phyator, a swimming hole in the Beruushan Gorge.

Was this... one of Omeka's memories?

She turned the device horizontal to lengthen the view as it redirected toward an off-screen voice, revealing a small child.

Herself.

Young Remy dashed past the viewpoint and flew from the rock on which they stood. Voices called congratulations as her head emerged from the water.

It *was* a memory—one Remy knew well. This was the last time their family was together, just moments before the explosion.

The blurry screen focused on the two adults below as they cheered for Omeka, encouraging her to jump. And with one final look at her beaming sister, she launched herself into the air and plummeted to her family's ovation.

Remy's mouth tilted into a half-smile. Seeing herself happy—so brimming with joy—it filled her with a warmth she had been lacking for some time. And this past feeling helped her recognize one current.

Sixxis had become family, just like Omeka said. All these people had—even Bilanthia.

As much as Remy wanted to sit there and sift through the files, she was needed elsewhere. There were already multiple Guild ships on the Rixxonian surface, with likely more coming. They would need her assistance. She could not stand by.

Her eyes drifted to the probe sitting undisturbed on the engine room floor. And with it, a theory entered her mind.

Yes... perhaps there was something to it.

Invigorated by warmth, love, and a newfound, passionate desire to help her friends, Remy approached Omeka and squeezed her hand. "Goodbye, sister. Thank you for saving me."

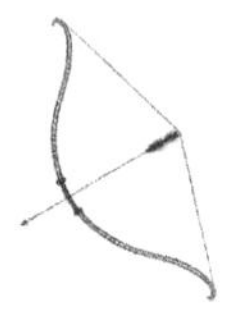

Chapter 43

"Don't move."

Hah—yeah right!

Grinning under the hand, Sixxis hopped up and shot his body down—but met only the resistance of an arm wrapped around his waist.

"Come on, Sixxis," he heard as he wobbled still. "I said *don't* move!"

Wait a minute...

Instead of going down this time, he spun—and came face to face with Adira. "It's you!"

"Shh"—Adira threw her eyes past him—"you're being too—"

Sixxis hurled his lips the small space between them, meeting hers in passion. And for just a moment, the jungle's dense chorus dissipated, taking with it all sense of danger as he closed his eyes and felt only her.

"Who's there?" came a voice, interrupting their moment.

Adira pulled back and looked Sixxis in the eyes, then dashed into the thicket.

Sixxis followed right behind her—but the ground disappeared as he slid through the brambles. Grasping over his head with one hand, throwing the other over his mouth to keep quiet, he managed to grab hold of a thick root and swing into a recessed area below, thudding onto the hard ground.

He winced and looked up at Adira, who mouthed, "Sorry," over the rustling above them.

Well, that wasn't the way Sixxis wanted that moment to end, but *thakk* if it wasn't the best moment of his life! All the fear, the worry, how much he missed her—it was gone.

"Hmph." Boots clomped the ground above them, fading away into the jungle noise.

Adira swept toward Sixxis and pressed their foreheads together. "It's good to see you," she said, pulling herself closer.

Sixxis' mouth tilted as he wrapped his arms around her. "I've been thinking about this moment since we left."

"As have I." She pulled back. "But I wish you'd come alone."

"Thought I'd bring some of the fun back," Sixxis replied, rubbing at the back of his head. "In case you were bored."

"Now isn't the time for jokes. Our people are in danger!"

Sixxis' expression darkened. "And if we don't do something, what's in store is *not* good." But the darkness didn't last long: his face stretched into his signature grin. "They said they found a bunch of us in one spot. Any idea where that is?"

"The"—her eyes narrowed—"why are you looking at me like that?"

"You're incredible. How many have you found?"

Adira smiled. "I'll tell you on the way to Therulin Glade." She jumped, grabbed the root, and swung up onto the shelf above.

"Therulin Glade?"

Her smile grew as she looked down at him. "Formerly the Forbidden Village."

Sixxis' face exploded—but he didn't have time to get excited for her. He needed to keep up, and they needed to *go*. So with a hop, he mirrored her movements on his way to the level above and pushed aside everything in his path until he came in step with her.

Adira rounded the tree with Sixxis matching her gait. "I've found twenty so far—in five separate groups! I—"

"We should probably get off the ground," said Sixxis. "Sorry, I want to hear about—"

"No—it's okay; you're right." She sighed, craning her neck. "Everything's too high."

Hah—*nothing* was too high!

Tapping a finger on his chin, Sixxis waltzed through a gateway of two mighty trunks. He leaned his back on one and stretched his neck up the other. "Give me a boost?"

Adira crossed to him, crouched, and laced her fingers into a basket.

"Three..." Sixxis planted a foot in her hands and bobbed at the knee. "Two... one..." He pushed off, taking the extra lift and kicking off the trunk to a higher branch. And when he landed, he hooked it with his knees and dangled back down. "I've got you."

Adira backed up and got a running start. She leapt up the tree, rebounded with the same fluidity, and reached a hand for his. Her feet met the opposite tree the moment they touched. "Now what?" she asked as they swayed still.

Sixxis double-pumped his eyebrows. "You climb me."

"You're impossible," she groaned. And with a vicious eye roll, she moved hand over hand up his body.

"And *you* aren't the only person to—"

Her knee knocked into his face—probably on purpose. "It's amazing you don't get it from everybody."

"Just a matter of time before I do."

As she came parallel with a strong enough branch, Adira reached off Sixxis, grabbed hold, and swung herself up. "I'll lead the way."

Sixxis fell in behind her as she leapt onto a thick bough and bounded off her toes to another, matching the rhythm of her steps as they danced through the understory.

"What's happening?" she asked. "Why are these people here?"

Sixxis picked up speed. "They're with those last guys." He hopped down a level, crossed under Adira, then rose up again, skipping forward in symmetry with her. "There's more to it, but Jag made their leader really mad, and he threatened to come and take our people—to take *you.* We got here as soon as we could."

"But Jag's all right? Seeing you alone, I worry about him."

"Yeah—took a few beatings, but he's okay; the doc fixed him up. He's just helping Remy with something."

"Doc? Remy?"

"Don't worry; you'll meet them soon. You'll like Remy, I think."

"So, the blue and orange beast," she said. "That was you?"

"What?"

"I saw two black beasts come from the sky, then one blue and orange, then more black."

"Ah—yep, that was us!"

"Six, you hear me?" hummed Jag.

Sixxis bounced forward a few more boughs and stopped. "I hear you!"

"What have you found out there?"

"Adira! And I overheard some Guild goons talking about a group of Rixxonians. We're heading there now."

"Where?"

"The Forbidden Village. It's thakkin' cool, Jag—she's found twenty people and re-named it Therulin Glade!"

Adira's feet pitter pattered behind him. "Wh—what? Are you speaking a different language?"

Sixxis snapped upright. So weird... he didn't even realize it, but sure enough: Adira sounded different from Jag. He really *was* speaking a different language. "I guess I am," he said in Rixxoninan.

"Who are you talking to?"

"Hang on, brother." Sixxis turned. "I'm talking to Jag."

Adira's head tilted. "What?"

"A lot's happened since the last eclipse. I promise I'll tell you everything."

"I..." she trailed off, eyeing him up and down. "Yes, you are a bit different." She smiled. "It suits you."

It didn't take long, but she'd found it in him. This past week, these experiences—they had him feeling so *alive!* Of course he missed Adira and thought about her all the time, but now he couldn't imagine a life back on Rixxon Prime, not anymore—not after the places he'd been and the things he'd seen.

"Six," Jag said, "I don't know where the village is. Can you—"

"You can use the tracker," Remy interrupted.

"What's that?" Jag asked

"I installed a tracking device in Sixxis' suit before the Merutan mission. I"—Remy cleared her throat—"I thought he would get lost in the forest."

Sixxis laughed. "Valid concern."

"I regret nothing."

"I bet you never do."

"Jag, there is a receiver in your suit. Rapidly tap your wrist interface four times, and—"

"I've got this, little one," Bo assured.

"We'll meet you there," Jag said

Sixxis looked to Adira, almost losing himself in her eyes. "Let's go save our people."

"Nice to be back"—Sixxis hopped down a platform, across the main avenue—"you know, *not* running for our lives."

"For now," said Adira, criss-crossing behind him. "But this..." She hopped to the ground and wandered forward. "The waning sunlight... It feels all too familiar."

A pit rose in Sixxis' stomach as he padded into the soft dirt. High above him, a distance that seemed much shorter than before, the moon crawled toward the sun.

The eclipse would start soon.

As he stepped onto the charred patch left by their last visit, hanging his head at the dead grass' crunch beneath his feet, Sixxis' mind transported him back to that night, when his parents died protecting their escape.

Familiar was right.

"Where is everyone?" he asked.

"Just up ahead." Adira took his hand. "In the villa."

His parents were so strong; though it was long ago, that fact had always clung to his mind. And now he had no choice but to step into their position. Could he protect these people like they did all those years ago?

"It's different this time," said Adira, either reading his mind or continuing her own thought from before. "This time we know what's coming."

And there it was—the *true* strength here, the strength that drew his father into battle all those years ago, the same that pushed Sixxis to flee, pulling his brother behind him.

"Come on," she said, tugging at him. "We may have gotten here first, but we don't have much time." She broke into a jog down the avenue, toward the Ancestor Tree standing resolute over the chief's villa. "We should get everyone out of here."

"I don't know about that," he said, running after her. "The Advocate's a persistent guy. He won't stop until he finds what he's looking for—which is *you*."

Adira slid to a stop beside the looming Tree. "What are you saying? That we can't escape?"

"No." He continued past her and turned. "But if we run, all we'll do is scatter again. We're stronger in numbers. We should make a stand."

"Are you crazy? You saw what that one man did at the farm."

"I *am* crazy, yes—but not in this case. Jag will be here soon, and Bo." He laughed. "Oh man, wait 'til you see *him.*"

Adira scowled. "I don't understand how you're so relaxed."

Relaxed? Hah!

"It's all an act," said Sixxis, turning for the villa's open door. "I'm really freaking out."

"That's... comforting, actually—in a strange way."

"I do what I—"

"Wait, Sixxis!"

Too late! A rope tightened around his ankle, ripping him off his feet and into the air, where he dangled and swayed upside down.

"Who's there?" A woman flew from the villa, her back-length braids whipping her body as she charged, arrow nocked and aimed at his face. "You're back!" she said to Adira, lowering her weapon.

"Yes—and I found help!"

The woman looked up at Sixxis' upside-down body—clearly unimpressed. "This?"

Adira nodded. "He doesn't look like much, but Sixxis was there when we fought the Thakk." Her lips folded into a radiant smile, shining in the deepening twilight. "He saved my life."

"Sixxis?" came another voice from inside the villa. "Wazzaru and Mara's boy?" A man emerged, much older than the rest of them. He was entirely bald. "This either bodes well or frighteningly bad for us." His eyes met Adira's. "What of the beasts? What is coming?"

"Nothing good."

Sixxis had rotated enough so his back was to them. "Hang on," he said, waiting to turn around. When he did, "Long story short, bad guys from different planets who want to kidnap you."

They needed a plan—but Jag was the planner, not him.

"Hands out." Adira bent down and pulled a dagger from her ankle sheath. She popped up, hopped off the doorframe, and cut the rope.

Stretching his arms down at the last second, Sixxis planted his hands and sprang to his feet. "Thanks for that."

"So you think we should fight?" Adira said, sheathing her dagger.

Sixxis nodded and threw up a fist.

"I like this one," laughed the other woman. "He's bold."

"Foolhardy's more like it," said Adira.

The woman laughed again. "I'm Peralla."

"And I am Gorren, founding member of the new chief's guard"—the man smiled at Sixxis—"and old friend of your parents. They would be proud of your determination to defend this place."

Sixxis dropped to a knee and bowed his head. "Gorren, it would be my honor to join the new chief's guard."

"Come on!" Adira's face glowed orange, matching her top bun as she shoved him. "Cut it out!"

"What?" he said, rocking to the side and then back up straight. "Got to protect what I love!"

"Love?" Peralla scoffed. "This is hardly the time for such trifles."

Sixxis shrugged. "I don't think you get to choose when it happens."

"Welcome, second member of the new chief's guard," said Gorren, pulling Sixxia to his feet.

"How are the children?" Adira asked.

"All three are in the false room," Gorren reported.

"And the traps?"

"By all the major entrances, and on all sides of the open avenue."

"Weapons?"

"We searched every hut in the village and took what we could. It's all inside."

Thakk—guess Jag's plan wasn't necessary after all. Adira had things covered!

She turned to him. "Will these people have explosive projectiles like the man at the farm?"

"From what I've seen"—Sixxis grimaced—"probably?"

"And from what you overheard, they're tracking us by our... heat?"

"Yeah—actually, let me check on that." He tilted his head and shifted languages, "Remy, you there?"

"Yes," Remy replied.

"The Guild said something about locating heat signatures. What does that mean?"

"They have scanners that detect the heat emanating from your bodies. Frankly, I am surprised they are effective, given this planet's climate."

Wait, did that mean—

"So if it's hotter, they might not be able to see us?"

"Perhaps. The scanners do not differentiate between living and nonliving matter; they merely recognize thermal energy."

High above, the eclipse folded more and more darkness onto the scene. And this time it'd be *their* advantage.

"Great!" Sixxis hopped a little. "Jag, Bo—you two close?"

"Should be," Jag replied.

Nodding, Sixxis turned back to the Rixxonians; both Gorren and Peralla's mouths hung open.

"In all my days..." Gorren muttered.

"Ah"—Sixxis scratched at the back of his head—"Sorry about that. It's a long story."

"What did you learn?" Adira asked.

"They're tracking our body heat, but *only* our heat. They can't tell what's us and what's just, uhh"—he shrugged—"hot."

"Real eloquent," said Peralla, rolling her eyes.

Sixxis ignored her, a savage grin plastered on his face. "I have an idea."

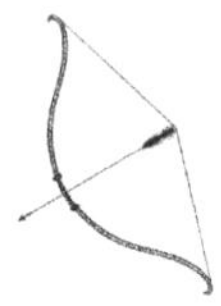

Chapter 44

"Sir!' The Lommorian agent snapped a salute, her yellow scales jumping off the endless green around her. "The final regiment will enter the atmosphere momentarily. We will be ready to march on the village within the hour."

"Good," replied the Laktilian operative. "How many Rixxonians are there?"

"Initial readings indicate twenty, maybe more. The heat and humidity are disrupting our estimates."

Twenty Rixxonians... Given his previous trouble with just three, the Advocate had spared no free hand in the assault. And given his recent assassination of Pert Gubora, all Guild resources were now in his control. So together, he gathered five of his appendages and three full regiments of agents

The Laktilian grinned a wide, vicious grin. "Sixty-five on twenty—good odds, don't you think?"

The agent responded with a grin of her own. "I do."

But the twenty Rixxonians were only part of the foreseen resistance. Shortly after his first ship arrived, another descended to the surface—presumably Jag and the others. It had taken long enough to gather ranks, so they would likely be in the village soon. That meant one all-out offensive, then odds and ends to take care of—because there was no longer any question: they had Omeka.

The Laktilian's grin stretched even wider.

This would be a fruitful stop indeed. They would collect as many Rixxonians as they could, then split ranks to claim the downed pod and his kidnapped appendage. And all the while, the Advocate labored in his workshop, repairing the fallen operatives and reinforcing their systems with *beautiful* tritonic steel.

Things would soon be right again. He would have Jag's mind and everything it held. Because while the Advocate had renounced his connection to Garrison—that *weak* human—he still craved the truth.

"Divide the agents into five equal groups," directed the Laktilian. "Have four form ranks and await further orders. Send the fifth to me."

The Lommorian snapped another salute. "Sir!" She scurried off, as the final dropship whirred into a nearby clearing.

Contingencies. Back-up plans. Failsafes.

The Advocate was not used to setting such things in place. But given his recent... *failures...* he could not underestimate his enemies any longer. Already they had crippled the Guild network, stolen his greatest creation, *and* managed to reactivate her—something that altogether baffled him. Because despite onerous study and rigorous experimentation, it took the Advocate *years* to grasp the technology behind his Intelligence. And even still, he didn't reach full understanding before gaining access to the Buyer's knowledge base. So how had they figured it out?

Were they... better than him?

No. He was *extraordinary.* Nobody compared in body, *or* in mind.

And he would soon be *better.*

They—or rather, *Remy*—simply got lucky. Now, he was merely heeding the advice of his late friend, Pert Gubora.

Careful... yes, he was being careful.

Chapter 45

Jag stretched his arm forward and swept it round to refocus their heading. A red light on his wrist blinked faster as he found the right direction. "This way." He tiptoed up an embankment.

"Remy wasn't kidding," said Bo, wiping a hand across his brow. "This place is muggy as hell. Gravity's real heavy, too. No wonder you're so fit—you work hard with every step and sweat it all out!"

Trees blocked every corner of Jag's vantage until they came to the hill's apex. There, two lines of flickering lights cut through the thinning undergrowth, dancing on the sides of the village avenue.

They'd arrived—and the cauldrons were lit?

"Six," he said, "you're drawing them right to us!"

"Don't worry," Sixxis replied, "I've got a plan."

Jag's head cocked back. "*You* have a plan?"

"I also find that difficult to believe," Remy added.

"Well, it's mostly Adira's plan," he admitted. "But I helped! The fire should confuse their heat detectors."

"That is..." Remy trailed off. "...brilliant, actually."

Sixxis snickered. "Jag, they're close. I need you and Bo to lure them down main street."

"How many are there?" Jag didn't exactly want to be the diversion—not again.

"Oh, a fair few. I've got eyes on the main group. They're coming in opposite the villa."

As his heart rate accelerated and pounded his chest, the tenderness in Jag's newly repaired ribs became more and more noticeable.

"Stand in front of the Ancestor Tree," Sixxis continued. "Have your weapon ready, but hold off as long as you can. Just taunt them."

Jag wasn't sure he could shoot the operatives, not after what he'd learned from Omeka. One way or another, they were alive. He couldn't hurt them—not while they had no control.

"I've seen them talking to each other. Remy, correct me if I'm wrong, but that should mean they're not all the Advocate."

"That is correct."

"Thakk yeah!" Sixxis celebrated. "That means most of these jerks are *choosing* to be here. And they've chosen the wrong planet to mess with, right Jag?"

"Right." Jag nodded, mostly to himself. Because *he* had no choice: it was time to fight. But how could he tell who was under the Advocate's control and who wasn't?

Bo stepped in beside him. "Have you ever killed anybody?"

"Just once."

"Pits—shouldn't've asked." He clapped him on the back, pushing him down the hill. "You'll do great!"

"Brother," Sixxis almost whispered, "it feels a lot like that night, doesn't it?"

Jag lifted his gaze up through a small break in the canopy, toward the darkened sky. With the rush of everything, he hadn't even taken a moment to consider it, but Sixxis was right. The lit cauldrons, the coming danger, the almost-full eclipse—all of it.

"Adira, tell him what you told me."

"I might feel like that night," came Adira's voice, speaking Rixxonian, "but this time we know what's coming. This time, it's no unseen enemy that merely wishes to scatter us. We face conquerors, invaders from a different world that threaten everything we hold dear and intend to take us from our home.

"And this time, we're not reacting. This time we're ready."

"Dunno what she just said"—Bo shrugged—"but it sounded impressive."

"Sixxis doesn't exaggerate when he says she's incredible," Jag said.

They hadn't even been gone one eclipse, and from the sound of it, Adira had really grown into her new role. Maybe that meant Jag could, too. But what role was that? Who was he, and what could he do?

Continuing down the hill, he came up beside a hut.

Jag didn't have all the answers, but he didn't need them right now. He just needed to step up, to protect this place and its people.

"We stand tall as trees," he muttered, nodding again to himself.

"You might want to come in through a window," said Sixxis.

Jag glanced into the empty home. "Why?"

"Just trust me."

"Enough for me," said Bo, squeezing his massive frame through the opening. "I assume the Ancestor Tree is the big one at the end of the road?"

The Ancestor Tree. The thing Jag clung to as Rinx soldiers marched down the avenue—the thing he'd defend with everything he had, like his parents before him.

"Yeah," he replied, climbing in after Bo, "that's it."

Jag crossed the dirt floor and stepped into the open, as darkness overtook everything but the cauldrons' fluttering firelight. He turned right, drawing his rifle and swiveling his head as they advanced toward the great Tree.

Silence enveloped their footsteps and the crackling fire, an overwhelming juxtaposition to Jag's last visit. He ran for his life down this same avenue just a week ago, under this same eclipse. Now he was back with new life, new identity.

...or was he the same?

"Is this the village your parents died protecting?" Bo whispered, drawing two pistols.

"This is it—where I grew up."

"Then we'll have to make 'em proud."

Jag slowed as he approached the Tree. Closing his eyes, he pressed a palm into its bark. "Mother, father—and mother, wherever you're buried—stay with me."

Warmth surged from the Tree, almost as if they were listening.

"May I?" Bo stretched a hand forward and caught Jag's eye, then too pressed a palm into the imposing trunk. "I see why you call this the Ancestor Tree." He closed his eyes. "They're here—all three of 'em. I can feel it."

Jag's looked up at him. "What do you mean?"

"Dunno 'bout any sorta afterlife, but there's something to be said about energies."

"Energies?"

Bo opened his eyes and nodded. "Our energies linger when we pass, staying with those we love, in the places that mean something to us, or sometimes in a place we know we'll be needed again someday. You felt something when you touched the Tree, didn't you?"

"Yeah."

He placed his enormous hand on Jag's shoulder and smiled. "We're not alone."

A twig snapped to their left.

"In more ways than one, apparently," whispered Jag, whipping and aiming at the sound.

"Wait for it..." said Sixxis.

Jag lowered his weapon. "What are—"

SWISH!

"Ahh!" yelled someone unseen.

"Hah!" Sixxis popped. "Don't fall too hard!"

WHOOSH! Jag whirled around—as a Guild agent disappeared into the ground.

"Sirs!" called out a voice from the hole. "Traps!"

But it was too late. Snaps and cracks broke the still of the scene as all around the avenue, Guild agent after Guild agent was yanked upside down, plunged into a pit, or thrown backward.

"Very clever, Jag!" yelled a deep, raspy voice. "I'm impressed you were able to get here so quickly!"

"Leave now!" Jag shouted back. "You won't be taking anyone today!"

"Ahh—you underestimate how many troops I have to spare!"

Just then, no less than ten agents—all in that standard Guild armor Jag had come to recognize—leapt onto the avenue from either side, past the few others caught in triggered traps. They formed ranks in two equal lines and advanced on Jag and Bo.

"Remember," barked the voice, "we want everyone *unharmed!*"

High in the canopy, clutching a vine, Sixxis hooked his toes round a branch. "Ready?" he said, glancing at the two Rixxonians on either side of him.

"Ready!" they replied in unison.

He glanced across the way—where Gorren and Peralla waited with their groups—then at Adira and her two beside him.

Talk about incredible. Sixxis hadn't seen this many jungle folk in one place since he was a kid!

He couldn't help but admire his people. Though they didn't range much in size or stature, each wore their blaze of orange hair in a unique way. Each was ready to fight, to do what they needed to keep themselves and their families safe.

And from what he'd seen in his travels so far, they had a pretty good chance!

"We're ready for you this time!" Jag yelled below.

"Careful what you say," replied the gravel-voiced operative. "Get them!"

As the agents picked up their pace, clomping their boots down the dirt path, Sixxis threw up a thumb. All the Rixxonians responded in turn.

Time to go!

"Yee-yee-yeeee!" Machete in hand, he leapt from his branch and swung toward the battle below. Greenery flashed by his flying frame until he reached the avenue, where it disappeared and was replaced with *other* green flashes—the other swinging Rixxonians. He grinned to himself and braced for impact.

SLICE—THUMP—THUD! In successive motions, he cut through one agent, kicked off another, and rebounded from a third, launching himself into a backflip. All around him, the others collided with the rows of agents, slamming feet into their bodies or pulling them from the ground.

Perfect timing: All ten Guild agents cleared from the avenue as Sixxis landed in a crouch at its center. Rising up, back to Jag and Bo, he whipped his head over his shoulder and tossed up a thumb. "Welcome to Therulin Glade!"

His two companions swung in and landed beside him, as did Gorren and his group. Together, the six Rixxonians faced down the road, where more troops broke into a run.

Sixxis grinned. "Bo—you're gonna like this part." He reared his head back. "Yee-yeeee!"

The agents continued their fast pursuit—but just before they hit the open part of the road, a jumble of heavy logs tumbled from the darkness above and drove them into the ground. Then came a rapid barrage of arrows, screaming through the trees to pick off those still standing.

"Eeyooo!" boomed a war cry from the canopy.

"Six," Jag yelled, "watch out!"

"Scatter!" Sixxis dove through the cauldrons as an energy blast left the ground behind him a sizzling pile of black. He whipped around. "Everyone good?"

"Yes!" reported Gorren, peeking from behind a cauldron on the other side.

"Change of plans," yelled the gravelly Guildsman, "fire at will, but aim to *injure*—not kill!"

Short surges of light erupted from all directions, a cacophony of gunfire that ensured anyone nearby would know: the Battle for Therulin Glade had begun.

"Time to move!" Jag yelled, launching an arrow down the avenue and engulfing the area in an explosion.

"About time—brace yerself!" Bo grabbed Jag and heaved him onto the chief's villa. "Cover us from up there!" he shouted, plodding off and offering Sixxis a hand up. "Pretty neat—"

SHOOP—THUD! Bo and Sixxis looked left; an agent toppled to the ground, arrow in his chest.

"Damn!" said Bo. "Nice shot, Jag!"

Sixxis took Bo's hand and sprang to his feet. "Glad you're here," he said, double-pumping his eyebrows. "Care to have a little fun?"

"A bunch of non-enhanced goons?" Spinning and stowing his guns, Bo laced his fingers and cracked his knuckles. "Been waitin' fer this!

Another arrow whizzed past them, piercing an agent in the brush to their left.

"Thanks, Jag—Sixxis, up top!" Bo crouched and cradled his hands, nodding to an agent on a high platform.

"Don't mind if I do!" Sixxis planted a foot in Bo's cradle and catapulted himself, drawing his second machete midair. He sliced at the agent as he soared over her and landed in a crouch.

"You definitely get style points for that one!" Bo hollered, running down the road between the lines of tiered huts.

"That was nothing!" Sixxis hollered back as more shots blew in from a higher platform across the avenue. "Bo—comin' down!" He bolted toward the edge and launched toward the big man.

Bo caught Sixxis' feet with all four hands and pitched him toward the high threat. "Tell yer people I'll cover 'em!"

With the assist, Sixxis just cleared the second tier's lip, slashing at the goon's legs as he passed. And as she toppled over the edge, he threw his voice at the avenue, "Gorren—take your folks and clear these guys outta here! The big guy'll cover you!"

"On me!" Gorren yelled in return. "Eeeyaaaa!" Bouncing about, leaping to and fro to avoid the flashing lights all around them, Gorren and his four drew their weapons and charged.

Just then, something caught Sixxis' eye—and it charred the platform as he dove aside. He spun to find his attacker.

Other side of the avenue—no problem!

Slotting back, he sprinted forward and threw his body across the way—but an arrow flew through their head before he got there. And as he landed, Adira and Peralla flipped onto the platform beside him.

"I had that covered," he said, mouth wrinkled.

"I don't think you did," Adira replied, sending his typical grin back his direction.

"Look out!" Peralla rolled behind them, drew her longbow, and fired through the darkness, nailing an almost unseen agent square in the forehead.

"Heh." Sixxis flitted his head between the women. "Who's the better shot?"

"Now's not the time," said Adira, rolling her eyes.

Peralla smirked. "Me, obviously."

Grinning, Sixxis stepped to the edge and looked over. If he thought it was incredible before, this was even better! The five Rixxonians rebounded off trunks, bungalows, and even Bo's big body as they cut down every agent that tried to sneak onto the road. And all the while, Bo took shot after shot—and it sure looked like he didn't miss.

"*Thakk*, our people are amazing," he marveled.

"Six," said an exasperated Jag, "I could use a hand!"

Sixxis threw his attention east—at the bevy of lights by the villa "Skies! We left Jag all alone over there!"

"On it!" Slinging her bow over her shoulder, Peralla took off toward the platform's other side, ran up the bough stretching beyond it, and tossed herself at a hanging vine. "Ee-ko-kooo!" The canopy rustled to life as her voice swelled into the trees. And she hit the avenue's center at a sprint with four Rixxonians right behind her.

Sixxis jogged after her, whistling in amazement. He turned to Adira. "Well, shall we—"

THUMP!

"Impressive show thus far," said the gravel-voiced operative, his breath hot on the back of Sixxis' neck.

Sixxis whirled around. "Wha—"

A shining, white hand came crashing into his head before he could finish, slamming him into the platform—then an arrow flew in and pierced that same hand.

With heavy blinks, Sixxis refocused as the woman he loved faced down the pale man.

"I am Adira, daughter of the late Salaf Therulin and Chieftain of the Rixxonian jungle." She pulled back her bowstring, aiming for his head. "You are not welcome here. Leave at once."

"Ohoho!" The operative ripped the arrow from his hand and applauded her, blue blood oozing from the wound. "You've gained a title since we last met!"

Adira didn't budge. "I've never seen you before in my life."

"I don't have time to explain."

Strong in her footing, Adira fired arrow after arrow at the operative running toward her—but everything bounced off his plated armor.

Thakk!

Sixxis lunged for his dropped machete and threw it at the charging man, piercing cleanly through his shoulder. But as one operative toppled forward and crashed into Adira, another landed on the platform beside Sixxis and lifted him by the throat.

"Well done," said the Laktilian, his tongue spitting from his mouth as he spoke. "Don't worry; it'll be over soon." He lifted his head. "Converge on the Quadmalian—shoot to kill!"

Sixxis grasped at the scaly arm, choking as he tried to get a look.

Four agents surrounded Bo, and he ducked to avoid a shot. While down low, he grabbed one of them by the leg, whirled her around—sweeping the remaining three off their feet—and slammed her into the ground. Then, whipping his weapons from his belt, he fired at them—one, two, three, four.

"Heh," Sixxis coughed, "you'll have to do better than that."

Two agents joined them on the platform, pointing their weapons at a disoriented Adira. And down below, four more agents surrounded Bo, this time keeping their distance.

"Such senseless violence," said the Laktilian. "I had hoped to bring you all with me *unharmed*, but it appears that won't be possible."

"If you don't leave now," Sixxis sputtered through his shrinking airway, "you'll be the only one who's harmed."

A smirk stretched across the Laktilian's pointed snout. "Don't you see? You can't—"

Red exploded from the agents' heads behind him.

"What?" He dropped Sixxis and whirled around.

"Move! Remy shouted.

"Adira—we gotta go!"

They scrambled to their feet and leapt in opposite directions—as *BOOM!* An enormous blast ripped into the night.

Chapter 46

For just a moment, the battle fell still.

Peering through her sniper scope, prone atop a hill adjacent to the village, Remy maintained focus on the Laktilian operative. The electroshock round she created with the probe's materials worked to perfection: The moment it impacted her target's skull, it exploded into a rippling bubble of electricity that crumpled his body and shot the others in all directions. Now, she needed only to confirm her theory.

Had the blast deactivated the Intelligence?

She held her aim on the Laktilian as long as she could justify, then redirected to inspect the battlefield. Sixxis and Adira had managed to escape and were out of view. The blast seemed to have distracted the nearby Guildsmen enough to give Bo and the Rixxonians the time they needed to clear the space, but more troops broke into a run toward them. And at the village's other end, the firefight raged on.

"Bo," Remy said, "to the west!"

"I see 'em!"

"Glad to hear you joining the fight," said Sixxis.

The corner of Remy's mouth twitched. "Well, it is already clear you would have died without me." She whipped her aim and fired a normal round, piercing an agent creeping behind Bo.

"Teamwork for the win!" Bo shouted, waving two arms in the air and firing pistols with his others. "Y'might wanna check on Jag."

Before doing that, Remy glanced at the Laktilian operative; still no movement. And so she pivoted her body to—

Something grabbed hold of her leg, yanking her back and tossing her down the hill's other side. She lost grip of her rifle as she tumbled through the thicket, rolling until she crashed into a large tree trunk.

A deep voice crept beneath the brush. "I'm disappointed in you, Remy. A perfect record—no incidents, no questions, not even a single sign of defiance—and you turn on us in an instant." A red, clawed hand hooked round her leg and pulled her from the ground.

The same Laktilian? No; this one's spines gathered differently.

"Such wasted potential," he said, shaking his head, holding her upside down in front of him. "You could have done great things—hell, you *have* done great things. Your breakthroughs in digging apparatuses alone set us forward ten years."

"I will *still* do great things," she replied, glaring up at him, "the first of which will be destroying you."

"Hah!" He whipped and threw her up the hill. "You still think you can win. It's quite entertaining."

Remy hit the ground hard—but the force of the earth only fortified her resolve. "Why have you done all of this?" she said, sitting up.

"It's a lonely existence, being as brilliant and capable as I am. And the further I push my boundaries, the less possible things become with just one body, one frame of reference." He held out and turned his hand, eyeing it with care. "It's the pursuit of *more* that drives me—a motivation to build on that brilliance." He looked straight at Remy. "You of all people understand."

Remy opened her mouth to speak, then closed it again—for she *did* understand. But she had recently learned there was more to it. "Your actions only drive you further into that lonely existence."

"I am not alone," said the operative, standing tall. "I share the thoughts, fears, and memories of—"

"But you control them. You take all sense of individuality from them. And you therefore do nothing but imprint their thoughts upon your own."

He scowled. "Clearly you *don't* understand."

Remy pressed to her feet and glowered down at him. "You are not as powerful as you imagine yourself to be. Surely even you recognize this after your recent struggles."

"I am *all*-powerful," he replied. "And I will—"

"You are misguided, lost. And your actions are unforgivable." She glanced at her rifle, six paces away.

"I wouldn't try it," he said, drawing and raising a pistol. Slowly, he walked the few steps between them and pressed its barrel into her forehead. "I don't want to kill you, Remy. I spent long enough fused with Omeka that I've grown... attached to you. And—"

"*Do not* invoke my sister's name." Anger swelled and spilled from her voice. "You are unworthy to have even shared her air."

"In her, you manipulated circuitry that took me years to master. With our minds combined, we would truly be unstoppable! And this attachment I feel toward you—it might even persuade me to let you keep conscious control. We'd just—"

"You are an abomination, a debasement of what it means to live." Remy pressed her forehead into his barrel, holding his attention as she reached for the sidearm hidden behind her leg. "And you are desperate: you know your days are numbered."

"Last chance," he said, narrowing his eyes. "Join me, or die."

"*You* are the only one who will die." She drew the sidearm and dropped to her rear in a single motion. Aiming up, bracing herself for what would surely be immense pain, she fired at his face.

BOOM!

The electroburst blasted the operative's body into the air—and flattened Remy into the ground. She lay paralyzed like before, only the effects were far stronger this time

She could not move, even in the slightest way.

"Remy!" Bo yelled. "You okay over there?"

All she could produce were a few faint mumbles.

"I'm on my way!"

"Watch out!" Jag slid down for a better shot and fired.

Peralla jumped and kicked off the agent behind her, shoving him from the roof as the arrow struck him. She landed beside Jag, nocked and ready. "You're a pretty good shot with that thing," she said, firing at an agent on the ground.

"Thanks." Jag surveyed the battle below. Things were starting to turn—and not in a good way. Remy had saved Sixxis and Adira, but with Bo now off helping her, the

Rixxonians had just Jag, Peralla, and Adira covering them. And that meant most of their ammunition wasn't strong enough to penetrate the Guild armor. At least Sixxis had rejoined the fight; his machetes could cut through anything.

"Six," Jag said, "you're no good on your own down there. Get back here—we can make a stand at the Ancestor Tree!"

"Be right there!" He turned to the others and pointed into the understory. They bounded from the avenue and zipped into the trees.

"Peralla," Jag said, "Take the gray-tipped arrows from my quiver." He whipped left and fired, as Peralla drew and fired in the other direction. Swiveling, they launched arrow after arrow in tandem, each slashing through its target.

Three operatives had hit the battle, but they'd left Jag alone so far. Given what he knew about the Advocate—and what Omeka said—that wouldn't last long.

"I don't think we can win this fight," Peralla said. "We should get out while we can."

Get out? No, Jag had done enough running. *He* had to stay—to see this through—but the Rixxonians didn't deserve to be a part of it. And the longer they fought, the longer it felt like they were falling into the Advocate's—

"You really shouldn't let others fight your battles for you, Jag."

Peralla whipped around, only to be hammered to the ground by a flash of yellow—a screaming, backhanded strike.

"Did you forget about me?" The Lommorian operative grabbed Jag's arm. "I *certainly* haven't forgotten about you!" She whipped and hurled him across the roof.

Jag tumbled down the slope until he could stabilize himself, then rolled onto his back. With an armor-piercing arrow still loaded, he aimed up at the operative.

"Go ahead," she goaded, stretching her arms out wide. "It will be but a mild injury for me, but it may end her *forever*."

Jag's finger twitched at the trigger.

"As I thought!" yelled the operative, rushing and gripping his leg. "You're too *weak*"—she threw him off the roof—"and predictable!"

All breath left Jag as he slammed into the Ancestor Tree and plummeted to the ground. Flat on his back, he writhed about in search of air as the battle spiraled away from them.

A Rixxonian swung in and collided with a group of agents—but one of them managed to grab her before she could swing away. Then a second Rixxonian plunged into them; another agent jumped up and severed his vine, sending him crashing into the dirt.

The Lommorian's boots hit the ground beside Jag's head. "You can end this right now," she said. "Promise to come with me—to join my Intelligence—and I will leave this world forever."

The sound of gunfire invaded Jag's earpiece. "Pits!" Bo called out between blasts. "We're pinned down over here!"

"Yee-yeeee!" Led by Sixxis, a group of four Rixxonians flipped onto the scene. But even though Sixxis cut down several Guildsmen and freed their captives, three jungle folk were ultimately taken in the scuffle and dragged into the surrounding brush.

"Tick tock, Jag," said the Lommorian, ignoring the battle and looking down at him. "The longer you wait, the more of your people I take."

Finally—Jag gulped in some air. "How do I know you're telling the truth?"

Adira plodded onto the villa roof and fired an arrow. It sliced through the operative's arm but didn't seem to phase her.

"We promised to always be honest with each other," she said, firing her pistol back without looking. "Remember?" She pointed it at Jag.

Several paces away, Sixxis ducked and dodged a few attacks, leaving another Rixxonian exposed. Agents dragged her away like the others.

"You won't just be helping me," continued the operative. "There's much to gain for you as well."

"Me?" Jag said.

She nodded, grin stretched wide across her beaked mouth. "I hold in my memory banks the only surviving records of your parents."

His parents... If Jag joined the Intelligence, he wouldn't just save Rixxon Prime. He'd finally know them—who they were, what they were like—he'd know *himself*. And if he didn't, that information might be lost forever.

The operative's gun exploded into a cloud of purple dust, as a machete came soaring straight through it.

"You're running out of goons, you goon," said Sixxis, brandishing his other machete.

Quiet gripped the square—as *PAT PAT*, Adira landed opposite Sixxis, arrow nocked.

"Heh," laughed the Lommorian. "So it's three against one."

"Make it four." Swinging in from a vine, a bald Rixxonian completed the cross surrounding the operative.

Jag stumbled to his feet. He'd been through too much to assume their strength in numbers would mean victory. The Advocate was too smart.

There was always something else.

"Gorren, how are things looking?" Adira asked.

"Not good," said the bald man. "Four have been captured, and I haven't seen Peralla for a time. She may have taken the others and fled."

"Hah!" spouted the operative. "Issues maintaining loyalty, miss chieftain?"

At this rate, all the Rixxonians would be taken. And who knew what would happen to Jag's crew? Were *they* safe?

"Gorren," said Sixxis, "go help the big guy."

"But—"

"Just go! We'll handle this."

Gorren bowed and took off down the avenue, joined by the last remaining Rixxonian.

"Clock's still ticking, Jag," said the operative.

Suddenly, a surge of warmth swelled up from the ground, into Jag's chest. And right then he knew: His parents *were* with him. And that meant he had to do what they—all three of them—did for him.

Because *this* was his fate—his grand purpose. Only *he* could end this.

"Leave them," he said, tossing his rifle, "and I'll come with you."

Sixxis hopped to his side. "Jag, what are you—"

"Just go, Six!" he yelled, sweeping his brother aside. "You and Adira get out of here!"

A pulsating hum invaded the area, trembling the grass and pulling at the air—as a big, black ship dropped into a hover beside the open roadway.

There was always something else.

"Impressed?" A new Lommorian operative emerged atop the villa. "I took your tactic and stalled. I now have a full vessel's weapon systems locked on you all."

"Leave them," Jag repeated, eyes locked on the operative before him.

"You did answer in time," she said in unison with the man on the roof, "and I am a being of my word."

Sixxis took a timid step forward. "Jag..."

"Just go," he said. "It's the only way."

Sixxis' mouth wrinkled. He backpedaled slowly, then turned and leapt from view.

Chapter 47

Sixxis finished his climb and came to a stop on a high bough. There, he looked down as Jag began following the operatives toward the ship.

"He can't really go with them, can he?" said Adira on a branch below.

No. He couldn't. There was no thakkin' way Sixxis was about to let Jag go—not like this.

"Unhand me!" yelled a voice—Gorren's. A group of agents wrestled him and another Rixxonian toward the ship.

"*Unity* will be arriving soon," Bilanthia said in Sixxis' earpiece. "I apologize for—"

"Stand down," said Jag.

Nope!

It was obvious what Sixxis needed to do. He concentrated on sending his message only to Bilanthia. "Don't listen to him. There's a big black ship over here, and I need you to light it up."

"Roger that!" Bilanthia replied.

Sixxis dropped down a level. "Do you trust me?" he said, back to Adira.

"Of course. Why?"

"I have to go." He turned and looked her in the eye. "And I need your help."

Her head tilted. "What do you mean?"

"Jag's the one he wants. If he goes now, who knows what will happen. If I go—well—he'll probably use me and the others to get Jag to come after us."

"But—"

"I know you and Jag are both telling me I need to think more before I do things, but there's no time to think this through."

"I..." Adira trailed off, peering into his eyes as tears welled in her own.

"It'll be okay—I promise." Sixxis approached her and pressed their foreheads together. "Besides, the chances of you two figuring out how to rescue me are way higher than you and me rescuing Jag." He planted a kiss on her cheek.

Adira threw herself closer and squeezed him tight, then pulled back. "What's your plan?"

"I want you to follow right behind me. Once we get to Jag, just grab him and get out of there." He grinned. "I'll take care of the goons."

"Arrival in one minute," Bilanthia reported.

Down below, the two Rixxonians had been herded into the ship. Jag's feet were just about to hit the ramp.

"Are you with me?" Sixxis asked, tiptoeing to the edge of his branch.

"Always."

He drew a deep, controlled breath. "I love you, Adira."

"I—"

"I'll make sure that monster doesn't do anything to our people." With that, he launched forward and grabbed a vine. Swinging to the ground, he hit the dirt at a sprint, charged up the ramp, and bolted into the ship. It didn't take him long to find Jag—and Adira was right behind him.

"Sorry, brother!" Sixxis ducked low and rammed his shoulder into Jag's captor—heaving him at the wall—then spun and threw a foot at the other operative's face.

The sudden attack sent Jag stumbling. "Six, what—"

"Jag"—Adira grabbed his arm—"we have to go!"

"But—"

The ship started to shake.

"Shit!" shouted the Lommorian operative. "Take off—now!"

A pulsating hum vibrated the floor. Sixxis dashed through the narrow corridors as the ship lifted from the ground—but ran out of luck as he came to the final room: four agents stood there, guns drawn on him and the captives.

"Six," said Jag, "what are you—"

"I'll be fine." He dropped his weapons and threw his hands up. "You'll come get me."

"But—"

"You'll figure it out," he said, nodding to himself. "I'm sure of it. This is far from ov—"

THUMP! A powerful strike sent Sixxis crashing into the ground. He blinked to refocus his watery eyes.

"You!" yelled the Lommorian operative, standing over him. "Despite how *touching* this is, I grow weary of you making things difficult." She lifted her boot and rammed it into his face.

ACT III

The Rescue Mission

Chapter 48

Sixxis—Sixxis had been taken.

Jag sat cross-legged in the soft grass, dwarfed by the Ancestor Tree before him. Sunlight seeped through the clear space above, but even as the welcome rays warmed his back, they illuminated the scorched bark that now covered over half the great Tree.

Skies, Six! Why'd he have to do that? It was supposed to be Jag on that ship—not him!

It was all Jag's fault, no doubt about it. Sixxis' kidnapping, Omeka's murder, the danger brought to Rixxon Prime, the death at Meru Plaza and on Palatia—at the center of everything were he and the Advocate. And while the Advocate's instability and weird obsession with him underlied each event, Jag hadn't exactly been an innocent bystander. *He* fired explosive arrows on Merutan; *he* pressed the Advocate and made him angry on Polt; and *he* built that rage even further talking to Omeka.

"Jag?" Remy's knee padded into the grass beside him.

Two weeks ago, he hadn't been to this village since the night they ran. Now he'd almost died here multiple times, leaving it battered and burnt in the wake of battle.

"We will get Sixxis back," she almost whispered.

Jag took a deep breath. "You don't know that. We don't know anything."

"For now, yes. But Omeka was able to retrieve us information. I will soon—"

"Soon is too late!" Jag popped to his feet. "We need to go now!"

"Hit the brakes there, Jag," said Bo, pumping his arms back and forth as he walked down *Zara's* ramp. "We're not ready to jump into things. We needa refuel and resupply at the very least."

Remy drifted upright. "And we cannot go until I finish analyzing the schematics, both of the Advocate's body and of the fortress on Polt."

Jag squinted. "...did you say fortress?"

"And Polt?" Bilanthia came striding down the ramp. "I'm unaware of any such structure on that planet."

Remy shook her head. "There is no mention of it in any Guild records. And given its sheer size, it seems virtually impossible that no one has detected even a byproduct of its presence." Her eyes narrowed. "Clearly, the Advocate has achieved yet another unprecedented technological feat..."

Tension rose from the tip of Jag's toes, through his body, and into each of his revving fists. "So he's taken seven Rixxonians—including Sixxis—and gone to a fortress that nobody even knew existed?"

An emerald hand came to rest on his shoulder. And as he turned to face her, Adira reminded him, "We stand tall."

Jag's mouth slammed shut. Even though she couldn't understand their words, she knew what was going on; she'd been there the whole time.

"What are you all talking about?" she asked. "Are we—"

A gentle whir descended from the sky.

Bo craned his neck at the endless, empty blue. "Is he back?"

"It doesn't appear so," said Bilanthia, similarly searching.

But Jag knew. "It's Elama!"

Of course it was—showing up too late.

"Give them space to land!"

The trees surrounding the avenue shook off bits of char and ash, which littered down to reveal the invisible, rounded frame of *Pioneer* settling in beside *Zara*. Four small portions of the grass depressed into the ground, and air hissed out as the ship trickled into view.

A Horranite woman came jogging down the lowering ramp. "Is everyone okay? We detected the Guild ships as they departed."

"Just watching, as usual?" Jag said, arms folded.

Elama stopped a few paces ahead of them, frowning. "I'm sorry?"

"While you were just sitting up there, Sixxis was taken—and six others!"

Remy stepped in beside him. "The Advocate intends to indoctrinate the Rixxonians into the *Intelligence*, as he calls it."

"Well"—Elama's brow lifted her face into a soft smile—"we'll just have to make sure that doesn't happen, won't we?"

"I'm sure *we* doesn't really mean *we,*" Jag said, glaring at her.

Elama's mouth wrinkled. "We will do all we can—I swear to you." Her half-smile fully faded. "How did things go with Omeka?"

"Your tactic revived her," Remy replied, "and she retrieved data for us."

"Excellent! What sort of data?"

"I have not yet analyzed it."

"Perhaps we might be of assistance in that endeavor." Elama tapped her wrist and held it to her face. "Torin, we have work to do."

"On my way, commander," crackled Torin's voice.

"Now hold on," said Remy. "I would very much—"

"Remy." Jag turned and locked eyes with her. "We need their help. And you need a break."

Remy started to say something, then closed her mouth and looked him up and down.

At this point, Jag had joined in Remy's suspicions. But also at this point, those suspicions didn't matter. All that mattered was getting Sixxis back. The Arbiters had already shown they understood the technology behind the Advocate, so they could handle Omeka's data. Like Remy said before: they were as necessary as they were dangerous.

She nodded. "I trust you."

"Could someone tell me what's going on?" Adira mumbled.

"Ah"—Elama tapped her wrist again—"Torin, please bring some solution."

"Yes, commander."

"It will not help right away," she said in Rixxonian, smiling, "but you will be understanding everyone in no time."

Adira caught Jag's eye. "I don't understand."

"It's okay—Six and I did it. It's how we can speak different languages. We learned them overnight."

"...overnight? But that seems impossible."

"It is quite possible, I assure you," said Elama with a chuckle. She turned to Remy. "The files are on your handheld, I presume?"

Remy nodded. "And we have recovered the body of an operative. I was able to channel the probe's electroshock energy into a bullet; I deactivated one other as well."

Elama's entire face widened as she beamed at Remy. "Fascinating! And brilliant execution on your part!"

"It was rather intuitive."

"How long will it take you to figure everything out?" Jag asked.

"It depends." Elama turned her smile to him. "But regardless, we will give you the most complete information we can assemble from the data points."

It depends? That wasn't an answer! The Advocate had gone too far, and they had no time to lose. Sixxis' life depended on it!

Jag curled his lip and—

"I know this is a difficult moment," Elama said before he could speak, "and I recognize how helpless you must feel with your brother being taken."

Helpless was right. Jag didn't want to wait, but he clearly had little choice. Even if he *did* go straight after the Advocate, he wasn't even sure what he'd do when he got there. He just wanted to get moving—because that meant moving closer to getting Sixxis back.

"Jag," she continued, "I think it's time you saw something."

"What?"

"The Guild was particularly interested in a set of coordinates on this planet, on both their last visit and this one. Based on what you told me regarding their search for that unique metal, I have a feeling I know what you might find if you go there."

Remy tugged at his arm. "I will come with you."

"That's okay, you—"

"Do you think I am going to let you do this alone?"

Jag stepped through the last bit of brush and into a clearing, a stark contrast to their previous hour's walk through the densest, most entangled part of the jungle he'd been. The grass shone a brilliant green, given life by an opening high in the canopy that allowed the sun's light passage.

He bent down and ran a hand through the grass. It was warm like the beams shining down on it, but also in a deeper, less tangible sense—like the warmth of the Ancestor Tree. It welcomed him instantly, despite the unwelcoming nature of the jungle depths.

Remy emerged from the thicket, holding fast to the onyx stone hanging around her neck. "We are close."

"I hope Sixxis is all right," said Jag, burying his fingers in the delicate blades.

"You know him better than I do, and I am confident he will make it through this."

Jag looked up. "You think?"

She nodded, then nodded him forward. "It is likely through that tunnel."

Jag floated upright and lifted his face to the sun one last time. He took a deep, cleansing breath—then plunged down the path between a mess of brambles and gnarled branches.

The trail constricted as they worked downhill, then expanded into a recessed glen. And on the other side of that glen, the metal orb sat lodged between three tree trunks, almost like it'd become part of the surrounding overgrowth.

"Jag?"

He rotated to face Remy. "Yeah?"

"...I did not say anything."

"Is it really you?"

Jag's limbs doubled in weight. He turned, slowly, and found someone standing outside the orb's open door: A woman, clad in a white jumpsuit. She was... small, but not as small as Remy. Her hair fell straight down past her shoulders.

"Mo—mother?"

"Oh, it really *is* you!" said the woman, clasping at her heart.

Remy stumbled back a step. "Impossible..."

"Oh, hello! Who might you be?"

Remy looked at Jag, clearly confused. And it was at this point he realized his mother was speaking Rixxonian: Remy couldn't understand her.

"This is Remy," Jag said.

She smiled. "Nice to meet you. My name is Ashley Hellickson."

Jag's mouth wrinkled. "Remy, I guess this is somehow Ashley... my mother."

Remy started to talk, then stopped and eyed them both. "I do not understand."

"Me neither," Jag said, face scrunched. "How are you here right now?"

"I'm not sure I'm really here, to be honest," Ashley said through a half-smile. "But a kind woman named Elama did promise me I'd be able to see you one last time." She took a step forward. "And just look at you!"

Remy approached, head atilt. She poked a finger at Ashley and scattered a collection of pixels. "As I thought..." she muttered, turning to Jag. "I will leave you to talk."

"You don't have to—"

"I will be just back there. Come to me when you are ready." She looked to Ashley, nodded, then turned and reentered the bramble tunnel.

Jag wandered across the glen as she disappeared from view. "I..." He came up beside the orb, running a hand along its cold, hard exterior. "I have so many questions."

Ashley's half-smile spread full. "What do you want to know?"

"You're from Earth?" he said, splaying his palm on the orb.

She nodded. "I was sent on a secret mission with two others to find life in the universe—to make contact with other sentient species."

"But as I understand it, Earth is really far away. How did you get here?"

"That's the question, isn't it?" Her mouth wrinkled, just as his always had. "One minute, we were traveling through space some ten light years from home. The next, my body felt like it was stretched beyond its limits. And once that was through, we were in a completely different place—a different galaxy."

"I don't understand."

"We didn't either," Ashley sighed. "We deemed it a *wormhole*, a wrinkle in space and time. We traveled through and popped out near here."

"And me..."

"You weren't planned"—tender affection exuded from her smile—"but oh, were you loved."

Jag leaned against the orb and folded his arms. "What do you mean I wasn't planned?"

"The wormhole changed everything. Though it lasted but a few seconds, I thought for sure I would die." She shut her eyes. "Coming face to face with mortality, then learning we'd never see home again..." Her eyes opened, gaze fixed past him, and she stepped past to follow it. "Though we never had much hope of a return journey, this was something different."

"Just like that?" Jag said. "You were just... here?"

Ashley nodded, still facing away. "We tried to go back through, of course—several times—but it seems it was a one-way tunnel. Or maybe it wasn't a tunnel at all. Maybe something just... happened." She turned, a half-smile tilting her mouth. "But good did come of it. In the face of all the uncertainty and fear, your father and I couldn't hold ourselves from each other anymore."

"Jason..."

Ashley's smile filled out once more. "Our training was long and rigorous, and through it all, we fell for each other. But given the importance and open-ended nature of our mission, we buried our feelings."

"What was he like?"

"He was a real goofball," she replied with a chuckle. "Always claimed his reason for accepting the mission was so he could make an alien friend."

Sounds like Jag's father and Sixxis would've gotten along.

Sixxis... maybe Jag could learn something from Ashley that would help get him back.

"What about the third crew member?" he said, pushing off the orb. "What about Garrison?"

Her eyes lit up. "The smartest, most driven man I ever knew. He was constantly improving himself, always pushing and striving for more."

Jag's head cocked back at the unexpected praise. "You speak so fondly about him."

"But of course! He was my longest and best friend. Such passion and loyalty..." Her smile faded; a single tear ran down her cheek.

"What is it?" Jag asked, stepping closer.

"Garrison was never the same after the wormhole, after I..." More tears trickled down her face.

Whatever she was about to say was important—that much was obvious. "What is it?" Jag said. "What happened to Garrison?"

She looked at him through watery eyes. "Why so many questions?" She sniffled. "Did he survive?" Her face brightened a touch. "Is he alive?"

Jag could've never prepared for meeting his mother out here, let alone this conversation. How could he tell her that her oldest friend had turned into a psychopathic, mind-enslaving cyborg?

"He's alive," Jag said, keeping the rest to himself.

"Oh, I'm *so* glad to hear that!" Ashley celebrated with a hop. "I do hope he's found happiness."

"What were you about to say?"

Still sniffling, she locked eyes with him. "I was terrified to tell him I was pregnant. When I did, he called me stupid, stormed off, and didn't come out of his cabin for days."

"Why would he do that?"

"We only had so many supplies. There was no guarantee we'd actually find life, so you were another mouth to feed that limited our chance at success. That, and a research station truly is no place for a baby." A smile stretched across her face once again. "But that didn't phase you. You were such a happy child."

She was trying to change the subject.

"If he was your best friend," Jag said, eyes still locked, "you know there was more to it."

Ashley looked away, down at the exposed roots running along the ground. "I knew of his deep feelings for me; I always had. That's why I was so terrified to tell him."

There it was, the truth—the *real* truth. Garrison loved Ashley, and Jag was the constant reminder that things never worked out between them.

"Mother..." Jag trailed off, unsure he wanted more truth. "How did you die?"

She sighed. "Like everything else, it happened quickly. One of our probes picked up footage of two humanoids on a nearby moon. For a moment, we reveled in the discovery. We'd finally found *life*!" Her lip quivered. "Our ship's hull started shaking within minutes: we were being attacked."

So Garrison wasn't to blame after all.

"One escape pod shorted out. Garrison hopped in the second and jetted off, but the third wasn't big enough to fit you, Jason, and myself." More tears welled in her eyes. "Jason stayed behind. You and I launched, and I watched our ship get split in half."

Jag's stomach sank, not because he'd learned of his parents' story—but because it seemed that amidst all his pain, Garrison's life ended just like Omeka's: at the hand of the Guild because he was in the wrong place at the wrong time. And just like Omeka, he was turned into something else, leaving behind everything he previously was.

"What happened then?" Jag asked.

"I remember a searing pain, then passing out. Later, I woke up. I think a lot happened, but all I recall is the immense fear I felt for *you*. Elama held my hand and promised you'd be safe, and that I would be able to see you one more time so long as I gave her my permission. Obviously, I did—then everything went dark."

"And you woke up here."

"Actually, I woke up once before. I spoke with a curious green man."

"...my father? Wazzaru?"

"Wazzaru—yes! I told him your name, and that people above would be watching over you, intending to come back someday when 'the time was right.' I also said he could tell no one what I shared."

Grand purpose... father must have told mother.

"It was incredible, really," Ashley continued. "I had no idea what I was saying; it just came out of me, like someone had programmed it in. But it didn't seem to phase Wazzaru. He just said, 'I understand that I do not understand, and I therefore will not question. Someday, something will come of this.'"

Through the winds of change, we stand tall as trees...

Jag's father clearly took the sayings to heart. And the sayings clearly defined Jag's life more than he ever gave them credit.

"It looks like he took great care of you," she said, treading past him, scattering her pixels as their shoulders brushed. "I'm so proud of you. All I wanted in those final moments was to give you the chance to live, to make your own choices—to be *you.*"

Jag sank to a crouch. "A lot's happened lately to make me question who I really am."

"You decide who you are, Jag."

He looked up at her, shocked that she'd repeated the Advocate's words.

"Choice is everything," she said. "It defines you more than anything else."

"My choices so far have brought me to a breaking point. I feel stuck—I'm not sure how to move forward."

Ashley turned to face him, that same smile stretched across her beautiful face. "Trust yourself. That's all you need."

"Trust myself..." His eyes drifted down, shutting as they reached the ground.

"If you see Garrison," she said, "tell him I'm sorry—and that he *is* good enough."

She was gone when Jag looked up. Once again, he was alone.

...but *was* he alone?

Remy waited just beyond the tunnel. Adira was back at the village with Bo, and Bilanthia. Collected in one place were all the people he cared for most—all except Sixxis.

Sixxis...

Despite having finally met his mother and gotten his answers, it was almost like none of it mattered anymore. Even during this conversation, one that would've been life changing just a week ago, he couldn't get his mind off his brother. Ever since the Advocate left—skies, ever since the whole ordeal with Remy and Omeka—Sixxis was all he could think about.

Because Sixxis was the only one always there. And now, Jag had a feeling Remy would be there—Bo and Bilanthia, too.

Had he found his place—his home—where he truly belonged?

Had he found... himself?

"Is she gone?"

Jag turned to find Remy encased in the tunnel. "Yeah."

"Are you... all right?"

He smiled. "Yeah."

Chapter 49

Jag looked up from the leatherbound book in his lap, as *Unity's* engines whirred to a calm stop. She pressed into the soft dirt, stabilizing herself on Therulin Glade's main avenue.

He felt the journal in his pocket the moment he took his seat. And the moment he opened it up—inspired to keep reading for the first time since this all got started—he grew ashamed. He'd put it away before they even hit Korrignolan, convinced it wouldn't tell him anything important.

With everything that had happened, he now understood how wrong he was.

He'd spent so much time and energy wondering where he came from, dwelling on the past and who it made him, he'd lost focus on what really mattered—and how *that* shaped his identity. Now as he read through his mother's words, her stories about Jag and Sixxis' childhood games and the bond they forged, everything hit him—in the most painful way.

Sixxis *had* to be okay. Jag wasn't sure what he'd do if something happened to him.

"I will see you inside," Remy said, rising from the seat in front of him. It was the first either of them had spoken since leaving the orb.

As she swung her legs over *Unity's* side wall and climbed down the ladder, Jag realized how much he'd grown to value and appreciate Remy. Like his brother, like his other companions—his new friends—she stood by his side when he needed it most. Just being near her gave him the same sense of comfort as Sixxis. Skies, in some ways it gave him *more* comfort, probably because Sixxis was constantly moving, talking, joking—just being Sixxis.

Jag stayed in his seat as Remy's feet patted the avenue. She turned and crossed toward *Zara*, then clanked up the ramp and entered the cargo bay. "I wonder," she said, "do you understand me now?"

"Do you understand me now," Adira repeated. "Yes, I suppose I do."

"Fascinating."

"Did Jag come back with you?"

"Yes. I am sure he will be in soon."

"Did something happen?"

"I will let him tell you." Remy's footsteps softened, then disappeared.

Everything had happened so quickly since leaving Rixxon Prime. Jag went from living his life unaware of anything else in the universe, to getting swept up into the stars, traveling to four other worlds, and meeting a man who has "known" him longer than his own family. Oh, and he'd gotten the shit kicked out of him a few times. And according to the news from Merutan and Palatia, all it did was *delay* widespread destruction—not *prevent* it.

Exhaling big, he mounted the ladder and climbed to the ground. His feet dragged as he approached *Zara*.

The Advocate had gone too far. Taking Sixxis was one thing, but six innocent Rixxonians? And all this after he released the Thakk, causing pain and suffering to countless mountain folk.

Jag stopped in the center of the avenue. To his right, the blackened Ancestor Tree stood tall, seemingly stronger than ever. To his left, the fractured, three-storied bungalows reached into the canopy, joining the verdant ceiling above.

This place was more than his home—it was a part of him. And it was in danger, just as it was when he left in the first place.

Head held high, steps filled with purpose, he started again for *Zara*.

Ashley claimed Garrison to be a good person, but that didn't exactly align with Jag's experience. Still, it begged the question: Could he be brought back, like Omeka? Would he be someone else, or were he and the Advocate one in the same?

Jag's boots plunked up the ramp and into the cargo bay, where he found Adira sitting on the steps. She'd released her hair from its usual tight bun, flowing it down past her shoulders. But her radiant beauty betrayed the somber energy spilling out of her.

"How are you holding up?" he asked.

She shook her head. "I'm starting to think I should've come with you the first time. Then I wouldn't have brought all these people here to the glade. And Sixxis..." She looked down, splayed her fingers on her forehead, and ran them through her hair. "Sixxis might not have—"

"I'll get Sixxis back. That's a promise."

"Take me with you," she said, leaping to her feet. "Please!"

"Are you sure?"

She turned and stretched her neck back, taking in *Zara*'s metallic interior. "It's not just about Sixxis. Our people were taken. This man—what did you say his name is?"

"The Advocate."

"The Advocate has turned everything we know on its head."

Jag sighed. "You have no idea."

"What do you mean?"

"He told me where I'm from—a planet called Earth—and proceeded to explain how he's *also* human; that's what we're called apparently. Then he asked a lot about my mother."

"Your mother?"

"I saw her, Adira," Jag muttered, staring forward at nothing in particular.

Adira's head tilted. "You saw her? What do you mean? When?"

"Just now, in the jungle." His eyes met hers. "I talked to her."

"Did you find what you've been searching for?"

Jag's mouth wrinkled as he nodded. "But not in the way I expected."

"What do you mean?"

The elevator doors hummed open, and Bilanthia came striding out. "Is it true?" he asked, sweeping toward Adira. "Can you understand us now?"

She nodded.

"Splendid!" he celebrated, rubbing his enormous hands together. "I must admit: I'm not great at keeping still, especially at such high-tension times. I was wondering if I might talk to you—to perhaps occupy both our minds?"

"You want to talk to *me*?" she asked.

"Why yes! From what I've gathered, you are a chieftain, no? I am *very* eager to learn about the history and society of this beautiful planet!"

Her lips curved into a soft smile. "It really is beautiful, isn't it?"

"Truly one of a kind," added Elama, emerging from the engine room, still projected as a Horranite. She came to a stop beside Bilanthia, a kind expression emanating from beneath her cheek horns. "Perhaps this is good timing. Jag, I would love a word if you would allow it."

Jag nodded.

"Shall we walk?" she said, stepping back and gesturing outside.

Jag fell in line behind her. She led him down the ramp and onto the avenue, coming to a stop before the scarred Ancestor Tree. A moment passed before either of them spoke.

"It is a magnificent tree," she said, gazing up the mighty trunk. "So strong despite all that's happened." Her gaze fell to Jag. "Much like you."

Jag just looked back at her.

"I'm sorry—for everything. I haven't been the most present through all of this. It's uncharted territory, even for me. I have tried to be as supportive as I feel I can."

"How did you do it?"

"I'm sorry?"

"My mother, in the glen." He walked forward and placed a hand on the Tree. "Was it really her?"

"As much of her as possible."

Jag closed his eyes, feeling the energy flowing from the bark.

"When we found you, there was no hope of saving her. But I was able to codify what remained of her mind and install it in a transmitter, set to activate when it detected your genetic signal."

"So she's just been... waiting there?" He turned and looked up at her. "For me?"

"Not exactly. Her mind remained dormant between transmissions. To her, no time passed."

"Except when she talked to my father."

"Yes." Elama smiled. "The transmitter was also set to activate the first time someone came near—so she could explain."

Jag dropped to a crouch and pressed a hand into the ground. "My mother—my other mother—the last thing she said to me was something about some 'grand purpose.'" He squeezed the dirt, picking up a handful. "My whole life, I thought there was something to that. But now I see that it was you all along."

"Ah—Wazzaru must have told her. I suppose that was to be expected." With a sigh, Elama placed a gentle hand on his shoulder. "I'm sorry if my references to fate have caused you stress. Perhaps I might clarify."

Jag released the dirt and stood, locking eyes with her as she drew a piece of paper from her pocket.

She held it forward. "Your mother was clutching this when we found you."

It was a photograph, torn on one side. In it, he recognized Ashley, the woman he'd just met in the glen. The man beside her—well, he looked a lot like Jag.

"My..."

Elama nodded. "And a third."

He looked closer at the torn side. At its base, a single foot remained of the third person.

"Turn it over."

He found something written on the back:

J A G

Jason Ashley Garrison

"My... name?"

"Your mother named you after the only family she thought you'd ever know."

Family... and according to Ashley, that included Garrison.

"When I say fate has more in store for you, I merely mean that I see major events—past, present, even future—cascading from your existence. As far as what *will* happen, that is impossible to predict because it hinges solely on you."

"On my choices," he said, echoing Ashley's words.

Elama nodded. "You're a good person, Jag. And as much as it may be difficult to see or understand, I care deeply about you. Please know that."

There it was again: the undeniable warmth flowing from Elama, the same warmth that set Jag's trust in her so early on. Despite all that had happened since—all the frustration and feeling of abandonment—his suspicions evaporated in that moment. He couldn't help but believe her.

"In any case, Torin and I have things we must discuss with Remy." She smiled. "It will be a bit, still. Perhaps you should try to relax?"

Fate. Grand Purpose. Choice.

Jag slid the photograph into the journal and laid his head back, resting it on *Zara's* metal topside. He'd been up here since the conversation with Elama, gazing through the break in the canopy, lost in thought. Only the loudness was more manageable. For the first time on this adventure, the quiet afforded him space to think—to take everything in and decide how he'd proceed.

Getting Sixxis back was obviously top priority. Next were stopping the Advocate and toppling the Guild. But stopping the Advocate seemed much more loaded now. Jag almost felt a responsibility to Garrison—to help him find himself once again.

But what could Jag do?

"Ah—here y'are!" said Bo, climbing up the last bit of *Zara's* body. "Been lookin' fer you." He pounded to a seat beside Jag. "You doin' okay? I know with Sixxis gone, it's—"

"I'm okay," Jag said.

Bo gazed up with him and whistled. "This place sure is stunning."

"I used to seek out spots like this, where you have an unobstructed view of the sky." He set the journal down and stretched his hands behind his head. "Like I was looking for something out there."

"Well, y'sure as pits found somethin', didn't ya?"

"More than something." He drew a deep breath in through his nose, then let it out through his mouth. "That stuff you said about energies... is it just about when you die?"

"Nah," said Bo, brushing a hand aside. "Energies are everywhere, serving every purpose. They can guide us, comfort us, warn us, you name it."

Jag closed his eyes. "On the day this all started, I couldn't shake my anxiety. And then I ran into a Guild operative, who I later learned was connected to the Advocate—who I now know is the only other human in this galaxy."

"That sounds about right. You felt his presence—like somethin' was comin' for ya."

Jag sat up and hugged his knees. "What if it wasn't the coming danger I was feeling? What if it was Garrison reaching out to me, begging to be released?"

"I s'pose it's possible."

His eyes fell on the journal. "For a minute there, I thought it was fate, but now I'm not so sure." He looked up at Bo. "Do you believe in fate?"

"Sometimes," he said, rolling his head and cracking his neck. "Other times, no. But I don't dwell on it. I can't control what the universe has in store."

"So you just go with it?"

"Basically." Bo shrugged. "Ain't nothin' that's definite. That's about all I know—and all I need to know."

Through the winds of change...

"The day she died, my mother rambled on about my grand purpose. I locked into that my whole life, and today, I learned it was just because of Elama—because my mother knew someone was watching and would come for me."

"Well thakk," said Bo. "Talk about a screeching halt to what you've believed for years."

"Hah—are you saying thakk now?"

"Eh"—Bo shrugged again—"thought I'd try it out in honor of Sixxis. Still isn't quite mine."

Jag had spent so much time in his head that he hadn't even appreciated his brother's levity. Thakk wasn't just a word he liked saying. It was something he used to lighten an otherwise pitch-black concept—something Jag desperately needed in his life. Plus, the word *was* fun to say. Jag kind of liked it.

And *thakk,* did he miss Sixxis.

"Team," Elama's voice buzzed into his ear, "please join Torin and myself at the holodeck."

Chapter 50

"We have finished analyzing the data procured by Omeka."

Jag stood across the holotable from Elama. All around the deck, his companions—Remy, Bo, Bilanthia, even Adira—fixed their eyes on her as she spoke.

"The Advocate has retreated to a remote valley on Polt."

Remy caught Jag's eye. "I find it hard to believe that he is able to disguise his movements on such a heavily trafficked world."

"It's quite ingenious, really," Elama replied, "not to mention *fascinating*."

What? How could she be taking this so lightly?

Torin tapped the table, dimming the cabin lights to a faded purple. "Ages ago, this valley was home to a host of lakes."

A circle of mountains appeared atop the table, plunging down toward a wide basin with bodies of water strewn about.

"As time drew on, Polt's warming temperatures dried the lake beds."

The lakes shrunk as Torin spoke.

"The resulting impact on the surrounding atmosphere was devastating. Overwhelming amounts of arsenic and other noxious elements permeated the air, ravaging the landscape."

Remy's eyes widened. "The Posaltika Basin."

Torin nodded. "Because the valley is significantly lower in elevation than the remainder of the planet, the rest of Polt was unaffected."

"*This* is the fascinating part," Elama added. "The low temperatures of the valley kept all that contaminated air close to the surface, rendering the entire basin a toxic wasteland.

Not only that, but the sheer density of the particles make it all but impossible to navigate. It is now a deep and desolate desert covered by impenetrable, poisonous fog!"

"A perfect place for a secret fortress," Bilanthia concluded.

Torin tapped the table. "Given the blueprints we've recovered, 'fortress' is an apt signifier for the structure."

Three circular levels established the base of the image that appeared, rising in height like a set of steps. They met an eight-sided prism at their center.

"That doesn't look terribly inviting," said Bo.

Jag walked forward and leaned his hands on the table, squinting at the ominous projection. "How do we get in?"

"This is the main entrance," said Torin, as a diminutive pair of double doors on the lowest level glowed green and made it evident how massive the fortress was. "We also have the hangar bay doors, which open here."

The upper half of one of the structure's eight sides glowed green.

"So the front door and the door to all their ships," Jag said.

Torin nodded. "And the entrance beside the roof landing pad."

A single light blinked atop the prism.

"Hah!" Bo spouted. "Not much better."

Jag leaned in closer. "Are there any other options?"

"If I may," began Elama, as a collection of yellow tubes appeared beneath the ground, "the structure's ventilation and filtration system is complex and expansive." She ran her spindled finger along a pair of pipes branching from the central network, out into the surrounding sand. "If you enter through this tubing, you may avoid detection."

"Despite the locale," said Remy, again catching Jag's eye, "I still have trouble seeing how the Advocate has been able to hide the existence of this fortress. The ventilation system alone would be detectable by even the most basic planetary scan."

"Yes..." Elama replied. "Like his hive mind, this is a troubling development."

"Whatever the circumstances," Jag said, "this is where we are." He nodded to Elama. "We'll take the tubes. And once we're in, we'll need to free Sixxis and the other captives, then deal with the Advocate."

"And by 'deal with the Advocate,'" said Remy, "you mean disable each and every one of his operatives. Should even a single being connected to the Intelligence escape, we will have failed."

"Should probably blow up all their ships, then," Bo offered. "That way nobody can fly off when we're not looking."

Bilanthia scratched at his horns. "I've heard whispers of a secret Guild fortress. If they're true, its memory banks contain *every* Guild record, including many that do not exist elsewhere. We should obtain any and all information we can. With ample evidence, perhaps we can finally convince the Legislature to disband the organization."

Jag sighed. "And this is all made more complicated by the fact that there are real people still alive under the Advocate's control—ah." He turned to Adira. "Sorry, this probably isn't easy to follow."

"I don't need all the details." She nodded, the table's lights filling her eyes. "Just tell me what to do."

"Aww pits—you're comin' with us?" Bo pumped a set of arms into the air. "No wonder Sixxis is so into you. You're one helluva lady!"

"Sixxis..." She smiled. "...talks about me?"

"Well a'course! S'what love does to people—or so I figure." He scratched his head. "Don't think I've ever been in love myself."

Adira's cheeks flushed a shade closer to her cascading hair as Remy refocused them, "Elama, have you had the chance to look at my prototype, and at the captured operative? Will a second high-impact electroshock revive the indoctrinated like it did Omeka?"

"In some cases, likely yes," she replied, folding her arms. "In others, no."

"Explain."

"I hope it's okay that we scanned both the recovered operative... and Omeka."

Remy started to say something, then stopped herself. She nodded.

"With these two subjects alone, the variance in the Advocate's work is on full display. Where Omeka had two central processors, the other had just one; however, neither's organic form was strong enough to sustain life without the network's assistance."

Jag squinted. "Can you two bring us along, please?"

"Yes!" Elama replied with a jump. "I apologize. There are two major factors at play: the state of the organic being and the deepness of the network's integration."

"But there is no way for us to detect either in the heat of battle," Remy finished. "So we must fire on all operatives—once to deactivate, then again, knowing the second blast *could* revive them." She looked to Elama. "Correct?"

"Just to be safe, I would increase the charge—and aim for the head—but yes. Those falling under the necessary criteria should have the capability of regaining themselves."

"But the Intelligence will still be present."

Elama nodded. "Each infected piece must come out. In some ways, the network's physical circuitry functions similarly to advanced prosthetics." She turned to Bilanthia. "Torin can show you how to identify which systems are compromised."

"I presume I will need to replace anything I remove?" Bilanthia clarified, still rubbing at his horns.

"Yes."

"I can certainly bring supplies and try," he said, raising his ridged browline. "We'll need to stop by my foundation's storehouse on Horran."

"We needa make a stop anyway," said Bo. "Gotta refill the water tanks and fuel up."

"I also require supplies," added Remy.

"It would be best we do all this without causing a commotion." Bilanthia rubbed his horns some more, then snapped his fingers. "I know just who to call." His brow then furrowed. "But how do we know this will all work? There's far too much *could* and *should* in this inquiry."

"I do not like the uncertainty, perhaps more than any of you." Remy turned to him and repeated her sister's words, "But could and should are as good as we can hope for right now."

"Ducts and tubes, electroshock bullets, chance of bodily harm from your own weapons"—Bo's entire face stretched into a savage grin—"this mission's starting to sound *fun*!"

Jag matched his grin. "Glad you're having a good time."

"I will create our munitions," Remy said. "Bullets are easy enough—they will be fired from a distance." She turned to Jag. "I will set your arrows to go off on a short timer so you can clear out."

"Jag's not the only archer here," said Adira, raising her hand. "I'll take some of those arrows. I also have quite a bit of experience making them, if you need some help. I'm good with my hands."

Remy nodded. "Thank you."

"Torin," Jag said, eyeing the projection, "can you highlight where the captives are likely being held?"

Red lights illuminated the hallway behind the double doors. The words DETENTION AREA appeared.

"Right by the exit—that should make it easy. Can we get *Zara* down there to load them up?"

"The planetary radar will detect any ships entering the atmosphere," Elama said. "It will need to be deactivated."

"Where is the central control room?" Remy asked.

Jag's tongue stuck out, running along his lower lip as a small region in the central structure glowed red and grew a label. "Can you deactivate the radar from there?"

"Affirmative. I can also duplicate and download all their files. But it will take time."

"Uhh"—one set of arms still folded, Bo pushed off the wall and walked into the light—"y'all are skippin' something. How can you deactivate the radar for *Zara* without bein' seen yerself? How will *you* get down there?"

"We can help with that." From her pocket, Elama produced a pair of what looked like metal bracelets. "Put these on," she said, tossing them to Jag, "then throw your arms over your head in an x."

Jag caught the objects and turned them over in his hand, then clicked one over each wrist. "Like this?"

She nodded. "It's best if you put some power into it."

Widening his stance, Jag took a deep breath and threw his arms up—and instantly, a yellow light buzzed over his head, falling down and around his upper body.

Remy's eyes exploded open. "What is this?"

"A kinetic energy barrier," replied Elama, beaming. "Do you like it?"

"Incredible..."

"Not only will it give you a defensive boost in battle, it will allow you to enter the planet's atmosphere without a vessel, thereby avoiding detection."

Bo's mouth twisted to the side. "What, you just expect us to jump to the surface from space?"

"Essentially."

"Count me outta that," he said, waving a hand to the side. "I'll bring *Zara* down."

"I'm afraid I'm much too old for such a task," chuckled Bilanthia. "I will also stay behind."

"What about you?" Jag asked Adira.

"Just tell me what to do."

"Okay." Jag pointed at the tube end sticking into the desert. "We jump down and enter here. Remy, you make your way to the control center. Adira, go with her and watch her back."

"On it!" replied Adira, flashing a determined look at Remy.

"I'll head to the detention area and get ready to help everyone escape." He leaned in closer. "Looks like it's a hallway. Bo, Bilanthia, I want you to come knock on the front door when you're down. We can flank them."

"I would suggest heeding Bo's advice and detonating as many ships as you can—as soon as possible," offered Elama. "Torin, *Pioneer*, and I can wait in orbit in case any attempt to escape, but we cannot shoot them all down."

Jag grinned. "The exploding arrows you made me should do the trick. Once we're clear, I'll meet up with Remy and Adira, then we'll head to the hangar and start wreaking havoc."

"Three of you in one place will likely draw out the Advocate." Elama nodded to Torin, who triple-tapped the table to pull up a hologram of the villain. "After analyzing his schematics, we have found four areas composed entirely of organic matter: just under his rib cage on his right side, his groin area, portions of his neck, and a small stretch between his bionic arm and torso." Each area glowed red as she mentioned it.

"So much for weaknesses," said Jag. "That doesn't make things much easier."

"We found something else *quite* interesting," Elama continued. "There is a black box embedded in his neural network."

"Black box?"

"In simple terms, we cannot see what's inside. It could store any numbers of files or processes, but there's no—"

"I think I know what's inside," Jag said.

There was only one answer—and maybe it was *the* answer.

"He keeps saying he 'doesn't remember.' I think he has memories locked away in there."

Elama inspected Jag's face, the hologram, then Jag's face again. "It is *quite* difficult to erase organically produced memories. If he truly cannot remember, it's possible you are correct."

"Can we break through?"

She grimaced. "This is one of the deepest, most intricate firewalls I have ever seen. Whoever created it—presumably Pert Gubora—had no intention of those memories ever surfacing again. That said, it *does* look like the barrier has weakened."

Ashley—she had to be the key.

"I know what to do."

"Very well," said Elama, hopping and clapping her Horranite hands together. "That's the plan, then!"

Torin tapped the table and moved for the hall. "Doctor, if you would please follow me."

"I'll set course for Horran," said Bo, boarding the lift.

"Elama," Jag said, "do you think there's a chance we can save Garrison?"

Remy stepped forward. "I beg your pardon? There is no *save* in this scenario. The Advocate—"

"He's in pain, Remy; always has been. And I think he used that black box to block it out."

Remy narrowed her eyes. "Pain may spur us to commit such acts, but it is no excuse."

"I'm not—"

"By simply *suggesting* we might save him, you are excusing him."

"To be honest," said Elama, "I'm not sure what will happen if you're able to break the firewall. Your mother was twenty-nine years old when we found her, so we can only assume Garrison was around the same age. That means you would be releasing approximately twenty-nine years of suppressed memories all at once. If they are rooted in such pain—especially given how quickly the synthetic mind analyzes and processes information—he may overload instantaneously."

"Good riddance," Remy scoffed.

But it didn't matter to Jag. He knew the black box was their only hope. He could only hold out that *somewhere* in there was the man his mother had nothing but good things to say about. If not, well, then they could just end things.

One way or another, Jag would free Garrison from his pain. Just like one way or another, he'd get his brother back.

Chapter 51

Remy glanced over her shoulder, hip pressed into one of the tables in *Zara's* engine room. "Would you mind assisting me?"

After three more diagonal slashes, Adira sheathed her daggers at her ankles and bounded to Remy's side in just two steps. "What can I do?"

It had been some time since they reached Horran, and already they had refueled. Jag, Bo, and Bilanthia would soon be back with the remainder of the supplies, but Remy had enough to get started—and she had no intention of delaying.

"I would like to push these two tables together to create ample work space."

"Got it." Adira crouched beside her and gripped the table's edge with her long fingers. "One... two... three!"

They heaved one table into the other, accentuating the horrendous screeching noise with a loud *BANG*.

"Thank you," said Remy, straightening out and patting her thighs.

"Think they'll be back soon?" Adira asked. "I really could've helped!"

"Some things have... happened lately. It is best you are not seen.

Certainly, with the assault on Merutan and the video footage of their preceding altercation on the capitol steps, the general public of Horran would not have reacted positively to a Rixxonian. Her staying behind was the best option.

"Sorry." Adira leaned against the table. "Things are a little loud right now."

Remy lifted an eyebrow, because it was in fact quite *quiet*. "I do not hear anything."

"Right. And that's making it worse."

Remy opened her mouth to speak, then closed it again. Jag and Sixxis both trusted Adira, and she seemed fine enough. Perhaps Remy could trust her as well.

Perhaps they could... talk.

"Do you mean it is loud... inside your head?"

Lips pursed, Adira nodded. "I can't stop thinking about it. I want to help, but I have no idea what I'm doing out here. So I just spiral around all the worst things I can imagine—about the worst ways I can lose Sixxis."

Sixxis... he had become far too important for Remy to give up on him. She cleared her throat and stood tall. "I have no intention of allowing anything to happen to Sixxis."

A tear fell down Adira's cheek as she looked at Remy. "He told me I would like you."

"He..." Remy sighed. "Other than my sister, I have not had many friends in my life. Though I was cold and distant, Sixxis took to and expressed care for me almost instantly."

Warmth buoyed Adira's emerald-green smile. "That sounds like him."

"Jag has also become a friend, which strengthens my resolve to keep Sixxis from harm."

"He told me about your sister. I'm so sorry."

While other motivating factors had since joined in Remy's mind, it all began with the murder and subsequent enslavement of her sister. And so every fiber of her being combined within to drive her toward one outcome: she would kill the Advocate. But now as that thought re-entered her mind—or more accurately, swelled to the front of her mind, for it was always there—she grew guilty.

She had spoken strongly—perhaps too strongly—when Jag mused about helping Garrison. For all they knew, Pert Gubora took his agency just as the Advocate had come to take it from others. And given his now-synthetic mind, whatever pain, fear, or inadequacy he felt over what happened were likely codified into his operating system. What's more, if he truly were missing his memories, he would have no concept of where those feelings came from.

Remy shuddered, thinking of the fog ingraining itself permanently into her perception. In itself, it was consuming, uncomfortable, but she knew its emptiness came from the vacuum left by her sister's death. Were its origins unknown, how would she feel?

She would likely choose *not* to feel.

"I lost family recently, too," said Adira, placing a kind hand on Remy's shoulder.

In a way, Remy was no different from the Advocate.

While she never lost access to her memories, she *did* lose all sense of emotion regarding them—and most other things for that matter. And in that, she lost an enormous part of herself.

Like the Advocate, she was not *whole*.

It was not until this last week that she realized it. But seeing Omeka again... *feeling* her for the last time... it brought everything back. And it cloaked her existence in pain and sadness.

"My father was a great man," Adira continued. "And already his death wasn't in vain. Thanks to him, I'm unifying our people, something that hasn't happened for generations."

Remy smiled—for the first time in a long time, a full smile—for Omeka's death was also not in vain. "Without my sister, we would not have even been able to *find* the Advocate, let alone stand a chance at defeating him. She helped us all, and now"—she picked up Omeka's daggers and offered them to Adira—"she will help you."

Adira took one in hand and turned it over, eyeing it with awe. "Were these hers?"

"Technically, they belonged to the Advocate." Remy clicked the button on the other's hilt. A band of blue electricity buzzed around the blade's edge. "I thought you might return them to him."

Adira jumped back and pressed the button on her dagger, then slashed and twirled it around. As it hummed about, zipping to and fro in the air, its buzzing sounds folded perfectly into the gentle whir of the engine. It was quite peaceful, relaxing.

Remy drew a deep breath, for the engine room had regained its sense of calm. Though still pained, she had received her peace, her acceptance of Omeka's fate—and she had seen the way forward. But that way forward involved Sixxis.

Alive.

"Oi, Doc," echoed Bo's voice from the cargo area, "lemme get that!"

"These will be a drastic upgrade on your current weapons." Remy deactivated her dagger, then walked and placed it in Adira's hand. "Use them to bring Sixxis back."

Jag ducked and jumped to the side, avoiding two of Bo's punches—but the big man's sweeping third arm got him, clapping him on the back and sending him stumbling.

"Gotta admit," said Bo, "that last one was just 'cuz I could—and 'cuz I was tired." He pounded into the floor and leaned back on all four hands. "Think it's best we rest up 'til we get there; don't think more practicing is gonna do you any good."

Who knew if *any* of it was doing Jag good? They'd been sparring since they left Horran, and he didn't feel any stronger, no more prepared—at least not in the physical sense. He was prepared in his mind because he'd identified the two worst outcomes of the situation: Sixxis' death or his.

Or Adira's.

Or Remy's, Bo's, or Bilanthia's.

Thakk—okay, so maybe he hadn't quite made it there mentally either. But that wasn't going to keep him. He may not have been prepared, but he was *ready.*

"Bo," said Bilanthia, sitting atop one of his mobile surgical stations by the elevator, "are you all right?"

Bo stroked at *Zara's* metal flooring. "Ko-Ra would be proud'a you, old girl."

Bilanthia leaned forward. "I'm sorry—did you say something?"

"Don't you worry," Bo said. "I'll make sure nothin' happens to you."

"This plan has her out of harm's way the entire time," said Jag, wiping sweat from his brow and dropping to a seat on the steps.

Bo shut his eyes tight. "I just can't have anything happen 'ta her. She's more than a ship." He sighed. "She's all I have left of my sister."

"Sister?" Jag said. "You have a sister?"

He nodded. "Ko-Ra."

"Ko-Ra..." Bilanthia repeated, his gaze trailing off with his voice.

Bo raised a single eyebrow. "You okay, Doc?"

"Yes yes," he said with a jump. "Ko-Ra is a lovely name. I apologize; I must have gotten a bit lost in it."

Bo shot a playful eye at Jag. "You're a real oddball, Doc. I like having you around."

"I like *being* around," Bilanthia replied, a crooked smile forming beneath his horns.

"Did you lose her in the scattering?" Jag asked.

"Yeah. We were on opposite sides of the city when it happened, so we couldn't connect before evacuation. I had no idea where she went, but I knew what to look for." Bo stroked the floor again, this time with an open palm. "*Zara* here was Ko-Ra's before me. She never would'a parted with her, so when I found her in a scrapyard on Korrignolan, I knew."

"That's it? You just accepted it without any proof?"

Bo shrugged. "Galaxy's a big place, Jag. Proof's hard enough to find on a single continent, let alone across star systems."

"Yes," added Bilanthia, "the odds of finding truth in this universe are far lower than your experience has shown, I'm afraid." He scratched at his chin. "Though I *am* starting to believe that the longer we spend our time around you, the more truth we will discover."

Things had been going ridiculously fast—that was for sure. And Jag had learned something every step of the way, about himself, his past, about the galaxy.

"Speaking of, Doc," said Bo, "been meanin'ta ask: what was all that about Pert Gubora a while ago?"

That's right. Bilanthia got all heated about the Advocate killing Gubora. Jag had completely forgotten.

"Ah yes," said the doctor, rubbing his hands together. "Pert Gubora and I are old partners—even old friends, despite our divergent paths. Many of the supplies we just pulled from my storehouse are based on prototypes we created together."

"You worked together?" Jag said.

He nodded. "He was not an evil man at his core, merely one driven by a powerful blend of curiosity and ambition. *That* is what fueled him to start ignoring regulations in our work, a practice I removed myself from the moment I recognized what he was doing."

"It sounds like you respect him a lot."

"I would not be where I am today without him. He was brilliant—and incredibly loyal—but also quite guarded. If the Advocate truly did murder him, that means they were close enough for him to feel entirely safe."

So the Advocate and Gubora were... friends? What sort of friend would lock someone's memories away?

"Why didn't you say something before?" Jag asked.

"I live my life by a certain set of guidelines. One of them is to never offer information until necessary."

"I don't get it."

"Had you known of my past connections with Gubora at the outset, you may not have trusted me. But learning of them now, you feel no threat. Yes?"

He was right—Jag knew Bilanthia was in it for the right reasons.

"Makes sense t'me," Bo said with a shrug. "We all got a past, don't we Doc?"

"Right! Sometimes it's relevant, other times it's not."

"And sometimes, you needa keep it alive. That's why I can't lose *Zara*, you guys. She can get scratched up and all, but she needs to come out okay—just like every other member of the team."

Jag's eyes drifted between his companions, two men that had become something much more than a team. "I'm still not sure what convinced you both to come with me in the first place," he said, "but I'm glad you did."

"You are a rather intriguing person, Jag," said Bilanthia. "Though I did have other reasons, my decision to come along was driven by *you*."

"But I thought it was Remy who—"

"Her involvement played a part, yes—but it was *you* who tipped the scales, the moment you said you wanted to 'do the right thing.'" He smiled. "Many people understand what the right thing is, but few possess the personal wherewithal to *do* anything about it."

Jag wasn't sure if *he* really understood. "I'm just trying my best."

"And *that* is all anyone can ask for." Bilanthia's smile stretched wider. "You see, Jag, I followed you because I was intrigued. I am *still* intrigued. And I will continue following you because I trust your intentions."

Jag's mouth wrinkled.

"You have been seeking your own answers and agenda, yes, but all wrapped in this mission to better the galaxy as a whole. You may not see it, but you're a lot like me!"

"For what it's worth," said Bo, raising a hand, "I see it. Y'all are a couple of impressive, beautiful men."

"Anyway"—Bilanthia hopped to the floor—"shall we check to see what our engineers have made for us?"

"Ooh!" Rolling onto his back, Bo squeezed his body into a ball before popping all six limbs out and lumbering to his feet. "Definitely curious to see!" He crossed to Jag and offered his hand—and a single eyebrow pump. "New toys."

They made their way to the engine room, finding Remy and Adira beneath the glowing, blue cylinder on its far side. The air in the room was much less tense than it was on Jag's last visit. In fact, even though Sixxis was gone—even though they had yet to truly succeed in any collision with the Advocate—there seemed to be an odd sense of optimism amongst the crew.

Was it optimism? No, probably not. Nobody was doubting or downplaying the danger of the mission. Everyone knew what challenges lay ahead.

Maybe it was determination. They all had a personal reason to see the Advocate fall—everyone except Bo that is. But he seemed content making sure his new friends got what they needed.

Was that it?

"Good timing," said Remy, stepping out wide and gesturing to the table cluster beside her—to rows of blue bullets and bundles of blue-tipped arrows. "We have finished our preparations. I made a few adjustments to my previous prototype; the munitions should be more stable."

"Ah, and ya' made plenty!" Bo shoved Jag and Bilanthia behind him and plodded forward. "S'good; this coming fight feels like a rare four-pistol affair. I'll need a lot of ammo."

Jag wandered toward the right side of the table, eyes fixed on an arrow bundle. He bent over to get a closer look at the tips. "So these will explode?"

"Affirmative," Remy replied. "The moment each hits its target, it will trigger a burst of electromagnetic energy on a three-second delay—and a sizable one at that. You will want to clear out of the blast range whenever you fire."

"But it won't hurt us if we get hit, right?" Adira clarified from the table's other side.

"Not directly, but you will be stunned: you will be unable to influence how you fall."

"We made these, too," said Adira, holding up one of the special arrows.

"You brought them..." Jag took a step toward her, eyeing the small, simple things that started it all.

"Since he wanted them so badly"—Adira grinned at Remy—"we thought we'd bring them to him."

"And they'll blow up like the others?"

"Affirmative," said Remy. "They are extra strong, built for the Advocate himself."

Jag pricked his finger on the tip. "If Sixxis were here, he'd demand that we test it on him."

Remy's mouth tilted. "And he would not stop demanding until we agreed."

That was the truth. Sixxis was relentless when he decided he wanted to do something.

"If I am being honest," she continued, "I am curious to see it myself. Perhaps we should honor his suggestion?"

"What's this—Remy advocating for a little fun?" Bo didn't skip a beat. He ripped one of the guns from the table, loaded a bullet, and held it over his head. "Who wants to shoot me first?"

"I will," said Remy, holding out her hand.

Bo gave her the pistol and jogged out a ways, then turned and opened his arms wide. "Where you gonna hit me, just so I'm ready?"

Remy extended her arm, steadying as she aimed. "I will shoot the floor a few paces in front of you."

"Won't the burst interfere with *Zara*'s systems?" Bilanthia asked.

"Negative. I designed this specific pulse to require organic matter to adopt a charge."

"You can do that?" Jag said.

"It is quite simple, really." She pulled the trigger—and *BOOM!*

A good distance away, Jag's feet lifted from the ground; he clambered to restabilize. After breaking so many bones in such a short time, he could've really stood to avoid getting thrown around so much.

Across the room, laying on his back with his arms in the same position as before, Bo mumbled something incoherent.

"Is he... stuck?" Jag stepped in for a closer look.

"I told you," Remy said, lowering the gun to her side. "He is stunned."

"For how—"

"Yeeooow—that was wild!" Bo curled his arms into his body and rolled up to a seat. "Who's next?"

"I will pass," said Remy.

"No thanks," added Adira.

Jag shook his head. "Nope."

"I'm much too old for this," said Bilanthia with a chuckle.

"What!?" Bo threw his hands into the air. "You're gonna just—"

Remy yawned, stretching her hands behind her back and lacing her fingers. "I am quite tired," she said, turning to Adira. "You must be as well. Shall I show you to the beds?"

"Yes, please!"

"Well pits," said Bo, watching them trot off. "My stake in this mission just grew a bit."

Jag lifted his brow. "Why's that?"

"I think I just caught a glimpse of my role here when Sixxis isn't around."

Chapter 52

It was time.

Everything that had happened—seemingly in Jag's entire life—built up to this moment. But was he ready to rise to the challenge, to save his brother and his people—to defeat the Advocate?

Standing before the elevator in *Zara's* upper corridor, he eyed Remy and Adira. "Ready?"

Remy nodded.

"Ready!" said Adira, spinning her new daggers and stowing them in her ankle sheaths.

"Bo, Bilanthia, any sign of Elama?"

"Nothing on the radar," Bilanthia reported.

Remy shook her head. "The Arbiters' support of our efforts is tenuous at best."

She wasn't wrong. Despite Jag's rekindled trust in Elama, her inconsistent presence kept him wary. Because even though she was so helpful just hours ago, this was another instance of her disappearing without explanation. What if a ship got away before they made it to the hangar? Or worse, what if a ship got away, and they didn't even *notice*? Nothing good—that was for sure.

"Looks like we go on without them." Jag left out the rest of his thoughts.

"Y'all sure everything's bolted down in the cargo bay?" Bo asked.

Remy engaged her helmet. "Affirmative."

Elama *did* outfit Adira for the mission; at least that was something. Shifting about in her armored suit, she scowled as she patted at the collar. "Where's the—"

Her helmet whizzed over her head—and Jag couldn't help but laugh. "You look *exactly* like Sixxis did the first time *he* tried the suit!" He engaged his own helmet. "Bo, we're ready; go ahead and open the door."

"Yessir!"

Zara rumbled and banged.

"Bay open; atmospheric, gravitational, and life support conditions deregulated."

Nodding to himself, Jag stepped onto the elevator; Remy and Adira took their places by his side as the door closed; and before he realized, it opened again to reveal the familiar scene of the cargo bay—this time consumed by the black expanse before them.

Suddenly weightless, the three floated upward. And in the distance, the orange, ringed body of Polt stood strong and silent, beckoning them forward.

"This is it, everyone," Jag said, looking first to Adira, then to Remy. "Five of us, ready to fight a fight most people in the galaxy don't even know is happening. And yet it doesn't feel like an exaggeration to say that the lives of countless people hang in the balance. We've seen what the Advocate can do by himself, and we absolutely cannot allow him to grow his ranks—because before long, he'll be unstoppable.

"We have our plan, but I won't for a second tell you it's going to be easy. We can only assume that everyone down there—every single person coming against us—will be connected to him. Which means every fight will be like the one on Merutan, like the one at the tower.

"He may have the advantage in numbers, and we may be infiltrating *his* base, but we have something he doesn't have: each other." He looked down at Remy, catching her eye through their tinted visors. "You've all shown me that home can mean a lot of things. For those people down there, it means Rixxon Prime." He paused.

"For me, it's you all—and that includes Sixxis. So let's go get him back!"

"Yeehoo!" hollered Bo. "Solid speech!"

"Yes." Remy nodded. "Well said." She guided herself to the back wall and crouched parallel to the ground. "If there is nothing else." With another nod, she shoved off the wall, through the bay, and into space.

"Last eclipse, I could have never predicted this is where I'd be." Adira repeated Remy's motions, shrugging as she fell still on the wall. "No sense getting nervous now. Probably best to be like Sixxis in this situation, don't you think?" She pushed off.

Now alone, Jag took a moment to embrace the immense stillness of the void. There were times in the jungle he felt small—and he *definitely* felt small in the mountains—but this...

Just like that, he found himself back atop the rocky Rixxonian plateau, gazing out over the farm and far-off treeline. Because here he was, once again overlooking something so vast, so far beyond himself.

Something that was in danger—something that needed *his* help.

He positioned himself like the others before him, coming to a crouch on the wall beside the elevator. And with a single exhalation, he launched into the abyss.

"Remember to make your adjustments before entering the atmosphere," Remy warned.

Arms glued to his sides, Jag tested his left and right thrusters. The rectangular "runway," as Remy called it when explaining the interior helmet display, tilted side to side, changing colors based on how well his trajectory matched his target landing spot.

"Green means go," he repeated to himself, making small adjustments to straighten out.

Adira was a true inspiration; how she was out here doing this was beyond Jag. Even Remy, who'd just barely learned the possibilities behind this kinetic barrier—that was about to be the *one* thing keeping them from burning to bits—was handling everything so well. Jag hadn't handled much of anything well so far.

At least he'd survived.

A small speck on the orange canvas began to glow yellow: Remy had engaged her barrier and entered the planetary shield. Jag made a few more directional adjustments as Adira too began to glow. And when he started to feel the heat, he crossed his arms in front of his accelerating body to brace for entry.

Despite the barrier's protective buffer, the temperature rose in and on virtually every part of Jag's body. What if he caught fire? *Could* he catch fire? That would be quite the end to the mission—his blazing body plummeting toward the planet, turning to dust and poofing into the sand.

He closed his eyes and drew a deep breath. Because from everything Elama and Remy told him, he'd be both safe and unable to do anything until he broke through the atmosphere.

Seriously. How was Adira handling this so well?

An enormous popping sound—just like Remy described it—was all the signal Jag needed. He burst his eyes open and threw his arms to his sides, resuming his adjustments.

Down below, Remy had already deployed her parachute and entered the valley's haze. Because Jag was so locked on his display, Adira's parachute startled him as it exploded backward—and he leaned a little too heavily on his right thruster.

HONK! HONK! "Warning," said his suit, the runway blinking red. "You are off course."

"Thakk!" Jag smashed the left thruster, promptly forcing his body into a rotation as he dipped below the basin's peaks. "Skies thakk!" He smashed the right thruster to stop spinning, then alternated pumps on both sides, trying to stabilize and recenter his body without flipping over—as the word *ENGAGE* flashed on his display.

But the runway was still orange!

"Jag, deploy your chute immediately!" Remy ordered.

"Almost there..." The eerie, gray cloud had overtaken Jag's periphery; he could almost *feel* the poisonous air, it was so thick. But he kept his focus glued on the display, and with just one more pump, his runway turned green—so he pulled the cord to throw his parachute. Slowing down just enough to keep from breaking on impact, he plodded into the sand, stomping foot over foot and tumbling forward onto his face.

Remy's voice cut through the fog. "Jag!"

"Well"—he rolled onto his back—"that could've gone better." The mist in the valley was overwhelming; he could see, but not very far.

Then Remy appeared, running toward him. "Are you all right?"

"Yeah." He pushed to his knees and shrugged off his parachute. "Where's—"

"G—gah!" Flailing about, her frame obscured by the haze, Adira just got more and more tangled in her chute's cords. "Get it off. GET IT OFF!" She whipped a dagger from her ankle. Its blue electricity glowed through the fog as she sliced herself free.

"I sincerely hope this is not a sign of what is to come," said Remy.

"We're just getting it out of our systems," Jag replied, a haggard grin beneath his helmet.

"Bo, Doctor"—she turned and held a small rod in the air—"we have landed safely."

"Glad t'hear it!" said Bo.

"I see no increased commotion in the region," added Bilanthia. "Though we likely can't rely on radar."

"Keep your helmets on," Remy directed. "The Arbiters may have abandoned us in this endeavor, but Elama's assessment of the air was accurate. It will take time to kill you, but it will weaken you quickly."

Jag drifted to his feet and patted red sand from his thighs, realizing just how cold it was in the basin—and how barren. A chill ran down his spine as his eyes wandered up a nearby dune. No plant or animal life, not even a sound save some whistling wind.

There was nothing but red desert.

Good thing Remy knew where to go. "I took the liberty of adding the planetary map and fortress blueprint to your suits' tracking systems." She tapped her wrist four times to initialize the same receiver Jag used on Rixxon Prime to find Sixxis. "They are set in order of your objectives."

Jag quadruple-tapped his wrist, bringing on the same blinking light; it pointed him up the dune he'd already inspected. "Guess we climb," he said, starting the trudge.

It was a tough walk uphill. Each step sank into the sand, and the frigid, toxic air didn't exactly help. Neither did the intense wind that thankfully weakened as they drew higher.

Eventually, they reached the top, engulfed in near silence. And the bizarre fortress was still nowhere to be seen in the haze.

"The vent should be close," said Remy, standing tall in her small frame, sweeping an arm about to refocus their heading. "This way." She started down the dune's other side.

"Sure wish we could've walked *up* this side," Jag said as he fell in behind her. "Much less steep."

"They are equally terrible," she replied.

"You won't hear me arguing," Adira said from the back of the line. "If this is what other worlds are like, I'm fine staying on Rixxon Prime forever."

"They are not all like this."

"I know I've seen a few beautiful places already," Jag agreed. "I—"

Something hissed to his left. Throwing his attention, he found a swirling, red cloud cutting through the fog, toward their position. "What is—"

"Sandstorm." Remy picked up her pace. "We can do nothing to avoid it. That said, there is almost nothing out here, so the only things flying about will be sand. We will be in no real danger so long as we stay close and keep our bodies low. It will, however, be incredibly unpleasant."

Of course! This was all they needed—to run into a sandstorm right when they were sneaking into the Advocate's base.

Jag hustled down the hill to get closer to Remy as the storm overtook them, lessening his already low visibility. Clicks and clacks filled his ears as the sand whipped at his body, the only sounds not consumed by the howling wind that might've thrown him off his feet were they not dug so deeply into the ground.

They trekked on without speaking, huddled together and hanging onto each other as they waded through the sand, doing everything possible to keep the pelting particles from throwing them off course.

"We are close," Remy yelled, holding the beacon forward.

Jag straightened out to look over her shoulder. "I don't see anything."

"We must—"

The ground rumbled—then *HISS!* Air screamed up from the ground a short ways ahead of them.

"Hurry!" Remy bolted for the billowing cloud.

Unsure what was happening, Jag followed, with Adira right behind him. They came to Remy's side as the hissing stopped.

"Quickly"—she pointed at a closing hole in the sand—"we must get in. Otherwise, we will need to wait for the next cycle."

Just realizing the storm had lessened with the air surge, Jag stood up. "Why did—"

"Now!" she said, shoving him toward the hole.

Still confused, Jag hustled up the hill and jumped feet first into the closing gap. Ribbed, metal tubing gave him a bumpy ride until it disappeared and deposited him into a massive shaft. He thankfully was quick enough to react: he reoriented himself, landed on his feet, and tucked into a roll. Remy landed in the same way behind him, and Adira absorbed the fall, clicking gracefully on the steel flooring.

"We have thirty minutes before the next cycle," said Remy, brushing sand from her legs. "We must enter the fortress before then."

Jag rolled his neck around, taking in the dark, metallic space. "What happens if we don't make it out in thirty minutes?"

"There are at least four ways we could die."

"What!?" he said, eyes darting at her. "Why didn't you tell us that ahead of time?"

"I thought it would be faster to simply tell you where we needed to go and how long we had to get out—rather than explain the inner workings of this immensely complicated exhaust system and how they continuously interact with the surrounding atmosphere to create a habitable space." She nodded. "We will be fine. You trust me, yes?"

Chapter 53

"This should be it." Remy drifted left, toward a dripping ladder just in front of the damp side wall. She turned to Jag. "And it is where we part ways: at the top, you will go left, and we will go right."

"Got it," he replied.

"Once we get clear of the shaft, it will be safe to remove our helmets."

"Good," said Adira. "I hate this thing."

Remy was not terribly keen on the helmets either, nor the full-armored suit. Even in the cold of space, she preferred to not cover every portion of her body. Doing so was far too restrictive.

"I'll go up first," offered Jag.

Remy nodded. "We should avoid firing any electroshock rounds until absolutely necessary. Just the sound of a single burst will likely alert the Advocate to our presence."

"And we'd like to keep from doing that for as long as possible."

Remy nodded again. "I also suggest we not attempt to revive any operatives until we have the support of Bo and the doctor. From what I understand, and from our experience with Omeka, any such attempt has a chance of bringing the Advocate back."

"Just to clarify," said Adira, propping a hand on her hip, "I *shouldn't* use those daggers on anyone we run into?"

"Affirmative." Remy glowered beneath her helmet. "Save them for the Advocate himself."

"What's this?" Jag said, leaning in and inspecting an unidentified goop on the ladder.

Remy wiped across a rung, then rubbed the gunky substance between her fingers. "Something that is likely unsafe for your bare skin. I would hypothesize it is a liquified amalgam of the basin's toxic air and the synthetic atmosphere of the fortress."

Adira scratched her head. "I don't follow."

"I never do," Jag said, placing a hand on the ladder.

"Wait." Remy grabbed his arm. "I... apologize for how I spoke when you asked Elama about Garrison."

"It's okay. I—"

"No." Gaze focused on him, she shook her head. "It was rude and insensitive. There is clearly a connection between you two, and all of his technology is far beyond even me. Perhaps we can—"

"Remy." Care and kindness exuded from Jag's palm as he placed it on her shoulder. "It's all right. We'll do what we need to do, and we'll do it together."

Remy opened her mouth to speak, then closed it again. She nodded.

"Let's get to it," he said, beginning his climb. Adira started up just below him.

With one hand on the ladder, Remy took a long look down the tunnel. It filled her with an instant, bitter rage—for it much resembled the mining shaft in which her sister drowned. But different from before, she found her rage mitigated by something else.

Was it... pity? For Garrison?

Regardless, it gave her control over her emotions. She channeled this into a first powerful step up.

The clinking of their feet echoed in the deep, dank conduit, joining the sounds of the liquified, atmospheric concoction as it dripped onto the steel tubing. Feeling a sense of comfort from the metallic melody, knowing full well they would not be long for this serene quiet, Remy savored the space.

Then Jag reached the top.

"Turn the wheel to your left," she said.

TH-THUNK! The sound reverberated down the tunnel.

"Here goes," Jag said, hoisting the cover and sticking his head through. He glanced both ways. "We're clear."

Following her companions, Remy pulled herself into the dimly lit, silver-plated corridor. As Jag then shut the cover behind them, she stowed her helmet and ran a hand through her hair, pushing it off to its correct side. Jag and Adira too stowed their helmets, each drawing in a relieved breath of unobstructed, clean air.

"It is time," Remy said, turning and eyeing the slight incline in the hallway before her. She took a few steps and looked down to the side. "Take care of yourself, Jag."

"I will. You two watch out for each other."

"I'll make sure nothing happens to her," said Adira.

"And I, her." With that, Remy started up the corridor, hand at the ready on her sidearm. Adira kept her head on a swivel beside her.

The enormous swing in temperature between the shaft and fortress proper was enough to distract even the most focused of minds. But command over her mind was perhaps the quality of which Remy was most proud. And so onward she drew, determined to see the mission succeed.

Holding her arm forward, she scanned the three options of an upcoming fork. "Left up ahead," she whispered. "Then we—"

The subtle sound of footsteps pittered in, coming from the opposite direction.

"Quickly—into that room!" Despite her hushed instructions, Remy dashed to the side wall, engaged her magnetized boots, and tiptoed up its surface.

"I like that plan better," said Adira, launching up the opposite wall and kicking into the rafters, where she grabbed onto a pipe and planted her feet across the hall.

Together, the two held themselves parallel to the floor as three operatives rounded the corner: A Lommorian, a Horranite, and a lavender-furred Velandisite. They walked in line, one behind the other in perfect harmony—because there weren't three of them at all. They were all *him,* and that made their coordinated movement *repulsive.*

A bead of sweat dripped to the tip of Remy's nose. Following it with her eyes, fearing even the slightest sound might alert the Advocate and every iteration of him, she held her breath and brought a hand below her face. The sweat hit her palm as the operatives passed below. And when they disappeared from view, she gasped for air.

"That was close," she said, catching her breath as she walked down the wall.

Adira relaxed her legs and dropped. "I *really* don't like how quiet they are."

"All the more reason to release them from his control." Remy deactivated her boots and started back for the fork. The hallway stretched long around the corner. A doorway stood open at its far end, others spaced along its sides. "The control room should be—"

A Laktilian passed by the far doorway, and Remy whipped back around the corner. "We will not be able to enter without removing the operative," she said, reaching for her rifle.

"Let me see." Light on her feet, Adira darted down the hall at a diagonal and ducked into the first open doorway. And after repeating her actions to reach the next on the opposite side, she stuck her head out to get a look. "I count two. How are you at range?"

"Exceptional." Dropping to a knee, Remy leaned out and aimed her barrel down the hall.

"Heh—me, too." Adira drew her longbow and nocked an electroshock arrow.

"It appears to be a circular chamber. We will need to wait until both pass by the door at the same time, on opposite sides of the room. I will take the far operative."

Adira nodded. "Just tell me when."

A moment passed, then, "Now!" Remy held her breath and took aim at the operative on the room's far side, a chalk-white person with charcoal hair pulled into a tight bun. Her shot roared into the fortress as Adira's arrow tore through the air, each hitting its target squarely in the side of the head. The first burst came immediately, the other three seconds later.

Remy hit the button to collapse her rifle, stowed it behind her lower back, and broke into a sprint—for the battle had begun. She charged forward, convinced they had removed all threats from the area.

But she was wrong.

Firing erupted from the control room as a third operative—one previously hidden by the narrow door frame—leaned into the open and discharged his weapon. Remy considered shooting back for a brief moment, but her hesitation removed the chance. She was forced to dive into an open room on the side.

"Damn! There is—"

The barrage of blows disappeared—then *BOOM!*

Unsure what had happened, Remy stayed still, back against the wall.

"You did a great job on these arrows!" Adira said as she appeared in the doorway, slinging her longbow over her back. "They're incredibly balanced."

"I"—Remy shifted her eyes, then peeked into the hallway—"thank you."

Adira stepped back and gestured forward. "I'm right behind you."

First Jag and Sixxis, now Adira. The Rixxonians were an incredibly capable people. Quite impressive.

Remy continued forward, this time more slowly and with her sidearm in hand. It appeared there were indeed only three operatives present, an observation confirmed when she and Adira crossed through the doorway.

Branching out from their position, a grated walkway circled the space, with four sets of stairs drawing down to a suspended central platform. There was no floor or ceiling: on the central platform stood a large terminal, with wires, tubes, and pipes stretching both up and down the humongous, open shaft. And at their feet, the bodies of both the Laktilian and the third operative—another Lommorian—lay still and lifeless.

Remy chose not to dwell on the operatives, for they would soon be returned to their original selves. "I will get to work at once. Please keep your eyes open."

"On it!"

"Jag," Remy said, "we have reached the control room."

"I think I heard," Jag said, ducking into a room as the quick thumping of boots neared him. "That explains the commotion down here." He checked his heading with the tracker and waited for them to pass.

"I have disabled the radar and unlocked the main doors," Remy reported.

"Roger that," Bo replied. "On our way!"

So far, Jag's trip through the fortress had been quiet. He had yet to run into any operatives—or anyone at all for that matter. The boots running past were the first signs of life he'd found since parting ways with Remy and Adira.

Something about that didn't feel right.

Worrying about it wouldn't get him anywhere, so he continued down the corridor, crossbow loaded and ready in case he *did* run into someone. But just as before, there was nobody. He traveled undisturbed through the fortress for fifteen minutes. And for fifteen minutes, he questioned Sixxis' safety.

Was he all right? Would Jag rescue him, only to find that the Advocate had already merged their minds? That would without a doubt be the *worst* possible outcome.

Checking in with the tracker, Jag realized that in his swirling thoughts, he'd just about made it to his destination without noticing: one more right turn.

"I'm at the detention area," he reported.

"And we'll be at the door momentarily," added Bo.

"Got it! I'll make sure you're clear." Jag leaned out and looked down the long, expansive hall, toward the massive set of double doors on the other side.

It was completely empty.

"We're all clear," he said.

"That was quick!"

He whirled back, slamming his body into the wall. "Remy, if there are prisoners down here, don't you think there would be guards?"

"Hold please," she replied.

None of this made sense. Everything had been *way* too easy. Jag was starting to—

"No..."

He snapped upright. "No, what?"

"Bo—do not open the door!"

Chapter 54

The double doors whooshed open, filling the otherwise quiet space as Jag engaged his helmet and peeked around the corner. Just outside, at the distant end of the long corridor, Bo and Bilanthia each stood behind one of the doctor's mobile gurneys.

"Remy," Jag said, "what are you—"

A Lommorian woman emerged from a door halfway down the hall, clapping slowly as her black-armored boots plodded on the floor. She turned to Bo and Bilanthia when she came to the its center. "Welcome, my friends!" she said, lifting her arms in a wide gesture. "I must say, you're quite predictable."

More operatives filed out to join her.

"Pits!" Bo shoved Bilanthia out the door and fired a shot, then kicked his gurney over and dropped behind it. His electroshock round struck the lead woman's head, its ensuing blast blowing her backward and hurling the remaining operatives into the walls.

Seeing his chance, Jag darted into the corridor and ducked into an empty cell, then leaned out to take it all in: Six downed operatives, sixteen cells between him and the exit—including his and the empty one across the hall. That meant fourteen potential hiding spots to check. So as the operatives in the hall groaned, clearly recovering from being stunned, he took advantage of his closing window and dashed for the next set of doors.

"Oh no you don't!" yelled Bo, peeking over the downed gurney. He popped up and fired, as another operative leaned into the hallway adjacent to Jag.

"Bo, get down!" Jag yelled, taking aim as shots exploded toward the big man.

The operative whipped around—and met an arrow in his forehead. "Jag!" He dropped his arms and stood upright. "Maybe you're not so predicta—"

The electroburst *BOOMED* through the hallway, crumpling the operative to the floor as Jag ducked into his cell and pressed against the wall.

"Thanks for that!" called Bo.

"No problem!" Jag replied. "I—"

A fist rammed into the side of his helmet, shooting him to the ground. Blindsided, he had no chance at orienting himself to his attacker—but it didn't matter. A foot came hammering into his stomach before he could even react. Rifle in hand, he flopped onto his back and blinked to refocus.

Yet another Lommorian stood over him, gun drawn. "You're full of surprises, aren't you?"

"I guess humans can be pretty clever, can't they?" Jag heaved his body to the side and fired off a wild arrow, coming nowhere close to hitting the operative—but striking the ceiling.

He braced himself.

"Hah!" laughed the operative. "How—"

BOOM! Her body buckled under the blast.

Already prone, Jag didn't get nearly as much of the burst—but it did leave him stunned. And so he lay on the ground, unable to move anything but his eyes, shifting them between the stunned operative and those breaking into the hall toward his companions.

"Doc," Bo hollered, still taking cover behind the toppled gurney, "you okay over there?"

"I am fine, yes!"

"Still got that piece I gave you?"

"Yes, although—"

"I'm gonna need you to pretend you're not there for a while. When I say so, I want you to fire down the hallway at anything."

"A—anything?"

"Yeah, Doc." Bo hopped up and fired near two operatives running down the wall. "Go crazy!" Both launched forward, and he sent consecutive shots at their heads as they hit the ground.

The scene erupted into a furious flurry of lights and explosions. The operatives scattered out and advanced on Bo, using the corridor's width to their advantage.

Still struggling to regain control, Jag glued his focus on the operative in his cell. He swore a finger twitched, but nothing else had moved. It was just a waiting game at—

He splayed his fingers—recovering first—then pulled an arrow from his quiver, threw himself at the stunned operative, and drove it into the back of her head. And then as quickly as he could, he grabbed his weapon and dove into the hall.

BOOM!

He skipped into the cell as the burst subsided, then loaded three arrows, pushed out three quick breaths, and pivoted back into the hall. Advancing on the rear of the operative scatter, he shot them one, two, three across the width of the ceiling. Six bodies buckled to the ground like the previous—but the victory was short lived.

A Horranite came slashing at Jag with a short blade.

Jumping back, he dropped to a shallow lunge and held his rifle overhead to catch the attack before it sliced into him. "I thought you'd want to kill me yourself."

"You still don't get it," replied the operative, kicking him backward. "All these people *are* me."

"No." Jag stood tall. "There's something of Garrison's locked away inside you—*just* you. I know you're missing those memories. I can—"

"Ah!" hollered the woman, clutching her head as she dropped to a knee. Every operative in the hall did the same behind her.

Seizing the opportunity, Bo jumped up and took careful aim, but he could only disable two operatives before the others started to recover.

Jag only managed one. And before he knew it, an even scatter stood before him in the corridor, all weapons fixed on his position. Opposite them, a similar group closed in on an exposed Bo.

"Doc," he said, "I think it's almost—"

One by one, something pushed and pulled Jag's operatives out of the hallway. And then a Lommorian woman—the same who gave the initial greeting—came charging at him.

He scrambled, fumbling to load up and take aim.

"Not me, you idiot!" Veering left, she threw her open palm into an operative's throat—completely upending him—and slammed his body into the ground. "Them!"

"Now, Doc!"

"Go for the ceiling!" Jag yelled.

Bilanthia leapt into the open and howled as he shot round after round in a sweeping motion across the ceiling.

Electrobursts detonated all around the space—as a light screamed past Jag's face. Whirling about to fire on its source, he struck another operative as the Lommorian woman grabbed his arm and pulled him into a cell.

"Is that moron trying to kill us!?" she said.

Jag lifted an eyebrow. "Are you—"

"Not the Advocate, no." She peeked into the hall, then returned her attention to Jag. "Name's Lorrie. Whatever you're doing, it's working; I have control again."

"You don't feel him trying to break in?"

Lorrie scowled. "What? No! He's definitely gone. I feel normal—like myself."

"The other person we revived had to fight him off, so—"

"My link wasn't too deep. Unlike some of the others who were dying when he took them, I was a volunteer."

"You... volunteered?"

"Yep," Lorrie said, peeking back into the hall. "Came with my friends, Werth and Morban." She yanked her head back as a shot came searing past her. "That would be Morban."

"But why would you volunteer?"

"The Advocate promised a place in his personal regiment. Why wouldn't we?"

"So—"

"This really isn't the time, don't you think? Just know that I'm me, and that I'm here to help."

"I..." Jag nodded. "Glad to have you back."

"Doc!" Bo yelled. "Stop!"

Jag and Lorrie peeped into the hall, as what *was* an overwhelming swell of explosions faded to nothing more than the occasional spark.

"I'm goin' out!" Rising to his feet, shrugging off his coat, Bo ran down the corridor with a pistol in each hand. And after making it a ways, he turned and walked backward, swiveling his head, shooting at one operative after the other.

Lorrie's head cocked back. "Damn—he's a good shot with all four hands."

A shot seared past Jag.

"Morban!" Lorrie yelled, shoving past and breaking into a run toward a recovering Lommorian.

The operative's eyes widened. "How did you—"

"Nope—not Morban!" She lowered her shoulder and barreled into her—lifting her up and pounding her into the ground—then straddled her body and pummeled her face. "Damn you, Advocate! You've messed with the wrong crew, and you've pissed off the wrong person!"

Lorrie, stop!" Jag yelled. "You're only hurting Morban at this point!"

"Hey you!" she yelled at Bo. "Toss me one of those!"

"What the—"

"It's okay," Jag said. "She's with us."

"*Man*, this shit is confusing." Bo shoveled a sidearm to Lorrie before turning to finish his cleanup job.

"Today will be the end of you, Advocate," she said, pressing the pistol into Morban's head.

"Lorrie!" Jag called out. "You—"

BOOM! Her body flew up and back, crashing into the far wall.

"That seemed a little unnecessary." Bo came up beside Jag and holstered his remaining weapons. "I think we're clear down here," he said, stretching his hands forward and cracking his knuckles.

Jag shuffled down the hallway, through the sea of bodies littering his path.

Twenty-four, an even two dozen.

"You'll have your work cut out for you, Bilanthia," he said.

"In more ways than one, I'm afraid." Across the way, the doctor inspected his wrecked equipment.

"Well, we've got Lorrie now, and that gives me hope that we can actually bring these people back." Jag threw his crossbow over his shoulder. "Remy, how's it going up there?"

"We're—"

Explosions rang into Jag's ear.

"Skies—I've gotta get up there! Bo, can you stay and help Bilanthia?"

"Yeah, I'll stick to the plan and watch the doc."

"I can help." Over where she'd landed, Lorrie pulled herself to her hands and knees. "Or rather *we* can—once I find Werth and Morban."

Bo folded his arms. "I dunno about that."

"We know the lower levels of this place really well," Lorrie said, pressing to her feet. "We can clear them out while you keep doing what you're doing."

"We'll take all the help we can get," Jag said. "Use our electroshock rounds; we don't want to hurt anyone more than we need to."

"How noble," she mocked, rolling her eyes. "But you saved me, so you're the boss. We'll bring everyone back here."

"Here!" Bo tossed her another pistol. "I'm keepin' two."

"You may have mine," offered Bilanthia. "I think I've shot it enough for one day."

Jag held an arm toward Bo. "Good luck."

"Likewise." He tapped Jag's forearm with his own. "I'll see you in the hangar."

Jag tore off running.

Chapter 55

The firing stopped—then *BOOM!*

"Remy!" Adira hopped from the upper ring to the center platform, skipping over the steps and dropping to a knee. "Are you okay?"

Determined to leave no information uncovered, Remy was furiously combing the Guild database when Jag called—and when an operative caught them by surprise. Because of her exposed position on the suspended platform, she had no choice but to drop below his sight line. She had since been flat on her stomach, hands over her neck.

"I am okay," she said, picking up her head and rolling to a seat. "Is he—"

"Taken care of! But there will be others." Adira threw a glance over her shoulder. "How much more time do you need?"

"Fifteen minutes," Remy estimated, pushing to her feet.

"Okay. I'll do my best to—"

Adira's ears perked up. Her head darted side to side. "Why are there eight entrances!?" She sprang from her position, floating up and touching down on the upper ring, then pressed her ear beside a doorway.

"What are you—"

"Shh!" Circling the room, she listened to every entrance until one gave her pause. "This one." She moved to the next. "Here, too."

Remy dropped low. "Two groups, one in each hall."

"Tell me when one's about to cross into the room."

Remy nodded and pressed up just enough to peer across the floor. A group of three operatives jogged toward them in one hall, a pair in the other.

The pair drew close before long.

"Now!" she said, pointing to the right doorway.

With incredible fluidity and finesse, Adira nocked an arrow and spun to face down the further group of three. She released—striking the center operative's forehead—then skipped to the side and vaulted into a backflip over the other entrance.

BOOM!

Flying through the air, she drew another arrow and—just as the first of the pair crossed the threshold—drove it into his head.

Remy took off in the opposite direction, hoping to avoid the—

BOOM!

The blast propelled her body up the last few steps, leaving her otherwise unaffected. But as she picked herself up to get her bearings, she could not locate Adira. Across the way lay the two operatives, one twitching slightly, the other still. But no—

"Remy, down here!"

The voice drew her attention to three green fingers latched onto the platform's edge. "No!" she yelled, running to assist—but the stirring operative opposite them caught her eye. "Hold, please."

Remy stood, ripping her rifle from behind her back and extending it in one motion. She cocked the barrel back to shorten its range and retract the scope, then aimed first at the two in the hall. She fired at each of their heads, pivoted, then took the final, easy shot. And as the trio of bursts then thundered through the shaft, she tossed her weapon aside and dropped to her stomach—but she was not strong enough. "Jag, where are you?"

"Moving as fast as I can!"

Damn. What could she do? Perhaps—

"I must revive an operative," she said, popping up, drawing her sidearm, and rounding the platform.

"But I thought—"

"I will not lose anyone else!"

BOOM!

...after a moment of absolute silence, the chalk-white operative's eyes fluttered open. They sat up, patting at their body, confusion evident on their face. "Ho—holy shit! I'm alive!"

"Yes, and I need your assistance!" Remy turned and ran.

"I don't even know if"—they pulled a leg out from beneath their body—"never mind; I can move. Right behind you!"

Coming back to Adira, Remy again dropped to her stomach. "Help me pull her up!"

"You got it!" They dropped and stretched down.

"One… two… three!" Adira lunged, throwing her arm toward the second pair of hands. And with the combined strength of her two helpers, she made it high enough to get a better grip and pull herself to safety.

"You two are *incredible*!" said the former operative, flopping onto their back. "I'm J'Nia, by the way." They sat up and let their shimmery hair loose from its bun, then shook out and ran their hands through it several times. "Feels good to be me again—especially now that I know what *me* is."

Brow lifted, Adira looked at Remy, then back at J'Nia. "What do you mean?"

They shrugged. "Had a bit of an existential crisis in there. Really came to grips with life, what it means, and all that shit." Their face twisted in on itself. "Then again, it's hard to say whether I was actually alive or not; maybe calling it an existential crisis isn't right."

"You are alive now," said Remy, "and my understanding is that you comprehended everything that happened. So, I would agree with classifying it as such."

J'Nia tilted their head and smiled, running their messy, voluminous hair down the side of their face. "It's a real hell being trapped with nothing but your thoughts and a show you can't change."

"A… show?" Now Adira tilted her head.

"Oh, yeah! You're from that planet—Rixxon Prime, right?"

Adira nodded.

"Well, a show is basically a moving picture with sound that tells a story."

"We do not have time for this." Remy drew her sidearm and thrusted it at J'Nia. "Can you help keep watch?"

"Nuh-uh—nope!" they said, scooting back and throwing their hands up. "I learned a lot about who I am these last six months, and who I am doesn't shoot people."

Remy's arm fell limp. "Of course," she grunted. "I revived a pacifist."

"Nah, nothing like that." J'Nia hopped to their feet. "More like I just don't do guns. Zero interest, ya know?"

Remy scowled. "I do not—"

CLANK CLANK—from the hall.

"Really don't think we have a ton of options," said Adira, head whipping to the side.

Remy let out a heavy sigh, then gestured to the terminal. "How are you with this database?"

J'Nia grinned. "I know the system really well."

"Good. Can you make sure all the files upload to the drive I plugged in?"

"Yup!"

"We will cover you."

Skipping steps, Jag bounded up the final flight of stairs and crept toward the corridor entrance. As with his trip down to the detention area, he hadn't run into much resistance. He had a feeling that would change soon, though.

He ducked beside the open doorway to double-check his loadout and confirm his heading: straight out the door, up the ramp, and to the left. Prepping to toss his body into the hall, he threw out three breaths—then realized he wasn't alone; quick, heavy footsteps approached his door from the right, then turned and headed down the hall.

So their backs were to him.

Grinning, Jag whipped into the doorway and fired at them both—but his face wiped clean when he saw that he'd missed one.

BOOM!

Unwilling to chance it, he broke into a sprint toward the lumped body of the still-functioning operative. Closing in fast, arrow in hand, he readied his strike—but then gunfire blew in from the hall's other side. With no other choice, he dove into a room on his right, then hopped back to the door for a look.

The new enemy—another Lommorian—helped the previously stunned operative to his feet in the corridor, pointing her weapon at the one Jag didn't miss.

"I wouldn't do that, Garrison," he said, stepping into the hall, arrow locked in.

Weapon fixed, the Lommorian smirked over her shoulder. "How'd you do it?"

"Do what?"

"You're restoring these people to their original consciousness. I must say, even when I felt Omeka rooting around during our conversation, I could have never predicted you'd figure out something like *this.*"

So he knew about Omeka. And that meant he knew they were coming. Then again, pretty much everything so far proved that.

Jag pulled his weapon in closer and moved for the trigger. "I don't think I need to tell you how brilliant Remy is."

"Hah—no, I suppose you don't. In any case, removing this person means one less you can turn on me."

"You shoot, so do I."

"You clearly don't understand the situation, do you?"

Jag glared.

"Alone," said both operatives in eerie unison, "you can hit only one of me."

"Good thing he's not alone." Adira rolled into the hall on their other side, bow drawn. "I've got the talker!"

With a yell, Jag fired on the unclaimed operative. The arrows struck their targets simultaneously, the bursts echoing out as he ducked back into his room. And right when the sound dissipated, he rolled into the hall. "Adira!"

"Sounded like you could use a hand," she said, grinning as he jogged toward her.

Jag slowed as he approached and threw up his forearm. "Your timing was perfect."

Adira tapped it with hers. "The control room is just up here," she said, turning and throwing the bow over her shoulder as she rounded the corner.

"Are you sure it's safe?" he asked, hesitant to stow his weapon.

"Yeah. We've pretty well cleared out the place by now. We were just about to revive everyone when I heard you down the hall."

"How do you know you've cleared it out?"

"Remy will fill you in."

Jag followed her into the control room and wheeled to a stop, crossbow still drawn—and when he saw someone he didn't know at the central terminal, he pulled the sights to his face.

"Whoa whoa whoa!" they said, throwing their arms into the air. "Friend! I'm a friend!"

"Glad to see you alive."

Turning, Jag lowered his weapon. "Remy!"

"Without me"—Adira shoved him—"he wouldn't be."

Remy smiled. "That makes two of us."

"I would guess three of us," added the other person, "but I haven't been super with it the whole time." They offered Jag a fist. "I'm J'Nia."

Unsure how to respond, Jag mirrored her. "Jag."

They bumped his fist. "I already know you."

"Welcome to the team," he said with a nod.

"Beats the hell outta the team I used to play fo—ah!" J'Nia clutched at their head and dropped to the ground.

The others waited, weapons at the ready as J'Nia writhed about, hollering out in agony. Then they fell still.

"...what was *that*?" shuddered out from their trembling body.

Remy's gaze darted to Jag. "That would be the Advocate trying to break through."

"Break... through?" J'Nia looked up, tears welling in their eyes. "You mean I might fall back into the Intelligence?"

"Not if we can help it," said Jag, jogging to their side and offering a hand.

"Yes," Remy added. "You must be strong. Hold him off and make your way to the detention area. Our people will help you."

"I'm"—J'Nia sniffled—"I'm not a very strong person."

"Alone, none of us are truly strong." Remy and J'Nia locked eyes. "But together we are. And together, we can rid the galaxy of all instances of the Advocate."

Half of J'Nia's mouth formed a smile. "Together," she repeated, taking Jag's hand.

Jag pulled them up and turned to Remy. "What's the situation?"

"It is clear the Advocate knew we were coming."

"Yeah. He just told me he could feel Omeka 'rooting around.'"

Remy nodded. "Security cameras indicate nobody on the levels between here and the detention area, or between here and the hangar; however, they also reveal our blueprints to be false."

Jag gasped. "How's that possible?"

"The Advocate must have altered the file when he discovered Omeka's intent."

"Any idea where he is? Does he have the captives?"

"I can answer that," offered J'Nia, rubbing at their head. "Last I saw, he had everyone up in the hangar."

"Good—we're headed there anyway." Jag stood tall. "Bilanthia, how are things down there?"

"We are almost caught up," he replied, "but Lorrie and her team continue to bring more from the lower levels."

"Lorrie?" Adira asked.

Jag nodded. "Any chance you could make it up here?"

"I'm afraid I'm not terribly mobile anymore."

J'Nia was already starting to feel the effects of the Intelligence, so they didn't have much time; they needed to get her down there. Not even Remy knew what would happen were someone revived and overtaken again.

Damn the Advocate!

Of course he knew they were coming—and *of course* he was toying with them, giving them what they were looking for while keeping complete control of the situation. But Jag questioned how effectively the villain could split his attention. Was it really possible that the Advocate held his conversation with Jag, tried to overtake Omeka, altered the blueprints, *and* controlled the operatives in the Rixxonian jungle, all at the same time? How long could he keep this up? None of the fights in the fortress had been like the ones before. He seemed... weaker. Distracted.

Confidence surged within Jag. Coupled with this realization, the conversation with Ashley had him feeling like they were *finally* a step ahead. And the Advocate clearly wasn't expecting the burst weapons and their ability to restore consciousness, so that was a few steps further.

For the first time since his fated hunting session with Sixxis, they were ahead in the game—because that was just it.

"It's all a game to him."

Remy's head tilted. "Jag?"

He turned to J'Nia. "Did he change anything else about the blueprints?"

"A *ton*! Like, there are actually seven entrances into the fortress, not including the"—their face twisted—"how'd you guys get in here anyway?"

"Ventilation," Remy replied.

"Gross," they said, scrunching their face. "Well yeah, he was funneling you to the detention area since he knew that's where you'd want to go anyway, what with the prisoners and all. Must not've thought to check the filtration system." They laughed. "You know, it really is fun watching you all do your thing, just one-upping each other."

"And right now, we're a step ahead," said Jag. "What's the *actual* fastest way to the detention area from here?"

J'Nia shrugged a guilty shrug, then pointed down one of the halls. "There's an elevator. Goes right to it."

Jag breathed out the heaviest of sighs, expelling all his frustration over how long it took him to get to the control room. "Are you okay to go on your own?"

"Yeah. It'll take like four minutes."

"Of course it will," he said, rolling his eyes. "Remy, do we have everything we need here?"

"Affirmative."

"Then we three go to the hangar." Jag dropped his expectant gaze on J'Nia.

Smiling contentedly, they took a beat to get it. "Oh!" they said, jumping. "The way from here to the hangar should be the same. All he really did was cover up all entrances but one, delete the elevators, and hide info about the power system."

"I thought you said he changed 'a ton,'" Jag said, squinting.

"I did! This place has a lot of elevators."

"Why did he hide the power system information?" Remy asked.

"Because you can blow the whole core with like two buttons in here." J'Nia floated toward the terminal and pointed at a blue nob. "Actually, you just press *that* twice."

Jag grinned. "That will get Sixxis excited."

"Then let's go tell him," Adira said with her own grin.

Remy looked to J'Nia and nodded. "Take care of yourself."

J'Nia's face flushed as they smiled at the others. Then that smile tilted further into laughter, toppling them forward. They grabbed at their knees to keep from falling.

Wholly perplexed, Jag shifted his eyes from Remy to Adira. "What's so funny?"

J'Nia fell silent, glanced at Jag's confused face—then exploded into another bout. "Sorry," they said after a bit, wiping their face and sniffling. "I just think it's hilarious you all thought this *massive* fortress had only *one* entrance."

Chapter 56

Planting his foot at platform's edge, the Advocate gazed down at the expansive hangar.

"What if you just fell right now?" mocked Sixxis from behind. "That would be a pretty unexpected end to all this."

Unexpected... Jag and his friends had done several unexpected things. They were clever enough to enter the fortress undetected, but returning control of the operatives to their original hosts? And the paralyzing burst—brilliant! Half the time, the Advocate could do nothing but stare as he lost connection.

It made no sense. It simply wasn't possible that they could discover how to restore consciousness *and* create seemingly endless amounts of ammunition for it in the short time since Rixxon Prime. The Intelligence was far too advanced for Remy to comprehend so quickly.

"Anything going on down there?"

The Advocate snapped upright with a huff. "You're irritating." He turned to face his collection of specimens; Sixxis sat hugging his knees in their midst. "But if you must know, yes: your brother and friends are here."

"Is Adira with them?"

They'd outsmarted him. Once again, the Advocate had come to a crux and found himself inadequate, not good enough. Even the Intelligence—this creation that was both far beyond him and made him far beyond himself—was bested and being dismantled. It just confirmed how he'd always felt, because this too had happened before.

Because no matter how hard he tried, everything was taken from him at some point.

"Hello?" said Sixxis, waving at him. "Did Adira come?"

"Your girlfriend?" The Advocate scowled. "Yes, she is here."

"She *does* love me!"

Suddenly, the Advocate's ears screamed inside him. Clutching at his head, he pounded a knee into the platform.

All this time—this effort spread across multiple minds and situations—it wore on him with each passing minute. He'd felt his focus deteriorating for a while now. And because operating the connection across long distances had exhausted him in the past, he thought bringing all his appendages to one place would make things easier.

It did *not*.

Perhaps it was progressive fatigue from splitting himself further and further. Operating one consciousness was difficult enough—the Advocate commanded seventy-four. But until recently, he almost never did anything taxing in more than three places at once. Now this entire day—every twist and turn had been taxing!

He'd stretched himself too thin. And because of it, he'd been caught off guard.

Of course he knew his opponents would put up a good fight, but he certainly did *not* expect his operatives to turn against him. No... that was a surprise. Now his regiment was much smaller. And yet the Advocate felt *strong*, unsure whether it was a result of releasing different focus areas—or something deeper, as if with each deactivated appendage, a piece of him returned after time away from his body. Whatever it was, he became that much more *himself* with each successive loss.

Perhaps it was the operatives weighing him down all this time. After all, *he* was good enough. *He* was magnificent, the advocate of a new race!

He could try it.

Yes... if things seemed dire, he would try it—he would sever the link.

"You okay over there?"

The Advocate's eyes shifted toward his green aggravation. "Yes."

"I don't get it; you're usually real talkative."

He hovered to his feet, tensing his fists and feeling his power. "I'm sort of busy. I hope you're not upset that I'm skipping out on one of our *riveting* conversations!"

"Honestly?" Sixxis shrugged. "I'm just impatient—want to know what's going on."

"Pah!" released the Advocate, turning his back and striding for the platform's edge. "Your brother may have caught me by surprise, but I always expected him to make it this far. And this is as far as he'll go—as far as you'll *all* go."

Chapter 57

Jag led the way down their final corridor. Its barriers stretched wider and higher as they progressed, until the left side disappeared entirely. "I'm guessing this is it?" he said, pressing against the wall beside the opening.

"Yes," Remy confirmed from the rear of the line.

"Okay." Jag inched his head past the doorframe. "Let's get a—"

CRACK!

He rolled back to safety—as a bullet seared into the opposite wall.

"What did you see?" Remy asked.

"Ships," he said between breaths, "lots of them: two even rows along the sides of the ground level."

"Where did the shot come from?"

"Straight ahead. High platform."

"What else did you see?"

He shook his head. "Nothing."

"Well," said Adira, drawing her bow, "I think we know there are more bad guys than that."

There were *definitely* more than that. And they were probably all hiding, waiting in dark corners, ready to strike—because this really *was* a game. The Advocate had guided their movements through the fortress, and now they'd drawn to the final stage.

Jag grinned. "Adira, what did you say about being like Sixxis?"

"Feels right in this situation," she replied, returning the expression.

Jag's grin widened as he dropped to a crouch. He unloaded his electroshock arrows and replaced them with red-tipped, exploding ones. "We go out one, two, three." Standing, he gestured through the opening with his head. "Adira, you first. There are some ships just that way, small enough you should be able to get on top in one jump. Get up there and call out any movement you see."

Adira aimed her bow forward and plucked at its string. "I'll try to take a few out, too."

"I'll go next," Jag continued. "Start blowing up the ships on the other side and find some cover. Remy, then you can find the shooter, take them out, and come duck down with me."

"Very well." She whipped out her rifle. "I am ready."

"So am I," Adira added.

Jag's threw up a fist. "Run fast!"

"Always do!" Adira burst through the doorway at a diagonal, drawing the shooter's attention. She skipped forward, her movements too quick to be caught as she drew toward the right line of ships.

After the second shot cracked and echoed through the hangar, Jag rolled in and turned the opposite diagonal. Lofting an arrow at the first ship in the line, he bolted for a stack of crates and ducked behind them—as an electroshock burst rang out from across the towering hangar. "Remy, I've—"

Jag whipped to the side as something came grabbing at his arm—then didn't hesitate. He spun back, pulled a blue arrow from his quiver, and drove it into his attacker's head. Stuck with nowhere to go from there, he pulled the operative over his cover and ducked down—and the burst propelled him and all three crates into the air.

The metal luckily blocked the shock, so Jag maintained full control of his body as he crashed into the floor. He then threw his attention to the steel boxes screaming toward him. Darting to the side, he narrowly avoided being crushed by one before ducking behind another. And when everything fell still again, he peeked over his cover.

"You are taking too long." Dropping to a knee, Remy rotated into the open and took mere seconds to locate the enemy sniper. As her electroburst echoed through the hangar, she darted past Jag and dipped behind one of the ejected crates.

"Nice shot!" said Adira, leaping out from behind the first ship in the far line. She sprinted toward the next, sprang up on top, and dropped to her stomach. "I took out one over here."

"Me, too," said Jag. "What else do you see?" Seated, back pressed against his crate, he watched out of the corner of his eye as Adira crawled forward.

Her head swiveled side to side. "Nothing."

Nothing? How was that possible?

Jag leaned to the side of the crate. His eyes traced the silver flooring down the depressed aisle between the two ship lines, past the metal wall that rose up twice his height before leveling out to form the far platform, and up the enormous, black partition that stretched to the ceiling.

They were alone.

He popped to his feet. "Where—"

"Welcome, my friends!" boomed the Advocate's voice through the cavernous hangar. "You've done well so far, but I'm afraid this is the end of the line for you."

Whirring sounds replaced the villain's voice, as the black partition split at the center to reveal multiple tiers of platforms stacking up to the even higher vaulted ceiling.

A small, black figure stepped toward the edge of the top terrace. "Do you like my collection?" said the Advocate, gesturing to the sea of spacecraft lining the levels below him. "They're as varied as I am."

Two operatives fanned out from behind him and took their places, one on each side. Their motions were mirrored by two operatives on the level below them, and on the next, and on the next, all the way to the ground level. Two by two, the collection of people from all ends of the galaxy—of all shapes, sizes, and colors—stretched a vertical line from floor to ceiling, putting the full spectrum of existence on display.

On another occasion, seeing all the different kinds of people would have been fascinating to Jag, one who'd only ever seen a green Rixxonian until recently—but not today. Today it was appalling. Because today, one man had taken choice from these people and forced them into one mind—forced them to be the same.

"Jag," Remy said, breaking him from his trance. "This cover is not sufficient. We must either retreat or push to the first wall."

"No sense going back." Holding his crossbow close, Jag planted a hand on the ground. "Let's go!" He shoved himself up, fired an explosive arrow at an empty space on the platform, and sprinted for the other end of the base level.

"So hasty!" taunted the Advocate.

Remy stowed her rifle and ran after Jag—as gunfire erupted from the platforms above, scorching through the space and into the floor around their feet.

A few operatives fired at Adira, still laying atop her ship. She managed to avoid getting hit as she skipped to the ground and ducked below the next in the line. "Well," she said, "this just got a whole lot worse."

Jag slid into a crouch and pressed his back against the wall. "So much for destroying all the ships in the hangar. We'll just have to be careful and make sure none get away."

"The ships are the least of our worries," said Remy, ducking beside him. "If we cannot—"

Shots volleyed toward Adira as seemingly every operative turned their attention on her. The ship's wing sparked and crackled above her.

"Adira!" Jag shouted. "Get out of there!"

She bounded forward—as the wing bent under its own weight and fell right where she was huddled.

"Thakk!" With three quick breaths, Jag spun out and fired two explosive arrows at nothing in particular—but in the direction of the operatives—hoping to cause enough confusion to distract the Advocate. "Get over here, NOW!" he yelled as they impacted.

Seizing her opening, Adira charged out from her new hiding place and joined the two of them. Gunfire resumed on and around their location.

"I can hear all a'that down here," said Bo. "Y'all okay?"

Jag looked down the line and received a nod from each of his companions. "We're pinned down, but nobody's hurt." He glanced at Remy, mouth wrinkled.

There *had* to be another trick on the altered blueprint.

"Hey, Bilanthia—is J'Nia near you?"

"Been listenin' the whole time," J'Nia replied. "Bo and the doc rigged all the comms to play through *Zara's* external speakers."

"Are there any entrances to the hangar other than the main hallway?"

"None from the interior, no. It's just that, the exterior bay door, and the elevator."

"Wait, I thought you said—"

"Don't get excited. There are two elevators. One goes up the platforms, the other goes from the top platform to the roof pad."

Skies—there went that idea. How could they not have seen this coming? They walked right in, even though they knew it was a trap. Thakk, they *ran* right in!

"Hey Bo," said J'Nia. "you by the control room yet?"

"Just passed through, why?"

But there was no other way. Sixxis was up there, and they had to get him back. And if the Advocate had already—

"Can you turn around and go open the bay door? The master control touchscreen is super easy to use."

The hangar fell silent.

"You want me to—"

"You can't duck there forever," teased the Advocate. "Why don't you come out and—"

What if Jag couldn't save Sixxis? Even if they managed to defeat the Advocate and all his operatives today, all would be lost if something happened to his brother.

"Yeah," said J'Nia, "I want you to open the door and—"

"—really do just wish to talk," continued the Advocate. "Come out now, and—"

The conversation between J'Nia and Bo, the Advocate's pedestaled speech, and Jag's own inner commentary swarmed his consciousness. His mind fogged over as everything washed into a sea of ambiguity.

It was too much.

He clutched at his chest and sank to a seat. And for what felt like several minutes, he struggled to keep breathing paced with his beating heart.

Remy's voice cut through the fog. "Jag."

He looked up. Ever so slightly, she waved in and out of focus as she gestured to her helmet.

Good thinking; the suit had air in it. Maybe that would help him breathe better.

He engaged his helmet, and the relief was incredible—but brief. Sinking to the side, he propped himself up and gasped for air.

This was it. It was all about to—

Chapter 58

An enormous *KACHUNK* silenced the space, dispelling Jag's misted mind and focusing his eyes on the hangar-bay door—as *Unity* flew in and proceeded to fire on the levels above.

"What?" Jag moved his head side to side, looking to each of his companions, searching desperately for his survival instincts to take back over. "Bilanthia?"

"Nah, it's me," J'Nia replied. "Now's your chance, Bo!"

"Way ahead'a ya!" *THUMP THUMP THUMP.*

"Jag." Adira placed a hand on his shoulder. "We stand—"

"Tall as trees," he finished with a haggard smile.

"Are you all right?" asked Remy from his other side.

"I'm back," he said, choosing his words carefully—because he was *not* all right. He wouldn't be until they got to Sixxis.

Bo's thumping slowed to a stop. "What're you sittin' around for?" he said, hoisting Jag to his feet. "Time to climb!"

"My specialty," said Adira, launching up onto the platform.

"J'Nia, please come pick me up," said Remy, rising upright as *Unity* zipped into a flip from her strafed attack position. She pointed to a high ledge tucked into the wall by the entrance. "I will provide support from afar. Bo, would you please give me a boost?"

"My pleasure, little one." As *Unity* came to hovering rest beside them, Bo lifted Remy by the feet so she could jump on top. There, she engaged her magnetic boots.

"Those are neat," said J'Nia.

"Thank you."

Unity tore away from the ground, continuing her attack as Bo ran back to Jag. "Your turn; I'll boost you up the platform."

"What about you?"

Back to the wall, he crouched and formed a basket with all four hands. "Haven't figured that out yet."

"J'Nia." Jag placed his hands on the big man's shoulders and pressed a foot into the basket. "I assume the Advocate turned off the elevator in here?"

"Nailed it," they replied. "At least the one between levels. The roof elevator is still on."

"That's not much help," Bo grunted, heaving Jag onto the platform. "Guess I'll find the long way."

Jag pulled himself up and grinned back down. "See you up there."

"Bet yer third armpit!" Bo lumbered off down the wall.

Whipping around, Jag met the full force of the scene. He counted seven layers of platforms, evenly spaced up to the top. On each lay blazing hunks of metal—former ships in the wake of *Unity's* bombardment—but the vertical center remained unscathed. J'Nia was clearly prioritizing everything but the operatives in their attack, probably in hopes of not killing anyone able to be revived.

The fact that the Advocate was in no real danger wouldn't be lost on him long.

Behind Jag, *Unity* came to rest by the far side wall—as the shooting resumed, all sights directed at her.

"Go!" Remy shouted as she rolled onto the platform.

The tiny vessel zipped off to the side, drawing the gunfire with her.

Turning back, Jag eyed the platforms and locked in on the highest, non-burning area he could. He loaded his cable arrow and launched it toward the third floor's ceiling, pulling himself off the ground.

Adira jumped onto a platform outside the partition as he whizzed past. "Hey—no fair!" She fired an arrow and hopped up to the second level.

The ascent's first electroburst broke into the hangar as Jag's feet hit the metal. Arming himself with a full chain of blue arrows, he crouched and shuffled toward the platform's center, passing two burning heaps of metal before dipping behind a smoldering pile of debris. There, he peeked out, took aim, and fired.

BOOM!

But that was only one operative; there were at least two on each level. He jumped up and searched for signs of the others.

"Two behind you!" Adira called out from a ledge on the outer wall.

Jag spun to find an operative running straight at him. He set his feet and aimed for the head—as another arrow whizzed past him and struck the same operative in the shoulder.

"Skies!" said Adira. "Went for the same one!"

"You Rixxonians are such a *nuisance!*" A volley of gunfire accompanied the shrill voice, screaming past Jag—right at Adira.

"Sorry!" she said, leaping down a level, avoiding certain death as the platform charred and fractured behind her.

Jag dropped to the ground as the shooting turned on *him*. He hadn't gotten a good look where the voice came from, so a quick shot was out of the question. He could try for an area burst, but that probably wouldn't work with the delay; he'd pop up and shoot, only to get taken out before it even went off. So he went for the safe route: he pulled an arrow, clicked to arm it, waited a moment, then tossed it over his shoulder toward where he thought the operative was.

"Gah!" they yelled.

BOOM!

Then from elsewhere, "Your burst weapons are so *irritating!*"

Still unable to pinpoint their location, Jag was out of options. "I'll drop my weapon if you drop yours."

"Why not?" A resounding *WLANG* revealed the operative's location.

Rifle in hand, Jag stood to find a pistol pointed at him. But before he could react, the gill-faced, green person threw their hands up.

"I was being safe," they said, tossing their weapon to the ground. "Thought for sure you'd try to trick me."

Jag walked round his cover, holding his rifle away from his body. "Fair fight?" he said, tossing it to the ground as he took timid steps forward.

The operative stood up straight. "Fair fight."

WHOOSH! Two portions of the ceiling opened, and a new operative dropped down through each.

"Just you and me," they all three said, advancing on him slowly.

Reaching his rifle wasn't an option, so he'd have to fight. Good thing he'd practiced against Bo's four arms. What would two more on top of that be?

The first operative came sprinting toward Jag, swinging an arm at his head. Jag ducked the attack as it passed, then jumped to the side and squared off as the second operative brought two consecutive hooks at his face. He blocked them both, then drilled his fist into the operative's side body.

"Not bad," came another voice from behind him—along with a punch in the kidneys.

Taking the hit, wincing with the pain, Jag whirled around and hurled his elbow at the new attacker. The operative avoided the blow—but didn't see the fist coming behind it. Jag hammered them in the temple, then rebounded and brought an uppercut at their reeling head.

Another operative bear-hugged him from behind, squeezing and lifting him from the ground. "You've been practicing, haven't you?"

"It helps when less of you is metal!" Jag threw his head back, crashing into his captor's face and sending them staggering back. He landed alert and ready on his feet, only to find all three operatives closing in on him.

"This doesn't look very fair!" Barreling out from behind the burning wreckage, Bo lowered his shoulder and rammed into the closest operative, then grabbed and heaved them at one of the others with all four hands. "Saw some a' that—nice work!" He plodded toward his pile of two. "I'll take these ones."

Jag turned to face down the remaining enemy—the green, gill-faced one. "Just you and me," he mocked, glancing behind them to locate his rifle. He had no intention of keeping up the fair-fight guise for long.

"Oh, you're *hilarious!*" Gills flaring, arm stretched to the side, the operative charged him.

Jag dropped to his knees to evade the hit, then popped up and took off toward his rifle. Grabbing it, he whipped around and—

CRACK—BOOM! A wave of energy pushed his body back a few steps.

"We do not have time for your fist fights," said Remy. "I—ah!" Lights exploded from the levels above, all headed straight for her position on the far-off platform.

Then *Unity* burst in and came to rest below. "Jump!" J'Nia yelled.

"I've been hit," Remy replied.

"Roll off, then. I'll catch you!"

"You'd best get her ta' safety," Bo yelled as two bursts rang through Jag's ears. "I ain't losin' my Remy today!"

"Count on it!" *Unity* lowered with Remy's falling body, giving her a soft catch before whisking her below and out of view.

"Think we drew 'em down here," said Bo, coming to Jag's side. "I heard voices coming from the other end of the platform." He pointed up through one of the holes. "Time to go."

"I've got it this time," Jag replied with a nod. He loaded and fired his cable arrow through the opening, then pulled himself up. When he landed, he turned back and offered his rifle. "You're—"

A gun pressed into his back. Hot breath washed over his neck as a voice hissed, "Surprise."

Below, five operatives filed out and surrounded Bo, their weapons fixed on him.

"Pits," he said, raising all four hands. "Okay, okay. I give."

"Adira, are you all right?" Jag asked.

"Yeah, I'm fine. Cornered, though. Sorry!"

"It was a mighty effort, Jag," said the voice in his ear, "but it's over now. Why don't you come up so we can have that chat?"

Chapter 59

Jag dropped his rifle.

"That's a good lad," said the Laktilian operative. "Now follow me." They escorted Jag to a door at the platform's rear, where they placed their hand on a small glass terminal to open it. "I'll give you one final moment alone to reconsider my proposition."

Jag scowled. "And lose control of my own consciousness?"

"I'd rethink my tone on your way up," said the operative, kicking him through the door. "Your friends' lives might depend on it."

"You're insane to think anyone would ever join you willingly."

"Hah—they *always* join me willingly."

The door zipped shut. An eerie quiet consumed Jag's reality.

Walking forward, he positioned himself at the room's center. A series of u-shaped staircases showed the way up—three levels between him and the top platform, where the Advocate waited.

Three levels to get things in order.

"Bilanthia," he said, starting his climb, "how are things down there?"

"All operatives on the lower levels and in the control room have been accounted for, and we were successful in reviving and assisting about half of them."

"It wasn't easy," added Lorrie. "Not everyone was happy to break free of the Intelligence. A few even fought back, thinking they'd stay in that monster's good graces if they stopped us."

"Yes," Bilanthia continued. "Lorrie and her team have been astoundingly helpful. I do not think we could have done this without them."

"J'Nia, either." Jag rounded the corner, onto the next set of stairs. "Remy, are you all right?"

"I am here with the doctor. J'Nia fled the hangar the moment you were captured."

"Good. How's she look, Bilanthia?"

"She will be unable to walk on her own for a time, but she will make a full recovery."

"Glad to hear it. Remy, you just lay low for the rest of the mission, okay?"

"Affirmative. I... I am sorry."

Jag stopped. "Don't be. We wouldn't have made it this far without you."

"I—"

"It's okay, Remy. You can count on us to finish this." A moment passed, and he continued up the stairs. "We're going to need *Zara* up here."

"I'm afraid my hands are quite full at the moment," said Bilanthia. "I—"

"Gotta be honest," J'Nia interrupted, "since the moment I saw this ship, all I've been thinking about is when I'll get to commune with her."

Jag started taking the steps two at a time. "Commune?"

"She's the most beautiful ship I've ever seen—and that's sayin' a lot. I *really* wanna fly with her."

"Bo, I don't know if you're able to respond, but I don't think we have any other choice."

"Whattya mean?" asked J'Nia. "I'm a damn good pilot—you saw!"

"He's just really protective of her."

"Oh. Well that's fair."

"Bilanthia, how long will it take you to get packed up and ready to move?"

"Ten minutes," he replied. "More or less."

"Easy. This guy loves to talk, so you'll have plenty of time." Jag rounded another curve and slowed his pace. "J'Nia, there'll be a moment up there—a signal—and when it happens, I want you to bust into the hangar. We'll get the captives to you."

"We can pour out and make sure the lower levels are clear," offered Lorrie. "Make sure not even a *piece* of him escapes."

"Good thinking! Thanks, Lorrie. And thanks for all your help."

"No problem—so long as you kill that bastard."

Would it come to that? After everything, Jag still wasn't sure he wanted the Advocate dead. More accurately, he wasn't sure about Garrison. The Advocate, yes; he needed to go. But Garrison? There was something deeper at work here, something that made Pert Gubora go to great lengths to keep his memories away from the galaxy.

...or was he keeping them from Garrison?

"Jag," said J'Nia, "what's the signal gonna be?"

"I don't know yet, but I'll make sure it's obvious."

"Hah!" Lorrie popped. "I can't tell if you're brilliant or stupid."

Brilliant... Ashley described Garrison as brilliant. She said he was her oldest friend, one of the best people she'd ever known. So how did he become the Advocate, a monstrous *shell* of a person?

Jag nodded to himself. "I'll think of something. And when you hear me say the word 'Ashley,' that'll be your cue that it's coming."

"Ashley it is!" celebrated J'Nia. "See you in a few, boo boo."

Jag and the Advocate had been going at each other back and forth, trying to uncover the same mystery—one neither of them could help the other solve. Now with Ashley's words, Jag had his answers. He could share those with the Advocate, but that didn't feel right. Garrison needed to *remember*—not be told.

He reached the final landing and slowed to a stop. A simple door stood polished and cold before him: one final obstacle keeping him from his brother, one final barrier dividing him from his fated confrontation with the Advocate.

He took a step, and it whizzed to the side. A narrow walkway extended forward, connecting to the enormous central platform.

"We stand tall as trees," Jag muttered to himself. And with a deep breath, he walked out to fill his grand purpose.

Sixxis was his top priority—and he found him! Forward and to the left, his brother sat in the back center of a huddled group of captives. And to the right, Adira and Bo knelt heads down, each with an operative's gun pressed into their back.

"I must say: I'm impressed."

Jag's eyes darted toward the voice and found the Advocate standing tall, illuminated by the bright lights shining down from the vaulted ceiling. A glistening, black mask hid his face. "Nice helmet."

"Ah, do you like it? Tritonic steel. Exceedingly light and thin, yet impenetrable—although you know that already." The Advocate held up one of the special arrows. Its silvery frame shimmered in the light. "I appreciate you returning this to me."

"That arrow belonged to my mother."

"No!" yelled the Advocate, throwing it into the pile of confiscated weapons. "In all my years of searching, the only sources of this metal I found are the remains of the Earth vessels. It belongs to *me.*"

"So that really *is* the only reason you came to Rixxon Prime."

"Indeed. It is a beautiful steel—the strongest substance I've ever encountered. Its lustrous material lines the circuits and nerve endings in my body." He held up his right arm; it too glistened. "And other parts of me."

Sixxis locked eyes with Jag—and right as he did, gave the double-eyebrow-pumped grin that only Sixxis would give in this situation. The Advocate clearly hadn't done anything to him yet. That was good.

What *wasn't* good was the operative standing above him holding a grenade.

"You seem a bit distracted," said the Advocate. "Then again, I'm sure this isn't how you hoped your reunion would look."

"It's actually pretty close to what I expected," Jag replied, returning his brother's grin. "You underestimate the number of times Sixxis has gotten himself into trouble over the years. I'm used to finding him in situations like this."

"Hah!" Sixxis' face scrunched. "Definitely deserved that."

Jag's grin faded as his eyes fell across the rest of the captives. Mixed in among the Rixxonians were several others of all different species, many of them emaciated and ill.

"I presume you've had enough time to think?" said the Advocate.

"I did—and I have questions. What do you mean they always join you willingly?"

"The Intelligence requires a willing mind to sync."

Jag squinted. "What about Omeka?"

"There's a brief time on either end of death where the mind will latch onto anything that will help it survive."

"So you *can* just kill people and take what you want."

The Advocate folded his arms. "I'm not in the business of stealing lives, Jag. As much as you may believe it, I'm no monster. I offer people a shot at something better—or a second chance. "

"And what about these people?" Jag said, gesturing to the captives.

"They'll be willing soon enough."

"In case you don't speak ass-bastard," said Lorrie, "he's starving them until their only choices are to join him or die."

"What's it like joining minds with someone?" Jag continued.

"One moment, you are you. The next, you inherit another person's skills, knowledge, and thoughts. And you don't just inherit what they can do—you obtain every bit of training, practice, study, and experience that developed it." The Advocate turned his back and walked to the opposite platform edge. "It's quite beautiful, really. And through it, I've become so much more than what Gubora... made all those years ago."

"Why did you do it?" Jag asked.

"Do what?"

"Kill him."

The Advocate's head drooped. "I thought he stole my memories from me. But as it turns out"—his head twitched—"Garrison *asked* him to."

"Why?"

"He was in pain..." The Advocate whipped around. "Why are you so curious all of a sudden? This is not what we're here to discuss."

Jag's head drifted up, eyes panning the ceiling high above. Row upon row of arched metal beams streamed from each side of the expansive hangar, meeting at the center.

"I think I've answered enough of your questions. It's time for you to answer mine."

As Jag's gaze rounded down the far wall, it lingered on Adira; ever so subtly, she unsheathed the daggers from her hidden ankle scabbards. Always ready for the right moment—just like at the farm.

And that moment was coming.

"I won't be accepting your offer," Jag said, "but I'm curious if you'll accept mine."

"Hah! You have your own proposition now, do you?"

"If you let me help you—let me help Garrison—we won't have to destroy you today."

This time, the Advocate's laugh was no short burst: it reverberated through the hangar, bouncing off the walls and echoing into the ceiling. "You must have gotten hit on the head—because the way I see it, this is an unwinnable fight for you."

"We've got a pretty good track record when it comes to unwinnable fights." Jag caught his brother's eye and gave a subtle nod to the ceiling. "Six, remember the Thakk?"

A grin stretched across Sixxis' face. "Of course I do. It was thakkin' epic!"

"I'm sorry," the Advocate let out between laughs, "but I would call myself more of a challenge than some *beast*."

"We're in position," J'Nia reported.

Perfect timing.

"You're not much of a challenge," Jag goaded. "Not really."

The Advocate's head cocked back. "Excuse me?"

"This is *your* last chance. You won't make it out of this. You're not good enough—not as you are now."

The villain doubled over and gripped at his head. "No. I am *extraordinary.*"

"Just let it go, Garrison. I can help you remember."

"Stop."

"You're not alone anymore. Or you at least don't have to be."

"*...stop.*"

"Stop what? I just want to help, Garrison. It's not too—"

"Garrison is dead." The Advocate's body drifted upright. "He was weak. He didn't just *ask* Gubora to remove his memories—he *begged.* That day, he ceased to exist."

"Garrison was in pain," Jag said. "He'd just seen everything he knew destroyed. Don't you understand that?"

"How did you—"

"He cared about my mother—about *Ashley*—and she was gone, just like that."

The Advocate's head twitched. "Ashley..."

"You've lost everything about yourself. She wouldn't even recognize you."

His body snapped toward Jag. "You don't—"

"What would she say if she saw you today?"

"I"—his head twitched again, then again—"I don't—"

"She'd be ashamed of you."

And just then, something overtook the Advocate: he froze.

"Now!" Jag yelled.

Sixxis popped up, ripped the grenade from his captor's dormant hand, and activated it.

BEEP!

The Advocate regained control. "What are—"

Adira's daggers hummed to life. She cut her restraints and swept her legs, upending the operatives behind her and Bo.

BEEP BEEP!

"Showtime." Sixxis hurled the grenade at the ceiling.

BEEP BEEP BEEP!

The explosion shattered into the hangar, splintering the beams high above. Metallic debris rained down all around them—the biggest piece coming straight for the Advocate.

"Shit!" He dove and rolled toward Adira as she cut Bo's restraints. Rising to his feet as wreckage continued to fall, he drew his sword and held it to the side as it too hummed to life. "Those daggers are *mine!*"

"Then come and get them!" Adira said, slotting into a ready stance.

The two operatives latched onto Bo—but he shed their grasp by bursting his four arms outward. He plodded toward the weapon pile and grabbed Sixxis' machete. "Here!" he yelled, tossing it and picking up one of his sidearms. And as he turned, he fired at the two operatives' heads.

BOOM! The bursts propelled him back a ways, where he hit the ground hard.

"You!" shouted the Advocate, turning and storming toward the stunned Quadmalian.

"Nope!" Sixxis shot a leg back, kicked his operative in the chest, and bounded off them toward his fallen weapon. With two more skips, he scooped it up and thudded onto the platform between Bo and the Advocate. "You won't get any closer to my bud here."

"That machete belongs to *me!*"

"No," he said, twirling it and setting his feet. "It was my father's final gift to me."

Jag stepped forward, lining up opposite Sixxis and flanking his foe as the final pieces of the ceiling slammed into the platform. "You're outnumbered, Garrison."

"There are more of me down—"

Zara tore into the hangar behind him, her front end cocking upward as she roared to a stop and opened her rear door.

"This ends now, you bastard!" echoed Lorrie's voice.

And *THUMP!* Adira landed to the Advocate's right, completing the triangle around him, flourishing her buzzing daggers.

"You really are full of surprises today," he grunted.

Jag swept an arm behind him. "Bo, get the captives out of here."

"But—"

"These people can't even walk." Many in the scattered group hadn't even moved. "You can carry the most."

Bo pushed to his feet and shook his head out. "Are you—"

"Just do it! We can take him for now." Jag pointed at Bo as he instructed the captives in Rixxonian, "Help him—"

"Enough!" screamed the Advocate, throwing his arms outward.

Chapter 60

In an instant, every remaining operative collapsed to the hangar deck. Lowering his arms, the Advocate cracked his neck to one side, then the other.

Jag's eyes shifted between Sixxis and Adira. "What did you just do?"

He held the buzzing sword above his bionic arm and sneered. "You taught me something today," he said, pressing the blade toward his arm; sparks leapt from his metallic flesh. "It seems splitting my mind had adverse side effects I was unaware of. But as you returned piece after piece of me to my body today, I felt myself growing *stronger.* Now, I am just *me.*"

"Wha—"

"I am the superior being. And once you're all dead, I will enhance my design and rebuild!" The Advocate launched at Jag, raising his weapon overhead.

Jag dropped to a knee, activated his kinetic barrier, and stopped the buzzing tip a split second before it sliced through him.

"My my, what a marvelous shield! Remy has outdone herself yet again." The Advocate brought his glistening helmet close to the glowing yellow barrier. "You will not win."

The tritonic steel machete came to rest below the buzzing sword.

"It's like he said." Sixxis' face glowed in the blue electricity. "We've got a pretty good track record." He forced the sword up and punched the Advocate right in his helmeted face.

"Jag," said Adira, tossing a dagger to him as Sixxis leapt over the Advocate.

"Up you go," said Bo, hoisting a captive onto his shoulder. "You three be careful!" With the added weight of five—one on each shoulder, one on his back, and two cradled in his arms—he hauled himself across the platform, past where Jag, Sixxis, and Adira circled the Advocate. A trail of Rixxonians helped the others behind him.

"He's no Thakk, Jag," said Sixxis, brandishing his machete.

"You've got that right."

"Oh get on with it!" The Advocate lunged.

Jag jumped to the side and brought a swift punch toward the organic flesh on his side, then ducked down and swept him from his feet.

Diving into the fray, Sixxis swung downward—but the Advocate caught the machete with his tritonic steel hand. He ripped it from his grasp, kicked him square in the chest, and sprang to his feet.

Then Adira went on the offensive.

The Advocate parried dagger strike after dagger strike with his two weapons until Jag joined in—but he held his ground even then. Sparks flew every which way as the electric bands clashed and buzzed. And as his opponents grew tired, the Advocate seized his opening: he grabbed Adira by the leg and whirled her around, crashing her body into Jag's.

The two of them slammed into the ground.

"Don't you see?" he said, pounding his chest. "I do not tire the way you organic beings do!"

"Good thing there's three of us then, huh?" Sixxis bounded into the fight, spinning his body and bringing a powerful kick to the villain's back.

The Advocate stumbled forward, then redirected back toward his new opponent, slashing horizontally at his stomach.

With a grin, the unarmed Sixxis hopped back to dodge the attack. Using his agility and athletic prowess, he narrowly avoided three more strikes before the buzzing sword sliced through his armor and singed the skin above his ankle.

"We need to get those arrows!" Jag yelled.

"On it!" Adira tossed her dagger to him and bounded off.

"One down," said the Advocate, raising the machete over his head.

Jag hurled himself between them, clasping the plunging weapon between his banded daggers. The jumping sparks scalded his face as he held the attack with all his strength.

"You are so *aggravating*!" The Advocate swung at Jag with his own electrified blade—but Sixxis was there. Despite his pain, he sprang up and wrapped himself around the swinging arm.

The three of them struggled in their entangled position, each wrestling for control over the other. With everything he had, Jag tried to pull the machete from the Advocate's mechanized hand. Meanwhile, Sixxis used his body to hold back the attack and keep his brother from certain death.

But the Advocate's enhancements served him well. He held his own for an impressive amount of time, then simply said, "Goodbye."

He released the machete.

With the resistance suddenly gone, Jag tumbled forward. The blade flew through the air, a dagger still wedged in its side.

Bionic arm finally freed, the Advocate brought a haymaker crashing into Sixxis's head, plunging him into the platform. He turned to Jag and attempted the same attack—but Jag was ready. He ducked the blow and launched forward, tackling the Advocate to the ground.

But it was no use—the Advocate was too strong. He tossed Jag aside and stood over him, poised to strike.

SHOOP! A special arrow whizzed through his shoulder; his body seized; and Jag seized his opportunity. He drove his dagger into the Advocate's side.

"Agh!" Ripping his sidearm from its holster, the Advocate fired on Adira's position while slashing horizontally at Jag.

Jag activated his barrier just long enough to deflect the blow upward, exposing his opponent's wounded side. He grabbed the protruding dagger and pulled it across his body.

Blood poured from the wound.

"You're not alone, Garrison. It doesn't have to end like—"

"Don't you *ever* stop!?"

Enraged, the Advocate seemed to lose all control. Jag had little difficulty dodging and deflect blow after blow as his attacks became wilder and more telegraphed. And with every opening, he jabbed at the gushing wound, exploiting the weakness as much as he could.

But the Advocate finally landed a hit: after having another downward slash deflected by the barrier, he reversed his momentum and threw a forceful uppercut at Jag's chin.

The impact blurred Jag's vision as he staggered back. He blinked wildly in an attempt to focus, but it was taking too long. And so with no other option, he dropped to a crouch and held the shield over his head.

Sixxis lunged for the Advocate to help his brother—but the Advocate saw it coming. He whirled around and struck at the first thing he could find.

And his blade pierced cleanly through Sixxis' thigh. Hollering out, he grasped at the Advocate's hand as it lifted him by the throat.

Still dazed, Jag could do nothing but watch the swirling image of his brother being strangled. He tried to speak—but before he did, the second dagger came whizzing in, searing into the Advocate's shoulder beside the arrow.

"You'll regret that," said Adira, shining machete in hand as her green body blurred into frame. She clashed with the Advocate.

Useless until he could see straight, Jag crawled for the final arrow. Metal clanked on metal behind him as Adira held her own better than he and Sixxis did together.

Finally—*just* as he located his rifle and loaded the last special arrow—his eyes recentered and refocused. He whipped around to find the Advocate standing over Adira's fallen body, arm raised above his head.

So he didn't hesitate.

Jag's arrow pierced through the villain's bionic arm. Electricity surged up his body, freezing him in place.

And Adira didn't hesitate.

She pounced on the dropped machete and sliced up through the injured soft tissue connecting the Advocate's bionic arm to his shoulder. A combination of sparks, blood, and other fluids oozed from the wound as the limb fell from his body.

"YOU!" With what looked like everything he had, the Advocate brought a kick careening into Adira's side, then turned to Jag. "And YOU!" He broke into a sprint, pumping his remaining arm.

Jag scrambled to load another arrow, feeling his life nearing its end with each passing moment. He wasn't going to make it in time.

The Advocate drew his sidearm as he ran, aiming right for him. "It's over for you."

BOOM!

Chapter 61

BUZZ.

Garrison rolled over and tapped the terminal beside his bed.

Why'd he even bother setting the alarm? He wasn't going to sleep. After all, today was a banner day! Today marked 365 days—*one full year* since he learned Ashley was pregnant. Which meant one full year with no response to his desperate attempts to get off the ship—not even an indication that anyone received his messages.

Maybe humanity really *was* alone in the universe.

Garrison's mind didn't get much time to wander. *Shuriken* was too small a research station to allow for any meaningful amount of acoustic separation, and the kid was crying—again.

It was already a lousy day. The mindless shrieking wasn't going to help.

"Dawn," Garrison sighed, fading soft light into the tiny, undecorated cabin. He sat up and slid his feet to the cold ground, then closed his eyes and started massaging his face.

Four years ago, he was handpicked to explore the cosmos and make that ever-elusive first contact. The mission was slated to last a maximum of thirty years, depending on their level of success locating life.

Then they stumbled through the wormhole.

With another sigh, Garrison stepped into his light-blue jumpsuit and zipped it up over his body. Tapping the wall console, he exited his cabin and followed the narrow hall to the open central chamber.

Jason meandered about the mess with the boy in his arms.

With zero interest in any friendly morning conversation, Garrison tiptoed toward the collection of screens at his probe control station on the right wall.

"Oh good," Jason said, crossing the room just before he sat down. "Can you watch him for a sec?"

Garrison turned to face two of the three beings in his solitary existence. "Fine."

"Thanks!" Jason pressed the child into his arms and scurried back to the mess.

Dropping into a seat, Garrison propped the boy up on an adjacent chair. "Sorry to say it, kid," he whispered, "but you will be forever tied to my misery."

The baby tilted his head and locked into a momentary staring contest, then reached his hands forward.

Garrison squinted. "You're relentless—I'll give you that. No matter how hard I try to stay away, you always come for me."

"Success!" Jason shouted from his knees, head still in a storage unit. He crawled out and crossed back to them. "Little J, how about some crackers?"

"Things are getting more complicated now, aren't they?" Garrison asked, an amiable tone betraying his irritation with Jason's existence.

Jason took the child in his arms. "I'll say! We didn't set out with food for four—and we *definitely* didn't plan on raising a child onboard. Now that he needs more than his mom can give, I'm trying to get creative!"

"What's creative about giving him crackers?"

Jason was an idiot—more of a child than the actual child onboard. Yet he somehow managed to catch Ashley's eye.

His warm smile indicated a complete failure in detecting Garrison's sarcasm. "I guess nothing." He turned and headed for his cabin.

"Good morning, Garrison," hummed Ashley's voice from the other side of the research table in the room's center. In his effort to remain unseen, he hadn't even noticed she was there.

"Hi, Ash." He tapped his terminals alive. "You look busy. Sleep last night?"

"I woke up early," she replied, holding a clump of soil to her eye with a pair of forceps. "I was wide awake after lulling him back to sleep, so I started analyzing yesterday's samples."

"Any good news?"

Ashley shook her head. "One more planet studied, and we still haven't found anywhere capable of sustaining life." She stuck the forceps in her mouth, removed a clip from behind her head, and let her hair cascade down over her shoulders.

Damn.

Even today—the worst of days—she was just as beautiful as when Garrison met her. And she wasn't just beautiful. Brains, confidence, ambition, kindness—she had it all. She was just... perfect. It's why Garrison had always wanted more from their relationship. And when he discovered she was to be one of his teammates on this mission, he thought he finally had his chance.

That obviously didn't work out.

"How are you?" she asked, taking the seat by him.

"It's just another day," Garrison lied. "I'm starting to think we may never make contact."

Ashley smiled. "What did we say on launch day?"

While fleeting, these moments helped Garrison feel positive about things. Ashley's eyes whisked him away into a world of possibility—a world where he saw their success.

"That there's a zero percent chance there's no other sentient life in the universe," he said.

Her smile widened, then her gaze fell to the ground. "I can't stop thinking about it again."

The wormhole... yeah, Garrison thought about that a lot, too. Not because of how terrifying it was—because it's when everything changed.

He'd noticed Ashley and Jason getting closer throughout training, but he figured they—like him—understood the gravity of their mission and could keep it in their pants. But it seems the brush with death was all they needed to abandon reason and conceive a child 2.5 million light years away from home.

Garrison needed to leave the moment Ashley told him. He transmitted a false distress signal in every possible direction that day, and he'd sent the same signal many times since.

"Garrison?" she said.

They left Earth with so much promise and hope. Garrison was a part of something great—something that would impact every human in existence. Now he was a part of *nothing.* He was just Garrison, alone on this crew of four—playing house.

"G—Garrison..." Ashley stammered.

"What's up, Ash?" he said, shaking his head out. "Is something—"

She pointed at the terminal behind him.

It couldn't be...

Two humanoids in black suits shone through the screen. One drew an object from its belt and handed it to the other—then the screen went black.

...had they finally done it?

"Where's that probe?" Ashley asked.

"The moon on the other side of the planet."

"This is huge!" she yelled, exploding from her seat. "See if you can get it back online. I'll go get Jason!" She charged out of the room.

Garrison triggered a diagnostics test, then hustled to the corner, grabbed another probe from the bin, and brought it back to the terminal. As he waited, he admired the beautiful simplicity of its tritonic steel exterior.

Tritonic steel—the whole reason they made it this far.

A chime signaled the test's completion.

"All systems online," he read aloud in disbelief. "Manual deactivation." He ran it again; the second test produced identical results.

Now was his chance!

Throwing a glance over his shoulder, Garrison scooted to the comm station and recorded the next iteration of his message: "Hello, my name is Garrison Trapp. My crew and I are stranded with no hope of returning home. Please help us!"

Pleased with himself, Garrison leaned back and grinned. He'd recorded with *just enough* distress. It should've gotten the message across even if the receiver couldn't understand him.

It was *finally* happening!

Ashley rushed back to his side with Jason and the boy in tow. "What did you find?"

"It was deactivated manually," he relayed. "I'm going to send another—"

BANG! The ship shook.

"What was that?" said Jason. "Did we hit some—"

BANG!

Garrison pounded at his keyboard to pull up the ship's schematics.

BANG!

"Warning," said *Shuriken,* engaging the red emergency lights, "hull integrity compromised."

BANG!

Air rushed from their position, pulling at their bodies as the void's vacuum tried to suck them into space. But before anyone moved far, the emergency partition activated and barricaded them from *Shuriken's* now-lost portion.

"Whoever that was," Garrison said. "They clearly didn't want to be seen. We need to get out of—"

"There's something headed this way," Ashley said, having pulled up the radar on a separate screen. "It's coming fast!"

"I don't understand," said Jason. "Why would—"

Another wing blasted from *Shuriken's* body, furiously tugging at the crew until the next containment door closed.

"No time to understand!" Garrison yelled, throwing his chair aside and sprinting for an escape pod. He hit the button and whisked the door open, then whipped around to find the others still sitting down. "Come on you two! There's—"

BANG!

This hit *finally* jolted Jason and Ashley to their feet. They rushed toward the other pods.

About damn time!

Garrison threw himself into his pod's single seat and started the launch sequence. "You two had better be right behind me!" The door shut in front of him. And moments later—just staring at Ashley through the glass—he blew backward into the abyss.

That's when he saw it.

Two ships—not unlike ones he'd seen in movies back on Earth—flew circles around *Shuriken*, firing red flashes at her hull. Then one of them stopped; a green beam of light zipped from its body, extending into the space below *Shuriken*; and that light swung up through her midsection and disappeared.

Shuriken—Garrison's only connection to Earth—split down the middle and drifted apart.

"No..."

He didn't notice another pod launching before it happened.

"No!"

Maybe none of this would've happened if he didn't send that message. Maybe they'd still be alive. Maybe they'd all be together.

"NO!"

Garrison collapsed back into the seat, as pain, fear, guilt—it all consumed him at once. He thought he was alone before—when he had Ashley, Jason, and the kid—but this was something else.

And he wasn't just alone. He was the *reason* they died.

He couldn't do it. It was the *one* thing he wanted most of all—to keep Ashley safe. And when it mattered most, he wasn't good enough. He was inadequate, incapable, powerless.

Everything had been taken from him.

Chapter 62

Stunned, frozen in place on the ground, Jag struggled to regain control of his body. Between his blurred vision, the fast-paced fight, and the sudden, unexpected burst, he wasn't sure what had happened—but he was alive.

"It appears your design is not flawless."

His eyes followed the voice to find Remy hobbling across a far bridge, a crutch pressed beneath her arm. Her rifle lay behind her on the elevator platform.

"By my calculations, that hit to your exposed inner circuitry has overloaded your systems and rendered you inert."

Wiggling his fingers free of the burst's effects, Jag felt the warmth of mobility expand through his body. He rolled over to take in the scene.

The Advocate lay still on his side.

"I told you I would kill you," Remy said, stopping next to him and kicking his armor to retract the helmet.

"Th... thank you."

Jag lurched up to a seat. "Garrison?"

"Yes."

He pressed himself up and walked toward them—then remembered his brother. "Sixxis!"

"I've got him," said Adira, already jogging his way.

"Don't worry about me," Sixxis added. "Do what you need to do."

"It was my fault," said Garrison, a single tear running down his face. "Our ship was attacked because of me." He shut his eyes. "She *died* because of me."

Jag took his place by Remy's side.

"Ashley, I..." Garrison drew in a big breath. "I loved her—from the moment I met her. I thought our fate was sealed when we signed up for the mission. We'd travel the stars, make first contact, and together change humanity as we knew it."

A lump rose in Jag's throat. "And then—"

"Jason," he said. "Your *father* ruined everything."

"It was the wormhole," Jag corrected.

Garrison's eyes popped open. "How do you know about that?"

"I saw her, Garrison," he replied, breathing deeply, "on Rixxon Prime. I *talked* to her."

"Impossible."

"It is true," said Remy. "I saw her as well."

"She had nothing but great things to say about you," Jag continued. "She said you were brilliant, the smartest, most driven person she ever knew. And that you were her longest and best friend."

"Our probes didn't have tracking tech installed in them." Another tear fell down Garrison's cheek, followed by a spark and a head twitch. He squeezed his eyes shut. "The Guild ships that destroyed *Shuriken* came in response to *my* message. I led them straight to us."

"You can't have—"

"I was reckless. It wasn't the first time I sent a message out in hopes of finding someone. I just..."

He paused, then glanced up at Jag.

"The moment you were born, I felt so alone. I tried to get away from you as fast as I could. And I got her killed because of it."

Jag looked him in the eye, the eye of a man he would never truly know.

"I couldn't save her. And knowing it was my fault, I became consumed, trapped in my thoughts, feelings, and fears—so much so that when Gubora fused my mind with a synthetic one, that loneliness and inadequacy became encoded within me. They drove me, and I lost sight of my way—my *why*."

Such pain... No wonder he asked Gubora to remove all memory of it.

"I fell into the same traps as so many on Earth," Garrison continued, staring forward. "Greed, hatred, anger, enslavement—I became everything I despised about our kind. You, on the other hand..." He looked up through his tears. "You've grown into quite the representative of humanity."

"I don't understand," Jag said, shaking his head.

"When you meet others, you will."

Jag's mouth wrinkled. "She told me to tell you something."

For the last time, Garrison's eyes lit up.

"She said she's sorry... and that you *are* enough."

Garrison smiled. "Ashley would... be... proud..."

What life remained left his body, as Garrison and the Advocate fell dead for the final time.

For a moment, Jag mourned the loss of the only other human he'd ever meet—then he remembered his brother. "Six!" He took off running.

Sixxis lay on the ground, resting his head on Adira's lap. Purple blood oozed from the edges of the blade sticking through his leg. "It actually doesn't hurt all that much."

"It looks awful," said Adira.

"I bet the doc will have no problem fixing me up." Sixxis laughed. "You should've seen Jag after our other fights!"

Jag grinned. *"Finally*—someone else took the beating this time!" His mouth folded into a hesitant half-smile. "You saved my life more than once."

"It's what brothers are for. And besides"—Sixxis tossed a thumb back at Adira—"she saved us both"—then threw a finger at Remy—"and she's the real hero. She saved us all."

"We are a team," said Remy, crutching up behind Jag. "None of us would have survived without each other."

"We're friends," Jag corrected. "Family even." And with that, his eyes swept across the three people before him. "I'm glad you're okay, Six."

"Yeesh—me, too!" Sixxis replied. "Would've hated to get stuck with that guy in my head."

Remy grinned. "Perhaps merging with your absurd thinking processes would have forced the Advocate to take himself a little less seriously."

A smile stretched across Jag's face, because they really *had* become his new family—somehow thanks to Garrison, his former family who'd finally found his time to rest. Along with Ashley, Jason, and his parents from Rixxon Prime, Garrison would stay in the back of Jag's mind forever as one of the people who helped make him who he was. As for who he *would be* going forward, well, that was for him to decide.

And no matter what came his way, he'd stand tall.

On the ground a few paces away, Sixxis' machete drew Jag's eye. Its formerly smooth, knifelike edge was now peppered in all manner of sharp indentations. "Six, check it out."

Sixxis' eyes exploded open so hard they threw his head back. "I'm only a little upset. It looks thakkin' awesome!"

"Only *you* would admire your battered blade while another impales your leg," said Remy.

She had that right.

Chapter 63

Jag stood off on the base level of the massive hangar. He rolled his head around in a slow circle, back the other way, then let it hang as he puffed out a huge breath.

With the danger gone, Bilanthia had conscripted all able bodies to help pull out every box, table, and surface to give ample space for treating the indoctrinated. And so *Zara's* interior spilled out from her rear cargo door. Remy assisted with purging all traces of the Intelligence, while Adira tended to the ill and injured.

"Jag."

Lifting his head, he turned to find Lorrie.

"All former operatives have been accounted for." Two more Lommorians stood behind her on either side, one significantly smaller than the other.

"Thanks, Lorrie," Jag said with a nod. He looked past her. "You must be Werth and Morban."

"Yep," said the smaller one.

"Yep," echoed the other in a much deeper tone.

"Thanks for all your help, you three. We wouldn't have won without you."

"Hah!" Lorrie slapped a hand on his shoulder. "Something tells me you would've figured it out." She slotted a foot back and folded her arms. "You're pretty damn impressive."

"He's nothing without me," said Remy, crutching toward them with a crooked smile pressed onto her lips. "But the same can be said for me."

"And in the end, they realized the true reward was friendship." Lorrie rolled her eyes. "Come on you two—take some goddamned credit!"

Remy looked up at Jag. "Unfortunately, our job is far from over. There are still functioning Guild installations all over the galaxy. It will take time for news of Pert Gubora and the Advocate's death to spread, but once it does, it is only a matter of time before someone else steps in to take control. The infrastructure is too powerful to allow anyone to do so."

"She's right," Lorrie agreed. "And if I'm reading between the lines, she's proposing we get out there and start wreaking some serious havoc." Her mouth twisted into a devious smile. "I would very much like to help with that." She turned. "What about you, Morban?"

"Yes!" said the smaller one.

"Werth?"

"I will be reborn in the blood of all who fly the Guild banner."

...that was a little intense.

"We could certainly use the extra hands," Jag said, squinting at them.

"If you're taking applications for new crew members"—J'Nia ran toward them—"please please *please* consider me!"

"You passed *Zara's* test," Bo said behind her. "That's enough for me."

J'Nia screeched to a halt and turned around to face him. "You guys are great and all, but she's the *real* reason I wanna come if I'm being honest."

"Bahaha—you got good taste, that's fer sure!"

"You don't need taste to see how beautiful she is."

"Butter me up all you want," he said with a wink. "It'll still be a while before I let you pilot her again."

J'Nia's whole body sank. "Copilot?" they said with a shrug.

"I've got the doc."

"Oh, she can take my position," said Bilanthia over his shoulder from a nearby table. "I wouldn't mind taking on the role of crew chef. Bo, I am just *dying* to recreate some Quadmalian cuisine for you!"

"You can cook Quadmalian!?" On cue, the big man's stomach grumbled. "Where'd you learn that!?"

"I"—Bilanthia dropped a tool—"my my—sorry, I must focus."

"I bet Sixxis will be happy about this, too," Jag said.

"Happy about what?" Arm around Adira, Sixxis hopped over on his good leg and sat on a metal crate.

"Bilanthia is going to be the crew chef."

"Yes!" he said, slapping his good leg. Then his face grew more serious. "So Elama never showed up."

"It is all very convenient," said Remy. "I believe she was using us to hide their involvement in the Advocate's actions."

"I actually might have some information about that." Sixxis cleared his throat. "I had a little conversation with the Advocate while we were on our way here. He said he couldn't figure out the hive thingy until about six months ago, when someone called 'the Buyer' donated resources and knowledge to the Guild in some sort of exchange."

Jag's jaw dropped. "That must be the new investor he mentioned. Did he tell you anything about this person?"

"All he said was that she used voice transmission."

"So someone communicating on a voice-only channel offered unmatchable technology?" Jag shook his head. It sure as thakk didn't look good.

"This all but confirms our suspicions," said Remy, hand clenching to a fist. "The Arbiters are far more involved than Elama has let on."

Was it true? Did the Arbiters use them to cover up their mistakes? Did they both create the Advocate and outfit the team that destroyed him?

Something didn't sit right, but Jag couldn't put his finger on it. In all his interactions with her, he couldn't help but trust Elama—but every step revealed that it was all deeper than previously thought.

"Perhaps I can find a recording in the Advocate's memory banks," Remy continued, "to confirm the Buyer was indeed Elama."

Lorrie folded her arms. "Sorry, but that won't work. Gubora did all the coordinating with the Buyer. The Advocate never even talked to her."

"Very well," said Remy, narrowing her eyes. "But I will analyze his memory banks nonetheless."

Jag nodded. His trust in Remy went *way* further than his trust in Elama. "I'm sure if we keep taking down Guild installations, we'll learn more as we go."

"Starting with this one." Remy turned to Sixxis. "Would you like to trigger the destruction of this fortress?"

A savage, Sixxis-style grin stretched across his entire face. "Do you have to ask?"

EPILOGUE

Vic rounded the final switchback of her pre-dawn trail run and took in the path ahead. Like almost every other morning, there was nobody in sight, so she did the usual: picked up her pace as she descended toward the wider path leading out to the road.

With her hair pulled into a tight bun low on her head, the crisp, mid-November air cooled her exposed neck, giving her body the equilibrium needed to push itself for the final sretch of her ritualistic six-mile jog through the mountains. Leaves crunched as she continued her gradual acceleration, then burst into a full sprint off the incline. And for precisely two-fifths of a mile, every thought left her brain. All focus dwelt on her steady breathing as her feet clapped the dirt, matching cadence with the rapid, metronomic motions of her pumping arms.

Vic's feet pounded the pavement as she hit the road and slowed to a steady walk. She started for home, stopping her sportwatch at thirty-six minutes—almost on the dot.

She'd memorized every twist and turn of this trail, every rock and root. And like clockwork, she'd fine-tuned and mastered her body's response to each element. Nothing caught her by surprise, not here, not like it did when—

Her ringtone echoed in her mind; she'd been wearing earbuds at the start of this morning's run before choosing the sounds of nature over her audiobook. Unsure who could *possibly* be calling so early, she glanced at her watchface and read the name.

It was Hammer. Son of a bitch.

Naturally, Vic couldn't refuse a call from her old CO. She tapped the green button to accept the call. "Well if it isn't the old goat himself!"

"Hah!" he chortled. "You sure know how to make a man feel welcome, Vic! How was your run?"

"Brisk." She continued down the road and got straight to the point. "To what do I owe the pleasure?"

"I assume this line isn't secure?"

"You know it isn't." She stopped. "But Hammer—that shouldn't matter."

Despite her relatively young age, it had been a year—almost to the day—since Victoria "Vic" Thomas left MARSOC. It was the war that drove her out. After seeing firsthand humanity's limitless capacity for inflicting pain and terror on each other, she opted for the quiet life. Now she stayed in the solitude of her cabin in the Uinta mountains of northern Utah.

"I need to talk to you about something," Hammer said.

"I'm retired," Vic replied, starting for home. "You know that."

"And *you* know that I respect the hell outta that. I wouldn't be coming to you if this wasn't important." He blew out a deep breath. "There's big things going on, Vic—bigger than all of us."

"Nothing the team's never seen before I'm sure."

"This is unlike anything *anyone's* seen. And the team can't know about it—not yet anyway. Your place still secure?"

"Yes."

"Let's talk when you get home." He disconnected the call.

Trent Hammer was a strange person—that much was certain—but even this was off brand. It wasn't like him to keep things from his team, and it was even less like him to be so cryptic. Even in discrete situations with sensitive information, tact wasn't exactly his strong suit. Then again, he *was* good at exaggerating things.

As Vic's house came into view, she shrugged off the mystery and continued on. She'd know soon enough; no need to worry about it. She'd go home, whip up a quick breakfast, and—

Seeing the front door ajar, every ounce of Vic's training activated within her.

She dropped to a crouch and hustled across the road, then ducked beside the wooden staircase and reached for the handgun hidden beneath the steps—all without making a sound. Bringing her head level with the raised porch, she eyed the door.

Movement: someone was inside.

Vic dropped down, pressed her back into the porch supports, and waited. When she had her chance, she'd—

"Vic, you back yet?" called a voice from inside.

It was Hammer.

"Son of a bitch," she muttered, hiding the gun back under the steps.

"I heard that!" Resounding thumps accompanied the creaky front door as it swung open, revealing Hammer's broad, sturdy frame. "I may be gettin' older, but my hearing hasn't dropped off one bit!"

"Well," said Vic, walking up the steps, "you *are* a son of a bitch, so..." She raised a single eyebrow and offered a crooked smile. "It's good to see you."

Hammer grinned, calling attention to the massive scar running vertically across his left eye. "Sorry to barge in—really. The moment you tendered your resignation, I had every intention of leaving you alone."

"Intention means nothing without follow through," Vic said, brushing past him through the door. "You of all people know that."

Hammer lumbered after her. "You're not wrong. But once you hear what I have to say"—his grin returned—"you might actually give me a damn break for once."

"We'll see about that." Crossing into the kitchen, Vic opened the fridge and popped a can of sparkling water. "Well? Get on with it."

"You might want to be sitting down for this," Hammer said, turning and heading for the living room.

Vic followed, entering the room as he plopped his massive body on the sofa. "What's going on?" She lowered herself into an armchair. "You're being even weirder than usual."

"Vic," Hammer exhaled, leaning forward, "as far as I know, only fiften people on the entire planet have heard what I'm about to tell you—beyond all the world leaders, of course."

"Quit dancing around the point, y'old goat."

"You know Abernathy Enterprises, right?"

"Of course." Vic sat back and took a sip of her sparkling water. "Tritonic steel manufacturers; inventors of the first faster-than-light engine."

Hammer nodded. "Twenty-one years ago, they sent an undisclosed mission into space with the express purpose of making contact. Three crew members left with little expectation of a return voyage. Whole thing was very hush hush."

Vic crossed her legs.

"The crew went into sleep stasis for two years. Just hours after waking up, they hit something they didn't expect."

"Aliens?" she said, one eyebrow raised.

He shook his head. "A wormhole."

"Hah! Have you been reading science fiction, Hammer?"

"It's real, Vic. I've seen the reports. One minute, the IGPS.—that's the intergalactic positioning system—showed them in one place. The next, they were all the way in the Andromeda Galaxy."

She squinted. "That's—"

"2.5 million light years away from Earth."

Vic considered saying more, then just nodded. "Go on."

"For the next year or so, the crew studied every planet they came across, desperately searching for other sentient species—then everything suddenly went dark. Comms disappeared, and the IGPS. failed. After a while, the folks at Abernathy Enterprises shut the operation down and vowed to tell nobody."

"Why would they do that?"

"They'd just sent three twenty-somethings to their deaths, Vic. And not just *any* twenty-somethings, either. These were bright kids."

She took a few gulps this time, chugging until her can was empty. "I don't see what this has to do with me."

"Last week, a terminal from the lost ship was reactivated. One of the crew members logged in, and the moment he did, facial recognition authenticated him and sent stills back to Abernathy Enterprises."

Vic jolted forward. "He's alive?"

"More than alive, it seems," said Hammer. "He had metal plating lining parts of his head and neck."

"Interesting," she said, sitting back again. "But I still don't see how this applies to me."

"The world's coming together, Vic. For the first time in history, the whole of humanity is uniting for a greater cause." Hammer locked eyes with her. "We're sending a group out to the location of the wormhole—to go through and look for him. We're going to find what happened, and we're going to make contact—for *real* this time."

"How noble," she scoffed. "Do you really think the world can work together on this?"

"Only if they have a worthy leader."

"Hah! So that's why you're here?"

Hammer nodded. “They asked me for my best—and that’s you. Always has been, always will be.”

“Wh—“

“You’ve seen what humanity is capable of on every scale and in virtually every arena. And through it all, you’ve maintained unmatched integrity, grit, and most importantly, composure.”

Once again, Hammer locked eyes with Vic. “I can’t think of a better person to represent our species.”

Author Note

Thank you—from the core of my being—for reading *Identity Crisis*. I hope you enjoyed geting to know Jag, Sixxis, Remy, Bo, and Bilanthia as much as I did, and I hope you'll consider leaving a review.

This book is my first ever publication, and it's much more than something I spent a few years creating—it's a part of me, a critical piece of my own identity. And I'm so glad I was given the opportunity to share it (and by extension myself) with you.

I started this story years ago—August 2015—on a whim. I was working two jobs but had a fair bit of time to myself at one of them (and my boss explicitly said he didn't care what I did with that time so long as everything around the office got done). So I started writing. I put together about seven chapters of what I thought was a pretty cool story.

Then things got busy. I lost some steam as I planned the next phase of my life, which ultimately brought me halfway across the US and into grad school. And when that was done, I just wanted a break. I took a year off, during which I headed to the southern tip of the Appalachian Trail and started walking north.

All told, I hiked a third of the trail (737 miles) in about seven weeks. And that story started spinning back into my mind when I was out there. It'd been a while since I had the mental space for it, and I was excited to find the opportunity to dive back in. (It helped that I'd met a pretty spectacular gal who was very encouraging about my writing.) I still didn't get the chance to open it back up for a bit—though I *did* marry that gal, move further across the country, and start my first full year of teaching

Then came the 2020 pandemic, the sudden global shutdown, and the inevitable existential crisis we all faced (at least me—I obviously can't speak for you).

Let's just say that in my exile, I channeled my energy into creating something. The result was the first draft of this book—and that draft changed *everything*. It launched a passion I never knew I had.

You see, I'd always been a creator. To that point in my life, this part of me manifested itself in music. I'd been directing choirs, composing and arranging here and there as I expressed myself and helped others do the same. But I found something new in writing. I found a world—no, a string of worlds waiting to be created through my words, old friends I'd always been fascinated by but had never given the proper personal emphasis.

I committed right away. I put full steam and stock into storytelling, left my teaching job, and found a position as a contract writer, editor, and instructional designer. Skip forward two and a half years, and I've fully changed careers into learning and development, written a book, and concepted/outlined/plotted at least ten more to run in series with it. One way or another, I write every day.

It's been a long road these last couple years, learning all about novel creation, story structure, and the ins and outs of writing I'd never spent the intentional time studying. Though this story fluctuated in priority along the way, my work on it never stopped. It was a constant in my life. And so through my career shift, wading through the pandemic, and starting a new life with my partner, building this new world was an ever-present effort that propelled me forward.

And now, the fact that this book is out in the world—right here in your hand—that simple fact to me is the sign that I've made it. I've created something and learned so much about myself in the process.

And there's much more to come!

With all that, I'm always looking to grow and improve. I would love nothing more than to make a career out of storytelling, and I can't do that without your feedback. **So please—consider leaving an honest review and sharing with me your thoughts and feelings about this story**. I will read and take to heart each piece of feedback—for real. After all, these stories are just as much for you as they are for me.

This book is just the beginning of my writing journey, one that promises many new worlds in the years to come. And I would love nothing more than for you to join me—so **let's stay in touch!**

Find me on the web at my website: https://claytonpulsipher.com. There, you can **sign up for my mailing list** to stay up to date with all the latest news, sneak peeks, and exclusive goodies—right in your email inbox. You can otherwise follow along or drop me a note on social media:

Instagram: @clayton_pulsipher
Facebook: clayton.pulsipher23
Twitter: @clay_pulsipher

Coming Soon

Be on the lookout for *Subterfuge: Part Two of the Arbiter Trilogy*—coming 2024.

Printed in Great Britain
by Amazon